Change of Heart

"Walsh has penned another endearing novel set in Loves Park, Colo. The emotions are occasionally raw but always truly real."
ROMANTIC TIMES

"*Change of Heart* is a beautifully written, enlightening, and tragic story. . . . This novel is a must-read for lovers of contemporary romance."
RADIANT LIT

Paper Hearts

"Walsh pens a quaint, small-town love story . . . [with] enough plot twists to make this enjoyable to the end."
PUBLISHERS WEEKLY

"Be prepared to be swept away by this delightful romance about healing the heart, forgiveness, [and] following your dreams . . ."
FRESH FICTION

"Walsh writes a small-town setting, a sweet, slow-building romance between two likable characters and a host of eclectic secondary characters."
ROMANTIC TIMES

"Well written and charming."
NOVEL REVIEWS

"A masterful word painting, *A Sweethaven Summer* is a story of loss, regret, forgiveness, and restoration. Novel Rocket and I give it our highest recommendation. It's a five-star must-read."

ANE MULLIGAN, PRESIDENT, NOVEL ROCKET

"This book captivated me from the first paragraphs. Bittersweet memories, long-kept secrets, the timeless friendships of women— and a touch of sweet romance. Beautifully written and peopled with characters who became my friends, this debut novel is one for my keeper shelf—and, I hope, the first of many to come from Courtney Walsh's pen."

DEBORAH RANEY, AUTHOR OF THE CHICORY INN NOVELS SERIES

"*A Sweethaven Summer* is a sweet debut, filled with characters whose hopes, dreams, and regrets are relevant and relatable. A great book club read!"

SUSAN MEISSNER, AUTHOR OF *A FALL OF MARIGOLDS*

"*A Sweethaven Summer* is a stunning debut. . . . With a voice that sparkles, Courtney Walsh captured my heart in this tender story of forgiveness and new beginnings. It's certainly a great beginning for this talented author."

CARLA STEWART, AUTHOR OF *THE HATMAKER'S HEART*

"Courtney Walsh weaves a captivating tale that taps into the universal desire for belonging and happiness. This delightful debut has a bit of mystery, a bit of romance, a beautiful setting, and an intriguing cast of characters."

MEGAN DIMARIA, AUTHOR OF *SEARCHING FOR SPICE*

"*A Sweethaven Summer* shines with moments of hope and tenderness. With interesting characters, a delightful setting, and a compelling plot, this is one of those stories that stays with you."

TINA ANN FORKNER, AUTHOR OF *RUBY AMONG US*

A Sweethaven Homecoming

"Courtney Walsh puts the sweet in Sweethaven. If you're looking for an uplifting, hope-filled story filled with characters you'll feel like you know, *A Sweethaven Homecoming* has it!"

MARYBETH WHALEN, AUTHOR OF *THE BRIDGE TENDER*

"*A Sweethaven Homecoming* is a triumph! With the foundations of family, love, and faith, The Circle grows through heartbreak, loss, and betrayal and emerges renewed in their love for one another and, most of all, their love of themselves."

SUSAN OPEL, CREATIVE EDITOR, *PAPER CRAFTS* MAGAZINE

A Sweethaven Christmas

"Readers will smell the pine of Christmas trees and the aromas of holiday food and will hold close the friendships they develop with the characters."

ROMANTIC TIMES

"Walsh's compelling writing style creates unforgettable characters readers come to know and love, while her story lines contend with issues common to us all. . . . Even though the ending is emotional (keep [a] box of Kleenex handy), it's a story of hope, goodwill, and good friends that is perfect for the Christmas season."

EXAMINER.COM

JUST LOOK UP

ALSO BY COURTNEY WALSH

Paper Hearts

Change of Heart

A Sweethaven Summer

A Sweethaven Homecoming

A Sweethaven Christmas

Just Look Up

a novel

COURTNEY
WALSH

Tyndale House Publishers, Inc.
Carol Stream, Illinois

Visit Tyndale online at www.tyndale.com.

Visit Courtney Walsh's website at www.courtneywalshwrites.com.

TYNDALE and Tyndale's quill logo are registered trademarks of Tyndale House Publishers, Inc.

Just Look Up

Designed by Jennifer Ghionzoli

Edited by Danika King

Published in association with the literary agency of Natasha Kern Literary Agency, Inc., P.O. Box 1069, White Salmon, WA 98672.

Just Look Up is a work of fiction. Where real people, events, establishments, organizations, or locales appear, they are used fictitiously. All other elements of the novel are drawn from the author's imagination.

For information about special discounts for bulk purchases, please contact Tyndale House Publishers at csresponse@tyndale.com or call 800-323-9400.

Library of Congress Cataloging-in-Publication Data

Names: Walsh, Courtney, date, author.
Title: Just look up / Courtney Walsh.
Description: Carol Stream, Illinois : Tyndale House Publishers, Inc., [2017]
Identifiers: LCCN 2017001940 | ISBN 9781496421487 (softcover)
Subjects: | GSAFD: Christian fiction. | Love stories.
Classification: LCC PS3623.A4455 J87 2017 | DDC 813/.6—dc23 LC record available at https://lccn.loc.gov/2017001940

Printed in the United States of America

23   22   21   20   19   18   17
7   6   5   4   3   2   1

For my daughter, Sophia.
Look up. That's where the good stuff is.

CHAPTER

1

JUST BREATHE.

Lane Kelley rested her hand on her knee, willing it to stop bouncing. She watched from behind her desk as Marshall ushered the client—a young guy in jeans who appeared to be valiantly attempting a goatee, albeit unsuccessfully—through the glass doors of the conference room at JB Sweet & Associates, the interior design firm where she worked as one of many designers.

You can do this. It's what you've been working for.

The chance of a lifetime.

That's what Marshall had called it—*the chance of a lifetime.* *"You're one of five people in the company who will get to be part of this project, Lane. The higher-ups are watching. This is huge. You're not going to get an opportunity like this again."*

She understood. She'd been pursuing this since she started at the design firm seven years ago as part of her senior seminar at Northwestern. She hadn't expected to stay here this long, but she quickly found a home at JB Sweet, and she was good at what she did.

The last seven years had gone by in a blur, leaving Lane with half-remembered moments of creating branded environments for new and established companies by using her artistic abilities and her love of interior design. Her college internship had turned into a career—one that afforded her a luxury loft in the city, a shared personal assistant, and now the chance to become the next creative director at JB Sweet.

Chloe welcomed the goatee guy—Ashton—and the rest of the team from Solar into the meeting room and flashed Lane her trademark oh-my-goodness eyes. Chloe understood, more than anyone, what this meeting meant to Lane. In some ways, this would be *their* promotion. After all, if Lane did get the position, she'd already promised that her first request would be for Chloe to move up with her.

Chloe gave Lane one more knowing nod as she passed by again, and Lane actually considered pinching herself.

This was the moment she'd been dreaming of—a chance to win over the execs at Solar, to convince them that yes, they very much should give JB Sweet & Associates the honor of designing and branding their new business space, because yes, she and her team would work round the clock to make sure the branded space would reflect Solar's unique, casual-yet-trendy style.

"They love our aesthetic," Marshall had told her. *"I mean, bring your A game, but expect good things. According to Ashton, the whole team is leaning our way."*

And that was *before* her pitch. All she had to do was *not* mess it up.

She'd run through her presentation well into the wee hours of the morning, starting in on the caffeine around 4 a.m. She was ready. Excited, if a little jittery. Her designs were great. She could do this. She could wow them.

And yet, thinking of it now, she felt rocking-on-a-boat-in-choppy-waters sick. She'd never had a chance this big in her life.

Don't mess this up, Lane.

The rest of the executives from Solar, a tech company in the *Forbes* top ten last year, filed past. They shook hands with Marshall and the others from her team as they walked through the door. But not Lane. She was still at her desk, busy trying not to throw up.

Stay in control. These guys have no idea that your nerves are taking you out to the woodshed. No one can make you feel inferior in this arena. This isn't high school. This is where you shine.

The guys from Solar—she could only call them "guys" because not a single one of them actually looked like a man—all resembled their fearless leader, Ashton, aka Mr. Wanna Goatee. Jeans, hoodies, Converse One Stars. No suits for this company. Somehow she found that more intimidating, not less. After all, she'd never been the trendy type.

She shoved aside the unwelcome image of a sweater that didn't quite cover a protruding midsection.

"Honey, I tried to tell you, you shouldn't wear clothes that are so tight."

She'd been aching for sympathy, but her mother had only given empty *I-told-you-so*s and the sour taste of disapproval. She hadn't meant to disregard Lane's feelings; she just wanted to help. At least that's what Lane tried to tell herself.

Nobody here knows about that.

Marshall looked terribly outdated next to the Solar execs with his white button-down and geometrically patterned red tie. Handsome in his own way, yet everyone in the room aged twenty years in the presence of their fetus-clients.

Marshall broke away from the others and headed her way.

Her phone pinged, and she glanced at it almost without thinking. Instantly she wished she hadn't.

"What is it?" Marshall asked when he reached her. "You have that look."

She tapped on the notification. She'd set her phone up to alert her whenever a competing design firm posted something on social media, and this was a big one.

"Julia Baumann." She looked up at Marshall. "You didn't tell me Innovate was pitching your friend Ashton, too." She showed Marshall the photo, a cozy image of Julia Baumann and the goatee guy in the next room. "The caption says, 'Sweet things are happening for Innovate. Details coming soon.'" She frowned. "There's a winking emoji and *sweet* is in all caps. Is she sending a message to us?"

He took the phone from her and read the post for himself. "I'm sure you're reading too much into this."

"I thought you said we practically had this one 'in the bag.'"

Marshall shrugged. "We do, Lane. Maybe she's trying to get under your skin."

Well, that would be juvenile. Lane groaned. She didn't want to think about Innovate just before she walked into that room. Julia Baumann had a way of swiping clients right out from under her, and it was starting to feel personal. Lane found most of the design community open and friendly—encouraging, even—but Julia was none of those things.

Lane took another glance at the photo. "They look awfully friendly, Marshall, and you know Julia probably had a solid pitch."

"Maybe." Marshall squeezed her hand. "But ours is going to blow them away."

He couldn't possibly know that. She thought back to their many long team meetings—how many times had Marshall deferred to her, chosen her ideas and trusted her vision? What if he'd been wrong to do so? What if she'd misunderstood Solar and gone in completely the wrong direction?

No. She shook her insecurities away. Their pitch was ready—and it was on point. JB Sweet himself would have to take note once she presented her plans. She'd finally get that promotion and maybe even take a little vacation to celebrate.

She'd never taken a vacation.

"Come on, forget Innovate. You're ready for the big leagues." Marshall walked her over to the small huddle at the end of the room where the rest of their team had gathered.

She barely listened as Marshall gave the team his version of a pep talk. He scanned the circle and was met with overenthusiastic nodding from everyone but Lane. She didn't do overenthusiastic. She did focus. She did the game face. She did control.

And she did it well.

"Lane, you okay?"

"I'm ready." She didn't bother trying to explain her readiness or convincing Marshall she really meant it. That's what weak women did. And she never wanted to be one of those again.

"Okay. We'll start in just a few minutes. Knock 'em dead, guys." Marshall waited until the others had dispersed, then turned his attention back to Lane. "You feel good?"

She nodded as she ran through her pitch in her mind.

"Remember, this is the chance—"

"Of a lifetime." She cut him off. "I know." *Don't remind me. I'm nervous enough as it is.*

"I went out on a limb to give you this meeting, Lane. You're up to this, right?" He raised a brow as if issuing a challenge.

"You know I'm up to this." She clicked her phone's screen off, wishing she could click off the sick feeling in her stomach that easily.

"That's my girl." He clapped a hand on her shoulder. Like she was one of the guys. Very professional.

She had to hand it to him—he was doing an excellent job of keeping their relationship hidden. Even she found it hard to believe he had any romantic feelings for her at all.

"You go ahead," she told Marshall. "I'll be right there."

Breathe. She was running through her opening one last time when her phone pinged again, and as if she were programmed to do so, she pulled it out and glanced at it.

Julia had posted another image, this one a photo of the mock-up Innovate had presented to Solar only hours ago. The caption read, *We're calling it "Solarvate." Can't wait to get started.*

Lane's mouth went dry, her stomach hollow. The image on the screen looked so elegant, so regal, so not what she had planned for this pitch meeting.

"You ready?" Chloe stood at her side, looking a little more tired than usual, the way she often did after one of their all-nighters. Lane made a mental note to get her assistant a gift certificate for a massage or give her some time off to thank her for being so helpful. Chloe had probably seen Julia's posts too. She kept tabs on them the same way Lane did. But Lane had to believe Solar hadn't made up their mind already. If they had, would they really be sitting here in JB Sweet's conference room?

She did a quick survey of Julia's design, then turned her phone to vibrate. "I'm ready."

Chloe nodded and moved out of the way as Lane passed by. She smoothed her black dress pants and sat down next to Marshall.

After everyone was seated, JB called the meeting to order. The Solar executives, with their Starbucks to-go cups, their casual shoes, their bordering-on-shaggy hair and impress-me expressions, all turned their attention to the man. Marshall might've aged twenty years in the presence of the Solar execs, but next to them, JB seemed downright prehistoric.

Lane had always found him to be a quirky kind of man, one who used words like *fellow* and had a bushy white mustache that made her doubt the presence of an upper lip at all. Ashton should take a few pointers from JB. That man knew how to grow facial hair.

Lane half listened to JB's introduction of Solar—stating facts she'd already researched on her own. Next, JB gave a short pitch about why his firm was the best to take on the massive task of creating and designing a branded space for a cutting-edge tech business like Solar.

JB assured them that the space they had planned for Solar was not only functional but truly creative at its core—something the artistic Solar execs would certainly appreciate. JB was nothing if not an excellent salesman. Maybe that's why this *fellow* was still running the show after all these years.

Lane glanced down at her tablet, mentally reciting her opening lines, when the phone in the bag near her feet lit up, vibrating loudly enough to pull Miles's attention.

"Might want to silence that thing," her coworker hissed.

She fished the phone out of her bag and pressed the button to stop the noise before anyone else noticed, but not before she saw that it was her mother calling. She sent the call to voice mail. She supposed she was due for her monthly guilt-trip phone call—it had been at least that long since she'd spoken to her mom.

In her hand, the phone started vibrating again.

Mom, you have the worst timing.

She hit the button to shut it up, then turned off the power.

Marshall took JB's spot at the front of the room and introduced himself. "I think we're ready to begin." He glanced at Lane.

Just breathe. Part of her, she supposed, would always feel like a fraud. Most days, despite her Northwestern education and years of experience, Lane still felt like she was playing dress-up in the closet of someone much older, much thinner, and much more professional than she ever felt.

And yet she'd mastered the art of playing this part perfectly, as if she were born for the role.

". . . and we're sure you'll be as impressed with her as we are. Lane Kelley." Marshall spoke her name, pulling her out of her own head.

She met his eyes and he leaned forward as if to will her out of her seat.

Had time suddenly stopped moving?

Lane stood, taking her place next to the big screen. *You can do this.* She flipped open the cover of her tablet and drew in a deep breath as the image of a mood board that perfectly captured their design popped up on the screen beside her.

She'd created the image herself. Most people were visual, and the images, all of them, needed to conjure the same feelings the space itself would. Every item on the mood board had been carefully—painstakingly—chosen.

Lane knew Solar inside and out, she reminded herself. She'd read every article, every blurb, every tweet and Facebook post that had anything to do with the business this team had built. She was wrapped up in the details—and it was about to pay off.

In spades.

She had her game face on. As she stood there, every insecurity melted away. They were in her world now, and here, she knew how to get things done.

Lane was about to deliver her first sentence when the glass door of the conference room opened and Chloe appeared. She wore an apologetic look on her face and Lane knew her well enough to tell she wasn't happy to steal the attention.

"I'm sorry to interrupt." Chloe looked at Lane. "Lane, you've got a phone call."

"Can't it wait?" Marshall spoke through clenched teeth, doing a bad job of pretending he wasn't annoyed.

Chloe's face fell. "I'm afraid not."

Marshall pressed his lips together and glared at Lane, telepathically communicating the words undoubtedly running through his mind: *Don't screw this up.*

"Can you take a message, Chloe?" Lane asked. "I'm just getting ready to begin."

"I don't think—"

"Take a message," Marshall cut her off.

"There's been an accident, Lane," Chloe said. "You need to take the call."

NATE WAS HER FAVORITE BROTHER. He always had been. He'd been the one who stuck up for her when everything went sideways. And when she heard her mother's voice on the other end of the phone, the floodgate of memories opened and it all came rushing back.

His earnest face. His knit brow. His pleading words. *"How could you do this to Lane?"* It was as if he knew nothing would ever be the same again. And he'd been right.

"Lane, it's Nate," her mother had said when Lane picked up the phone. "We need you to come home."

"What about Nate? What's going on?" She leaned against Chloe's desk, her gaze wandering through the glass of the conference room, where Marshall now stood next to the screen, stalling for time.

Lane pinched the space just between her eyebrows, trying to focus on her mother's voice on the other end of the line.

Her mother started to cry. "There was an accident last night. He's in the ICU. You need to come home, Lane."

This couldn't be happening. *Please, God, not Nate.* Her heavy sigh matched her heart.

Marshall glanced at her from where he stood and she quickly turned away.

"The ICU?" She did her best to steady her voice, unsure how she was going to persuade Marshall to give her a few days off. Convincing Solar to hire them was only the first part of the job—if they won the account, their workload would double, maybe even triple. And if she knew Marshall, and she did, their deadline would be a tight one. He would overpromise. Talk big like he did.

And Lane wouldn't sleep for the next six months.

Marshall didn't care about family emergencies. He cared about results. If she couldn't deliver them, he'd find someone who could.

"Tell me what happened, Mom," Lane said.

"It was a motorcycle accident. Nate and that stupid motorcycle," her mom said. "A truck swerved over the center line and into his lane, and when he tried to get out of the way, he lost control and ended up colliding with a telephone pole."

"Why didn't you call me last night?" Lane tried not to sound accusatory.

"We didn't know how serious it was until this morning," her mom said. "You know Nate—he's been in and out of the emergency room since he was a little boy."

"Was he wearing a helmet?" Lane asked, thinking back to Nate's eighteenth birthday, when he announced he'd purchased a motor-cycle with his own money. Their mother had been furious, but Nate's argument that he was an adult now eventually won out. She'd made him promise he wouldn't ride without a helmet—a promise he only sometimes kept.

"Yes, thank goodness," her mom said. "But they don't know . . ."

"Mom?"

Her tears had apparently overtaken her. Lane heard a commotion on the other end.

"Mom?" As if raising her voice would make her mother pick the phone back up.

"Lane?"

"Jer?"

"You should come home."

She felt the pinprick at the edges of her heart. "She's not just overreacting? You know how she is."

Her youngest brother sighed. "He's not conscious, Lane. He's in a coma. Broke his right arm and leg and two ribs." A pause, then Jeremy spoke in a lower tone. "He's in bad shape."

She sank into Chloe's chair as she thought of the last time she'd seen Nate. Two years ago at Christmas, and only because he came to the city and she felt obligated.

She should've done better. Nate wasn't the one who betrayed her.

"Let me see what I can do," Lane said. "I'm in the middle of a couple of big projects here." She didn't want to think about Nate in a hospital bed. Or what it would be like walking into the waiting room and coming face-to-face with family she hadn't seen in months—years. Here, at work, was where she belonged. She was comfortable here. Competent. And people knew that about her. Harbor Pointe didn't hold even a sliver of that assurance.

She pictured Jeremy standing in the middle of the Harbor Pointe Hospital, surrounded by their parents, their oldest brother, Noah, and his family, and Nate's never-ending line of friends. How would she find the courage to insert herself into the fray? The image from one of those Discovery Channel shows popped into her head—salmon working so hard against the natural order of things, swimming against the flow and seemingly getting nowhere unless they were willing to jump upstream.

She'd always found it hard to be the salmon.

"Lane." Jer's voice was quiet, yet firm. "This isn't a 'let me see if I can work it into my schedule' kind of thing. This is a 'drop everything and get here' kind of thing."

His words robbed Lane of the air in her lungs. She had a feeling it was something like that. Denying it wouldn't make it go away. She rubbed her temple and closed her eyes, willing the dull ache in her head to fade.

"What are you saying, Jer?" She heard the crack in her voice.

A quiet beat; then, "Just get home, Lane. Today." And then he was gone.

As her mind floundered, she placed the receiver back in the cradle on Chloe's desk. Seconds later, Chloe appeared at Lane's side as if she'd been watching her from some unknown hiding place, waiting to pounce the second Lane hung up. "What is it?" Her eyes were wide.

Lane stared at the floor. "I have to go home."

Chloe tossed her long auburn hair behind her shoulder as Lane raised her chin to meet her gaze. "What's wrong?" In that moment, there was no trace of Chloe's usual sharp-witted sense of humor—only genuine concern in her eyes.

But that made everything seem more real—and Lane didn't want to believe any of it. She couldn't form a reply.

Lane started toward her cubicle, her head doing a pirouette, her palms cold and clammy. Marshall was probably glaring at her in his mind despite maintaining his composure in front of JB and the others. She'd let him down.

God, please don't let Nate die.

"What can I do?" Chloe asked as Lane reached her desk and started gathering her things.

"Just help me reschedule whatever's on my calendar for the next couple of days," Lane said, tucking her laptop into its case.

Chloe turned her attention to her tablet. "I can do that." She tapped the screen a few times. "You've got a meeting with Mrs. Pim this afternoon and a phone call with *Chicago Woman* magazine after that."

Lane rubbed her forehead. "I forgot."

"I'll reschedule," Chloe said. "I'll make sure they know it was an emergency."

Lane dropped into her desk chair. "What about Solar?" Unwanted tears sprang to her eyes as she saw everything she'd worked so hard for vanishing into thin air. And yet a part of her knew it was the phone call that had made her truly emotional.

She just didn't want to think about that right now.

"I'll go in and explain what happened. Let's see if we can get them back in a few days." Chloe's smile revealed perfectly straight and professionally whitened teeth. Chloe ran a fashion blog, one that was doing surprisingly well. Lane supposed that's why her assistant had practically become her personal shopper. Chloe said it was fun to dress her boss, especially since she could shop on someone else's dime.

Lane had never much enjoyed shopping. Years of finding nothing in her size had sullied the experience, she supposed.

Lane sighed. "But they've already met with Julia Baumann at Innovate. If they don't hear our pitch today, they probably aren't going to hear it at all."

"I think Miles was talking to them just now. I'm sure the team can handle it."

Lane stifled a groan. Miles would handle it all right. And he'd weasel his way into her promotion too—he'd been after it all year.

"I know. It's just that this was my pitch."

"I'm sure they'll understand," Chloe said, though she and Lane both knew better. That's not how this business worked. The odds of a second chance were slim.

Her assistant stilled. "So what happened, Lane? Is everything okay?"

Lane didn't discuss her family—not even with Chloe—and she wasn't about to start now. "I think it'll be fine, but thanks for your concern." Even as she said the words, she felt like a liar. She wasn't even remotely sure everything was going to be fine. She wouldn't know until she got there and saw her brother for herself.

Chloe probably saw right through her, but she knew better than to press Lane.

She stood, gathered the last of her things, and turned to Chloe. "Can you let everyone know they can reach me on my cell?"

"Of course, Lane, but if you need a couple days off, take them," Chloe said. "It's not like you haven't earned it."

Lane stiffened as her friend attempted a hug that turned awkward. "Thanks."

"Is there anything else I can do?" Chloe's face had fallen as if the gravity of the situation had pulled the buoyancy from her eyes. Somehow Lane knew that now she wasn't asking as an assistant—she was asking as a friend.

"Thanks, Chlo," Lane said. "But no. I'll let you know if I think of anything."

Chloe gave her one brave nod and Lane started down the hallway toward the elevator.

"Where are you going?"

Marshall's voice stopped her, but she didn't immediately turn around. She could sense that Chloe had stepped into Lane's cubicle, no doubt desperately wishing she could disappear.

Slowly Lane faced him. "I have a family emergency."

She could imagine how it sounded, given that Marshall knew nothing about her family—even after working together for seven years and dating each other for five months. He was as much in the dark as everyone, but that didn't make what she said any less true.

His hands were attached to his hips, his gaze holding hers hostage. "Come into my office." He walked past her, down the hall toward the very room where they'd shared their first kiss only a few short months ago. Marshall confessed his feelings had been growing for her despite the fact that he'd been in a serious relationship with someone else for three years.

"That's all over now, though," he'd told her. *"And I thought maybe we could have a drink together after work sometime."*

She'd been hesitant at first since she'd worked so hard to be taken seriously, but his quiet persistence won her over in the end. Sometimes she thought maybe she was just tired of being alone, but then she remembered the side of Marshall no one else ever got to see. He was charming always, but with her, when other people weren't around, it was more than that. He was attentive and thoughtful and he told her she was beautiful.

Mostly, though, her affection for him lacked the kind of intoxication new romance sometimes brings, which meant Lane could enjoy their relationship without having to be afraid of the deep pain of losing it.

Her heart was secure—and that was the most important thing.

They'd kept their romance quiet, given Lane's ambitions of becoming a creative director one day.

Now, sitting on the sofa in his office, blinds drawn, she didn't know if she was here as an employee or a girlfriend.

He sat down next to her. "What's going on? We've got a room full of really important people in there, and you're bolting for the door."

She stared at her hands, folded in her lap. "I told you. Family emergency."

He leaned closer. "Can you give me a little more than that?"

No. She couldn't. She didn't want to invite Marshall into that world—a world that didn't make sense, even to her. "It's complicated."

He scratched his head just behind his ear and shifted on the sofa. "You've got to explain this to me, Lane."

"I need a couple of personal days," she said. "You know I wouldn't ask if it weren't important."

His eyebrows shot up. "Right now? In the middle of the biggest project you've worked on since you started here? You blew it in there. The team had to cover for you."

She held his gaze. "But that's what it means to be a part of a team, isn't it?"

Marshall studied her. "You know what I'm talking about. This was your chance to show off a little—you say you want to be a creative director; then you walk out of a pitch meeting with Solar? Not a good decision."

"You know I didn't just 'walk out,'" she said.

"Do I?" he asked. "You've told me nothing about that phone call. For that matter, you've told me nothing about your family."

"I admit the timing is less than ideal." She hoped her attempt to change the subject would hold. She could feel him studying her as if his glare would break her down, make her spill the whole sad story.

"I need more than this if I'm going to give you a few days off," he said. "I'm talking as your team leader now."

She shot him a look. "Marshall, please."

He shrugged as if to ask what else he was supposed to do.

"You're pulling rank to extract information on my personal life."

The tight look on his face softened. "I thought *I* was your personal life."

She looked away. "My brother was in an accident. I need to go home and make sure he's okay."

"You have a brother?"

"I have three brothers." She stood. "And I have to go now."

He stood in front of her, took her hands, and forced her to look at him. He pushed her dark hair behind her ear and waited until he had her eyes. She hated how vulnerable it made her feel. Her wall was usually fully intact—unable to be scaled.

The memories of Nate must've thrown her off.

"How long will you be gone?" he asked.

"A couple of days at most," she said, thankful he'd chosen to stay on topic.

"You know what I'm up against here. And you can't afford to throw this opportunity away."

Lane didn't say anything.

"I'm going to have to be able to get ahold of you," Marshall said.

"I'll keep my phone with me."

"I already talked to Ashton about another meeting. We gave him just enough to entice him to come back and hear you deliver it the way we'd planned. I asked him if we could have until Monday."

"And?"

"He said they'd hold off making decisions until you were available." Marshall grinned. "And I think I can hold JB off too."

Monday. That was a week away. Nate would be better by then, though. That should be fine.

"Thank you, Marshall," Lane said. "For getting me a second chance."

"Of course." He pulled her into a stilted hug. "Just hurry back, okay?" He kissed her, but she barely responded. They were at work, after all, and frankly, she had other things on her mind.

She rushed out of JB Sweet & Associates, mentally packing for her trip to Harbor Pointe and willing away the deep sense of dread that had balled itself into a tight knot at the base of her stomach.

CHAPTER

3

RYAN BROOKS WOKE UP in a hospital bed in a small room at Harbor Pointe Hospital.

"You're awake." A tall, thin nurse with salt-and-pepper hair, wearing pink scrubs and round glasses, eyed him from behind the computer screen. Her name—Elaine—had been stitched onto the scrubs top. "How are you feeling?"

He wasn't sure. The last thing he remembered was sitting on a bed in the emergency room. He winced as a sharp pain shot through his temples and across the back of his skull.

"Headache?"

He nodded. "I'm fine."

"Sure you are, tough guy," the nurse said. "You were admitted last night for observation—do you remember that?"

Vaguely. "Yeah."

"And you remember the accident?"

"Do you know how my friend is?"

"Right now my only concern is you." She entered something on the computer, then came over to examine his leg. This hospital stay wasn't pleasant, but at least he was conscious, and he didn't think he could say the same for Nate.

"Do you know how long this is going to be?" he asked, doing his best not to sound like a jerk.

The expression on her face told him not to mess with her. "You could have been killed last night. The least you can do is let me check your stitches."

Great. Could he ask her to hurry up with it already? He wanted to check on Nate. Last thing he remembered was seeing him rolled off on a stretcher into an ambulance—and his buddy wasn't responding.

"They said you hit your head?" Her gravelly voice reminded him of a cartoon character, one who smoked too many cigarettes.

"I was wearing a helmet."

"Doesn't mean there was no damage. We did a CT scan last night, and you don't have a concussion—"

"Great, so I can leave."

"But the doctor is still going to want to see you before we let you go." She gave him a wry grin. "You might as well sit back and relax. You're going to be here for a while."

"I've already been here for a while." Ryan let out a long sigh and stared at the ceiling. His head throbbed and he felt groggy—probably from the beat-down he'd had from the pavement.

He rested his head back on a too-soft pillow and drew in a deep breath. That unmistakable hospital smell wouldn't let him forget—even for a moment—where he was, and his memory, replaying images from the accident on a continuous loop, wouldn't let him forget where he'd been.

The truck swerved over the line. Nate skidded across the asphalt. The sound of Nate's bike slamming into the telephone pole as Ryan tried to regain control of his own bike, missing the same pole by inches.

Inches between him and death.

Again.

So many close calls and yet here he was, walking around with bumps and bruises while so many of his friends were six feet underground.

Something about it seemed unfair. He should be in the coma, not Nate. Not the guy whose family was probably pacing the hallway outside his room praying for complete healing.

Hadn't Ryan left death behind on the other side of the world? Had it followed him back here from Afghanistan?

He shook the thoughts from his mind, willing away the images that seemed intent on tormenting him.

After the Kelleys' traditional Sunday dinner yesterday afternoon, the topic had turned to the Cedar Grove vacation cottages. Nate's dad, Frank, asked about the work it took to restore a dozen rundown cottages, and Noah wanted to know about Ryan's investors.

"The deadline's coming up," Ryan told them. "They'll be back to walk through the cottages in about a month, to check on the progress and make sure we're ready for tourist season."

"And heaven knows we need help with tourist season," Frank had said. Both Frank and Noah Kelley ran businesses that heavily relied on tourism, just like many of the residents in Harbor Pointe. And they all knew tourism as a whole was down, since so many of the vacation homes had been bought up by people who left them vacant for much of the year.

"That's what I'm hoping," Ryan said. "Cedar Grove would help get new people in here."

"It could be great for our economy," Frank agreed. "I knew it was a good investment."

He was one of the first to invest in Ryan's dream. For the briefest moment, Ryan felt like the man was a proud father. Frank clapped him on the shoulder. Would Ryan ever be able to repay his kindness?

"I won't let you down," he said. "You or the other investors. I know you're all counting on me." They weren't the only ones. He had a lot riding on Cedar Grove. He had the plans drawn up, yes, but there was still so much to do.

"You look exhausted, man," Nate had said.

"Yeah, but it'll be worth it." Especially that first week after he opened—when he'd be hosting his most important guests.

"Back to the grind tomorrow," Nate said, that goofy grin on his face. "You should probably make the most of the weekend."

Ryan knew exactly what he meant. The two of them had spent hours riding over the last two years. They knew the highway with all its turns as if they'd committed them to memory. Riding made Ryan feel alive—it was about the only thing that did.

They drove along the lake, taking in the views, driving faster than they should, but when they passed the Harbor Pointe city limits and entered Newman, Ryan grew distracted. Newman with all its memories, its secrets—they whispered to him as soon as he saw Scooter's, the red barn–turned–bar on the edge of town.

Every time they took this route, his whole body tensed until they cleared Newman on the other side.

They drove right past the high school, the ball fields, the trailer park, Ryan battling the memories he'd worked hard to bury the entire time. While Harbor Pointe oozed charm and drew in tourists from all over the Midwest, Newman, only miles up the highway, had very little to offer anybody. Even residents had to drive twenty minutes in either direction for shopping options or jobs.

How badly he'd wanted to get out of there.

They reached the next town, then the next, and Ryan could finally relax, but they'd have to drive back through on their way home.

Dusk. That golden hour when eyes played tricks, giving flat pavement a confusing shine and casting shadows on things that weren't there.

But it wasn't the time of day that had caused Nate's accident, because shadows weren't objects that came out of nowhere and forced other drivers off the road.

They'd just passed the sign for Newman—five miles away. Maybe it was a memory of something that had slowed Ryan down, but Nate didn't notice. His speed remained steady, putting a bit of distance between their two bikes.

If they'd been side by side when the truck in the other lane crossed the centerline, one or both of them would probably be dead right now.

Ryan flinched as the nurse rebandaged his wound. The gash in his leg was nothing compared to Nate's injuries, and he'd known that almost immediately.

He'd watched, horrified, as the truck in the other lane veered just as it was about to pass them. Nate swerved to get out of the way, but he quickly lost control of his bike before colliding with the pole. Ryan also had to swerve to keep from hitting Nate, and when he did, he came down hard on the pavement, slicing up his calf and hitting his head on the ground. The impact, even with his helmet on, had been enough to knock him out for at least a minute.

If he thought about it, he could put himself back there, lying on the pavement, eyes fluttering open behind the darkness of his helmet. It had felt like waking up from a fog, like he'd been given anesthesia and there was still just enough in his system to keep him from feeling coherent.

He was pulling the helmet off without sitting up when the brake lights of the truck, now stopped in the middle of the road, caught his attention. The driver was probably going to pull over and park, come see how they were, call 911.

Ryan's head throbbed, and pain shot through his right leg. Beside him, he could see Nate's bike—what was left of it—but Nate wasn't moving.

He tried to call out for help, but he didn't have a voice. He didn't have words. His head felt heavy and thick, difficult to hold upright.

The brake lights on the pickup truck flickered. Why wasn't the driver getting out? The engine revved and it started moving. Was he just going to leave them there, like roadkill on the side of the highway?

I should get the license plate.

He squinted, trying to get a good view of it, but his eyes wouldn't focus.

Blue Ford pickup truck. Rust around the back tire on the driver's side.

Ryan opened his eyes, feeling as if the oxygen had just been sucked out of the room. The image of the truck in the middle of the road raced back.

Blue Ford pickup truck.

Newman.

Scooter's Pub just a few blocks away.

In the waning light of day, he couldn't be certain. He didn't know for sure. Lots of people had trucks in Newman. Lots of people drove through Newman.

"Ryan?"

Without his realizing it, a doctor had entered the small room in Harbor Pointe Hospital. Ryan had met him last night but didn't remember his name.

"How are you feeling today? Your breathing is labored and you're sweating."

Not from my injuries; from my memories.

"I'm okay," he said. "Headache is all."

The doctor took out a penlight and shone it in Ryan's eyes.

His eyes refocused and he saw the man's name tag. Dr. Tambor. Still didn't ring a bell. Maybe he hadn't been paying very close attention last night. "Do you know how my friend is? Nate Kelley?"

Dr. Tambor and the nurse exchanged a look.

"What was that for?"

"I'll check on your friend's condition," Dr. Tambor said. "But right now I'm concerned about yours." Were they trained to give that answer?

Dr. Tambor then asked a series of questions, which Ryan answered as best he could. All the while, Elaine took some notes on the computer.

"I'd like to run a few more tests." Dr. Tambor glanced at Ryan.

"Just to be safe. I want to rule out an internal bleed or bruising on the brain. I'm glad you were wearing a helmet, son."

Son. Why did his stomach tighten at the word?

"Just sit tight and we'll be with you soon."

"I'm finished here too." Elaine stood.

"Can you find out about Nate?" A thick fog seemed to have moved into Ryan's head, like a cloud that covered the sun.

"I'll see what I can do." Elaine patted his arm. "You're very lucky to be alive, young man."

Ryan looked away. He'd heard that before.

And somehow he didn't feel lucky at all.

CHAPTER

4

THE DRIVE TO HARBOR POINTE felt anything but familiar. Lane almost took the wrong exit twice. It had been years since she'd been back home, and if she was honest, she wished she could keep it that way. She glanced at Otis. The French bulldog lay in the passenger seat, snoozing happily. He had no idea what they were in for.

She'd left Harbor Pointe for Northwestern when she was eighteen. Her grades, test scores, and extracurricular activities won her a spot on the university's freshman roster and a substantial scholarship. People could say what they wanted to about Lane Kelley, but no one could say she wasn't smart. She felt like she'd just hit the jackpot. A ticket out of town.

Harbor Pointe might be a quiet escape for most people like her, people with demanding jobs and little rest, but it was the exact opposite for Lane. Every bad memory she had was rolled up in one big ball squarely positioned at the center of Harbor Pointe.

She'd been born in the wrong place, she was convinced—and her quick acclimation to city life proved it. Since graduation day, work had been her only priority. Somehow she'd deluded herself into believing she'd never have to face this place again.

She should've known better.

In her backseat were two bags packed with whatever necessities she could grab on her way out the door, including a half-full bag of food for Otis.

She hadn't intended to get a dog. In fact, she didn't really like dogs, and whenever Otis licked her, her skin broke out in hives. But she had to admit this tiny creature somehow made her feel less alone. Chloe must've known she needed that.

The woman who was paid to assist her really had become one of Lane's only friends.

She realized how pathetic that was.

When Chloe had shown up at Lane's door with Otis, both wearing matching puppy-dog eyes, Lane distinctly remembered the question *What is she thinking?* racing through her mind.

Chloe's eyebrows drew down in a pitiful display. "My landlord won't let me keep him."

"Why are you bringing him here?"

"Because you own your loft," Chloe said, crossing the threshold into Lane's apartment. "And because I thought you might like him."

Lane found out later that Chloe had purposely found this dog at the shelter and brought him straight over to Lane's house. He'd been a gift—a thoughtful one. Lane had hired a dog walker to take care of the creature during her long work hours.

Chloe knew more about Lane than Lane wanted to admit. For one thing, she'd suspected Lane's relationship with Marshall almost from the beginning and hinted that she knew about it. But she'd never told a soul and, from what Lane could see, never judged her for it.

She'd also tried—more than once—to probe Lane about her family. Lane had managed to stay tight-lipped. No sense dragging her assistant into the crazy mixed-up world Lane had all but exited. But more than that, she understood the things Lane didn't say. She must have sensed Lane was lonely or decided she was pathetic, but either way, Lane had gotten Otis out of the deal.

And that had turned out to be a very good thing.

She did her best to stay focused on the road, but her mind hadn't settled down since she hung up the phone with Jeremy.

She'd been reliving the last time she spoke to Nate, two Christmases ago. He said he was in town to visit friends and wanted to say hi and beg her in person to come home this year.

"Don't you miss it at all?" His face was so earnest, the kind of guy you knew was good just by looking at him. "You can't stay away forever."

Watch me.

He'd taken her silence as the hint that it was and changed the subject, then spent the rest of their visit catching her up on his—and only his—latest news. The rest of it, she didn't want or need to know. She gave him a vague breakdown of her life—loft apartment in Chicago, worker bee at JB Sweet with hopes of one day being named creative director, no relationships to speak of (who has time for romance?). She left out the parts about her insomnia and her obsessive relationship with the elliptical machine.

Before Nate left, he stood in her doorway like an awkward teenager not sure what to do next. He turned to her—*earnest eyes*—and asked once more. "For me, Lane? Come back for me? It's not the same without you."

Years of sitting on the roof waiting for Nate to come home from whatever social outing he'd been at flashed through her mind. He'd always been so popular and well-liked, and he'd always told her to come along with him. They were only a year apart in age—it would've been a natural fit. "I'll make sure you're not stuck alone in some corner."

She'd never gone. Instead, she spent her weekend evenings throughout high school reading—on the roof outside her bedroom when the weather was nice enough. And when he returned, he'd crawl out of his window next to hers and answer her questions about the party, school dance, football game, or homecoming celebration he'd just come from.

Those conversations were, to this day, some of her favorites.

She was *this close* to agreeing, just because it was Nate asking. And when she said, "I'll think about it," she meant it, but they both knew better.

They weren't close anymore—not like they used to be—and maybe that made her dread this trip all the more. It was obligation, not heart, that brought her home.

The thought shamed her. Nate had proven his loyalty to her in a way no one else had, but she'd tossed his relationship out on the trash pile with the rest of them.

It was unfair, but she hadn't thought so until now, in the face of tragedy. What did that say about her?

Her phone buzzed in the cup holder and Otis sat up. She glanced down and saw that it was Chloe, who'd been instructed to keep her updated on any important developments in the Solar campaign. Or anything else at the office Lane should know about.

She picked up the phone. Miles McQuerry is acting project manager in your absence.

Lane's stomach rolled over. Seriously? Marshall put Miles in charge? Miles was the epitome of a cutthroat businessman, and it was Lane's throat he was after.

"Great," she said into her phone, watching as the word magically appeared in the text box. "Watch him like a hawk."

Miles would make the most of these circumstances, and Lane knew it. She knew it because if the roles were reversed, she would do the same.

She groaned as she stuck the phone back in the cup holder. Otis growled a response. She'd get to the hospital, make sure her brother was okay, and then she'd return to the city as soon as possible. She had to—or everything she'd been working for would go up in flames.

Besides, Nate was invincible—Jeremy and her mom must've forgotten.

Knowing he was in the ICU certainly made it easy to forget.

After three hours of driving, Lane exited the highway for Harbor Pointe, Michigan. The signs promised "peace" and "quiet." She supposed it was true for most people—it was hard for a town with so little to do to offer anything but peace and quiet. Growing up in a tourist town, she had a revolving door of summer friends. She'd come to realize she much preferred being in the city surrounded by busy go-getters than on the beaches of Lake Michigan surrounded by lazy vacationers.

Even though it had been years since she'd been back, she could still recite the script from one of her more tolerable summer jobs—Harbor Pointe tour guide. Somehow standing up at the front of the harbor trolley and giving newcomers the rundown didn't intimidate her at all. She just pretended she was someone else for a while as she narrated the trolley's route toward the water. So many of the town's activities revolved around the lake.

"Vacationers love our water sports, boating charters, and lighthouse tours, but be careful after dark. Some say the old harbor lighthouse is haunted by the ghost of a lighthouse keeper who disappeared at sea during a storm in the spring of 1953." She'd used her best newscaster's voice as she delivered the script and tried her hardest to make the stories interesting.

After the lake tour, they'd head toward town. *"Of course, after a full day on the water, you'll want to explore our thriving food industry. Harbor Pointe is home to thirty-two different locally owned eateries, including Summers Cheese, one of my personal favorites, which is the perfect stop after you visit one of the three beautiful wineries in the area."*

Lane realized she'd been speaking out loud to no one but Otis and felt instantly embarrassed. Especially the way she'd added in the bit about Summers, plugging the family business like someone with a personal stake in it. She supposed some things would be with her forever, no matter how much time passed. After repeating those words numerous times a day for several summers, they were embedded in her memory, a permanent reminder of everything Harbor Pointe was supposed to be.

She drove through downtown, which still looked a lot like a movie set that had been frozen in time. She turned onto Main Street and wondered how it was possible nobody had lobbied to repaint the brightly colored storefronts that lined either side of the street. The town was quiet this time of year—not quite tourist season—but unless everything had changed, the locals were gearing up for the influx of people who would join them for the summer.

The cottages and vacation homes in and around Harbor Pointe would soon be rented out or occupied by those who spent their summers away from "real life," lazing on the beaches and living what Lane's mother referred to as a "simple life."

She always said people came to Harbor Pointe for days, maybe weeks, for a taste of what the Kelley family got to have all year long. She'd made it all sound so appealing, but Lane had never been convinced.

Besides, for people like the Kelleys, summer was just a busier work season. While everyone else escaped from the demands of a stressful life, those who ran businesses in Harbor Pointe worked to make sure all their needs were met. The line drawn between the vacationers and the townies was a thick one, edged deep in the fabric of the town, the way the Berlin Wall split the capital of Germany in two. Only someone as naive as Lane had once been would ever think it didn't matter, that friendships could withstand such a concrete separation.

She knew better now.

Only her siblings seemed able to bridge that gap—it had never been a gift Lane had possessed. Another way she was so different from the rest of them.

Her phone buzzed. She picked it up as she turned down Sweetwater Lane toward Harbor Pointe Hospital.

Told Mrs. Pim about your emergency. She asked if she could text you a few photos. I told her it might be good not to bother you right now, but you should probably expect her pictures.

Mrs. Pim. Lane had been the point person on the rebranding

of the woman's restaurants throughout the city, and even though they'd technically finished the project months ago, the woman still called at least three times a week.

Chloe was going above and beyond, and Lane knew it. She found the contact for her favorite spa in her phone and dialed it.

"I'd like to make an appointment for my assist—my friend—to get a forty-five-minute massage with Ruby."

Ruby had magic fingers. At least that's what she'd heard. Lane rarely had time to have someone work the knots out of her back anymore.

She gave the girl on the other end Chloe's name and told her to charge the credit card they had on file for Lane.

"Can you call and tell her about the appointment?" Lane asked. "Just let her know it's taken care of and her only instruction is to forget about everything for an hour."

"Of course. Will there be anything else? An appointment for yourself, maybe?"

"No, that's all." Never mind that Lane would desperately love to forget about everything for an hour herself. But now, more than ever, she did not have time for that.

She hung up the phone, wishing she could see Chloe's face when she got the call from the salon. Marshall might not give Lane the accolades she deserved, but Lane had come to appreciate people who did their jobs well. She'd learned how very rare it was.

The hospital came into view and she quickly found a parking place near a patch of grass for Otis's sake. She attached a leash to his collar and led him outside, checking her Twitter feed as she let him do his business. Miles's most recent tweet popped up as she scrolled.

Never waste an opportunity.

Frustration snapped within her, giving her insides a tight squeeze. Something about it felt personal, like he had posted it just for Lane's benefit, flaunting the fact that he fully intended to steal that promotion right out from under her.

Lane started back for the car, still staring at her phone. She shouldn't be thinking about work. She glanced at the hospital building, willing her heart to focus on why she was here.

She began to text Chloe as she walked toward her car, trying to decide how to say thank you to her assistant without giving away the surprise she'd arranged. She reached the sidewalk and was nearly to her car when a man's voice pulled her attention.

"Look up!" he called out. Lane jerked her head up just in time to realize she'd stepped straight into the path of an oncoming biker, who, judging by his tone, wasn't happy about it. "Watch where you're going!"

"Sorry!" she called after him, but he didn't respond.

That was the other thing about Harbor Pointe. The foot and bike traffic.

"Downtown Harbor Pointe is what's known as a walking village, with many residents and visitors opting not to drive motorized vehicles for the duration of summer. This gives the village a calm, relaxed vibe that hearkens back to simpler times, the times we're all trying to capture as life threatens to pass us by."

The words from her tour-guide days had invaded her memory, unwelcome but oh, so true. She hadn't known it then; she'd simply been reciting a script. But now she had a better understanding of the contrast between her hometown and the fast-paced professional world.

Still, there were far too many ghosts here for Lane to ever find peace—and that didn't even include the one in the harbor lighthouse.

She tucked her phone away and got Otis situated in the backseat, cracking the windows as she did. She was thankful the early May weather was cool. Otherwise she'd have to bring her dog into the hospital, and something told her he wouldn't be welcome.

She turned toward the hospital. Perhaps she'd been dreading this more than she wanted to admit. The uncomfortable reunion, the clashing personalities, the too-loud banter, the guilt trip her mom would lay on, the embarrassing way her family would have taken over the waiting room, the snide comments about how she couldn't extract herself from the city even for a weekend or Christmas—"and you know how your mother loves Christmas."

And Lindsay. She absolutely dreaded coming face-to-face with Lindsay.

But even more than all those things, she was terrified of seeing for herself just how badly her brother had been hurt. The tone of Jeremy's voice when he told her to drop everything and get there—it was urgent. It spoke volumes.

Sunlight streamed in through the large windows at the front of the hospital lobby, a contradiction mixing bright light and happiness with the dark worry and sadness that seeped down the corridors.

A stop at the front desk told Lane that Nate was in room 352. He could only have two visitors at a time, and the front desk volunteer was fairly certain he'd had a steady stream since he was first brought in last night.

"I'm sure," Lane said.

"Seems like that boy is quite popular." The woman smiled. "We're praying for him."

Yes, Nate always was the popular one. Everyone loved him and he knew it. The image of his grin invaded the corners of her mind. She missed that smile, that charming "Yes, I do know how good-looking I am and you're powerless to turn away until I've gotten what I want" smile. With that expression on his face, Nate could convince anyone to do anything for him—it was like a superpower. She remembered countless times he'd used his powers to stay up past bedtime, turn in homework after the due date, go to school late, get access to the community swimming pool after hours. . . . She almost laughed thinking about it. Almost.

She found herself standing outside the elevator, though she had little memory of getting herself there.

She pressed the button with the 3 on it, bracing herself for what came next. Her social anxiety was at an all-time high as the doors to the elevator snapped shut. A hollowness seemed to have been carved out of the center of her chest, leaving it open and exposed. She leaned against the wall of the elevator and drew in a very deep breath.

"Maybe you could help me with this? I mean, if we're still okay. . . ."

Her prayer was fast and fleeting, as most of her prayers were these days. Another thing she didn't really have time for. She had to believe God understood. He knew how important her job was, after all. And God liked hard work. Right?

She pulled out her phone and scrolled through her Twitter feed—out of habit more than interest.

The elevator stopped, then shifted. *Maybe it'll get stuck and I'll be locked in here all day.*

But the bell dinged and the car righted itself. No such luck.

Lane clicked the phone's screen off and wished she could teleport to Nate's bedside.

She smoothed her blouse, pulling her suit jacket around her a little tighter. Then her eyes fell to her pointed black heels. The doors started to open and the sound of voices infiltrated the silence of the little box where she stood. Slowly the doors slid out of the way, landing her directly in front of one of the two people she would've been content never to see again. Lindsay.

Just breathe.

CHAPTER

5

LANE INHALED the kind of breath she imagined a woman in labor would breathe, slow and deep, meant to steady wobbly knees and nerves that didn't stand a chance against the situation in front of her. A breath that would have to carry her through until she was finally able to walk out of the hospital—whenever that was.

The onslaught of unwanted—and unwelcome—emotions all attached to memories she'd done very well to bury wound up and punched her squarely in the jaw. She knew Lindsay would be here, some part of her knew, but she'd hoped she could get by without having to face her. At least not first thing.

"Are you getting out?" Lindsay's brow twitched and Lane stepped out of the elevator and into the hallway. Her phone buzzed.

Can you e-mail me the market research on Solar's competition? Need to find a couple of statistics JB asked for.

Marshall's text couldn't have come in five minutes earlier? Lane glanced at Lindsay, who stood in the center of the hallway like an out-of-place freshman at her first high school dance.

Lane almost excused herself, then remembered she didn't owe

Lindsay the same common courtesy she would've given any other human being on the planet. She didn't owe Lindsay anything.

She stepped off to the side and did a quick search of her e-mail, found the one Marshall wanted—which she'd already sent him, complete with the market research—and forwarded it to him.

"Lane?"

Even before she glanced up, she recognized her mother's voice behind her. She turned and saw the older woman walking toward her with outstretched arms. "Oh, thank goodness you're here. Lindsay, why didn't you tell me your sister had arrived?"

Lindsay turned away.

Before she knew it, Lane was wrapped in a tight hug. Her hands found her mother's back, and they rested there lamely until Lane counted to three and pulled away.

"Let me look at you," her mom said.

Dottie Kelley had always worn her dark hair short, but now flecks of gray showed her age, and while her skin had held up remarkably well, there were slight rainbow-shaped wrinkles framing her eyes—eyes that seemed to glimmer a bit as she took in the sight of her daughter.

"You look so professional."

Lane glanced down at her black dress pants and pin-striped blouse. Her heels made her considerably taller than her mom, who seemed smaller somehow, her larger-than-life personality lying dormant, most likely because of the accident.

"And thin. Lindsay, isn't she thin?"

Lane cringed. *Don't ask Lindsay anything about how I look. Don't remind me that she is the pretty one and I'm the smart one. Don't remind me of what that cost me.*

"How's Nate?" Lane asked, switching her oversize bag from one shoulder to the other.

"About the same." Her mom's eyes filled with tears.

A pair of reading glasses hung on a chain around her mother's neck, and despite the nice temperature outside, she wore a loose shawl around her shoulders. In fact, everything her mom wore was loose, as if she had something against clothing that touched her skin.

Mom had always been small—slight, even. Lane could still remember praying that somehow, miraculously, her much sturdier frame would magically transform into her mother's. But she had her dad's genes too, and there was nothing delicate about those.

"He's going to be okay," Lane said, aware that she had absolutely no proof to back up her statement.

Mom nodded as if Lane's ignorance didn't matter. They were choosing to believe Nate would be all right. "Why are we standing in the hallway?" Her mom tossed Lindsay a glance.

"I'm waiting on . . ." Lindsay's voice trailed off.

Mom's face froze for a second as if someone hit the Pause button on a video image of her.

Lane looked away. Lindsay was at the elevator waiting on someone. It didn't take a genius to figure out whom.

"Come into the waiting room, Lane." Mom motioned for Lane to follow her down the quiet hallway toward the noisier waiting room. "You can say hi to everyone and then I'll take you to see Nate."

Lane watched her own feet as each one moved forward involuntarily, methodically obeying her mother's words. Seeing Lindsay had rattled loose all the boxes she'd stuffed at the back of the closet of her mind.

She didn't want to be here. She didn't want to make small talk with family members she didn't really know. She didn't want to pretend she was fine sitting in the same room with Lindsay. She didn't want to spend another minute disappointing her mother for being *too* busy, *too* focused, and now, apparently *too* thin.

And even though she hated herself for it, she didn't want to see Nate. Not in a hospital bed with tubes breathing for him. She wanted to go on believing he was out there happily pushing his own boundaries, riding his motorcycle or bungee jumping or traveling the world. That was the life she'd invented for him, pieced together by what little she'd gathered from social media and their few sparse conversations over the years.

She didn't want to see that things had taken a turn for him, landing him broken and bruised in a medically induced coma.

"Everyone's been here since we first got word," Mom was saying and Lane forced herself to listen. "Jer has hardly left Nate's side— you know how he looks up to both of the boys."

Lane knew. Everyone looked up to Nate and Noah—especially Jeremy.

Before they reached the waiting room, Lane heard her family. They'd never adopted the idea of "inside voices." Her mom laced her arm through Lane's and squeezed. "I'm glad you're finally home."

She hadn't lingered on the *finally*, but Lane's own guilt emphasized the word. Harmless in theory, and yet it said so much.

Her phone buzzed in her pocket. She pulled it out with her free hand just as they crossed the threshold into the waiting room.

Lane, was really hoping you would make it out today. The tile they delivered is just not right. Wanted you to see it in person. Sending a picture so you can see for yourself.

Mrs. Pim.

"What is it?" Mom asked, watching as Lane tucked the phone in her purse.

"Just work," Lane said, not wanting to explain any of it to her mother, who would most certainly not understand.

She'd text Mrs. Pim back as soon as she got a free moment.

The phone buzzed again.

Lane reached for it, but her mom tugged on her linked arm. "It can wait, Lane."

A knot tied itself in the center of her stomach. Her mom, with her lackadaisical approach to life, would never understand that some things couldn't wait. In Harbor Pointe, everything waited.

Her mom had never been an "I like everything in its place" kind of person. She was the type who took life as it came. To that end,

Dottie Kelley had always been a mystery to her eldest daughter, who was very much the opposite of her mother.

In Dottie's world, everyone was happy and fine and good and because of that, she found it nearly impossible to understand Lane's heartache. Even when Lane was a kid, Dottie simply couldn't believe that anyone would ever hurt her feelings. Rather than entertaining the thought, even for a moment, she'd give her blanket rationalization: "I'm sure they didn't mean it, honey."

Hadn't they? Lane was certain they had. Surely her own sister had—what else did she think would happen? But then, maybe Lane's feelings were never a consideration to Lindsay.

Her thoughts were interrupted as they entered the room and she found a group of people standing together in a circle, praying.

Her mother tugged her close and grabbed her hand. "We've been praying for your brother round the clock."

Lane believed it. The intensity of their prayers only made her realize the gravity of Nate's condition—and it shamed her to think of the selfish sort-of prayer she'd mumbled in the elevator on the way up here.

The mood in the room was something close to somber, which was rare for a family like hers. How serious was her brother's condition for it to have cast such a dark cloud?

After the prayer ended, Lane didn't rush to raise her bowed head. Instead, she took a step out of the circle, careful not to draw attention to herself.

Seconds later, she was greeted by a loud welcome from her father, brothers, and extended family. One look at her and they shouted her name like they'd been planning it "on three." Instantly the too-small waiting room felt overly cramped with the Kelley family and many of Nate's friends tucked inside like crayons in a box. Somehow she felt like the one that didn't quite fit in its place.

And just like that, Lane was fourteen again, the wallflower, wishing she could run home and lock herself in her bedroom with a book.

You're not that girl anymore.

She'd made sure of it. She'd done everything she could to eliminate every trace of the girl she'd been, to transform herself into a businesswoman with an incredible career. She'd gotten out of Harbor Pointe, and she'd made something of herself.

So why did she still feel out of place and anxious?

She hugged her bag closer as if she could hide behind it, but she knew better. Her dad pulled her into one of his famous bear hugs, clapping her on the back with a little too much force.

"My daughter, the big-city girl," he said with another clap. "I thought I'd never see you again." He pulled away but kept his hands on her arms, studying her up and down. "Look how fancy you are."

"And thin," Mom said. "Isn't she thin?"

"Too thin," Dad said.

There's no such thing. Lane felt the heat rush to her cheeks. She didn't like them all staring at her. Half of the people she couldn't place or hadn't met, and those she did know, she hadn't seen in so long they also felt like strangers.

She should be better about keeping in touch—and yet she had a new life now. She couldn't help it if she didn't fit in here. Surely they weren't surprised—she never really had.

Her phone buzzed again, and if only to exhale, she pulled it out of her bag and stared at the screen.

Miles is pushing a new angle for the campaign.

She frowned and texted back: To who?

Marshall. He's working him over pretty good.

Lane sighed. She didn't even know how to respond, but the news hit her like a sucker punch.

"You going to sit on that thing all day?" Jeremy stood in front of her seeming too grown-up to be her little brother. He had facial hair, for pete's sake. He looked like an actual man.

"It's just work." Lane forced herself to step into his outstretched arms.

A crash from the other side of the room drew everyone's attention. Lane watched as a little boy ran away from a stack of magazines he had presumably knocked onto the floor.

"Oh, Jett, honey, stop." Dottie rushed over to the boy.

"That kid's name is Jett?" Lane asked.

"He's a handful," Jer said, his voice low.

"Who does he belong to?"

"Lindsay and Jasper," Jeremy said. "They don't believe in discipline, only in *logic* and *reasoning* . . ." His voice trailed off and he turned toward her. "I'm sorry, Lane. I wasn't thinking."

She held up her hand to silence him. "It's fine. Even I know there's no reasoning with a three-year-old." Lane swallowed the bile that pooled at the back of her throat. "They really should do a better job of watching their kid."

Jer shrugged. "Probably figure someone will make sure he doesn't break anything."

That always was Lindsay's way—push off her responsibilities on everyone else. She was too much "fun" to be bothered with actual responsibility.

"Where's Noah?" She looked around, but her oldest brother wasn't in the waiting room.

"With Nate." Jer stuffed his hands in his pockets, and for a brief moment a flash of the little boy she'd known returned. "You should go see him."

Lane looked away.

Their mother had made the rounds like a hostess at a party. She checked on every family member, every friend, asking if anyone needed anything.

No one did.

When she returned to Lane, she wrapped an arm around her. "I can't believe you're actually here. Not happy it took something like this to get you back, but you're home, so I'm not complaining."

Lane didn't respond. Her mother's "not complaining" sounded a lot like complaining.

"Should we reintroduce Lane to everyone?" Mom turned her attention to Jeremy.

"No," Lane said a little too quickly. "That won't be necessary."

"But it's been so long, Lane," Mom said.

Lane prayed for something heavy to fall out of the sky and land on top of her. She wasn't picky—an anvil or a piano or a giant boulder would work just fine.

"I think Lane probably wants to go see Nate, Ma," Jer said.

Lane gave a quick nod. "I should do that." Her mouth had gone dry.

"Right," Mom said. "Let me see where we are in the shift schedule."

"The what?" Lane asked, not sure she wanted to know.

"He's had so many visitors, but he can only have two at a time in his room, so we broke it down into shifts." She said it like it was the most obvious thing in the world.

"I think Lane might need to go to the front of the line," Jer said. He'd gotten sensible over the years. She was grateful for that.

Mom's eyes went blank.

"Mom." Lane couldn't believe she actually had to think about this.

"No, of course, you're right." Mom turned toward the room. "Now, who should we pair you up with?"

"Can I go by myself?" Would she need to take a number to visit her brother in the hospital?

Mom frowned. "You're disrupting the system here, Lane."

"Well, it's a ridiculous system," Lane said without thinking.

Jer gave her a nudge. She knew her mother was just trying to make sense of everything that had happened. If creating a system for visitors to follow helped her pass the difficult minutes until Nate woke up, who was she to criticize?

It occurred to Lane that her mother's usual take-life-as-it-comes attitude was nowhere to be seen right now. In its place, all Lane saw was a need to control something—anything—when everything was so out of her control.

Lane could relate to that. She should be more sympathetic.

"Of course." Mom walked away and pulled a sheet of paper off the window next to the door. She scribbled something on the sheet, then motioned for Lane to follow her. Lane glanced at Jer, who said nothing more, and she left the waiting room, escaping to the quiet hallway.

This part of the hospital was white. Fluorescent. Cold.

They walked down the hall, the silence reminding her of a library. If Lane did have something to say, she most certainly would've whispered it. Speaking out loud seemed like some sort of violation.

"Here we are." Mom stopped in front of a room with a partially open door. "You'll have to tell Noah and Em their time's up."

"Mom, I'm not sure the hospital adheres to these rules quite as strictly as you think," Lane said. "You can come in for a minute."

Mom shook her head. "They have rules for a reason."

"I understand, but you should be able to stay with your son. No matter who else comes to visit."

It wasn't like her mom. At least not what Lane remembered of her mom. The Dottie Kelley she knew had an unending nonchalance. She expected that things would work out. She was the type of woman who "flitted."

It was these—and many other—qualities that had kept Lane from ever understanding her mother.

Mom pressed her lips together and glanced into the room. The door obstructed their view of everything except a monitor she could only assume was hooked up to her brother's limp body. Maybe that little machine was responsible for keeping him alive.

Her mother reached out and squeezed Lane's hand. "I'll go in next," she said. And then she walked away.

Lane watched for several seconds as her mom swished back down the hall in her loose skirt and flowing top. She'd aged fairly well, though Lane had to wonder if Nate's accident might change all that.

Already she seemed harried and stressed out, and that could age a person. Just look at every former president of the United States. When her mom rounded the corner and disappeared, Lane turned back toward the hospital room and pushed open the door. Noah sat in the chair right beside the bed, his wife, Emily, in the chair next to him. Noah and Emily met one summer when her family chose Harbor Pointe as their vacation destination. They were both heading into their senior year of college, so after one year of long distance, they spent the summer together and had lived here ever since.

Noah owned a water-sports rental business and Emily stayed home with their three kids, who were hopefully better behaved than Lindsay's son. Nate was the high school basketball coach and math teacher, and though he didn't have a wife, Lane had a feeling he'd only find one right here in Harbor Pointe.

Funny how this town had a way of sucking people back in.

Lane said a silent prayer of thanks that she'd managed to get out while she could.

Noah stared at her as if he didn't believe she was really there.

"Hey," she said.

"Pudge?"

Lane closed her eyes and pressed her lips together at the sound of the nickname, a thousand memories whirling through her mind. He hadn't meant it to hurt her, but even the smallest nick could reopen old wounds.

"Sorry," Noah said. "Guess I shouldn't call you that anymore."

Maybe you shouldn't have called me that ever.

"It's okay." She'd received the "harmless" nickname as a child, after all. At least, that's how her mother had described it when Lane asked her to make her brothers stop calling her that.

"Oh, it's a harmless nickname, Lane," she'd said. *"A term of endearment."*

"Well, I don't like it," Lane had said. She was in middle school,

and it was humiliating. Especially when her siblings used it in front of the other kids.

Noah had been something of a bully when they were kids—she had to remind herself he wasn't a kid anymore.

He drew her toward him for a hug and she squeezed his solid bicep. "Good grief, No—are you training for Mr. Universe or something?"

"CrossFit," he said. "Me and Emily both."

Lane glanced at Noah's beautiful wife and shrank at least four inches.

"Hi, Emily." She marveled at the gorgeous blonde and her ridiculously muscular body.

Lane had lost so much weight, and yet one hour back in Harbor Pointe and she was that fat, awkward teenager all over again. Especially around these two.

After several long seconds, Lane finally forced herself to look at Nate. Her dark-headed, dark-eyed brother lay perfectly still in the hospital bed, tubes covering his face and an IV stuck in his hand. He looked scruffy with his five o'clock shadow, and Lane could only imagine how angry he'd be when he woke up and found himself wearing a hospital gown.

"He looks small," Lane said, thinking less about his stature and more about his helplessness.

She expected a lump in her throat, tears in her eyes—something that proved she was still a part of the Kelley family—but nothing came. She felt wholly detached from the scene in front of her and she hated herself for it. She loved Nate. She should be terribly upset to see him like this.

When did you become so heartless?

"We can leave you alone. We've gone over our time, I'm sure." Emily turned to Noah. "I'll be in the hallway." As she passed by Lane, she gave her arm a soft, reassuring squeeze. Sisterly. "I'm glad you're home, Lane."

A spot of emotion lodged itself at the back of Lane's throat.

So this *makes you emotional? Your brother is fighting for his life and you've got nothing for him, but one squeeze from your fake sister and you turn to mush?*

Noah stood at the end of the bed, staring at Nate. "Told him to get rid of that bike."

"What happened?"

"Probably Nate being stupid," Noah said.

"Do we know that? Maybe it wasn't his fault." Lane didn't think they should criticize their comatose brother on the off chance he could hear them.

"It was his fault for getting the motorcycle in the first place." She stilled. "I'm sure he didn't mean for this to happen." She put a hand on her brother's arm. "Seriously? You've even got muscles in your forearm."

He raised an eyebrow as he looked down at her. "You can tell?" Noah tightened his arm muscles underneath her hand.

"It's kind of gross." Lane scrunched her face purposefully.

Noah laughed. "You should come to the gym with us. It's in Bay Ridge, but it's worth the drive. We're thinking about opening one up here."

"I don't think I'm cut out for that kind of gym," Lane said, thinking about how many hours she'd logged on the elliptical back home.

"I should go," Noah said. "Mom will probably give you another fifteen minutes before she sends someone else back."

"What's up with that?" Lane asked, frowning.

Noah shrugged. "I don't think she can stand to sit in here. She doesn't want to see him like this."

Lane's eyes fell on her brother—the one in the bed, not the one at her side. "I can't blame her for that."

"Also don't think she's admitted that this is as serious as it is." His face fell. "It might be the first time in her life she can't explain something away. She always had a knack for that."

Lane didn't know how to respond.

"You're sticking around for a few days, right? You have to come see the new store."

"Yeah." Lane glanced at Nate. "Looks like I'll be here a few days."

Noah gave her one more protective hug. "I'll talk to you in a little while."

She nodded and watched him exit the room, leaving her horribly alone with a brother she hadn't seen in too many months and might never get to speak to again.

CHAPTER

6

AFTER ANOTHER SEEMINGLY POINTLESS TEST, Dr. Tambor came back
to Ryan's room, apparently in the mood for small talk.

"Drove by Cedar Grove the other day," he said, eyeing the screen
with Ryan's results on it. "It's looking good, son."

"Thanks. Been a work in progress."

"When will you open?"

"A little over a month."

"Tight deadline." The doctor took off his glasses and closed the
folder.

"You're not kidding," Ryan said, trying not to think of how tight.

Cedar Grove was the most important thing he'd ever done, and
he had people counting on him to make a go of it. He had three
investors, including Frank Kelley. Local businessmen who liked
Ryan's plan to do his part in reinvigorating tourism in their town.
Their idea was to figure out a way to open up Harbor Pointe to a
whole new generation. The newspaper had done an article on Cedar
Grove, pitching the idea to the entire town. They were behind him.
And they were counting on him.

He couldn't let them down.

Then, and perhaps even more important, there were the guests he'd invited for his very first week. People he cared about. He didn't know what he'd expected when he'd sent out the invitations for a complimentary full week in a cottage on Lake Michigan, but he'd ended up with eleven booked cottages. And it couldn't just be any week away—it had to be exactly what he'd promised: an escape. A respite from difficult, sometimes-painful lives that deserved peace and relaxation.

He'd promised so much to so many people. He had to deliver.

"Getting close?"

The doctor sure had a lot of questions. Ryan reminded himself that he was a business owner now—everyone was a potential customer. After all, Dr. Tambor probably had family and they might need a place to rent for a week or two this summer.

"We're getting there. Just working on remodeling the last cottage."

"Think your team can carry on without you for a few days?"

Ryan's stomach dropped. "Not really." The project would come to a complete stop without him. They'd already fallen behind when winter decided to linger.

"I think we were right. It doesn't look serious, but I'm not sure you should jump right back into work," Dr. Tambor said. "You might have to let your team do the heavy lifting for a couple of days."

"Are you saying I can't be on the job site?"

"I'm saying you need to be careful. And you need to rest. You were in an accident, son." He sat on the stool beside Ryan's bed. "I want you to follow up with your regular doctor in a week."

Ryan sighed. He was all for rest, but not right now, not when he still had so much to do and not enough time to do it. "You said I don't have a concussion, right?"

Dr. Tambor studied him from behind his thin-framed glasses. "Yes, your scans are clear, but it was a nasty spill. Still not something to take lightly. There's a reason we kept you here overnight."

Ryan looked away. He'd been through combat—a bump on the head wasn't going to sideline him.

"You mentioned your head hurt. How is it now?"

"It hurts."

"I'll prescribe something for the pain."

"No." Ryan stared at the ceiling. "I don't need any drugs."

The doctor's brows knit together. "You don't have to be a tough guy here. It's okay to admit you're in pain and need something to relieve it."

"It's nothing I can't handle, Doc," Ryan said. "If it gets worse, I'll let you know." He wouldn't, of course, but the doctor didn't want to hear that right now.

"How about this: I'll call in the prescription and you can use it or not use it. That way, it's there if you need it."

Even still, he wouldn't use it.

"Why don't you get dressed and we'll get you out of here. I'll send Elaine back in with the paperwork and you'll be on your way. Your instructions are to rest and follow up with your doctor in a week. Got that?"

Ryan nodded. "Got it."

"Good." He stood. "Your friend is out of surgery and he's in critical condition on the third floor. They say he's stable for now, but he is in a coma. Doctors are hopeful, but it's going to be touch and go here for a few days. He wasn't as lucky as you, I'm afraid."

There was that word again. *Lucky.* His grandma Fred—short for Winnifred—would've told that doctor there was no such thing as luck. Only the hand of the Lord Almighty. She never did beat around the bush when it came to Jesus.

Odd he was remembering that now. Grandma Fred had died when Ryan was eight. How he remembered her at all sometimes seemed a mystery.

As the doctor left the room, Ryan heard a commotion from somewhere in the hallway. He recognized Hailey's voice immediately.

"Ryan Brooks? He was in an accident. Where is he?"

She sounded hysterical. Seconds—literally, seconds—later, she opened the door to his room and rushed over to where he sat. "Are you okay? What happened?"

"I'm fine, Hailey. Calm down. Didn't anyone tell you I was fine?"

"Mrs. K. left me a message. She said you two had been in an accident and then she started crying. I can't believe you didn't call me yourself."

"I didn't have my phone. I thought they'd let you know."

"I was out of town. I didn't get the message until this morning." Hailey's eyes were big and full of tears. "Are you okay?"

"I'm fine. Some stitches in my leg. Bump on my head. But I'm fine."

"What happened? Were you wearing a helmet? Was it your fault? Is Nate okay?" Hailey's chin quivered and she pushed her sandy-blonde hair out of her face.

"Which of those questions do you want me to answer first?" His head throbbed. He lay back on the bed and pressed his thumbs into his temples.

"You're not okay, are you?"

"I just have a headache." He closed his eyes for the briefest moment and saw the image of the blue pickup truck.

Hailey took his hand. "What is it, Ryan? You have that look on your face."

"What look?" He met her eyes.

She stilled. "The same look you had every time Dad got home from Scooter's when we were kids."

He stared at his sister. He still remembered when she called him in Afghanistan to tell him she was pregnant. She couldn't wait to get out of their house, to move in with her boyfriend, to escape from their dad.

He should've known that little fairy tale was doomed from the start. He should've protected her.

Hailey didn't need to hear about the fears that raced through his mind as he tried to piece together the scene of the accident. She needed to believe that he'd recover and that their past wasn't about to come back to haunt them.

"It's nothing; just shaken up, is all."

Her hug came out of nowhere and seemed almost involuntary. "I don't know what I would do if something happened to you."

He hugged her back, promised her everything would be fine— nothing was going to happen to him. But after yesterday, he was reminded that the promise was empty. He wasn't in control at all.

"I want to go check on Nate," he told her. "Nobody has been down here since right after they brought us in. I just need to make sure he's okay."

Hailey stared at him as if it were the last time she was going to see him.

"I'm fine, Hailey." But even as he said the words, his head throbbed.

"It could've been so much worse." Her eyes filled with tears, the kind that resulted from living the sort of life she had.

She was right. It could've been. But his grandma had taught him well, even at such a young age—he knew luck had nothing to do with it.

Thank you for protecting me. The silent prayer echoed through his mind as he gave Hailey one more reassuring hug.

"How are you going to get home?" She wiped her cheeks dry.

"I'll have Jer or Noah take me. It'll be fine."

The Kelley family had practically adopted Ryan and Hailey years ago. He didn't like to think about the way the family had first come into his life, but it was proof something good could come from something bad.

Frank had caught him trying to steal a sandwich at Summers, the cheese shop the Kelleys owned and operated. He'd gone in after school, riding his bike all the way from Newman. Frank must've known something wasn't right as soon as he walked in. After all, Ryan was in middle school and he didn't have a parent with him, and in retrospect, the man had probably learned to recognize a shoplifter.

Ryan wasn't a thief—he was just hungry.

Ryan thought about that day often. Frank slid between Ryan and his clean getaway with a knowing look on his face. "Haven't seen you in here before."

"I'm from Newman. Just passing through."

"Where are your parents?"

"Working." It was a lie. His dad was probably already at Scooter's, and by that time, he hadn't seen his mom in years.

"I see." Frank eyed him suspiciously.

Ryan swallowed, his mouth dry, his pulse racing with fear that he'd been caught.

"You know, I've been looking for some help in the back." Frank crossed his arms over his chest and peered down at the boy. "Easy stuff, really, some sorting, taking out the garbage, sweeping. Do you know how to do that stuff?"

"I think so."

"There's only one catch. I'd have to pay you in—" Frank waved his hands as he talked, as if the words he wanted needed to be wrangled in—"I'd have to pay you in sandwiches and chips, that sort of thing."

Ryan looked at the man, whose brow was raised in anticipation of his response. "That'd be okay."

"Yeah?"

"Sure."

"Good. I'm going to go to the back room and get some paper so I can make you a list of chores. You can eat while you read over it. Be right back."

Picturing it now, Ryan realized Frank had given him time to put back what he'd tried to steal. Frank made him a turkey sandwich on bakery white bread with freshly made cheddar cheese—something he bragged about as he put the meal together. He let Ryan pick out a bag of chips and a drink, sat him down at the counter, and left him alone to eat. In return, Ryan spent the afternoon sweeping out the back room, taking out the garbage, and cleaning the windows of the small cheese shop.

Ryan returned the next day and the next, diligently working on the list of chores in return for his only chance at dinner each day. When Frank noticed Ryan was saving half of his sandwich for his sister, he started giving him extra, making up reasons like "This bread baked too long in the oven" or "I need someone to try out this cheese."

Before long, Frank invited Ryan to youth group with Nate, then home for family dinners. As soon as Dottie found out what their home life was like, she treated both him and Hailey as if they were hers.

Not much had changed, even after all this time. The Kelleys made them feel like family, like they had somewhere they belonged.

"Okay, well, call me if that doesn't pan out and you need a ride." Hailey's comment pulled him back to the present.

"Will do."

She pulled a pair of aviator sunglasses from her purse. "You probably shouldn't drive at least for a few days."

"I don't have a concussion, Hailey. I'm fine."

"Still. You should be smart."

He would be smart. Smart enough to do what needed to be done so he didn't let down the people who mattered most. But not right now. Now, he needed to check on Nate.

When Ryan entered the hospital waiting room, it was even more crowded than he'd expected. That wasn't surprising. Nate was the kind of guy everyone loved.

Part of him wanted to go home—to stop thinking about the accident. He'd replayed it one too many times in his head already, and he still came up with that same feeling of dread.

Dottie spotted him from the other side of the room and rushed over. Just looking at her made him feel like he was lying.

But I don't even really know what I saw. Not for sure. I shouldn't say anything until I'm positive. Right?

"You're up." She drew the attention of the entire room, and now they were all focused on him. Normally that wouldn't have bothered him so much, but with his splitting headache and the flurry of questions racing through his mind, he didn't like it. He wanted everyone to go back to whatever it was they were doing before he walked in.

"We were down to see you a bit ago, and you were asleep. How are you feeling? Jer told me you had to get stitches." Dottie stared at him with the kind of maternal concern he'd only experienced because of her. It made him feel like he was nine years old and sitting in the ER waiting to get a cast set after falling off the monkey bars at the playground.

But when that had happened, his mother hadn't been there to look at him this way. He'd been rushed to the hospital by one of his friends' mothers—Mrs. Fowkes—and she mostly stayed on the phone, trying to track down his father.

"Try Scooter's," he'd heard her say quietly into the receiver. "That's where he is most evenings."

Everyone knew the truth about Martin Brooks.

She'd hung up the phone and gazed at him with big, sad eyes, pitying him for the hand life had dealt him.

"Any luck reaching the parents?" the nurse said when she reentered the room.

"I'm afraid not," Mrs. Fowkes said.

"We really need to get this arm set." The nurse turned to him. "Do you have any idea where your father might be?"

He glanced at Mrs. Fowkes, but she wouldn't meet his eyes. "Try Scooter's," he said. "That's where he is most evenings."

Mrs. Fowkes and the nurse wore matching expressions. They felt sorry for him—he could tell.

That's not how Dottie looked at him now. She was genuinely concerned for his well-being, as a mother would be for a son. She knew all about his parents, the way his mother had walked off when he and Hailey were little, leaving them with a man who had no business raising children. It had never mattered to Dottie. Not when she invited them over for Sunday dinner. Not when they showed up on her front porch in the middle of the night. Not when she made up beds in the living room and served them breakfast the next morning. And certainly not when she caught him smoking a cigarette behind her shed.

She'd made it very clear her rules applied to him as well—and he'd never smoked a cigarette again.

It was years she'd been doing these things for him and his sister, and never with an ounce of pity.

He updated her on his injuries, and then she hugged him. "I'm so glad you're okay." She pulled away and looked at him. "You should go see Nate. His sister's back there, but she's the only one and she's more than used her allotted time."

"She has an allotted time?"

Dottie whipped out a chart that allowed everyone fifteen minutes at a time but also ensured Nate wouldn't be alone.

Ryan didn't pretend to get it; he'd known Dottie long enough to understand she had her own way of doing things. He didn't think now was the time to ask questions.

"I don't want to intrude." Ryan was happy to take a seat in the waiting room with the others. He'd already seen Nate's accident up close. He didn't need to be reminded that he'd walked away unscathed by comparison.

Lucky.

The foggy image of the truck's taillights invaded his memory. He blinked, willing it away, but his head felt thick, almost like he didn't get to decide what images his mind lingered on.

"Are you okay?" Dottie put a hand on his shoulder. "Maybe you should sit down."

"I'm fine, Mrs. K.," he said. "My head is just aching, is all."

"Well, go in, see Nate, and then head home and go to sleep for a while." She frowned. "Or should you stay awake? What if the doctors are wrong and you do have a concussion? Maybe you should sleep at our house tonight."

He held up a hand—as if that could silence her.

"I don't want anything to happen to you. You live by yourself. Who will call 911?"

"I'll be fine. I promise. And I can wait out here till it's my turn to go see Nate."

"No, I insist," Dottie said. "Go on back. Tell Lane her time is up. I wouldn't mind spending some time with my daughter since I haven't seen her in, I don't know, over two years."

"Lane? I thought you meant Lindsay."

Dottie gave her head just one shake. "No. Lane. Hard to believe, right? Quite a blast from the past."

"It's been a long time." In spite of his throbbing head and the dread of seeing his friend lying helpless in a hospital bed, there was a slight tremor of excitement at the thought of encountering Lane Kelley again.

He hadn't seen her for years, but he'd thought about her often. How could he not? She'd been one of the few people who knew the truth about him and never seemed to care. He'd never been an outsider where Lane was concerned—maybe because in many ways, she felt like an outsider too. Even in her own family. Would she remember him the way he remembered her?

Lane had been so different from the rest of them. From everyone he knew, really. She was quiet, always reading, and Ryan had been intimidated—but intrigued—by her.

"I really don't mind waiting," Ryan said even as Dottie pushed him toward the door. Why did he suddenly feel nervous?

"Go."

Ryan reached Nate's room and stood outside for several long seconds. He didn't want to go in. But this was Nate. The least Ryan could do was say a prayer for him.

He pushed on the partially open door, surprised when it didn't make a sound. Nate's sister sat beside the bed, radiating apprehension. She didn't so much as stir, obviously unaware she was no longer alone. He should clear his throat or call out or something, but instead he watched her for a long minute.

Lane.

Nothing about her resembled the rest of the Kelley family, and nothing about her resembled the Lane Kelley he remembered.

Even as a girl, she'd always been so serious—Dottie told him once he was just about the only person who could make "her serious girl" smile.

Something about that singular comment had given him purpose at a time when he had none. He'd made it his daily goal to pull one great smile out of Lane Kelley. The days he succeeded, those were the days he lived for.

She sat straight at the side of the bed, legs crossed, unmoving. He knew little about what had become of the Kelleys' eldest daughter. She'd moved away for college while he was overseas and in the time since he'd returned, she hadn't been back.

He'd resigned himself to the fact that he'd likely never see her again, though he was happy to discover he'd been wrong.

Looking at her now, he remembered how strong-willed she was. No wonder it had been years since she'd been back. He had a feeling she could carry her grudge forever.

And honestly, part of him didn't blame her.

A buzzing sound jarred Lane back to life, and Ryan felt like a complete stalker for standing there as long as he had without alerting her to his presence. She reached down to her bag and pulled out her phone, then started tapping the screen. More buzzing. More tapping.

He watched for several seconds, marveling at the way she seemed to disappear into another world. She leaned over to return the phone to her bag, and as she did, she must've caught a glimpse of him out of the corner of her eye. She turned, an accusatory expression on her face.

"Who are you?"

Why did he feel like he'd just been caught doing something he shouldn't be doing? Because he'd been standing there for at least three minutes and hadn't spoken a word. Creeper.

"Hi, Lane."

She frowned, obviously trying to place him.

"Don't tell me you don't remember." He glanced at Nate, guilt tingling the back of his neck.

And you walked away again. How's that fair?

"Brooks?"

He knocked the thought away and turned his attention back to Nate's sister. "Been a long time."

She stood and faced him. There was a hint of the girl he remembered. Electric-blue eyes. Long, dark hair that fell in waves just past her shoulders and a sour expression that was possibly the only thing keeping her from being the most beautiful woman he'd ever seen.

But then, Lane had always been beautiful. She just didn't know it.

"How long have you been standing there?"

"Just a few minutes. Didn't want to intrude."

Her eyes narrowed as she sized him up.

"Your mom brought me back here." *What does that have to do with anything?*

Her phone buzzed, and like a cat watching a bird outside the window, she gave it her full attention. She took a step away from the bed, leaving an empty spot for him to fill. And yet, as he moved closer to Nate, everything within him wanted to run the other way. Nate was always the life of the party—the guy everyone wanted to be around. Seeing him lying lifelessly in this bed only stirred up the raw guilt he'd foolishly convinced himself wasn't there.

A nurse walked in, and Ryan stepped aside to make sure he was out of her way. He watched as she checked the machines hooked up to Nate. He understood nothing she did, and her face gave nothing away. Lane stood on the other side of the room, her back to him, tapping away on that stupid phone.

"How is he?" Ryan asked the nurse.

"Stable, but not out of the woods yet," the nurse said. "Weren't you the one who was with him when he crashed?"

Ryan stilled.

Out of the corner of his eye, he saw Lane turn. Despite her cold exterior, she seemed mildly interested in her brother's condition, or at least in Ryan's involvement in the accident.

"Uh, yes. I was." Ryan's voice was quiet.

"Must've been awful." The nurse adjusted one of the machines. "They said he's lucky to be alive. Maybe you are too?"

Yep. Lucky.

"I'll say a prayer for Nate. He was a couple of years ahead of me in school, but everyone always loved him."

"Sounds about right," Ryan said.

The nurse clicked a button on one of the other devices beside the bed, then glanced at Lane, standing in the corner like she felt suddenly out of place.

"Are you a relative?" she asked Lane.

Lane shifted. "He's my brother."

"Oh." The nurse's eyes widened as she stared at Nate's sister. "Wait a minute . . . Lane?"

Lane's eyes darted to Ryan, then hit the floor.

"It's me, Daisy. Daisy Marcus. Well, it's Daisy Teeter now. I married Pauly Teeter. You probably remember Pauly."

He didn't think Lane's body could get any tenser, but somehow it had. She shifted again, then wrapped her arms around herself. He watched her take a deep breath before meeting the nurse's eyes.

"I remember."

Ryan remembered too. Pauly Teeter was a first-class jerk. Ryan hadn't gone to school in Harbor Pointe, but he had a feeling, knowing how Lane had been teased, that Pauly Teeter might have been one of her worst bullies.

"Of course you do. You were in the same grade. Where have you been? You're never around anymore. If I looked as good as you do now, I'd come home to flaunt it all the time. You're like the caterpillar who went away and turned into a gorgeous butterfly. How'd you lose all that weight?"

Lane's eyes met the floor again.

"Heard you're a big shot something-or-other these days." Daisy had completely lost interest in Ryan and was now focused on Lane, who looked like she was barely enduring the attention.

He used the distraction as a chance to assess the grown-up version of the girl he used to know. Nobody had told him how striking she'd become, but maybe they didn't know. She was perfectly put together, as if someone was using her to demonstrate what a professional woman should look like. Dottie talked about Lane and her fancy job in the city, but it was a different thing to see her in person. He could tell just by looking at her—she'd made something of herself.

If he'd been intimidated by her before, he was downright terrified of her now. And yet, something about her standoffishness fascinated him.

"I work a lot." Lane looked like she'd rather be gnawing on wood chips than talking to this nurse.

"I heard something about your work." Daisy tried to fill in the blanks with whatever town gossip she'd heard but apparently came up empty. "What do you do again?"

Lane looked at Ryan helplessly. He could see her resolve faltering—how did Daisy not notice?

"Daisy, I was wondering if you could grab another blanket for Nate?" Ryan interrupted. "It's kind of cold in here."

Daisy pulled her attention from Lane with surprised eyes, but maybe it was enough to get the hint.

"Of course." She glanced back at Lane. "We should catch up sometime. It's been forever."

Lane's nod was less than enthusiastic. When Daisy finally left the room, a little bit of tension seemed to go with her. But only a little.

Lane stared at him for a few long seconds, and while anyone else might've thanked him for intervening, he had a feeling she wasn't about to give him the satisfaction. Any connection they'd had once upon a time was long gone.

"You were with Nate when he crashed?" she asked, breaking the much-preferred silence.

"We go out riding sometimes." He shoved his hands in his pockets, aware that she had him in her sights. "First time out this season. It was the first nice day."

"So that's a yes?"

He shot her a look. Hadn't he just saved her from the nosy nurse? Shouldn't she be nicer to him? "Yes, I was with him."

"Was it his fault?"

"It was an accident." Ryan felt like it would be better for them to stop talking. Her eyes threw him off. He was going to say something stupid.

"Nate has a reckless side." Lane turned toward her brother. "Maybe it was just a matter of time before it caught up with him."

Before he could correct her, the door swung open and Nate's parents walked in.

Dottie breezed over and stood next to Ryan, placing a hand on his arm, thoughtlessly, the way moms do with their sons whether they're grown or not. A gesture that came so naturally to her but meant so much to him. "Did you talk to him at all? They say that's good for patients in a coma."

Ryan glanced at Nate. "I didn't. The nurse was in here."

"Well, you'll talk to him later, then. I imagine you've gotten reacquainted with Lane." Ryan noticed Dottie didn't look at Nate, and he feared she might be in deep denial about her son's condition. He'd never known Dottie to be negative, but she was taking the optimism to a new level.

"Not exactly," Ryan said.

Frank Kelley let out a disapproving scoff. "Lane, where are your manners? You remember Ryan."

Lane's face went pale and she looked at the floor. Apparently she found the floor very interesting.

"There really wasn't time for small talk," Ryan said. "The nurse came in right after me."

Lane met Ryan's eyes for the briefest moment, then looked away. Why was he being so nice to her? She was *not* reciprocating.

"Well, Lane always had a soft spot for you, Ryan. You were so sweet to her." Dottie linked her arm through his and squeezed, focusing her attention on her daughter. "You remember how kind he was to you, Lane."

Again Lane's eyes found his, but she quickly averted them. Had she blocked it all out?

"You'd be proud of what he's become." Dottie was still talking. "Ryan is a wonderful addition to our little community. You should see how he's transformed—"

"She doesn't need to hear about me right now, Mrs. K.," Ryan cut in.

Dottie's face warmed into a soft smile. "We're just so proud of you, hon."

Moments like this, Ryan almost felt like he belonged to her, like it didn't matter how he'd grown up or whose son he was. It didn't matter that he belonged nowhere else.

The Kelleys were enamored with his war stories, supportive of the years he worked in construction, and now excited for his business venture. They seemed to respect the parts of his past he didn't want to discuss.

"I'm sure Lane would love to hear all about your projects," Dottie said.

He glanced at Lane, who was obviously unimpressed.

"Maybe later." He knew it wasn't the time or the place to discuss his dreams for Cedar Grove.

"This weekend, maybe," Dottie said. "We could even bring Lane over to your place for a little tour."

"I don't think I'll be here this weekend, Mom." Lane didn't meet her mother's eyes.

"What?" At his side, he could feel Dottie's shoulders fall.

"I can only take a few days off," Lane said.

"You don't have sick days built up in that big company of yours?" Dottie asked. "Or vacation days? *We* even give our employees vacation days, and if there was a family emergency, we wouldn't give it a second thought if they had to take some time off."

Lane's eyes were back on the floor. For someone who was clearly confident in many ways, there was still something about her that radiated insecurity.

"My company is different than your business, Mom," Lane said. "And I'm right in the middle of a big pitch, trying to land a huge client. My team is counting on me."

Dottie bristled at Lane's remark. "Well, Lane, your family is counting on you too."

"Mom."

"Forgive me if I think family is more important than work."

"It's not that simple," Lane said.

"I think it is. I think if your brother is in a coma, you should be able to spend more than a couple days with your family until you know everything is all right."

"It's so tense in here." Frank's trademark hand waving had begun. "We have to keep our spirits up—Nate wouldn't want you two fighting in his hospital room, and he wouldn't want everyone moping around here waiting for him to wake up. He's going to be fine."

Ryan's eyes happened to find Lane's as Frank said the words. He wasn't a mind reader, but judging by the look on her face, he wondered if she was thinking the same thing he was.

What if Nate doesn't wake up at all?

What if these people, this adoptive family of his, had to make a terrible decision about life support or organ donation? What if what he feared about the accident was true and when they discovered that truth, they'd make it clear Ryan had absolutely no business being there in that room like he was one of them?

Sometimes the truth of who he was smacked him in the face just when he was about to forget it.

The image of the blue truck raced through his mind.

This time, forgetting who he was wasn't going to be an option. And no amount of doing good would change that.

CHAPTER

AFTER HER ALLOTTED TIME WITH NATE, Lane slipped outside, not anxious to go back to the waiting room with the rest of Nate's visitors. Spring had descended on Harbor Pointe, and if Lane wasn't so anxious, she might've actually enjoyed the way the slightly cool breeze brushed through her hair.

She gathered Otis from the front seat of the car, attached him to his leash, and led him to the same grassy spot where she'd stopped before. She took out her phone and texted Chloe.

Any word on Solar?

Nothing more, but Marshall is in your cubicle looking over your designs for the atrium of their space.

Why?

He's trying to figure out how to tell you to give them an overhaul.

Lane wanted to throw her phone into the lake. What was Marshall thinking? The second she went out of town, he changed everything on her—what happened to this being her chance of a lifetime?

Marshall had her second-guessing work she'd been so proud of, and she hated that feeling.

She grabbed her laptop case with all of her work inside, returned an unhappy Otis to his makeshift bed in the car, and turned back toward the hospital.

She wanted to get behind the wheel and drive home, call a meeting with the Solar execs, and give the pitch she'd been planning to give that morning.

But her brother was lying in a bed on the third floor, unable to breathe on his own.

Heat rushed to Lane's cheeks. Work—even when it was hard—made sense to her. Sitting in that waiting room turned her into live bait for the ghosts of the past.

After all, it was only a matter of time before she saw him.

She'd be twitching and nervous if she sat up there, surrounded by a family of strangers but always with one eye on the door, ticking off the seconds until he finally showed up to play the part of dutiful husband.

It had been years since she'd seen him, years since they walked the campus of Northwestern together, years since she wished on that stupid star that somehow he would end up being the one.

Years since she'd foolishly believed he was.

The memories were years old and brand-new, but just like she had on that long-ago day, she shoved them out of her mind, refusing to feel any unwelcome emotion, the kind that made a girl weak. She'd never even cried. . . .

She sat down at a table in the lobby across from the gift shop on the hospital's main floor. Eventually she'd have to face everyone, but in that moment, she could hide. She had to hide; it was all she could muster.

She could pretend for a little while that her heart was fully recovered and the only things she had to worry about were her brother's condition and whether or not she'd destroyed her shot at this promotion.

For just a few moments there was nothing else to think about.

No Lindsay. No fear of running into *him*. No memories of the way that ring had looked on her finger.

Stop. One thing at a time. And some things never.

She pulled out her portfolio, laptop, and phone and positioned them just so on the table. She quickly checked her social media accounts—all of them. She'd set her posts for the week, but she liked to stay engaged. Her readers counted on it. Most of the interior designers at JB Sweet didn't bother with social media, but it had always been a part of Lane's plan to separate herself, to make a name for herself. Miles sent out the occasional tweet, but he didn't have half Lane's following. He didn't connect with people like she did.

She'd learned a lot about interior design working at that firm— and while she was no DIY goddess, she'd developed quite an online following for herself and for JB Sweet.

That had to count for something, didn't it?

She was responding to a question about installing a subway tile backsplash when she spotted Ryan across the lobby. She watched as he strolled toward the gift shop, unaware she was sitting there. Not that he'd care. Of course not. He was one of Nate's friends. Nate's friends had never paid a bit of attention to her.

Though that wasn't entirely true. More than once, Ryan had stuck up for her. He'd always been kind, even when the rest of the world wasn't. Come to think of it, they'd been friends too once.

Another friendship that had gone by the wayside.

She watched Ryan for a moment. She'd forgotten all about him, but looking at him now, she remembered the first time her dad had brought him home for dinner. Said he wanted the family to get to know his "newest employee," which even at her young age seemed odd to Lane, given that Ryan was barely thirteen at the time.

Over time and thanks to a few overheard conversations, Lane gathered that her father had brought Ryan home because some-how he believed their family could help him. She'd never asked for details, but it wasn't hard to figure out that things weren't great for

Ryan at home, and before long, he and Hailey were a staple in the Kelley family.

The Brooks kids joined them for camping trips and Sunday dinners. They sat with the Kelleys at church and camped out in their living room.

They were all friends, she supposed, the seven of them, though part of her was jealous at how easily Ryan had fit into a family that wasn't his. She'd been born a Kelley, but she couldn't feel more out of place.

Her senior year, Brooks went off to the Army and Lane hadn't seen him again until now.

Did he resent her for not keeping in touch?

She studied him without his knowledge from her spot across the lobby. She could tell Ryan was nothing like the guys she usually dealt with—men like Marshall and Miles. He wasn't even clean-shaven, and she'd never say so, but he could use a haircut. Chloe would probably call him "rugged." He wore a long-sleeved gray Henley underneath a washed-out blue T-shirt, the kind he'd probably had so long the material was now soft and worn.

He seemed to be limping, and his cargo pants had blood on them. Maybe Nate wasn't the only one who'd been injured.

She hadn't been nice to Ryan. He was probably worried and anxious about Nate, not to mention injured himself, and she'd lashed out at him like he didn't belong there, like he'd done something wrong.

She should apologize.

Her phone rang. Marshall. He knew how much she hated talking on the phone. She stared at it as if that would make the ringing stop, but finally took the call.

"Hello?"

"Hey." He paused. "How are things?"

He was calling to check on her? That was sweet—she wasn't used to sweet. It shamed her a bit, the way she'd been wishing away his phone call. "Fine. He's stable. Still critical, though."

There was another pause.

"Marshall?"

"Oh, good," he said absently as if he was doing something else. "Did you get a chance to look at the e-mail I sent?"

Now the pause was on her end. Was he calling to ask about her brother or to talk about work? "No, I must've missed it."

"Okay, when you get a second, take a look. I talked to one of the guys from Solar, and he gave me some insight into what they're looking for. Might need to tweak some of what you came up with before the next meeting. I explained it in my e-mail. You'll be back tomorrow, right?"

"Marshall, I've only been here for a few hours." Her mother's words rushed back at her. While she rarely agreed with her mom about anything—often just for the sake of disagreeing—the woman did have a point. If Summers Cheese Shop could take care of its employees, JB Sweet could take care of her. She'd never missed a day of work for anything until now. She didn't like feeling guilty for it.

"I understand, but you know what we're up against here," he said. "You've worked so hard for this account. I'd hate to see Innovate swipe it out from under you."

Maybe Innovate is more cut out for this one.

The words came out of nowhere and she swatted them away. She didn't believe that, not for a second. She wanted this. She needed it. She'd earned it.

"And what about Miles? Word is, he's working on a brand-new proposal."

Marshall went silent. Probably trying to think of how to spin this one—or how to fire Chloe for being more loyal to her than she was to him. "It never hurts to have more than one idea. But Miles isn't you, and his artistic eye is very limited. We know that, Lane, but if you're not here, I can't prove it to JB."

She pinched the bridge of her nose. Did Marshall have any shred of human decency?

"Lane?" Marshall sounded irritated. "Did you hear what I said? Innovate is going after this one hard. You want this account, don't you? This promotion?"

"Of course." A buzz of nervous energy settled in her core. "I just need a couple of days here," she said. Her stomach tied itself into a knot even as she spoke the words. It wasn't what she wanted, to stay in Harbor Pointe—not even for a couple of hours, let alone a couple of days.

He sighed—a heavy sigh filled with subtext. "Take them sparingly. You've got some stiff competition here, for Solar's account and for your promotion."

She rubbed her temple firmly as if that would make the pressure go away. "I'll check my e-mail and get back to you."

Lane hung up and let her head fall back on the chair. She closed her eyes for a long moment, a mix of emotions swirling inside her. Worry hung within her mind over her brother, over the account, over lingering memories of Lindsay and Jasper. It was the worst possible time for her to leave the office, and yet—

Before Lane could finish her thought, something hit her in the face—hard. She opened her eyes and saw a giggling Jett only a few feet away.

"Got you!" he hollered as he ran toward a Nerf football, which she could only assume was what had smacked her.

"That hurt!" Heat raced to Lane's cheek.

Jett picked up the football and turned toward Lane. She couldn't believe it—this terror of a child was going to throw it again.

"Don't even think about it." She held up her hands defensively.

He giggled like a psychopath and pulled his chubby hand back. Lane turned away, closing her eyes, but no ball came.

She peered in his direction through her fingers. He stood poised to throw the football straight at her, but behind him loomed Ryan Brooks, his much-larger hand covering the ball.

Jett looked up at Ryan, an undeniably terrified expression on his face.

"That's not very nice," Ryan said. "You shouldn't throw things at people—especially girls."

Obviously.

Jett let go of the ball and ran toward a teenage girl who was standing off to the side, engrossed in her phone. A babysitter? Cousin? Someone Lane didn't know.

Leave it to Lindsay to raise a little monster.

Ryan clapped his hand on the football like a man who'd played the game and took a few steps in her direction.

"Thanks," Lane said.

"Jett's not a bad kid," Ryan said. "Just gets excited. Like a puppy."

"Do you think they'll enroll him in obedience school?" Lane touched her cheek. Still hot and probably swelling. Amazing a so-called soft ball could hurt so badly.

"You've got to admit, though, he's got quite an arm."

She shot Ryan a look and saw the lazy grin on his face as he tossed the football from one hand to the other.

She didn't want to think about Jett. She didn't want to think about how he'd gotten Lindsay's wide blue eyes and Jasper's full lips.

"Did you really say he shouldn't hit people, 'especially girls'?"

Ryan shrugged. "Yeah. Kid's gotta learn."

"Isn't that kind of sexist?"

He stopped tossing the ball. "Nah, it's chivalrous."

Lane laughed. "Oh no. You've turned into one of *those* guys."

Ryan eyed her suspiciously. "What guys?"

"The type who thinks a woman needs a man to protect her."

"Oh, is that what I've turned into?" He raised his eyebrows.

She shrugged. "Looks like it. I never would've thought it was possible, but—" She motioned toward him, moving her hand from his knees to his torso as if his entire person was all the proof she needed.

His eyes narrowed and locked onto hers. "Don't tell me you've turned into one of those kind of women."

"The kind who can handle herself? Yeah, I have."

"The kind who won't let a man be a gentleman because she's intent on putting everyone in their place." He tossed the football in her direction and though she tried to catch it, she failed.

"I see you're still as clumsy as ever."

She bent down and picked up the ball. "You didn't give me any warning." She tossed it back. He caught it—of course.

She glanced toward the corner where Jett had run for protection and curled himself around the teenager. He now looked startlingly sweet. What a little con man.

"How've you been, Lane?"

The question took her off guard. She wasn't sure how to answer, not when it was Ryan asking. Even after all these years, she knew if she gave her canned, stock answer, he'd see right through her.

Lane's mom whisked off the elevator and into the lobby, a not-quite-welcome distraction and one that only slightly eased the tension between her and Ryan.

"I don't think she's sat down once since I got here," Lane said, more to herself than to him.

Her mom made a beeline for them but laser-focused her glare on Lane. "What are you doing down here?"

Lane could feel Ryan's eyes on her, almost like he'd wanted to ask her the same thing.

"I had some work to do," Lane said lamely.

Her mother stared at her. "Oh, Lane. You shouldn't have to work at a time like this."

Her phone buzzed. The slim device suddenly felt heavier in her hands. What could she say that her mother would possibly understand? Did she really need to remind her mom of all the reasons she might not want to sit in a waiting room with their family?

"Your dad and Jer are with Nate now. We want to make sure when he wakes up, he's not alone."

Ryan looked away, obviously thinking the same thing as Lane. She'd been around long enough to catch bits and pieces of her brother's condition, and it didn't seem that her mom fully comprehended the gravity of the situation. The question was, did Lane want to be the one to explain to her that it could be a while before they knew if Nate was going to survive at all? She pushed that thought straight out of her mind. That wasn't going to happen.

And she wasn't going to entertain the idea for a second. Not even in silence.

"You must be starving," her mom said.

"I'm fine." Lane had ignored her growling stomach more times than she could count, but eating felt so silly with Nate in critical condition.

"Ryan, would you take Lane over to Hazel's and make her eat something?"

"Mom, I'm fine," Lane repeated, her cheeks flushing at the thought of going anywhere alone with Ryan Brooks. What would they talk about? It would be like sitting down with a stranger. And Lane had never been good at small talk.

"You haven't eaten all day, have you?" Mom's tone accused.

Lane looked away.

"Probably haven't had anything of substance all week. And while you're home, I'm making it my mission to see that you are well fed."

"At a diner?" Lane and her mother obviously had different ideas of what eating well looked like.

"At a locally owned and operated restaurant with all kinds of wonderful choices." Her mother's tone was mock exasperated. "We call it farm to table, Lane. I would've thought someone as hip as you would've known that."

"I know that no one says *hip* anymore."

Dottie's mock exasperation turned real. "You know what I mean."

She did. And she also knew the importance of supporting the other local business owners—it had been a tradition in their family, and in all of Harbor Pointe, for as long as she could remember. Even in the city, Lane sought out small, family-run businesses. She supposed some of what she'd been taught had stuck.

"Ryan, you don't mind, do you? You could probably use something to eat yourself. Unless your head is still bothering you. Maybe you should go home and lie down. I can call Noah . . ." Lane's mom had turned into a ball of frenetic energy.

Ryan squeezed the football and avoided Lane's glare. "I don't mind, Mrs. K."

"Are you sure?"

"Yeah, I am sort of hungry."

"I knew I could count on you." Her whole face brightened as she said it. "Lane, be nice to this boy."

Now it was Lane who avoided looking at Ryan. She resented the implication that she would be anything other than nice, despite the fact that it only proved there were a few things her mother knew about her, even after all this time.

"Well, what are you waiting for?" Mom said. "Go eat. I'll send someone over if anything changes."

"Or you could just text us." Lane slung her bag over her shoulder.

"Please, Lane. You know how I hate cell phones."

Lane resisted the urge to sigh.

"It would do you good to put yours down once in a while too." She stared at the phone in Lane's hand as if that would punctuate her point.

Lane tucked it in her bag. "Happy?"

Her mom narrowed her gaze. "Only if I get a report that you eat the entire meal without looking at it once." Dottie tried to pretend she was teasing, but Lane knew she wasn't. Her mother had never mastered the art of innocent meddling.

"Mom, I just told you I'm in the middle of something really important at work and I can't just ignore my respons—"

"I know," she cut in and placed a maternal hand on Lane's arm. "But everyone deserves to eat a meal in peace. Ryan, make sure that phone stays in her bag, would you?"

He lifted his hands—one still holding the football—in a position of surrender. "I don't think I want to get in the middle of this one, Mrs. K."

Lane groaned. There was nothing she loved more than her mother's mothering. "I agreed to eat. Can we call that a win for your side?"

Her mom rolled her eyes in an overly dramatic fashion. "There are no sides, Lane. I'm on your side. I would think you'd know that by now."

Something shifted at the back of Lane's mind—a memory, shaken loose by her mother's words. And just like that, she was twelve again. By then it was clear that where Lane was concerned, her father's genes were more dominant than her mother's—and the women on the Kelley side were "sturdy," as the family called them. Lane wasn't stupid. Most of them were fat.

Lane grew so quickly, her mind didn't know how to catch up, and her lack of athleticism played a key role in her rapid weight gain during middle school, something that stuck with her throughout high school. She became an easy target.

How many times had she come home upset?

How many times had she found her mother unsympathetic?

"Oh, honey, I'm sure you're overreacting," she'd said. *"You're a beautiful girl, and anyone who says otherwise is just jealous. I think you're being overly sensitive."*

The words were hollow and did nothing to comfort her. Not then and not over the next several years when she became known as "the fat Kelley" while every one of her siblings was athletic or thin and popular.

Maybe her mother really was oblivious. Or maybe she was embarrassed by Lane's weight. One thing was certain—she didn't stick up for Lane. Not once. Instead, she tried to explain away Lane's pain. It was her way. Find some positive spin.

But when you were the one being teased, it was hard to find anything positive.

Lane hid all the way through high school, behind books, behind intelligence, behind her bedroom door, where she'd cried herself to sleep too many times.

But she wasn't that girl now. She'd transformed herself into a completely new person.

She'd done all the things she'd set out to do—proved to herself and everyone who'd doubted it that she *was* worth something.

So why did she still find that so hard to believe?

CHAPTER

"YOU DON'T HAVE TO GO WITH ME." Lane waited until her mom was gone before speaking to him.

Ryan watched as she packed up stacks of papers and notebooks and other things she'd spread across the table. Things that seemed *very important* to her, important enough to keep her down here instead of upstairs with her family. "I said I would."

"Do you always do everything you say?" She asked the question lightly like it had an obvious answer.

She was about to shove her laptop into its case, but she stopped and looked at him. "Oh, wow. You do, don't you?" Her eyes were crazy blue, practically glowing. She looked like she wanted to say something else but thought better of it. Maybe she was working on controlling her snark.

"I don't need a babysitter." Lane zipped her laptop case around her computer.

"I feel like I've heard that before."

She stopped and searched his gaze as if trying to put her memories of him back in order without all the pieces.

"You've always been kind of stubborn," he said.

"You've always been kind of pigheaded."

They glared at each other, Mexican-standoff style, for several silent seconds; then he finally took a step back and extended a hand in the direction of the front doors as though to say, *After you.*

She held on to his gaze, almost like she'd been challenged to look away and wasn't about to fail, as she walked past him through the lobby toward the front doors.

Why hadn't he told Mrs. K. he needed to go home and rest? She'd practically given him an out—why didn't he take it? Because he found it impossible to tell Dottie no, like a son who wanted to please, who wanted to keep his place in her good graces.

Or maybe because part of him wanted to spend time with Lane?

They'd almost reached the exit when Lane stopped so abruptly he nearly ran into her. She stood, wide-eyed and staring at the door.

"Jasper." She whispered his name, and if he'd been standing even a step farther away from her, he wouldn't have heard.

Jasper Grant walked toward them, still dressed in his suit from work. Ryan noticed that he barely glanced at his son, who was clicking through the channels on the television in the waiting room in an especially annoying way.

"Lane?" Jasper's stare matched Lane's.

She seemed frozen, incapable of moving.

Ryan waited for her to say something, but she only stood there. After a long tense moment, he spoke. "Hey, Jasper. Everyone's still upstairs."

Jasper didn't respond. He seemed unable to pull his gaze off of Nate's sister. Nate's sister who was not his wife.

Then, inexplicably, something came over Lane. She straightened, lifted her chin, and dropped her shoulders, attention fully on Jasper as she did. "Jasper."

"You look amazing," Jasper said inappropriately. His eyes darted to Ryan, then back to Lane. "How've you been?"

"We were just heading out," Lane said coldly. She glanced at Ryan. "You ready?"

"Sure." He glared at Jasper, then finally followed Lane out the door.

Outside, Ryan had to jog a few steps to catch up to her. She'd gotten farther than he would've expected in the heels she was wearing. When he reached her, he could see by her expression that coming face-to-face with Jasper had unraveled something inside her, but he could also tell by her body language that she did not want to talk about it.

"Are you okay?"

She shrugged. "Of course. Why wouldn't I be?"

He should feel comforted that some things about Lane hadn't changed. She was still as stubborn and serious as ever.

She walked quickly—like she was being chased by something—and after several minutes of that nonsense, he purposely slowed down. When she noticed he'd fallen behind, she stopped and looked at him.

"What's the matter?" she asked.

"Why are you in such a hurry?"

She didn't answer.

"This isn't Chicago—you can slow down."

She huffed off down the street. "I was taught to walk with a purpose."

"Well, your only purpose right now is to relax a little bit," he said.

"I don't have time to relax." She turned back toward him. "I don't really have time to be away from work—especially *here*—at all."

He watched as the weight of her own admission washed over her. Why especially *here*? Did she blame the whole town for her pain? To him, this place was like a safe haven—didn't she feel the peace the second she drove into town?

"Sorry; I didn't mean that," she said, even though he knew she did. "It's just been a long day." She stared off down the street, the waning light of the sun illuminating her face and making her look even more beautiful. If that was possible.

"Is it hard being back?"

She pressed her lips together, his question standing between them like an elephant. "It's fine. It'll just be good when I can get back to work." She clicked away, and he followed in silence. Lane had always been a tricky one when it came to her emotions. He couldn't push her—she wouldn't respond to his prodding. She never had. Instead, he'd just work on winning her over, one moment at a time.

After what felt like an eternity of walking in silence, they reached Hazel's, the turquoise-and-yellow diner squeezed in between two other businesses on Main Street. The sign in the window boasted, *Best Pie in the State of Michigan*.

"It's a pie place now?" Lane asked, reading the sign.

He was thankful for small talk—maybe for the first time in his life. "They've won all kinds of awards," Ryan said. "You should try the blueberry pie. It's made with fresh Harbor Pointe berries."

Lane glanced away. "I don't eat pie."

"Well, that's depressing."

She seemed surprised by his comment, but before she could offer a witty comeback, her cell phone chirped.

"I'm just going to take this quick." She stepped toward the stand-up chalkboard sign placed on the sidewalk just outside the door of the bright-turquoise café. It read, *Delicious Coffee at a Delicious Price*.

"I'll go get us a table." Ryan wasn't even sure she'd heard him, but she'd figure it out when she turned around and he was gone.

He entered Hazel's Kitchen, the old-school diner tourists and locals both loved. The place had more than just great pie. Pretty much everything he'd eaten there could've won an award—and as a single guy working long hours, he ate there more than he cared to let on. He stood just inside the door as waitresses zigzagged toward the open window to the kitchen, then back out to the long counter with tall stools evenly spaced from one end to the other. Beyond the counter, customers were scattered at booths or tables around the small, eclectic space.

"Brooks!" Jed Carrington, the town's mayor, sat at the counter, a cup of coffee and a slice of pie in front of him. He waved Ryan over.

Ryan wasn't sure he wanted to be roped into listening to another of the man's big ideas for Harbor Pointe, but it'd be rude not to at least say hello.

"Mayor."

"Heard about Nate Kelley."

Ryan gave a solemn nod, the image of that blue truck flashing in his mind, the sinking feeling of dread returning to his stomach.

"How's he doing? I heard you were with him when it happened."

As Ryan gave him the quick report, what little he understood, a few of the others seated nearby seemed to perk up. Ryan imagined the whole of Harbor Pointe was concerned about Nate. Another thing he loved about this town.

Behind him, the door opened, and he quickly lost Jed's attention and that of every other person who'd been listening to his update. His voice trailed off as he followed curious gazes toward the front door. Lane had stepped inside Hazel's Kitchen. Without even trying, she seemed to command attention just by walking into a room.

She had no idea how beautiful she was.

"Listen, Chloe, it's not going to do any good to get hysterical over—" She was still on the phone.

"Who is *that*?" Dean Fisher stared at Lane with stunned, hungry eyes. Was he salivating? Before Fisher got any wild ideas, Ryan moved toward her. Dean was the last thing she needed.

"Hey, Ryan." A woman wearing jeans and a Hazel's Kitchen T-shirt greeted him near the front door.

"Hey, Betsy." He smiled at her. He liked that the new owner of Hazel's recognized him, made him feel at home—a feeling he'd never take for granted, not even as an adult.

"You want your usual booth?"

"Sure, but there are two of us tonight." He motioned toward Lane, who finished her phone call and tucked her cell back inside her bag, where he imagined it would stay for only a few minutes.

"Sorry." She stepped closer to him. "It was work."

Her eyes found Betsy's and recognition seemed to wash over

them both, leaving Ryan feeling like he'd just stepped in the middle of something.

"Bets, you remember Lane Kelley?"

Betsy's smile was definitely forced. "I heard about Nate. I'm sorry."

"Thanks." Lane's attention was back on the floor.

After an awkward pause, Betsy picked up two menus. "Follow me."

He motioned for Lane to go first, confused when she hesitated for several seconds. She and Betsy were friends. At least he thought they were. He gave her a soft nudge, then followed her to a booth at the very rear of the restaurant.

Lane slid in, her back to the door, carefully avoiding eye contact with Betsy. Ryan sat down across from her and Betsy handed them their menus.

"Can I tell you our specials?" she asked.

Lane was glued to her menu.

"Sure." Ryan half listened as Betsy rattled off a number of dishes that would've normally made his mouth water. Something about sitting across from Lane, about her words on the street outside—"especially *here*"—about the tension between her and Betsy, had him thinking of other things besides his stomach.

Lane had always been something of a loner—but he'd had the impression she preferred it that way. Now he wasn't so sure.

What was her life now that her family wasn't a part of it?

"I'll send someone over with water and give you two a few minutes," Betsy said.

She disappeared, but something heavy still hung in the air above them, like a weighty cloud desperate to pour out buckets of rain.

"What was that about?" Ryan asked. "Weren't you two friends?"

Her eyes were still on the menu. "What's good here?"

He had to commend her for her impressive skill of changing the subject. Whatever had happened between her and Betsy Tanner, Lane did not want to talk about it. He started to wonder what else he'd missed while he was overseas—and why hadn't anyone filled him in?

"Everything is good since Betsy bought the place," Ryan said, eyeing the meat loaf platter on the menu.

"She *owns* this place?"

He nodded. "Bought it two years ago when Hazel retired. People drive hours for her pies. They did a write-up on the diner—and Betsy—in *Midwest Living* last summer. It's one of the top destinations in the Midwest."

"Seriously?" Lane's eyes darted toward Betsy, then back to him. "That's really great." It was the first twinkle of genuine happiness he'd seen in Lane since she arrived.

After a minute or two, another waitress showed up at their table and took their order. They didn't see Betsy again.

Lane ordered a grilled chicken salad, dressing on the side, and a glass of water. He decided on homemade pot roast with mashed potatoes and vegetables, as well as a cup of coffee.

Her phone buzzed, pulling her out of the world she was in and into another one altogether. She tapped on it for what felt like forever—wholly captivated by the words on the tiny screen. When she put it away, she looked surprised to find him watching her.

"What?"

"Have you ever thought of silencing that thing?"

"Not you too."

"Might not hurt to take your mom's advice," he said. "You never know what you're missing when you're focused on that phone all day."

"I'm sure you wouldn't understand what it's like to have a million people needing your attention every second of the day." She took a sip of water, a slice of lemon bobbing around in her glass.

"I take it Nate's accident came at a bad time for you?" The words were harsh and he regretted them instantly.

She glared at him. "Look, you're here because you feel like you owe it to my mother, but I'm actually perfectly capable of eating a meal by myself."

He didn't doubt it. "I'm sorry. That was out of line."

She watched him as though deciding whether or not to accept his apology.

"Seriously. I shouldn't have said that." This was not how he wanted things to go.

She took a sip and looked away, giving him a fraction of a second to admire those blue eyes and smooth skin—two things about her he'd always loved.

"Tell me about your job," he said.

She folded her hands on the table. "It's not very interesting."

"Try me."

"I work at a large interior design firm in the city called JB Sweet. I mostly work in branded environments."

"Branded environments?"

"Say you're a big company looking to move into a space. My team comes up with the design of that space to fit the company's brand. Lots of times we actually create the brand for the company and make sure all elements of it match."

She said it like it was no big deal, yet he had the distinct impression it was a very big deal to her.

"I'm guessing it's pretty time-consuming."

"You have no idea." Her phone buzzed and he lost her again. The waitress, a young girl with stringy blonde hair and a wad of gum in her mouth, brought them their food. As soon as Ryan inhaled the aroma of that pot roast, he realized how hungry he was.

"What about you? The last memory I have of you is waving good-bye the day you left for the Army."

"You promised to write to me while I was gone," he said.

She stopped chewing.

"You never did."

"I figured you had plenty of girls writing you letters, Brooks."

He smiled, not because he had plenty of girls writing him letters, but because she'd called him Brooks, the way she had when they were kids. The familiarity of it had always made him feel instantly close to her.

"I didn't think you even remembered me back in the hospital."

"Took me a minute." She looked away. "But then I got this horrible pain in my neck and it was like we'd never been apart."

He picked up a carrot and tossed it at her. Her eyes went wide and she laughed. "You're going to get us kicked out of here."

"Nah, I'm one of their best customers."

"So you moved to Harbor Pointe? You actually live here now?"

He sipped his coffee. How much of this did he want to get into with someone whose gaze held him captive like a prisoner of war?

"I guess I just needed a change."

That wasn't a lie. When he got home from overseas, he realized there was nothing for him in Newman—nothing but haunting memories and a dead-end life he had no interest in living. Harbor Pointe hadn't been his intended stop, but life had a funny way of changing course.

"That sounds ominous."

He shrugged. "It's not. I got home from Afghanistan and started working construction while I went to school. Took me longer than the traditional student, but I got my business degree."

"And do you still work construction?"

He studied her before answering. A construction worker wouldn't impress Lane, and yet he heard himself respond, "I guess you could say that," not wanting to sound pompous with tales of his new business venture.

The dull ache around his temples returned.

"Are you okay?" She stared at him. "You look like you're going to be sick."

Good to know he looked exactly how he felt.

"I'm fine. Just have a headache."

"From the accident?"

"I guess so."

She folded her hands on the table in front of her, examining him the way a cop might do when interrogating a suspect. "You never told me if it was Nate's fault."

"It was an accident," he said. "Truth is, I'm not sure what happened exactly. One minute we were on the road and the next, we were face-down on the pavement. A truck ran us right off the road. Nate collided with a telephone pole. I skidded right past him." He looked away.

"You were really—"

"Lucky, I know." His eyes found hers and she didn't break contact for several long seconds. Several long seconds of him feeling exposed, as if he'd said more of what mattered in those three words than he had since the day he returned from Afghanistan.

She took a drink, then did a quick once-over of Hazel's Kitchen. It was different from when she lived here, he knew. Betsy had put a lot of sweat equity into giving the restaurant a face-lift. He knew because he'd been the one to do most of the sweating.

"It's good you've stayed close with my family," she said, most likely because she couldn't think of anything else to say.

"They're the best. You're really fortunate to have them."

She didn't move, her expression still and unnerving. She didn't really *have them*, though, did she? But she could, if she wanted to. Did she see that?

"Nate and I are on the worship team together at church."

She stopped midbite. "What?"

"Don't sound so surprised. We've gotten pretty good."

She frowned. "Playing what?"

"Guitar."

"Nate plays guitar?" Her jaw went slack.

"How long has it actually been since you've talked to your family?"

She looked down. "Why do I have the feeling you already know the answer to that question?"

It was like a foghorn went off at the back of his mind ordering him to tread lightly. "Your mom said you've hardly been in town since you left for college—just a few times since then."

"Did she?" Her tone almost sounded like an accusation. "She have anything else to say on that subject?"

"Not really." He wouldn't tell her how often her name came up with the Kelley family, because when it did, it was clearly still a painful topic of conversation. He felt sorry for all of them, that this rift had grown so deep, like a valley between them, and for the briefest moment, he wondered if he could help mend it. He didn't like seeing them fractured the way they were. They belonged together, like it was when he was a kid.

"She did say you've had a lot of success at work."

"My work is important to me," Lane said.

"She's really proud of you."

Lane laughed. A humorless, sarcastic laugh. "I think you're thinking of one of my siblings."

"I know they miss seeing you. They all wish you'd come home more. I mean, work is important but so is your family, Lane."

"Really? They wish I'd come home more?" Lane's voice wavered, and for a split second he saw something other than steely stubbornness in her face. A pang of regret shattered inside him. He'd gone too far. He should've butted out.

"I didn't mean to—"

"Did they bother to tell you *why* I don't come home, or did they just make me out to be some self-centered workaholic who doesn't have time for my family?"

So much for treading lightly. He knew this was hard for her—why hadn't he let it go?

When he didn't respond, she pushed her plate away, covering it with her napkin.

"Lane, please."

"I'm not the evil one here, Brooks. I would've thought at least you might've been on my side." She threw a twenty-dollar bill down on the table and stood.

His eyes followed her as she made a quick, seamless exit, and as he turned his attention back to the table, he caught a glimpse of Betsy, staring at the door. Lane had been in town for only a few hours, and she'd completely disrupted the calm of Harbor Pointe.

And Ryan wanted to know why.

CHAPTER

9

IF LANE HADN'T BEEN WEARING HEELS, she might've started running as soon as the door of Hazel's Kitchen swung shut behind her. Coming back here had been a huge mistake. She should've known she wasn't strong enough to withstand the memories. Everywhere she turned, there was another one—Lindsay, Jasper, Betsy, and now even Brooks had turned maddening.

She walked toward the hospital. She'd go see Nate one more time and then she had to drive home. What else was she going to do? Sleep in her old bedroom in her parents' house? Wake up and have breakfast with Lindsay and Jasper and their terrorist of a son? She hadn't thought this through.

She glanced over her shoulder, thankful Brooks hadn't followed her. Maybe nobody had told him the truth about why she stayed away. Maybe she'd overreacted. She hated it when she did that.

Brooks had been to war. She hadn't even asked him about that. He was one of the best people she'd ever known—this happy-go-lucky kid who had no reason to smile or laugh or joke around but who always seemed to be doing just that. His optimism had shamed her more times than she could count—made her more aware of her own behavior. She'd always struggled to find the silver lining of a thing. Some things, she supposed, hadn't changed. Having her emotions too close to the surface brought out the worst in her, yet he should've left it alone. She didn't need to be reminded of what a bad daughter and sister she'd been. Seeing him, a boy who'd essentially grown up without his own parents, made her aware of that.

Her phone buzzed. Chloe.

Wanted to check on you. Are you doing okay? I've been worried about you all day.

Lane quickly texted back.

I'm fine. Just don't like being here or seeing my brother like this.

She stood in the doorway of his room and stared at him now, underneath a stiff white sheet and a hospital-issue blanket that did not look very warm. Daisy had never brought the second blanket Brooks had asked for.

Is he any better?

No change.

I looked up your brother on Facebook. Can't believe you've kept him from me until now, Lane. He's gorgeous. Any of his hot friends hanging around the waiting room?

The image of Brooks's "I don't have to try very hard to be gorgeous" vibe entered her mind. He'd always been unnervingly good-looking with his striking green eyes and a head full of messy hair the same color as beach sand. Then there was that five o'clock shadow, which, unfortunately, only made him better-looking. Just when she didn't think it was *possible* for him to get better-looking.

Your long pause speaks volumes.

I've only talked to one of my brother's friends, but he's pigheaded and annoying.

It wasn't exactly true. If anyone fit that description, it was Lane, and she knew it.

You didn't answer my question.

She stared at the phone, finally typing out her reply: Unfortunately, yes. He's ridiculously good-looking.

I knew it.

But he's pigheaded and annoying.

Uh-huh.

Lane put her phone away and took a few steps into the room, surprised to find it empty other than the machines breathing for her brother—the only thing that kept the room from being dead silent. Someone had turned the television on but left the sound muted as though the noise might bother Nate. She sank into the chair beside his bed, dropping her bag to the floor, and stared at him. Like all her siblings, Nate had been blessed with the near-perfect body of an athlete, but none of that mattered when you were fighting for your life.

She laid a hand over the top of Nate's and let out a deep, heavy sigh.

In a flash, she was fourteen again.

Every summer in Harbor Pointe started out the same way with a weekend that felt like one long parade, as families who owned summer cottages returned, a caravan of vehicles pulling into town one right after the other.

As was tradition, Lane and her siblings climbed out onto the roof of their large Victorian house and waved as their friends arrived. It was like Christmas morning, that first weekend, welcoming everyone back, seeing the friends they waited nine months out of every year to hang out with.

The next three months promised Lane lazy, sun-filled days at the lake with the same girls she'd always known. A tight-knit group of friends that made Lane feel like the luckiest girl in the world. But the summer she was fourteen, everything changed.

That summer, when the girls got out of their minivans, they didn't run straight to Lane's house and knock on the door. She sat on the roof, just outside her bedroom window, with her legs pulled up and her arms wrapped around them, watching as Noah, Nate, Lindsay, and Jeremy all ran off to the beach as their friends raced by to pick them up. It was still too cool to swim, but they'd gather on the dock and later build a bonfire.

It was tradition.

After waiting nearly an hour, Lane walked down to the beach by herself. She trudged up over the dunes, slipping her shoes off at the landing halfway down. The sun had just begun to dip down behind the horizon, and the bonfire blazed.

Lane stood off in the distance, watching her three friends, arms linked, hovering around the fire without her.

Why had they forgotten her?

Thinking about it now, Lane regretted going to the beach at all that day. She should've stayed up on her roof with her book until the sun went down, then sprawled out and watched the stars until she drifted off to sleep.

But she didn't. She walked over to Ashley, Maddie, and Sabrina, expecting their usual warm welcome, a hug, a series of giggles, and an "I've missed you so much."

Instead, Ashley stared at her for a long moment as if to ask, *Why are you touching me?* Lane pulled her hand off the girl's shoulder and glanced at Maddie and Sabrina, neither of whom would look at her.

"I was waiting for you guys." Lane's involuntary admission made her feel naked.

Ashley scoffed. "Why?"

Lane stuttered, emotionally wincing at the comment. "I thought we'd come to the beach together. Like always."

Ashley gave her a once-over, then walked away, Maddie and Sabrina trailing behind. Nate must've seen her face crumple because he swooped in as if out of thin air and whisked her off toward the wooden staircase built into the side of the dune before she lost it completely.

He wanted to know what happened, but Lane hadn't been able to give him an answer. She had no idea. She just knew her best friends suddenly weren't, and nobody seemed to care but him. He'd left his friends that night and spent the evening hanging out with her instead. She'd told him not to—told him to go back to the beach; she was fine. But he insisted on popping a bowl of popcorn and letting her pick the movie.

Miss Congeniality.

He said he didn't mind the chick flick because he got to see Sandra Bullock in that tight little dress after Michael Caine made her up to look like a beauty queen.

He could've been at the beach with his friends.

The manufactured breath of the machine at Nate's bedside caught her attention. She pressed her forehead to his hand. How could she even have considered leaving him like this? Nate—the brother who had always stuck up for her. The only one who stopped calling her Pudge because she asked him to. The one who'd told Lindsay what she was doing was wrong.

She couldn't leave now. Not when he was still fighting for his life.

No matter how much she hated being home.

Lane woke up the following day with a throbbing headache. She blamed Jett. She rolled over and looked at the clock. Not even 7 a.m. Why did it sound like her parents were having a party in the kitchen?

She'd stumbled in last night after her hospital visit, pulled on her pajamas, and fallen into bed without even bothering to turn on the light. But now, with the early morning sun streaming through the two east-facing windows, she realized her old room had been turned into a sewing room for her mother. There were still small traces of the room that it was when she lived here, but mostly it looked like a completely different space.

The door flew open with a start and Lane shot straight up in bed. Before her eyes focused, she was pelted twice in the forehead with something small and circular.

"Pow! Pow!"

Jett.

"Ow!" She held her hands up in front of her face.

"Got you!" The monster took off down the hallway.

What was he doing in her room before 7 a.m., and why did he have so much energy? Lane flung the covers off and tromped through the hallway, holding the two Nerf gun darts that had smacked her in the face.

She stormed her way down the stairs and into the kitchen, coming face-to-face with a room full of people. No wonder it sounded like a party—half the neighborhood was there. Most of them stood around the island, some were out in the eating porch, and she had everyone's attention, whether she wanted it or not.

Her eyes scanned the crowd. Noah and Emily, their kids, Lane's aunt Clarice, a couple of her mom's friends, a man Lane had never seen, and a few other familiar—but not really—people stared at her.

She imagined Jer and her dad were at the hospital, and as expected, Lindsay was absent. She'd dropped her kid off with her mom, but she hadn't stayed around. Nice.

"Lane, you're up!" Her mom sashayed over to her. "We were beginning to think you were going to sleep right through breakfast." Then she leaned closer to Lane and whispered, "Do you have a bra on?"

Lane folded her arms in front of her chest, wishing she could melt straight into the floor.

"Is that Pudge?"

Every muscle in Lane's body stiffened at the mention of the nickname in front of such a large group. Where was the Rewind button?

It was Doris Rhodes, their next-door neighbor, the one who'd called Lane to cat-sit every time she went out of town because "I know you're dependable and you don't have much else to do." Doris was a round woman herself with one daughter who'd grown up and left her ages ago. Lane had to commend that girl for making such a wise decision. Doris's husband had passed away when Lane was in high school, starting a trail of rumors that the old biddy had killed him herself with her nagging. Death by nagging seemed plausible once a person had met Doris.

"Hi, Mrs. Rhodes." Lane took a step back, wondering if it were possible to vanish into thin air.

"It's nice to see you're not so fat anymore," Doris said. "But still no wedding ring, I see. Holding out for Mr. Right? You shouldn't wait around forever, you know. Tick-tock."

"Our daughter is a career girl, Doris." Dottie handed Lane a cup of coffee, and Lane wanted to kiss the desperately needed caffeine. "Career girls don't have time for romance."

Her mother's words were benign, but her tone was not.

"Have you found a good church in the city?" Aunt Clarice asked. "It's so hard to find good churches nowadays, especially in the city. Cities are filled with so much sin. You probably haven't been in the good Lord's house since you were home last, have you? You have to be careful with your spirit, Pudge. You can't work your way into heaven, you know."

Ah, how Lane had *not* missed this.

Aunt Clarice had been a pastor's wife for as long as Lane could remember. Uncle Roger was the pastor of one of the churches in town, and he and Lane's dad spent every family function arguing about theology.

The Kelleys did not attend Uncle Roger's church.

The cacophony of voices swirled through the room.

"You probably don't think having a family is important, but in a flash, you'll be old like me, and . . ."

"You might be too thin, Lane. Do you eat? 'Course if you want to catch a man's eye, I suppose it's better to be too thin than too fat. You can let yourself go once the ring is on your finger." Pause for laughter.

"I heard you're mostly glued to that cell phone of yours, but studies show cell phones cause brain tumors. You shouldn't let that thing near your face."

"Mom, can I have another donut?"

Lane stood there in her lightweight pajama shorts and T-shirt, which she'd fished out of her suitcase in a state of exhaustion—and in the dark—last night when she got in, listening but not listening as they all fired their questions and opinions at her like Jett had fired the stupid Nerf gun that had gotten her out of bed in the first place. She stared across the room, trying to plan her escape. Noah and Emily's kids were now sprawled out in the living room looking blissfully unaware of what was going on in the kitchen, and Lane wished she could bypass all of this and join them. There was an oversize pillow next to the oldest one that looked awfully cozy. She doubted her niece and nephews would have opinions on her life. They'd probably let her just sit there and watch cartoons with them.

"Lane, did you hear me?" Her mom stared at her, waiting for a response to a question Lane hadn't caught.

"What?"

"Oh, Lane, I think that phone has completely ruined your ability to focus. I said, we've put you on the rotation."

"What rotation?"

"At the shop. We were going to close for the week, but your brothers offered to pitch in so we didn't lose the money. It's so tight this time of year, you know—well, actually, it's tight year-round now with tourism being down." Dottie's eyelids fluttered. "Are you listening to me?"

Lane didn't respond.

"You're going to have to help at the cheese shop and the farmers' market while you're here, maybe around the house a little, and then, of course, visiting Nate. We all need to do our part to keep his spirits up. Your father milked the cows this morning, but we want you to do it tomorrow. Noah will do it Thursday and then Jer; then we'll start all over."

The room stilled. She was amazed these people, who'd woken her with the sheer volume of their conversation, could be this quiet.

"I can't stay long enough for all that, Mom." She kept her voice low as if that would prevent the others from listening. Lane wished she could run out the door, get into her car, and drive straight back to Chicago. But the memory of Nate's unmoving face haunted her.

"You're not staying?" Doris squawked. "I thought for sure you'd change your mind."

"I told you." Aunt Clarice shook her head in a way that only older, disapproving women seemed to be able to.

"I have work," Lane said, her voice quiet.

The commentary started up again.

"All these young people do anymore is work, work, work . . ."

"Priorities out of whack . . ."

"Brother in the hospital for goodness' sake . . ."

Lane stopped listening, but as the bodies shifted around the room, a familiar silhouette appeared. Aunt Clarice took a step toward the donuts and Doris took a step toward the eating porch. Like the parting of the Red Sea, their movement revealed Ryan Brooks, who'd been sitting in a chair at the edge of the kitchen, hidden by the others, the whole time.

His eyes met hers, and Lane felt as exposed as she would have if someone had opened the door on her just as she'd stepped out of the shower.

Why was he here at this hour? Why was he sitting there all quiet and handsome? What must he think of her after hearing everything the others were saying? She was selfish, a workaholic, a former fat girl with a ticking clock.

But he already knew all those things, didn't he? And what did she care? It wasn't like she wanted to impress him or something. It was just Brooks.

Lane looked away, but as she did, he stood and moved into the kitchen.

"I'll take Lane's shifts," he said. "You can add them to mine."

Dottie waved him off. "That is far too much, Ryan. You have your own work to do."

Lane met his eyes again.

"I'd be happy to do it." He held Lane's gaze as he said the words.

Lane couldn't even protest—she didn't know what to say. He must have an ulterior motive or something and—*oh, my gosh, he's seeing me when I just woke up.* She set her untouched cup of coffee on the counter and left the room, anxious for this terrible, confusing nightmare to be over.

And even more anxious to eliminate the knowledge that Ryan's generous offer and pointed gaze hadn't only quieted the room; it had quieted the frenetic buzzing of anxiety that had seemed to be a constant undercurrent at Lane's center ever since the day she found out the truth about Lindsay and Jasper.

CHAPTER

10

"SHE'S VERY ODD," Doris Rhodes said when Lane walked out of the kitchen.

Ryan resisted the urge to go after her. Being here seemed to have her permanently on edge—or maybe she was just like that now. Edgy. He told himself his irrational desire to protect her came from a sense of duty to her family. After all, he owed the Kelleys a lot.

And yet a part of him knew it was more than that.

"It was very thoughtful of you to try and smooth things over with her, Ryan." Dottie poured herself a small glass of orange juice. "It's a shame she still has such a chip on her shoulder."

"Ma." Noah's tone sounded off a warning, and Ryan wished he'd already left. As much a part of the family as they made him feel, there were still some things that seemed best kept within their tight, blood-related circle. They did a good job of not discussing their dirty laundry in mixed company. He'd only put the whole mess together himself because he was observant—not because he'd been offered an explanation.

She held her hands up in surrender. "I'm just saying. Bitterness is the root of all evil. That's what the Bible says."

"I thought money was the root of all evil." Doris frowned. "Maybe evil has more than one root."

"Give her a break, Ma. This isn't easy for her either." Noah gave his mom a stern nod, and she seemed to take the hint because she didn't say another word.

Jett walked in, carrying an iPhone with a floral case that was definitely not a toy. He reared back as if he was going to throw it like a football, but Ryan snatched it from his hand before he could let it fly.

"Hey! No fair!"

Man, that kid needed some discipline. Ryan reminded himself that Jett was not his child and clenched his jaw to keep himself from talking to him like he was.

"Oh, Jett, that is not polite," Dottie said. "Why don't you go sit down with the other kids?"

"Why is he here so early?" Noah cracked four eggs into a bowl. "And where's Lindsay?"

Dottie shot him a look but didn't reply. Ryan understood what wasn't being said, and he hated that everything was so upside-down right now.

"I'm going to head out," Ryan said. "I've got to get back to the cottages."

"Ryan, are you sure it's a good idea for you to be working so soon after the accident? An almost concussion is nothing to fool around with. You could become a vegetable."

"I don't think that's true, Ma," Noah said without looking at her.

"Well, maybe not, but I still don't think it's a good idea." Dottie stuck the orange juice back in the fridge.

"I'll be fine. No real harm done." The pain in his head had mostly gone away. Besides, Ryan had a deadline. Investors. And lots of work to do. It seemed, in a way, the whole town was depending on him to single-handedly revitalize the tourism industry of Harbor

Pointe, though he knew that wasn't the case. Still, he had to get those cottages ready in time for opening day.

The phone in his hand—he recognized it as Lane's from her constant attention to it—vibrated. He glanced at the screen and saw a message from someone named Chloe.

Mrs. Pim is demanding to hear from you today about the drapes in the lounge. Apparently she's changed her mind again—shocker. But enough about work. . . . Any more run-ins with your brother's hot (annoying) friend?

Ryan shouldn't have read that, but even he had to admit, the phone was difficult to ignore.

"Well, if you must go, you should at least take something to eat." Dottie wrapped two donuts in a napkin and handed them to him. "And thank you so much for being here this early while we sorted out the schedule. We'll see you at the hospital later this afternoon."

The screen went dark and Ryan passed the phone to Dottie. "Sure will." He said his good-byes and walked out the door into the brisk spring air. He tried to ride his bicycle around Harbor Pointe as much as possible, but Dottie had wanted him there practically before the sun rose, so his worse-for-the-wear motorcycle waited for him in the driveway.

He stared at it for a brief moment, a part of him not wanting to get back on it.

Get a grip, man.

As he swung his leg over and sat on it, Lane appeared in the driveway near the garage, likely attempting an escape out the back door. A little black-and-white dog on a leash followed her out. She'd pulled her hair up into a ponytail and now wore a pair of running shorts and a tank top. He gave himself a fleeting moment to admire her curves.

He unhooked his helmet but didn't put it on. "You look cute." She frowned at him.

"I mean, it's a step up from those pajamas."

She shot him a look, but as her eyes hit the ground, he could've sworn he saw a smile. He'd crack through that tough exterior if it was the last thing he did. She tugged on the leash, but the dog seemed to have no interest in anything but the flowers beside the driveway.

"Yours?"

Another slight tug and the dog came to her side.

"Yeah, this is Otis." She scooped him up. "Noah took care of him for me last night, but he needs his exercise. He's a porker." The dog licked her chin.

"I didn't take you for an animal lover."

Another frown. "Why not?" She rubbed between the dog's ears. He shrugged. So far, all he'd witnessed was her cold shoulder. It was a different side of her, watching her with an animal that she obviously had great affection for.

When he didn't offer an explanation, her gaze wandered off behind him. "Thanks for offering to take my shifts, but I'll do it as long as I'm here. I just don't like that she assumes I have nothing important in my life. I mean, Nate is, of course, the most important thing right now, but I . . ." Her voice trailed off, her eyes focused on her Nikes—turquoise with a bright-pink swoosh. "Sometimes she's so ridiculous."

"She's coping," he said. "Best way she knows how."

Lane looked up but didn't respond.

"Going for a run or just running away?"

She laughed. "Maybe a little of both."

"You should head down to the new bike path. It'll take you right by the lake. Just start down Darby Lane that way and go right." He pointed in the direction of the path.

She stood with her hands on her hips and gave a quick nod. "You're not leading me into a mud pit or something, are you?"

He chuckled. "Why would I do that?"

"Payback for how I've treated you since I got here."

"Is that an apology?"

She raised an eyebrow. If it was, it was the only one he was going to get.

"I promise it's not a mud pit." Ryan buckled on his helmet. "There are a few rabid dogs, but you should be able to outrun them. Or at least beat them off with that attitude of yours."

"You're a funny guy."

He'd missed the playful banter they'd had once. As she looked away, he could see the amusement dancing in her otherwise-stony eyes.

He put the key in the ignition. "I gave your phone to your mom, by the way."

She patted herself. "I can't believe I forgot it." She eyed him. "How did you get it?"

"I didn't take it, if that's what you're thinking. Jett had it."

Lane shook her head. "That kid, I swear."

"Yeah, hopefully Dottie can't go through your text messages. She might find out something you don't want her to know." He winked at her, then started the bike. "See ya later."

She waved dismissively, and as he drove away, he found himself hoping that "later" came quickly.

Ryan headed down Darby Lane and turned right at Lake Shore Drive. Similar only in name to Chicago's bustling strip, this stretch of road ran along Lake Michigan and one of Harbor Pointe's beautiful, soft sand beaches. The beaches were what brought so many to Harbor Pointe, but it was the people who kept them coming back. At least that had been the case for Ryan.

After he'd left the Army, he needed to get his bearings—to try to forget the things he'd seen in Afghanistan and concentrate on a new life.

Compared to Newman, Harbor Pointe felt like a completely different universe. It was, he supposed. And if anyone here besides the Kelleys knew about his past, they certainly didn't let on or seem to care.

He'd walked through those early stateside days in foggy slow motion, trying to make sense of everything that had happened, suddenly faced with all the things he'd run away from the day he joined the Army. He'd hidden in a rented cottage for a week before he ever stepped foot in town. Then he ran out of groceries and decided to try Hazel's Kitchen.

He'd gone almost every day since.

Something about the town had captured him, as if when he stared out across the lake, the wind whispered over the water one word, meant just for him: *Stay.*

The week turned into a month, then a year. He'd found a job working construction and still managed to finish his business degree. He'd been back almost six years.

Now he was one of them. A local.

He drove to the other side of town, toward Cedar Grove with its rows of cottages in various stages of renovations. He'd lived on almost nothing for years so he could squirrel away every bit of money he could, almost as if he realized he was going to need it, though he didn't know what for.

When the owner of Cedar Grove died and they auctioned the place off, he was the only person who bid on it—the only person crazy enough, people said. But the prospect of turning this place into something that could benefit the community was good for everybody.

That was part of how he'd pitched the project to investors after using everything he'd saved on the purchase of the place. And a couple local businessmen—thanks largely to Frank's good word—took a chance. On him.

With a little more funding, he hoped to expand to Summers Bay next year with a whole new string of lakefront cottages.

But only if his investors were impressed with his work here. And only if he turned a profit.

He pulled up to the work site and met his contractor, Jerry Flanagan, in the street.

"Brooks, where do you want them to unload the stone?" Jerry hitched his thumb toward the front yard of the soon-to-be-finished cottage across the street from the model cottage where Ryan had been staying during the renovations. "Just in the yard?"

Ryan and Jerry fell into step as they approached the unfinished cottage. Jerry was one of those burly guys with a bushy beard and a beer belly, though Ryan had never known the man to drink anything stronger than Mountain Dew.

"Here's fine," Ryan said, motioning for the lanky guy delivering the stone to unload to the right of the walkway. The guy was tall and wiry, but his shirt was only partly tucked in and he didn't look like he'd showered yet this week. "Be careful with it," he hollered toward the cab of the delivery truck. He'd paid a fortune for that stone. It was perfect for the custom-built fireplace he had planned. The last thing he needed was for a sloppy delivery to hold him up.

A blue sedan turned onto his street and parked at the curb. Barb Lovejoy stepped out, her flame of red hair giving her away before Ryan ever saw her face. Barb's wide eyes and quick, birdlike movements were a bit off-putting, but she came highly recommended, and heaven knew he wouldn't be able to get the Cedar Grove cottages decorated without her.

"Didn't think I'd see you today," Ryan said as she approached. "Especially not this early."

"I knew you'd be out here now. Figured it was the best time to catch you in person." Barb's head darted around in quick, clipped movements as if connected to a string being pulled by a mischievous toddler.

Her eyes settled on him and she smiled—big teeth that almost didn't fit in her mouth and reminded Ryan, unfortunately, of a horse. "Place looks great, Ryan. You've done an amazing job."

He caught a whiff of her floral perfume. She'd applied it so liberally, he thought it might make him sneeze. "Thanks. Almost time for you to get in there and do your thing."

Her smile faded, whisking his away with it.

"What's wrong?"

"I'm so sorry, Ryan. That's what I came here to talk to you about." She clutched the floppy brown bag that hung on her shoulder, and her eyes welled up with tears. "I'm moving. My husband was offered the job of a lifetime in California. We leave next week."

Ryan tossed a glance at the nearly finished cottage behind him, then back to Barb. She was finally supposed to get started on decorating the cottages next week. It was the only way to get them ready in time. It had taken him months to find Barb in the first place. He didn't have time to launch a search for a new interior designer, and he didn't have the talent to whip something together on his own. Not even with the model—which Barb had already decorated—as a guide.

Ryan ran a hand over his chin, the whiskers scratching his palm. What was he going to do now?

"I took the liberty of putting together a few names for you." Barb rooted around in that giant bag of hers until she found a small note card. She handed it to him.

"Do you know I'm up against a deadline here?" Ryan stuffed the card in his pocket without looking at it.

"I know, Ryan. That's why I feel so badly about this." Barb's eyes fluttered open even wider as she said the words.

"Do you have anything else you can give me—color choices, fabrics, design ideas?"

Barb frowned. "We've just been so busy . . ."

Ryan sighed. She was supposed to have been working on this for a while now. "There's no way we can do this long-distance?" He was desperate now.

She shook her head. "I thought about that, but I'm not tech-savvy enough, and besides, I'll be in the middle of a move. You know how jarring that can be."

He stuck his hands on his hips and stared at the ground as if some magical answer might appear in the dirt underneath his work boots. "I get it. Thanks for letting me know."

"There are several very promising names on that list, Ryan. You're going to be fine."

He nodded, if only to let her know he was aware she'd spoken to him, even though he really just wanted her to go away.

"I'm excited to see what becomes of this place," Barb said. "I have no doubt you'll find a way to achieve exactly what you're hoping with these cottages—a place of rest for anyone who is weary."

"Thanks, Barb."

In the distance, he saw two figures moving toward them on bicycles. Was it already seven thirty?

"I'll leave you to get your day started." She hitched the bag up higher on her shoulder. "I really am sorry, Ryan."

"It'll be fine." There were those words again, empty as a fast-food container after a hungry man's meal. "Wish you all the best in California."

Ryan watched as she got back in her car and drove away; then he walked to the end of the gravel driveway that would eventually be paved with brick. He took a moment to glance along the shoreline at what he'd created, trying not to feel hopeless and like it was all about to implode.

Cedar Grove was his labor of love, and while he'd grown accustomed to telling people he saw a valuable business opportunity in purchasing the few run-down cottages and the land that went with them, he knew the truth—that renovating the old cottages had kept his mind occupied. Like therapy without the stuffy doctor peering at him over horn-rimmed glasses.

Sometimes he worried about finishing the last cottage—Esther, he'd named her. What would he do with the haunting memories when all his work was done? The nagging notion that he should be working through those with God, not with a hammer, entered his mind. As usual, he shoved it aside. Some things were better left buried.

Jack pedaled hard and fast, beating his mom up the hill with a cheer. "I won!" he shouted as he hopped off his bike and ran toward Ryan. "I beat Mom!"

Ryan lifted the seven-year-old into the air with a victory shout. "Saw it. You crushed it, buddy."

"Because I'm awesome!" Jack shouted as Ryan put him back on the ground.

Hailey slowed to a stop and smirked at the two of them. "I blame you for his inflated ego."

Ryan laughed. "Can't help it. Brooks boys are awesome."

Jack gave him a fist bump followed by a resounding "Yes!"

Hailey got off the bike, standing it up at the end of the driveway. "I see you haven't listened to a word your doctor said about taking it easy." She crossed her arms and glared at him.

"I'm fine, Hailey. Really."

His sister obviously wasn't buying it, but he really did feel almost back to normal.

"Esther's coming right along." She regarded the bones of the cottage. This one had been in the worst shape. They'd almost completely gutted and rebuilt it, and it was starting to look like a home again. They were a few weeks from finishing, but they'd made noticeable progress.

"I'm thinking she's going to get a teal mailbox." He winked at Hailey, who gave a quick gasp.

"In my honor?"

"No, in honor of Janice, the mail lady. She told me she liked teal."

Hailey punched him in the arm. "Don't be a smart aleck."

He laughed. Each of the white cottages was going to have a different-colored mailbox and a number of other design elements to make it special. Hailey was always bugging him about using teal—a girlie color he'd never pick out himself, but since his cottages had to appeal to women, he figured it wouldn't be a bad idea to listen to her just this once.

Besides, he liked to see her smile. He could still remember a time he wondered if he'd ever see her smile again.

The image of her standing on his doorstep two years ago with a then-five-year-old Jack and a black eye entered his mind the way it often did when he thought of Hailey. The image was always met with a protective anger. He'd made a promise never to let something like that happen to her again.

"How's Nate doing?" Hailey stared at him with those big green eyes that told him the accident had been too close for comfort.

Ryan filled her in on his friend's condition.

"They said it was a hit-and-run." Hailey stared off into the distance. "It must've been so scary."

"It was." Ryan ran a hand over his chin again, reminding himself that he should shave. He probably looked like a mess.

"Did you see the other car?"

Don't ask me that, Hailey. He couldn't lie to her. And yet, there was no way he could tell her his suspicions. Last night, replaying the accident in his head, he convinced himself his mind had been playing tricks on him. In the shadows of dusk, everything looked foreign. He couldn't be sure of anything—not enough to make accusations.

"It all happened so fast." He recounted the accident again, and when he finished, he heard Hailey exhale a breath he was sure she'd been holding since she'd walked out of the hospital the day before.

"I hate that motorcycle, Ryan." She steeled her jaw, looking up at him like a stubborn child intent on getting her way.

They wandered into the backyard, where a stunning view of Lake Michigan captured him as if for the first time. He'd never get tired of that view. They watched Jack run around for a few minutes, then sat down on a patio surrounded by overgrown shrubs. He'd get to those eventually.

"You gonna be ready to open?" Hailey asked, still watching Jack.

"I've got guests booked, so I'm going to have to be." Hailey knew how important that first week would be. She knew how much money he'd borrowed from people he actually cared about. She knew everything had to be perfect.

"Do you have enough guests to sustain this place for the summer?"

"We're about half-full," he said, though maybe *half* was generous. He didn't want to think about it. Somehow he had to believe it would fall into place.

"What about your website? You're going to need one, you know. That's how people find places like this."

Ryan groaned. "I've done pretty well with word of mouth."

Hailey squinted at him in the morning sun. "Half-full is not 'pretty well.' Some media attention wouldn't be a bad thing. What are you so worried about?"

Ryan waved her off. "I'm not worried about anything."

"You've made something really great here, Ryan. You shouldn't be afraid of celebrating that." She leveled her gaze. "He can't take this away from you. No one can."

He didn't want to talk about it. Pretending things were fine was much easier, and he didn't like to think about the way his desire to be off-the-charts successful conflicted with his need to keep the past in the past.

He didn't want anyone digging up what he'd worked so hard to bury.

If Cedar Grove took off—would he become part of the narrative? Would all the people who didn't seem to care where he'd come from find out the truth about Martin Brooks, about the mother who had run out on them, about the trailer where he'd spent most of his nights dreaming of the day he could throw a punch that rivaled his father's?

Sometimes, late at night, he'd get the feeling he needed to drive to Newman and check on things. He'd learned not to ignore the prompting of the Holy Spirit, so regardless of how much he did not want to go, he always did, careful not to let anyone—especially his dad—see him. Twice he'd dragged Martin out of Scooter's, unconscious, and gotten him back to his trailer without so much as a word. And every month, he left an unmarked envelope of cash in his mailbox.

But nobody knew about that.

How was it that after everything that man had done to them, Ryan still felt responsible for him?

"I think Cedar Grove is going to do just fine." *It'll be fine* had become his morning pep talk, and somehow, so far, it had been true. Maybe he really was "lucky."

Or maybe God really was watching out for him.

"Well, I like the idea of a teal mailbox for Esther. It'll give her character." Hailey stood. "Glad you finally listened to me."

"You want to help me pick out paint colors?"

"Don't you have someone to do that?"

"As of this morning, no."

Hailey groaned. "Why not?"

He told Hailey the whole story, which she digested with an expression of disbelief.

"She should've been working on these cottages as you guys finished them," Hailey said. Nothing like stating the obvious.

"Said the construction workers would interfere with her zen."

Hailey's expression turned sour. "I don't think that lady ever knew what she was doing in the first place."

"Well, that isn't going to help me now."

She clapped a hand on his shoulder. "Sorry, Bro. I can't really give you advice in this arena, unless you want everything painted teal." Hailey waggled her eyebrows. "With pops of red."

Ryan glanced at his watch. "Go get Jack and let's eat. If we don't hurry, he'll be late for school."

She motioned for the little boy to join them. He ran over, holding his hands out in front of him, one cupped over the other.

"Oh no, Jack, what do you have this time?" Hailey asked, stepping behind Ryan.

"A frog! Look! Can I keep him?"

"Absolutely not," Hailey said, backing away. "Absolutely, positively not. You are not bringing that disgusting thing into my house. Ryan, get rid of it."

Ryan took the frog. A small one who was undoubtedly confused by his whereabouts. "Hailey, you're such a baby. Let the kid have a pet frog if he wants one." He took the frog and shoved it toward her, stopping only inches from her face.

She screamed. "Ryan! Get that thing away from me or else!"

"Or else what?"

She ran off, leaving him with a frog and a boy who couldn't stop giggling. "You got her good that time."

He mussed Jack's hair. "I did, didn't I? But you've got to put this little guy back where you found him. We don't want your mom to have a heart attack, do we?"

Jack's face fell. "All right."

Up ahead, Hailey waited for them, arms crossed over her chest, a clear look of annoyance on her face. "I will get you back," she said when they caught up to her.

"I'd love to see you try."

CHAPTER

11

LANE PICKED UP OTIS and went back inside as soon as Ryan left, not only to calm the unwanted nerves that his presence had kicked up—was it the motorcycle that made her nervous or maybe the way he always seemed to be talking but never about the things he was actually thinking?—but also to figure out what had happened to her phone. First she checked her bedroom, but it was silly to think her mom would've actually put it back with Lane's things. Odds were better that Dottie had hidden it somewhere just to keep it away from her. Lane was surprised to find it buzzing on the counter in the midst of the continued chaos of the early morning party that had sprung up in the kitchen.

"It's like that phone has a magnetic pull on you." Her mom practically tsk-tsked.

Lane bit the inside of her cheek to keep from saying something regrettable. Goodness knows, her frustration had been building.

"How did this get down here?" Of course she already knew the answer. Passive-aggressive looked ugly on her.

"Oh, I think Jett got ahold of it. Ryan saved it for you," her mom said, unfazed by the invasion of privacy.

"You should really be nice to him, Lane." Doris shook a thick, wide-knuckled finger in Lane's face. "He's a very good man."

"And he's really good-looking." Noah's wife, Emily, glanced meaningfully at Lane as if they were old friends communicating through subtext, and for the briefest second Lane remembered how it felt to have a sister.

"Brooks?" Noah gave Emily that raised questioning eyebrow.

Emily grinned at Lane and took another drink of what Lane could only assume was a protein shake.

"You think Brooks is good-looking?"

Emily rolled her eyes. "Duh."

"How good-looking?" Noah seemed threatened.

"Not for me, hon. For Lane."

"That'd be weird. He's like her brother." Noah's height made his wife look even tinier.

"She's got three of those," Emily said. "She definitely doesn't need another one."

What Lane needed was an escape plan. "How do I keep that kid out of my room?" She had never really loved kids, and her sister's monster child reminded her why.

"'That kid' is your nephew, Lane." Her mom stopped wiping the counter and stared at her. "And he's actually very sweet. He's just rambunctious, like your brothers always were."

"No. If we'd acted like that, you would've resorted to the wooden spoon," Noah said.

"Oh, I would not have," Dottie protested, glancing at the others. Spanking was not appropriate discipline anymore—at least by society's standards.

"Remember the assembly line of spankings?" Lane's phone buzzed in her hand. "We all had to line up and get our crack one by one."

"Except Lindsay. Because she was always the one who told on us," Noah said.

"And because she was always the favorite." Lane couldn't ignore the sour taste in her mouth at the memory.

"You're making this up." Dottie looked at Doris, whose painted-on eyebrows somehow reflected the older woman's surprise. "This never happened."

"Like the time we started that bonfire in the backyard, but we almost burned down the shed."

"Now that I do remember," Dottie said.

Lane's phone buzzed again. And just when she was starting to feel her nerves settle. She glanced at Chloe's text.

OK, you don't want to talk about the hot guy, fine, but we do need to talk about Mrs. Pim. She called again. Marshall is expecting some changes on the Solar pitch before next week. Lane, are you going to be ready? How can I help?

Mrs. Pim? What about Mrs. Pim? She scrolled up and saw three missed texts, including one asking about Nate's "hot (annoying) friend." Good grief. What if Ryan had seen that? He wasn't only Nate's friend; he was hers. Sort of. But she didn't want him knowing she thought he was hot—it would just go to his head. Besides, Noah was right. He was like another brother to her.

How humiliating.

Her stomach rolled. Mrs. Pim was one of their best—and most high-maintenance—clients. Lane couldn't afford not to be there for her if she was having one of her many decorating crises. Sometimes Lane felt more like her therapist than her interior designer, but the woman always compensated Lane for her time.

The phone buzzed again.

Also, I assume you're the one I should thank for the me time at the spa. I know Marshall didn't set me up with that. Thanks, Lane. Really. Next time, you should come with me.

Wouldn't that be nice?

". . . that's all I'm saying."

Lane looked up. She struggled to comprehend the end of a conversation she'd been too distracted to hear.

"Well, do you disagree?" Her mom stared at her, and Lane felt like someone had just set a test in front of her and she didn't know any of the answers. Her mom must've gathered as much because she threw her hands up dramatically and turned away. "I think it would be a good idea to give Jett that phone of yours. He could throw it in the lake and we'd actually see your face once in a while instead of the top of your head."

Now she was just being absurd.

"I'm going for a run." Lane tucked her phone into the pocket of her shorts, stuck her earbuds in her ears, and walked out the door.

Outside, she drew in a deep breath. Her phone buzzed again. She sent Chloe a quick text to let her know she'd call after her run and hoped that would keep the constant buzzing to a minimum. Ryan had pointed her to the bike path, but when Lane started running, she found herself heading in the opposite direction—straight for town. Their house was on the edge of Harbor Pointe but still within city limits, which was, she supposed, why it was so strange to find three lone cows in their backyard.

When she was growing up, Myrtle, Gracie, and Lou had lived out there. She imagined the three that were now standing in the fenced-in yard chomping on grass and staring at her were probably called other names, but Lane didn't care to know what they were. She'd always been so mortified by these animals. They belonged on a farm, not behind an old Victorian in a lakeside town. She'd prayed—literally prayed!—that her dad would lose his obsession with cattle, but the longer he had the cows, the more he loved them. He began to use them in his marketing for the cheese shop. Soon, the Summers Cheese logo incorporated a rendering of Myrtle's face and the tagline "It doesn't get any fresher than this."

She ran through Harbor Pointe like she was competing at the Olympics, ignited by something unspeakable—a quiet, slow-burning rage that simmered just underneath her surface. It had been building since she pulled into town, and this was the only way she could think to squash it.

She craved that control she'd lost as soon as she crossed into town yesterday. Here, all sense of order was gone.

She headed toward Harbor Pointe's small downtown. Lane had never run these streets. When she'd lived here, she'd been much heavier and, sadly, lethargic. So much had changed once she went off to college. She "found herself."

Her feet hit the pavement at even intervals. Ah, yes, this felt good. It felt right. This was what she needed in order to get a grip on her spiraling emotions.

She'd started working out freshman year. Lost weight. Cared about what she looked like. Something about realizing she could have a second chance—that she didn't have to continue to be who she'd always been—inspired her somehow. So she became someone new.

Smart, capable, independent, and most important, *thin* Lane Kelley.

She was in control now. She had the whole world fooled. But at every turn, she wondered if someone would uncover her as the fraud she really was—an introverted chubby girl who should be hiding herself away in a closet somewhere with a good book and a pint of Ben & Jerry's.

The staccato of her footfalls quickened.

Someone *had* exposed her, hadn't they? The one person she'd trusted most. Why had she convinced herself it was safe to fall for him? Deep down, she was still Lane, no matter what size her jeans were, and girls like Lane didn't get the guy in the end.

She must've known that.

Her pace quickened and she struggled to get a deep breath. She worked out almost every day—her breathing shouldn't be this erratic.

None of it mattered now anyway. She was good at what she did. She worked. Work, work, work. Always something to do. Never a moment to allow her mind to be quiet—just the way she wanted it. It was the way she found her worth. Productivity.

So why did she still feel like an impostor? Like at any moment, it could all come crumbling down, and she'd be left with literally nothing but a too-expensive apartment and a French bulldog?

She ran past Sid's Barbershop, the general store, and Anita's Yarn Emporium, then crossed the street near the Forget-Me-Not Flower Shop and down toward the Hometown Creamery.

Breathe in. Breathe out. Something like electricity buzzed at her core. She still had so much to do. So much to prove. She picked up the pace.

As she turned the familiar corner, she approached Summers Cheese. The place where she'd spent hours of her life, learning the ins and outs of cheese making, dreaming about what it would be like if her dad had a normal job, like teacher or banker or policeman.

It was decidedly difficult for her to work in a place surrounded by cheese. Never mind that her lactose intolerance kept her from eating it; more than once kids found ways to compare her to Myrtle, and that was perhaps the worst part of all.

She stopped running and stared at it, her heart pounding, still unable to catch her breath.

She supposed now that she'd experienced more of life, she could appreciate the charm of a local cheese shop. In some ways, she could even relate to her father. He'd built his business from the ground up, which wasn't all that different from the career she'd built for herself.

She'd never seen a single similarity between them before.

The large, barnlike building looked a little worse for the wear. It could use fresh paint and some landscaping attention. The sign out front was weatherworn, its paint chipping. She should help. She should make this place better. What tourist wanted to buy their cheese in a run-down shop?

She should, but she wouldn't. She was better off on the outskirts of their lives, and besides, she hardly had time to handle her own responsibilities.

Lane met up with the bike path and ran along the lake, the bright-red lighthouse off in the distance. How many summers had the lighthouse been the thing anchoring her, reminding her that there were places to travel outside of Harbor Pointe, that one day she might be able to go away too, that things weren't always going to be painful and people weren't always going to be mean?

She didn't want to think about the way Maddie and Ashley and Sabrina had continued to treat her every summer after the one they'd first ostracized her. She didn't want to remember how they'd nicknamed her "Smelly Kelley" or how they'd snorted at her like a pen of pigs as she walked by—or how their teasing and insults had caught on with Lane's classmates and followed her throughout each school year. She didn't want to remember the day she walked home from the cheese shop, the summer after her freshman year, and saw photocopied pictures of herself haphazardly stapled to the lampposts all along Darby Lane. Someone had taken a photo of her in her bathing suit on the beach, taped it to a sheet of paper, and scribbled the words *Life in the Fat Lane* in bold, black handwriting above the image, then pasted copies all over town.

She'd torn them off one by one, only to find the girls at the end of the block, laughing, her own sister at their side. Lane's eyes met Lindsay's, and she tried to convey a broken *How could you?* But in return, she saw only weakness.

Lindsay the follower. No backbone. No original thoughts in her mind.

Lindsay had stared at Lane as she passed, her eyes confused, as though she were caught between two terrible choices—stick up for her sister and turn herself into an outcast or go along with these mean girls to avoid drawing their wrath toward herself.

Lindsay always did choose herself.

And while Lane would deny it to anyone who asked, that had broken her heart.

When she'd walked onto her front porch that day after what felt like a mile-long trek across a desert with no water, Betsy Tanner had been waiting for her with a stack of torn papers ripped down from other lampposts on the other side of town.

"I'm so sorry, Lane," Betsy had said. *"It's all so juvenile. We're in*

high school, for goodness' sake." Her eyes filled with the kind of tears only a person who understood could cry. Betsy had been the subject of Ashley's ridicule a couple summers before, and Lane had never stuck up for her. If she were honest, their treatment of Betsy made her feel like she was one of them, someone who didn't get made fun of, someone "cool."

She felt oddly distant from the memories now, as if the wall she'd put up around herself was enough to keep them from ever really hurting her again. As if time and distance from those things had given her perspective. Yet had they somehow contributed to the person she'd become?

Breathe in. Breathe out. It's not a race, Lane.

How much had changed that summer. Betsy became her only friend.

And Lane had thrown that away too.

Her phone buzzed. She pulled it out but didn't slow down.

Marshall had texted. Solar meeting officially set for Monday. Sending you the changes they've requested based on our preliminary meeting and the new direction Miles suggested. Will you be back by then?

She stumbled, disoriented and unable to keep her pace, falling in a heap on the pavement of the newly built bike path.

It had been so many years since she'd skinned a knee, she'd forgotten how it stung, but it all rushed back at her now as her eyes caught a glimpse of the angry red of her bloodied skin. A Barbie doll of a woman stopped to see if she was okay, still jogging in place as she offered Lane a hand. She said something, but Lane couldn't hear with her earbuds in. She pulled them out. "Sorry; what did you say?"

"I said you really shouldn't text and run at the same time," Barbie said. "It's dangerous."

Really? She couldn't win. Even strangers had an issue with her phone.

Lane bit back a snarky reply, forced herself to thank Barbie, and waved off her second attempt to help. "I'm fine."

She watched as the woman took off in the opposite direction, her long blonde ponytail swinging behind her.

Lane staggered over to a bench and sat down.

Next Monday suddenly had a stranglehold around her throat. It was too soon. She'd been optimistic in thinking she'd be able to work here. She hadn't even read over the changes Marshall wanted, but she had a feeling they were substantial. How could she possibly be ready to pitch something new to Solar by Monday?

But this wasn't the kind of opportunity you put off. This was the kind of opportunity you made room for. And Lane was accustomed to moving everything out of the way to accommodate work. It's what she did. Stayed up all hours if she needed to—anything to meet a deadline, to get it done.

The image of Nate in that hospital bed raced through her mind.

She stared at Marshall's words. Will you be back by then?

She quickly typed back, No way we can push that back a few days?

His reply came in immediately: Do you really want to make Solar jump through hoops for you? JB is paying attention to this one, Lane.

No. Of course not. She'd never made anyone jump through hoops for her—why would she start with the trendiest and largest client she'd ever had the chance to pitch to?

Marshall was right. It could be a deal breaker if she pushed him off. It sent the wrong message.

And yet . . . Nate. The one who'd told her to take the scholarship to Northwestern and get out of town. The one who'd told her being smart was better than being popular. The one who'd always stuck up for her, even if it meant sacrificing his own friendships.

The one who didn't go to Lindsay's wedding.

Lane shot off a quick text to Chloe asking her to make nice with Ashton's assistant and buy her a few more days. Marshall didn't need to dictate everything, did he?

She put the phone back in her pocket. She didn't want to think about it right now, but that didn't mean she wouldn't. That buzzy, anxious feeling stirred inside her. She'd only become aware of it recently, and sometimes Lane thought she was on the verge of spinning out of control. It was ridiculous. She was a professional. She thrived on stress. She liked to be busy.

But the timing of everything happening in her life at that moment could not have been worse. Like a perfect storm.

Her heart was still racing after her fall, and she could barely catch her breath. She'd let her nerves take over, forgotten everything her trainer had taught her about running, like it were her first time all over again. She'd gone too hard, too fast, like a crazy lunatic with no training at all. She'd used up everything she had right at the start, and now here she was, bloodied, humiliated, and not looking forward to the walk home.

In the distance, she could see the Cedar Grove cottages, where so many tourists had stayed over the years. Her mom found it important to call Lane at least once a month and keep her updated on all of Harbor Pointe's latest gossip, though Lane found it important to tune out what she said. Often these updates were left on her voice mail because sometimes Lane simply could not work up the energy to answer the phone.

She vaguely remembered that the former owner of Cedar Grove had died and someone else had purchased the place. Apparently the cottages were going to be completely remodeled, and "Oh, Lane, you could be the decorator. Come back here for a few weeks; work your magic at Cedar Grove. This is going to be quite the project. This little cottage community could bring more tourists to Harbor Pointe, and I know you haven't heard about all this, but we could really use that right now. We have our regulars, but the vacation homes have all been bought. There's nowhere for anyone new. Besides, it would give you a chance to do something nice for the town, and—"

Lane hadn't listened to the message all the way through.

She'd stopped listening to most of what Dottie said the day her sister stole her fiancé and her mother looked the other way.

CHAPTER

12

WEDNESDAY MORNING, Ryan woke up before the sun. He'd called every single name on the list Barb gave him, but all five of them were too booked to take on such a large project with a tight deadline.

His head throbbed from the worry of it. He hadn't come this far to fail. He had so much work to do, but it would have to wait.

He'd told Frank and Dottie he'd man the table at the midweek farmers' market for them so they could stay at the hospital. As soon as he had the thought, the image of Lane and her bright-blue eyes raced across his mind.

It was stupid that he wasted any time thinking about someone who was so obviously just counting the days until she could get back to her real life and forget she'd ever made this pit stop in Harbor Pointe.

Yesterday afternoon at the hospital, he'd found her in that same corner in the lobby, earbuds warning passersby to keep on walking. He disregarded messages like that, choosing instead to break the rules of social engagement as often as he could. He liked messing up her perfectly constructed world—a world he had obviously never fit into.

He'd pulled out the chair on the opposite side of the table and turned it around and straddled it, then stared at her for a full ten seconds until finally she glanced up and yanked the earbuds from her ears.

"What are you doing?" She sounded part flustered and part irritated, but there was also a hint of amusement. If he wasn't careful, he'd find himself living for that hint.

"What are *you* doing?"

"Working." She flipped her hands out over the mess of papers on the table.

"You do seem very busy."

"Are you going to tell me I should be up there in that zoo of a waiting room with the rest of them?"

"Instead of down here, hiding in this corner so no one can find you?"

"*You* found me." She met his eyes. He couldn't turn away.

"I knew where to look." He grinned at her.

"Does that mean you found me on purpose?"

"Would you think I was flirting if I said yes?"

"Of course not." Her eyes had widened.

"Oh." He frowned. "I must be off my game. I'm definitely flirting with you." He grinned at her and her cheeks turned pink.

"You're insane." She shook her head, and yet the twinkle of amusement hung around. It was all the encouragement he needed.

They talked about Nate for a few minutes. She hadn't seen him yet, but her turn was in about an hour. She hung out in the lobby because it was less distracting. That's what she said, anyway, but he didn't buy it. He knew she had other reasons for not wanting to be around her family; he just didn't want to bring those up.

"We should get coffee on purpose sometime." He glanced at the table where they were both sitting—separate but together—with their to-go cups.

Her shoulders stiffened. Uh-oh. He'd made it awkward. He talked too much.

"Or maybe we'll just keep running into each other." He was careful to keep his smile in place, though inside, he fought the humiliating feelings of rejection like everyone else. "Probably more exciting that way."

Her phone buzzed. She read the message and her fingers flew over the screen as she tapped out a reply.

"Work?"

"Mmm-hmm." She kept typing. "This is terrible." She'd muttered the words so quietly he knew they weren't intended for him.

He'd sat down quickly, but he slowly wandered away, leaving her with her phone, her thoughts, and her mumbling.

And now, a whole day later, he found himself still thinking about her and when he might get a chance to see her again. Stupid, really. He should take the hint.

Yet something told him Lane required persistence. It was like that with people who'd convinced themselves they didn't need anyone.

Besides, there was something dancing in those big blue eyes of hers that told him it was worth it not to let one little rejection make him give up for good.

He showered, dressed, and headed over to Hazel's for his usual morning meal. He parked his bike—the nonmotorized kind—outside, and as he walked in, he caught Betsy's eye. She nodded toward his usual booth, and he strolled over to it and sat down. The place was even fuller than usual, but he had the distinct feeling Betsy had saved his table for him.

He didn't need the menu and she didn't need to take his order. Another reason he loved this place.

"You're busy today," he said when she arrived at his table with a pot of coffee.

"Maybe tourist season is starting early this year." She filled his mug and he took a drink. "Let's hope so, anyway. How are the cottages coming along?"

He told her the good stuff first and then filled her in about Barb. Betsy was well connected—maybe she knew someone who could help him.

"Do you have your phone?" she asked when he finished.

He slid his old flip phone from his pocket, aware of the grimace on her face. "It makes phone calls same as yours."

She smiled and walked away. When she returned a few minutes later with his food, she handed over the fancy pocket computer she called a telephone. She'd pulled up a website and apparently expected him to look at it.

"What am I looking at?"

"This is a pretty well-known designer out of Chicago. She has a huge following on social media."

"Is that a big deal?"

Betsy sat across from him. "Yes, it means she's good. People really like her style and she's got great taste."

"It's a tight deadline, Bets. She's probably booked if she's that popular."

"Gee, that's the spirit." She took her phone and started tapping around on it while Ryan ate his sausage, egg, and cheese on an English muffin. She set the phone back on the table and pushed it toward him. "Tell me she doesn't have exactly the look you want."

He watched as she swiped through a series of photos of spaces that had a distinctly cottage feel to them. He'd worked so hard on the details in the construction and remodeling of each cottage— from the crown molding to the hand-scraped wood floors. Each detail had been carefully thought out. But now he had to throw someone in at the last minute to finish the cottages.

But the more photos Betsy showed him, the more he thought this designer would be even better than Barb would've been.

"Great, right?" Betsy grinned at him.

"Yeah. Do you have some magical connection to this designer?"

"No, but you do." She took out her notepad and scribbled something on it.

"I don't have any connections. Why do you think I'm asking you?" He stared at her blankly.

"This is Lane's site, Brooks. This is what she does."

He scrolled through the photos again. "Seriously?"

"Like I said—she's kind of a big deal."

He glanced at Betsy. "What's up with you two? I thought you were friends."

She shrugged. "We were. And now we're not."

"But you're referring me to her?"

"I can appreciate her talent." Betsy retrieved her phone and glanced at the image on the screen. "Besides, I have high hopes for Cedar Grove. It's going to be good for all of us."

The reminder squeezed something inside him.

"So, what, you think I should just ask her?"

Another shrug. "You could e-mail her, but you'd probably have to go to the library to send an e-mail, so face-to-face seems like a better bet."

He finished off his hash browns and took another swig of his coffee. "Probably. Thanks for the info." He handed her a ten-dollar bill and got up, stuffing his wallet back in his pocket. "I have to go. I'm working at the farmers' market today for Frank."

She stood. "How's Nate?"

"Have you been to see him?"

Betsy shook her head and pushed her glasses up on her face—something she did when she was nervous. She could carry on a perfectly normal conversation with just about anyone who walked through her doors at the diner, but whenever Nate was around, the girl turned mute. She probably didn't think anyone knew it, but her feelings for Nate had been obvious to Ryan almost since the day he'd moved to Harbor Pointe.

Ryan had been eating dinner alone after a long day on a job site, when Nate and some guys from the worship team strolled into Hazel's and sat down at a booth near the front. Betsy's face had turned crimson and she might've let out a slight gasp. Ryan didn't tease her about it—not then and especially not now. As far as he knew, Nate had no idea, but Ryan thought they'd be a great match. Betsy was cute but not exactly pretty, which might have been why she hesitated. Someone like Betsy didn't usually end up with someone like Nate Kelley. But she didn't realize that not all guys were completely shallow. Betsy was kind, and that trait seemed difficult to come by.

"You should go," he said. "He'd love knowing you were there."

"Oh, I'm sure he's got a waiting room full of people." She smiled even though her eyes had filled with tears. "Is he going to be okay?"

Ryan's heart dropped. He hoped so. He prayed so. His silent prayers seemed to be on a continuous loop in the back of his mind. *Please let him be okay, God.*

"I hope so, Bets." Ryan reached over and squeezed her shoulder. "But regardless, you should go see him."

"I don't want to be in the way."

"But you guys are friends. I'm sure it'd mean a lot to him to know you came by."

"I'll think about it." She sniffled.

Ryan gave her one last nod of encouragement and walked out. He rode toward the parking lot near the bike path where the farmers' market was set up each Wednesday and Saturday. The Harbor Market was a huge attraction during the summer, but locals enjoyed it as early as April.

He arrived at the Summers Cheese booth at six thirty and found Jeremy standing alone, typing something on his phone.

"Hey, man. What's up?" Ryan parked his bike behind the booth.

"Hey. Nothing, just waiting on Lane."

Ryan didn't like the visceral reaction he had at the mention of her name. "Lane?" Was she on the schedule for today?

"Yeah, I was just texting her. She's in the cheese truck."

"Lane is driving the cheese truck?" This he had to see. Lane had always hated working for the cheese shop, even at the farmers' market. She found the family business embarrassing. He'd assumed what little she knew about his family had colored her impression of him, too. After all, if a perfectly acceptable cheese shop was embarrassing, what did she think of someone with a drunk for a father?

A few seconds later, a shiny red refrigerated truck with a 3-D block of cheese on its roof drove into the alley behind the parking lot.

"Here she is." Jeremy moved toward the alley and guided Lane in as Ryan watched. He considered taking his phone out to catch a photo of her in that ridiculous vehicle but thought better of it.

She parked, got out, and glared at the two of them. When they didn't move, she opened the back doors of the van and motioned toward its contents.

"I loaded it all by myself, so you two can unload it." She pulled out her phone and once again she was in her own world.

"Should've called me. I would've come help." Jeremy moved past her, leaving Ryan staring at her for too many seconds.

"Should I have called you too?" She sounded wholly irritated.

"No. I don't even have my phone turned on."

She finally met his eyes.

He took a step closer to her, holding on to every bit of attention she gave him. "I prefer to look at people when I'm talking to them."

He let his gaze wander to her lips, then back up.

"Quit flirting with my sister and help me." Jer walked past him with a stack of cheeses.

Her cheeks reddened and she looked down. He watched for her smile, content that he would've found it if she hadn't turned away.

Ryan and Jeremy hauled numerous cheeses in a variety of sizes from the truck to the tables, one load after another, while Lane typed frantically on her phone.

As they worked, a number of local merchants stopped by to say hello, check on Nate, and buy their favorite kind of cheese "before the crowds."

Tilly Humphrey, the candle lady, waved from across the aisle. "Looks like we're neighbors today!"

Ryan and Jer both waved hello, but Lane didn't respond.

"Pudge, you should walk around with samples."

"What?" She looked horrified at Jeremy's suggestion.

"Dad always goes around, chatting up the other sellers. Gives them samples, checks out their products."

"I'm not doing that." She finally put her phone away.

"Why? You're a businesswoman now. Don't you have to talk to people on a daily basis?"

"That's different." She dug in her heels, more stubborn than anyone Ryan had ever seen.

"How? You're an adult—you should be over all that social anxiety garbage." Jeremy squinted at Ryan, who was trying—and failing—to pretend he couldn't hear the conversation going on right beside him. "You don't believe in that stuff, do you?"

Ryan glanced at Lane, whose face had turned pink and whose eyes were once again pointed at the ground.

"It could be a thing," Ryan said with a shrug.

Lane's eyes found his, but only for a moment.

"I'll keep unpacking. Jer, you go be Dad." Lane took a box from Jer's arms. "You're much better at it than I am."

Jeremy shook his head. "You know it's a wonder you've gotten as far as you have at that fancy job of yours. Do you hire people to talk for you?"

"Go away, Jer."

Jeremy gave Lane a shove, then grabbed a box marked *Samples* and headed across the aisle to Tilly, who wrapped her short arms around him in a welcoming, if invasive, hug. Jeremy didn't seem to mind. He'd inherited his father's charm and love for people.

Lane evidently had not. At least not for Harbor Pointe people.

She started unpacking the box she'd taken from Jer in silence and with so much force it was clear her brother's teasing had gotten under her skin.

"Talking is overrated." How did he break the ice with someone who seemed to be encased in it?

She lifted more cheese out of the box and dropped it on the table as if she hadn't heard him.

"Come on, do you really think your big, fancy job can compete with all of this?" His attempt to lighten the mood fell flat.

"I shouldn't be here." She'd mumbled the words. They were so quiet, he almost didn't hear her.

"At the market?"

"Here. In Harbor Pointe." She continued positioning packages on the table, roughly.

"What's going on, Lane?"

"Everything is a disaster. I need more time. I need to overhaul a design I thought was perfect, and I was hoping I'd get a few more days, but I just heard from my assistant and my boss says it's Monday or never. Monday! I can't even get a decent Wi-Fi signal here, and they want a new design by Monday." She slammed a block of cheese on the table, winding herself up with each word she spoke. "And I can't go work on it because I have to sell *cheese*—" she said it like a swearword—"at the farmers' market because my mother's guilt trips make me feel like I'm a ten-year-old who has no voice of her own."

Ryan half sat on the table and watched her, marveling at how quickly she spoke.

"And I swear, if one more person calls me Pudge, I am going to completely lose my mind. How much weight do I have to lose to make everyone forget I was ever fat in the first place?" She whisked her hands from her shoulders to her hips in one fluid motion as she said it, all the while holding a block of cheese. She plopped it on the table, then positioned it next to the others. "And this account—I can't lose this account. It could mean huge things for my career. Have you ever had an impossible deadline like this?" She gave him a look. "Of course you haven't. You're a contractor." He didn't correct her. "You build things and take your time doing it because *that* is what contractors do. I should know—I had to hire one when I renovated my loft. And it was sweet of you to ask me to coffee, but I have a boyfriend, and even though I don't love him, I don't think it would be right for me to go out to coffee with you when I'm supposed to be dating him, and I know you and I are only ever going to be just friends, but do you know what I mean?" She stopped talking as quickly as she'd started and stood completely still, staring at the blocks of cheese lined up on the table.

It was almost as if something had come over her without her permission and suddenly it was gone.

Now probably wasn't the best time to offer her a job designing Cedar Grove. In fact, that whole sliver of hope disappeared the second she started talking. Lane might be the best, but that meant she had no time for a rinky-dink project like his.

Slowly she turned toward him and he could see the horror of her outburst registering on her face—no trace of amusement in those baby blues now.

He imagined Lane Kelley didn't lose control very often. He tilted his head, knowing his silence made her uncomfortable and yet unable to help himself.

"I'm so sorry." Lane still clung to a package of cheese.

He watched her for a few long seconds. "You're hurting the cheese." He reached over and slowly pried her fingers off it. "Sounds like you needed to get a few things off your chest."

"I didn't." She turned, straightening the already-perfect line of packages on the table. "I absolutely didn't. I just need to find a way to get to work. I need to get back to work."

"Or you could take a few weeks off."

"Did you hear the part about the major client? The design overhaul? The career-making account?"

"I might've missed a few details because you were talking so fast." He took a step closer to her.

She spun around and found him standing only inches from her.

"Do you know anything about personal space?" She stepped back. He made her nervous—he could tell.

"I try not to live by too many rules." He grinned and reached across her to set a cheese block down on the table with the others. Her nearness, albeit withdrawn, sent his mind into a tailspin. What was it about this woman? He'd always had a bit of an infatuation with her—the shy, quiet bookworm who wouldn't give him, or anyone else, the time of day—but it was almost like those feelings had been plugged into an electrical socket and given a jolt.

Somehow it didn't deter him. Some of the hair had escaped her ponytail, and he wanted to brush it away from her face so badly his fingers itched

"I believe in rules." Lane's voice was quiet.

"Sounds to me like you need to break a few of your rules."

She straightened, folding her arms. "You don't know anything about me anymore, Brooks."

He opened a small container also marked *Samples* and popped a cheese curd into his mouth. "You're right, but I'd like to."

Her jaw went slack and she was off her guard again. It was so easy to throw her off-kilter, and he enjoyed it entirely too much.

"Are there any toothpicks in that truck?"

"Toothpicks?" She shook her head slightly as if to wake herself.

"For these samples?" He held up the container, giving it a slight shake.

"I-I think I saw some." She walked away, and he had to force himself not to watch her as she did.

The long line of booths had started to come to life as more people arrived and set up their merchandise on the tables. Jeremy had wandered all the way to the end of the lane, where Jensen's Dairy Farm had parked their big white delivery truck.

Ryan unfolded two chairs behind the sample table just as Lane returned with the cash box and a small container of toothpicks.

She handed them to him without a word and sat in one of the chairs, then disappeared behind her phone.

People began arriving, and the smell of fresh coffee filled the air. The Java Hut, parked nearby, was too tempting to resist.

"How about that coffee?" Ryan said, standing.

Lane looked up at him.

"I heard the part about the boyfriend, but it's just a cup of coffee, not a date. Want some?"

"Actually, yes." She leaned back in her chair. "But I'll get it."

He frowned. "I'm already up."

"You're better with people," she said. "If there are customers, I'd rather you handle them."

He knew she was introverted, but at the moment she almost seemed afraid.

"You take it black, right?"

He raised a brow. "Have you been spying on me?"

"I overheard you ordering at the hospital—don't be flattered. I just have a good memory."

He grinned. "Not flattered at all."

She snatched the ten-dollar bill from his hand and walked toward the Java Hut.

And once again he forced himself not to watch as she walked away.

CHAPTER

13

THE AROMA OF CHOCOLATE and hazelnut intertwined with the familiar smell of coffee as Lane stood in line outside the Java Hut, an old UPS truck that had been converted into a coffee stand.

The booth was just two down from Summers Cheese, and from a distance, she watched as people strolled over to talk to Brooks. He'd always had such a way about him—warm, easygoing, and charming. It drew people in. She could see it by the looks on their faces as they walked away from the booth.

She had none of those qualities. At least not here. At work, she'd managed to strike a balance, but take away the design element and it was like Lane's social skills disappeared. If anything, she was standoffish, maybe even off-putting. Her own shyness, or her fear of what people thought, kept her locked inside a box of expectations. Who she was versus who she used to be.

At one point, Ryan caught her staring, and before she could look away, he waved at her.

Why did he make her feel so exposed? There had been a time

when she'd felt completely comfortable around him. Even after a game of truth or dare had gone mortifyingly wrong, he'd managed to prevent any awkwardness, and he'd never made her feel like the butt of that joke.

Somehow the gap between them had grown so wide it was like starting over with someone she didn't know, and all of her insecurities were showing. It didn't help that he treated her as if he'd always known her. Ryan threw her off guard—and she didn't like being off guard.

Her phone buzzed.

Chloe. Just found out from Ashton's assistant that Ashton had agreed to give us a few extra days, but Marshall pushed for Monday. I'm sorry, Lane.

Lane's hand tightened around the phone as she processed her frustration. Why would he do that? He was forcing her to come back earlier than she wanted to, and he knew it.

Before she could fire off a heated text to Marshall, the girl in the brown coffee truck stuck her head out the window and shouted, "Can I help you?"

She grinned down at Lane, who forced herself to smile. "Just a medium black coffee and a skinny vanilla latte with no whipped cream."

The girl gave a quick nod, then got to work.

While she waited, Lane's eyes wandered back over to Summers as a young, pretty woman holding a little boy's hand approached the booth. The boy had a mop of thick blond hair that bounced as he ran straight into Ryan's arms. Ryan picked the kid up as if he weighed nothing and threw him over his shoulder, then somersaulted him back down onto the ground.

The woman had a familiarity with Ryan that told Lane she wasn't just another customer.

"Miss?" The coffee girl poked her head back out. "Your coffee." She handed Lane two cups.

"Thanks." Lane paid for the drinks, then turned back awkwardly, not wanting to interrupt what appeared to be a private conversation between Ryan and this woman and her child. *Their* child? She realized she didn't know Ryan at all anymore. What if he had a girlfriend? And a kid? What if he hadn't been flirting with her at all? How humiliating. Of course he wasn't flirting, no matter what he said. He was Brooks. She was Lane. They'd grown up together. He wasn't even an option in the romance department.

Brooks belonged with someone like this girl—cute, young, blonde. People would call them a beautiful family and it would be absolutely true.

He likely knew all about the disaster that was her love life—how the only guy who'd ever given her the time of day had dumped her for her younger, prettier sister—and he felt sorry for her. It was pity kindness, not flirtation.

She should've known that.

As she approached, the woman noticed her before Ryan did. She gave him a soft nudge and he stopped talking and turned toward Lane.

"Sorry to interrupt." Lane wished she could vanish. "Here's your coffee. I can man the table if you all want to walk around."

Ryan raised an eyebrow, probably thinking of how only moments ago she absolutely did not want to man the table. But the alternative—interrupting a moment between him and this woman—was far more humiliating than answering strangers' questions about cheese, which was saying something.

"Yeah, come walk around with us." The boy tugged at Ryan's arm.

Ryan made eye contact with Lane for a split second, then pulled the boy up as if he were using him to lift weights. "Sorry, buddy, I can't today. Promised my friend here I'd stay at the cheese booth."

She glanced at Ryan, who plunked the kid back down on the ground. Why wasn't anyone texting her now? An excuse to leave this awkward encounter would be so great. Lane was terrible at meeting new people, especially probably girlfriends of good-looking guys she'd mistakenly thought might be flirting with her.

The woman's skin was a light-bronze color that seemed to glow, her green eyes remarkably bright, her teeth perfect. Once upon a time, this woman would've been precisely the kind of person who intimidated Lane. She had to remind herself she wasn't fourteen anymore. This woman hadn't pinned her photo to lampposts or made pig noises at her.

The woman ran a hand through her long, wavy hair. "Lane, it's me—Hailey." She stuck out her hand as a greeting.

"Oh, sorry." Ryan shoved his hands in his pockets and turned his attention to Lane. "Forgot you guys probably don't recognize each other."

Hailey flashed Lane a toothy smile. "It's been a long time."

Hailey? Little bitty Hailey? And she had a son who was older than Jett.

"You know Ryan. He's always had terrible manners." She tossed a glance at Ryan. "You're living in Chicago, right?"

"I am."

"Ryan told me you were back."

"Did he?" Lane glanced at Ryan, who only smirked.

"If he gets too flirty, just give him a jab in the gut."

Lane glanced at him. "I don't think I have to worry about that."

Ryan met her eyes. "Oh no. You do."

Once again, Lane stumbled over her thoughts. Was he just teasing her? Surely he remembered how much she hated being teased.

"That monkey is Jack." Hailey nodded toward the boy, who had somehow climbed up onto Ryan's back and now hung there, one arm draped around Ryan's neck. "We moved here a few years ago, right after Ryan. You don't get back much, do you?"

Lane swallowed. Her mouth felt dry. "Not really, no."

"Probably like the city life better. Harbor Pointe is kind of sleepy. I thought about moving to Denver a while ago, but I'm a Midwest girl at heart."

Lane didn't know what to say. She suddenly remembered how chatty Hailey had always been. "Denver's nice."

"It's beautiful. The weather is perfect. I want to get out for a visit, but we haven't made time. Gosh, you've got the coolest hair.

I always wanted dark hair. Mine is naturally the color of old dishwater at Hazel's after a really long shift."

"Hailey works at Hazel's during the days." Ryan wrangled Jack, pulling him over to the other side of his obviously strong body.

"Oh, you know Betsy!" Hailey said. "She told me you guys went to school together. That's all she said when I asked about you."

Lane looked away. Betsy probably didn't want everyone to know how awfully Lane had treated her—how she'd accepted Betsy's friendship when it was convenient, then tossed it away when it wasn't.

The conversation lulled, but only for a second. Hailey didn't seem to appreciate silence.

"I didn't think I wanted to stay in a small town, but we really love it here. Everyone is so nice." A woman pushing a stroller caught Hailey's attention. "Hey, Tasha," Hailey said as she walked by.

"See what I mean?" She grinned. "And we just love your family. Jett and Jack go to school together. They're a few grades apart, but of course they play together at Sunday dinners."

For a split second, Lane had forgotten she was in a town where people knew Lindsay and Jasper and their perfect family. Her awkward lack of response halted the conversation, but her mind had gone blank.

Someone text me, please. She squeezed the phone in her hand as if she could make it so.

"On second thought, maybe we should go walk around." Ryan set Jack on the ground. "Do you want me to bring you back some homemade kettle corn?"

Lane frowned. "Thanks, but no."

"It's good stuff."

"I'm sure it is, but I don't eat kettle corn."

Hailey elbowed him. "That's why she looks so good." Then she turned to Lane. "I eat kettle corn." She laughed.

Ryan leaned in closer to Lane. "Another one of your rules?"

She turned away. This whole situation made her uncomfortable.

"Mom, can I have kettle corn?" Jack hollered as if his mom were on the other side of the market.

"Quiet, kid," Hailey said. "You don't need to yell."

"Let's go get a donut!" Jack said, this time slightly quieter than before.

"Hey, that's my line." A policeman with a familiar gait walked up to the booth and stood next to Hailey. He picked up a wrapped block of cheddar and turned it over in his hand.

Ryan stiffened. "Walker, how's it going?"

Walker? As in Walker Jones? Lane stepped back.

"Good. It's going good." Walker set the cheese down. "Morning, Hailey. You're looking beautiful this morning, as always. Ryan, your sister got all the looks in your family."

Lane begged to differ. Silently, anyway. Yes, Ryan and Hailey had the same eyes and the same propensity for talking too much, but his good looks could not be disputed.

"Can't argue there," Ryan said. "You probably remember Lane Kelley."

Walker's eyes landed on Lane, and after several seconds recognition washed over him. "Pudge?"

"It's Lane," Ryan corrected.

Well, that was nice of him.

"Right, sorry." He took a step back, put his hands on his hips, and ogled her without an ounce of shame. "Wow, who would've thought you'd turn out so hot?" His laugh reminded her of a big, drunk guy in a bar. "You had some pretty rough years there, but Mother Nature must've just been holding out on us."

"Walker." Ryan's tone sounded like a warning.

Lane's phone buzzed. *Thank you, Lord.* "I have to get this."

Her heart raced, and as she walked away, she heard Ryan say, "Dude, why are you such a jerk?"

"It was a compliment," Walker said. "I'm admiring her form."

"Well, don't."

Lane imagined Walker was staring at her as she walked away, but she wasn't about to turn and find out.

She glanced at her phone. Chloe again.

Any chance you'll be home earlier than you thought? I hate asking that because I think you should stay there as long as you need to. Just want to know when I should come to your place.

Lane glanced at Walker. Being here wasn't good for her for so many reasons.

I'm going to try to get out of here early. I'll text you when I know for sure. She sent off the text and pretended to have more to do on her phone, just to avoid any further conversation with Walker Jones.

"You know I'm just doing my job," Walker said, loud enough for Lane to hear, though she pretended she didn't.

"I already told you—and the other cop at the hospital—everything I remember," Ryan said.

Hailey grabbed Jack's hand. "I'll meet you later, Ryan."

He waved her off without actually looking at her, eyes still focused on Walker.

"Look, Brooks, you know I'm not accusing you of anything. We just need to find out exactly what happened. Nate's obviously not talking, and so far there were no other witnesses. Trying to do right by your friend."

Ryan bristled. "And I'm not?"

Before Walker could respond, Ryan tossed his coffee cup in the garbage and walked away in the same direction as Hailey.

Lane glanced up and found Walker staring at her. "In my experience, only guilty people storm off like that."

What was he saying? That Ryan was somehow responsible for what had happened to her brother?

"Maybe he just wanted to get away from you," Lane said, careful to hold the man's gaze like a person whose heart *wasn't* racing.

Walker's laugh sounded more like a scoff. "See ya later, Pudge."

He sauntered away, leaving Lane to watch the booth on her own, with a jumpy pulse and a mind full of questions about Ryan Brooks, Nate's accident, and what really happened that day.

ON THURSDAY, Ryan spent most of the day working on Esther with Jerry and the rest of the guys. The day had been a long one, and he couldn't get yesterday's visit from Walker Jones out of his mind. Walker was a first-class jerk for the way he'd talked to Lane, but it was his insistence on digging into the accident that had Ryan nervous.

Near the end of the day, he went to the hospital, making his way to Nate's room just as Noah was walking out.

"Any change?"

Noah shook his head. "I'm starting to wonder if he's ever going to wake up." They stood in the hallway outside Nate's room. "Walker came by again today. Any chance you remember anything more?"

Ryan shoved his hands in the pockets of his work jeans. He didn't want to lie to Noah—but how could he confess his suspicions when he wasn't sure? If he was right, would they all look at him differently? Would they blame him somehow for his father's stupidity? It wouldn't be the first time Martin Brooks's actions had tainted someone's view of Ryan.

"Brooks?"

"Sorry, I was going over it in my head." Ryan shrugged. "I wish I could remember more."

"We've got to get the guy who was driving that truck," Noah said. "And he better hope Walker finds him before I do."

Noah walked away, leaving Ryan standing alone in the hallway, feeling nauseous.

He entered the room, took a seat, and stared at Nate, guilt washing over him like a thick coat of mud.

"Oh, Ryan. I didn't know you were in here."

He turned and found Dottie standing in the doorway. "I just got here. Is it someone else's turn?"

She waved him off. "The nurses are a little more lenient than I thought. We've had people coming and going all day long. I don't ever want him to be alone, is all."

Ryan gave a soft nod and Dottie crossed over to the other side of the bed, still not looking at her son.

"How are you holding up?"

She sat down. "About as well as I can, I suppose. I just keep expecting to walk in here and find him awake and sitting up, wondering what all the fuss was about."

"Me too."

The sound of the machine's artificial breathing filled the silence between them.

"Thanks for being so kind to Lane," Dottie said.

He frowned. Did she expect him not to be kind to her?

"She's an angry person right now, I think. I'm guessing she hasn't exactly been friendly to you." She seemed to be sizing him up. "But then, you always were sweet to her, weren't you?"

"What can I say, Mrs. K.? I'm a sweet guy." He leaned back in his chair.

"You know I can see right through that charming facade you've got going on." She waggled a finger in his general direction.

He raised an eyebrow as if to say, *Do go on*, but Mrs. K. only stared at him, reading his mail without his permission.

Finally he looked away.

"What are you waiting for?"

For the first time since she sat down, she glanced at Nate. "Obviously tomorrow is promised to no one." Her voice hitched at the back of her throat at the implication. "You think you've got all the time in the world, but you don't. If you see a chance to be happy, you should take it. You deserve it, and my daughter could use someone good in her life."

"Thanks, Mrs. K., but—"

"She's working at the shop tomorrow. In case you wondered."

"You know she has a boyfriend," he said, deciding not to care that Lane's mom was far more observant than he'd given her credit for.

Dottie flicked her hand dismissively.

"I don't think she's interested in me."

She met his eyes. "Maybe not yet, but don't give up on her, okay? Lane is shy. Self-sufficient. She needs someone persistent. She's worth the work, isn't she?"

He grinned. Yes. She absolutely was. He'd known that since they were kids, but he and Lane were very different. Her with her stubbornness and him with his nonchalance. They'd drive each other crazy.

Still, he loved a challenge, even one that was nearly impossible.

"Besides, it's time you stopped dating all those tarts."

"Tarts?" Ryan laughed.

"All those ditzy, beautiful girls who get their news from *People* magazine."

She had a point. He definitely had a type, and Lane didn't fit it at all.

Lane was different. He had a feeling if he let himself, he could get lost in the whole idea of her. Maybe he *wasn't* up for this challenge.

"She's going back to Chicago, Mrs. K. I can't start a relationship with someone who has no interest in living here. You know my whole life is in Harbor Pointe. And I need to be here for Hailey and Jack."

Another hand flip. "If it's important, you'll find a way—"

"If not, you'll find an excuse. I know."

"Remember that, kiddo."

Oh, he'd remember. Lane got his mind spinning with so much noise that he'd fallen asleep with the image of her smile floating through his mind.

~~~

By Friday he could practically feel the time with Lane slipping away. Somehow he realized once she returned to Chicago, she wasn't going to come back. And though he knew that was probably for the best, at lunchtime he found himself standing in the parking lot of Summers Cheese, staring at the door and wondering what on earth he was doing.

She has a boyfriend. She is not interested in you.

More excuses.

He pulled the door open as if the words playing on repeat in his mind didn't matter at all.

Lane stood at the front counter wearing a long green apron and a ball cap, waiting on a customer who, by the looks of it, was very indecisive. Or maybe just interested in free samples.

"Can I try that one there?" The older woman pointed a bony, red-tipped finger at a chunk labeled *Tomato Basil Cheddar* and smiled at Lane.

Ryan stepped up beside the woman, catching Lane's eye—and her irritation. She'd always hated working at Summers, and he had a feeling needy customers weren't going to help.

"That's a good one," Ryan said. "But the four-year aged cheddar is even better."

"Oh?" The old woman turned to him, the smell of flowers and soap accosting his nostrils as she did.

"I'm in here every day. I'm telling you—" he pointed to the case—"that is the one you want."

"It is very good," the woman said. "I tried a sample of that earlier."

"You really can't go wrong with it, Mrs. . . . ?"

"Oh, you can call me Edna. We just got into town, so I wanted to stop by. My husband loves his cheese."

"Perfect. Lane, why don't you wrap up a block of that aged cheddar for my friend Edna here?"

Lane did as he said, an incredulous look on her face, then rang up Edna's order and sent her on her way. As the old woman walked out, the bell over the door jangled and Lane turned her attention back to Ryan.

"What was that?"

He leaned on the counter. They'd been here before. His turkey sandwich tradition had continued all the way through high school. Had Frank ever told the rest of them how Ryan had really come into their lives?

Ryan would work in the back for a couple of hours each day and Frank had Lane make him whatever he wanted in return. Did she know it was still usually the first—and only—time he'd eaten all day? Whatever lunch money he could scrape together always went to Hailey, so Summers kept him fed.

"You're like an old-lady whisperer. That was about to be her fifteenth sample."

Ryan laughed. "Don't you have a limit?"

She shrugged. "I'm just filling in."

"And you look very happy about it."

She groaned. "I'm having flashbacks—not the good kind." She pulled out a broom and came around the counter to sweep the floor underneath the few round tables set up in the space. Summers wasn't really a restaurant, but they did have a café menu, and occasionally customers needed a place to sit and eat.

"All your memories here can't be bad ones." He turned to face her. "I mean, I was in a lot of them, so how bad could they be?"

She glanced over and he grinned at her. If he could just get her to loosen up, remember how they'd been friends once, maybe he could chip away at the body armor she seemed to be wearing. Maybe he could even start to show her what she was missing by keeping all of them out of her life.

"All I remember is you showing up here to sweet-talk your way to free sandwiches."

"They were not free—I did my chores. Besides, your mom was right. You always had a soft spot for me."

"I just wanted to get you out of here as quickly as possible."

"Uh-huh."

She leaned over and swept the dirt into a dustpan. "What are you doing here now anyway? Don't you work?"

"It's time for lunch."

She dumped the contents of the dustpan into the trash can. "Let me guess, you came here to sweet-talk your way into a free sandwich?"

"Of course not." As she walked behind the counter, he faced her again. "I mean, unless you're offering."

"You're something else, Brooks, you know that?"

"That's what they tell me." He had to believe her annoyance with him was a put-on.

"Turkey with sharp cheddar and bacon?" She pulled the block of sharp cheddar out of the case and set it on the counter.

"Is there any other Summers sandwich?"

She shook her head as she put together the ingredients for what he was sure would be the best sandwich he'd had in a long time. Thick honey-wheat bread made at the bakery down the street, piled high with fresh deli turkey and topped with the best cheese he'd ever tasted. He hadn't come in for the food, but now that he thought about it, he was starving.

"Make one for yourself, too." He walked around to the other side of the counter. "Actually, let me make it for you."

She turned toward him, surprise on her face. "You can't be back here."

"Another one of your rules?"

She glanced toward the back, where he wondered if someone else was working. "One of my dad's rules."

"Your dad won't care." He walked over to the stand-up cooler and pulled out a container marked *Chicken Salad*.

He happened to know it was her all-time favorite, especially with a little salt and pepper.

"What are you doing?"

"I'm making you lunch." He gave her a shove with his elbow as if to clear space for himself at the counter where the sandwiches were made.

"I don't eat—"

But before she could finish, he put his hand on her lips, an action that came out of instinct but carried a weightier consequence than he expected.

Her eyes locked on his and stopped him in his tracks for a split second. What did he expect to happen? Did he think he could just touch her lips and feel nothing?

"No rules." He pulled his hand away. "It's your favorite; I remember."

She frowned. "Do you also remember me being overweight?"

He shrugged. "No. I just remember you being fun."

She gave a humorless laugh. "I was never fun."

"You really don't remember, do you?"

"What are you talking about?"

"The times we snuck down to the lake, all of us kids—except Lindsay because she was too young—and swam in the middle of the night? Or the bonfires on the beach at the start of every summer? The brown-bag concerts in the park your parents would drag us to and we always pretended to hate, but we ended up having the best time. You loved those concerts. And your dad always packed you this exact sandwich."

Her face fell.

"Those were some of my best memories."

"You and I remember those things differently," she said.

He studied her for several long seconds, resisting the urge to kiss her right there in the middle of the cheese shop.

"I hardly ever had fun as a kid." She turned back to the sandwich.

He'd heard about the teasing, but it wasn't until one night down at the beach that he witnessed it for himself. They were playing a game of truth or dare—an awful game he'd grown to hate—and someone thought it would be funny to dare him to kiss Lane. Her expression in that moment was one of sheer panic, but truth be told, he'd been wanting to kiss her for a while by then. They were in high school, and while he'd done his best to ignore it, he liked Lane. And not the way a brother likes a sister.

It wasn't the kind of dare he was dreading.

They both stood, the light of the fire illuminating their young faces, and he reached for her hand across the circle.

"You should've picked truth," she said.

Not a chance. Truth—for someone like Ryan Brooks—was much harder to deal with than any dare their friends could dream up.

He led her a short distance from the rest of the group, aware that in order for the dare to count, their kiss had to be witnessed by everyone. They stood at the base of the stairs built into the side of the dunes, his back to the circle, her standing right in front of him.

"This is ridiculous," she said. "You don't have to do this."

"What if I want to?"

Slowly their eyes met, but she quickly looked away, laughing off his comment. She was nervous, he could tell. He wondered if she'd ever been kissed.

He wished it hadn't taken a stupid game to get him to work up his courage.

"Are you okay?"

She nodded, staring at his chest. He lifted her chin, letting his hand slip down her neck and rest there.

"Let's just get this over with," she said.

But as he leaned closer, Walker Jones, the one who'd dared him to kiss her in the first place, came up beside them, a hand on each of their shoulders. "What's taking you so long, Brooks? We heard you liked bacon." He looked at Lane then and snorted at her—right in her face.

"Back off, Jones." Ryan pushed the other guy in the chest, forcing him to release his grip on both of them. "You're such a jerk."

Walker let out a loud burst of laughter, then called out to the rest of them, "It's not gonna happen. These two are disqualified."

Lane stood unmoving, as if his comments were cinder blocks tied to her ankles. He took her hand, but he had no words to comfort her after that.

"I'm fine, Brooks," she said. "I just want to go home. Alone."

Stupidly he let her go. In hindsight, he shouldn't have. He should've walked her home, stood on the front porch of the Kelleys' old Victorian, and told her that what he really wanted was to kiss her of his own free will—not because some idiot had dared him to as part of a cruel joke.

Instead he returned to the circle, feeling sick and trying hard not to punch Walker Jones square in the jaw.

CHAPTER

15

LANE WRAPPED RYAN'S SANDWICH and stuck a Summers sticker on the back to hold it together. As she did, she tried to calm her unsteady nerves. The traitorous things had gotten out of control as soon as Ryan's fingers touched her lips.

It was stupid. This was *Brooks.* He was practically a member of her family . . . yet she knew even a casual infatuation with him could lead her straight back to where she was after Jasper broke her heart.

She'd promised herself that would never happen again.

She was just jumpy. It wasn't because he still seemed to know her after all this time—or because he still wanted to be around her. Or because he remembered her favorite sandwich. They were friends. That was all. She needed to get used to having a guy for a friend again.

"Here's your sandwich." She held it out to him nonchalantly. At least she thought it was nonchalant. Could he hear her heart pounding?

He finished wrapping the paper around hers and held it up. "And here's yours."

She didn't eat bread. How could she say that without being chastised? "Now what?"

"Now you're going to come with me and we're going to eat our sandwiches."

Her phone buzzed in the pocket of her apron. For the briefest moment, she'd almost forgotten the insane amount of pressure she was under at work. "I really shouldn't, Brooks. I told my dad I'd cover while he's with Nate."

"Is Jimmy back there?"

"Yes."

"He can cover for an hour. Everyone deserves a lunch break."

A lunch break for her consisted of a Cobb salad with dressing on the side ordered by Chloe and eaten at her desk.

She glanced at her phone and saw Marshall's name on the screen. She didn't bother reading the message. At the moment, she didn't want to know what he had to say. He'd purposely handicapped her by keeping their next meeting on Monday when he very easily could've given her at least until Wednesday. Was he being selfish or thoughtless? Either way, it had her rethinking their entire relationship.

But then, being in Harbor Pointe had her rethinking a lot of things.

"Jimmy!" Ryan hollered.

Her dad's oldest employee appeared in the doorway of the back room.

"Can you cover the front for an hour?"

"Of course, Mr. Brooks!" He waved them off dismissively.

"See, Jimmy can handle it."

Lane shook her head. "You are a piece of work, you know that, Ryan Brooks?"

"I want to show you something." He grinned at her the way he sometimes had when they were kids. Most guys growing up in his shoes would've clammed up, closed themselves off, gotten into trouble. Somehow, his father's drinking had inspired the opposite in Brooks. He'd worked harder, laughed louder, and stayed out of trouble more than most boys his age.

Yet sometimes she could sense a dark cloud still hung overhead. As if some of it was just an act. How many people had actually seen the real Ryan Brooks?

She had. She was sure of it. There'd been a few rare, quiet moments over the years when he'd opened up in front of her. One time he told her the only place he felt safe was at their house.

Ryan grabbed two bags of chips—something else Lane didn't eat—and she took two bottles of water out of the refrigerator. They put it all in a Summers bag, and she pulled off her hat and apron and hung them on the hook by the back door.

Outside, she followed Ryan to the bike path and fell into step beside him as they walked parallel to the lake.

"Where are we going?"

"Can't you just enjoy the journey to get there?"

"Maybe once you tell me where *there* is."

He gave her a push. "You've gotta learn to relax, Kelley. When did you get so uptight?"

She laughed—not because she wanted to, but because she knew what he said was true. "I am not uptight."

"Prove it. Just enjoy the walk along the lake. Enjoy the boats in the marina, the lighthouse." He inched slightly closer to her and she bristled at his nearness. "Pretend for one hour that you have nothing to do."

She shoved him playfully. "You're crazy."

"But I'm cute. You gotta admit."

She looked away. See, like this. What was this? Was he flirting with her now? *Oh, my gosh.* Was she flirting with him? She wasn't good at this—any of it—but now that the thought had occurred to her, her pulse quickened—slight, but noticeable.

He didn't look at her like he saw her as a kid sister. It made her question her resolve.

As they walked, they talked about Nate, always on both of their minds. There wasn't much else to report. He was still in a coma, and the doctors were still closely monitoring him.

"What was Walker asking you about the other day at the farmers' market?"

Brooks's gaze stayed firmly in front of him. "He thinks I should remember more than I do, I guess."

Before she could ask him what exactly he remembered or assess for herself if he was hiding something, he nudged her with his shoulder and said, "Here. It's just up here."

"Cedar Grove?"

He jogged a few steps ahead of her, stopping in front of the Cedar Grove sign. New, by the looks of it, and very nice. She could see now that the cottages had been renovated, and one was still under construction. He turned toward her, hands stretched out as if presenting something.

"What?"

"This is what I wanted to show you."

She regarded him for a long moment, trying to determine why he had that goofy look on his face. "I'm pretty sure I've seen this before."

"Come here."

He led her toward one of the cottages and opened the door. She remembered Cedar Grove as cute but basic. It had gotten run-down, and by the time she moved away, it was the place out on the lake nobody really wanted to stay at anymore.

She could see someone had done a lot of work to change that perception. This cottage had been completely restored. With thick moldings and beautifully refinished hardwood floors, the place had a lot of promise.

"We knocked out a couple of walls to open it up—people really like an open floor plan. Makes it easier for the whole family to stay connected."

She ran a hand across the mantel over the brick fireplace. The whole place was like a blank canvas just waiting for the right artist to get ahold of it. Something inside her leapt at the idea.

But this wasn't the kind of interior design she did. She worked on branded spaces. For hotels. Businesses. Universities. Still, she could see light-gray paint on the walls, rattan shades on the windows, furniture designed to be functional as well as beautiful, placed—as Ryan had said—so a family could be together.

"Wait; what do you mean 'we'?" She faced him. "Have you been working on this project?"

He smiled. "This is my project."

"I don't understand."

"I bought this place, Lane. It's mine."

Her mouth opened. "Yours?"

"What do you think?"

With the open floor plan, the whole space was light, bright, and airy. She could see straight into the kitchen, where he'd installed brand-new white cabinets and beautiful white granite counters with swirls of gray in them, a perfect complement to the stainless steel appliances.

"I think it's amazing."

He grinned at her, then moved over to the counter and opened his sandwich. There was nowhere to sit, but apparently he was hungry. She, however, was not. At least not for bread. Or that's what she told herself to keep from devouring it.

"Come on; let's eat." He pulled her sandwich out of the bag and opened a bottle of water, sliding it toward her. "I've been wanting to show you this place since you came back to town."

"Really? Why?"

He glanced at her the way a child might when he sought the approval of someone in authority. He'd grown up with no approval from anyone that she knew of; maybe he just needed someone to tell him he'd done a good job.

"So you own all these cottages?"

He took a bite of his sandwich and nodded.

"Did you do the renovations yourself?"

Another nod.

"This is pretty amazing, Brooks. It's going to be a huge draw. This is what my mother was trying to tell me that day in the hospital. About what you've done for the community."

"She brags on me like she brags on you."

She waved him off. "She's never bragged on me."

"Lane, you have no idea. That woman talks about your accomplishments all the time. Thinks you're pretty amazing just living in Chicago, but working there too? And being a success? She knows you're doing something most of us are too afraid to do. You're the brave Kelley."

The thought stunned her. It was hardly true. She'd never felt brave a day in her life.

"Listen, I have an ulterior motive for bringing you out here." He washed down his bite with a swig of water.

She raised an eyebrow. "Oh, really?" she said dryly.

"I want to hire you."

"Hire me?"

He set his sandwich down, apparently so he could speak with both hands. "My interior designer quit, and Betsy gave me a link to your website. According to her, and your mom, you're kind of a big deal."

"Betsy gave you the link?"

He swallowed a bite and peered at her knowingly. "Yeah, you wanna tell me what happened there?"

"No."

"Fine, then just agree to help me out."

Lane took a drink of her water. "Ryan, I'm really flattered you thought of me, but this isn't the kind of project I usually do."

"But you could if you wanted to."

"You know how much work I have to do."

"You've told me." His face turned innocent. "And I thought about not even mentioning this to you, but then I thought maybe a change of pace is what you need."

Lane ran a hand through her hair. She hadn't expected this.

She turned and faced the main living room, the room she'd paint a dusty-gray color and accent with brightly colored, lake-inspired touches. She could see a white slipcovered sectional positioned to face the fireplace, and a couple of bright—maybe a little funky—club chairs off to the side.

No. She couldn't start decorating this place in her mind. She didn't have time to take on another project. But the screened-in porch off the back of the cottage caught her eye with its two wicker chairs and matching love seat, and she could practically see the rest of the space come together in her head with large white lights strung overhead and the perfect rug to pull it all together. It would be so different from what she'd been working on—it would be fun.

How long had it been since design was fun?

"Don't give me an answer right now," Ryan said. "Just think about it. But remember the greatest benefit of the whole project is the countless hours you'd get to spend with me."

She crossed her arms and glared at him. "Are you really this high on yourself or is it just a front?"

He shrugged. "We'll never know." He glanced at her unopened sandwich. "You're not going to eat that, are you?"

She scrunched her face and shook her head. "Sorry."

He opened it up and took a bite. "You have no idea what you're missing."

16

SUNDAY MORNING, a crash outside Lane's bedroom woke her with a start. She shot out of bed and opened the door, expecting to see Jett standing there in a pile of something he shouldn't be getting into. Instead, she found her father, whom she'd barely seen since she'd been home, standing beside the linen closet clumsily propping up a broken shelf.

"Did I wake you?" He turned toward her, his eyes wide.

"Frank, what on earth?" Her mother appeared in the hallway just outside the master bedroom, her wet hair flat around the edges of her face. "Did you break the linen closet?" When she noticed Lane standing there, it was almost as if she'd forgotten her eldest daughter was home at all. "Oh, Lane, you scared me. Good, you're up—we have church."

She couldn't be serious. Lane had already sat outside again for hours yesterday at the farmers' market—all in the name of cheese— and she had the sunburn to prove it. She'd even put in her time at the cheese shop. What else was she going to get roped into? Her mind searched for an excuse.

"Also, we need you to milk Daisy before we head out."

"What?" So far, she'd managed to avoid milking the cows.

"She needs milking. Noah took care of Wilhelmina and Ruthie, but he ran out of time before his big race this morning."

Her father still stood in the doorway of the linen closet, propping up the shelf with his shoulder.

"I can't," Lane said. "I'm going to see Nate and then I have to drive home. I've already been here way longer than I planned, and I have a presentation tomorrow."

Working here had proved impossible—any changes Marshall wanted had barely been implemented, leaving her with a load to do when she got home that afternoon.

She'd already resigned herself to the all-nighter ahead of her.

Her mother stiffened and her entire demeanor changed. "You haven't even been here a week."

"Mom, I'm sorry, but I have to get back. I've already explained what I'm up against at—"

"Work, I know." Her mom pressed her lips together and shook her head—barely—as if willing Lane's words away.

"Lane, at least stay for Sunday dinner," her dad said. "Church, then dinner. That's all. You'll be on the road by two."

"No, Frank, don't beg her." Her mom had turned into a martyr in the last five seconds, the way only a mother could. "If she doesn't want to be here with us, that's fine. She has her work."

"You say it like it's a bad thing," Lane said, wishing for the courage to say so much more.

Dottie sighed. "We're happy for you and proud of you, of course. You have a great career. But it seems to me that's the only thing you have."

This wasn't my first choice, remember? Is it my fault my sister is living the life I was supposed to live?

Lane drew in a deep breath and exhaled quietly. Why fight it?

She knew what she was going to do. She was going to milk a cow, go to church, then come back for family dinner, all because she could only find her backbone when she was standing in the office talking about some aspect of her job—never with her family.

"Are you going to stand like that for the rest of the morning, Frank?" Dottie glared at him, then disappeared into her bedroom, leaving Lane face-to-shoulder with her father, who looked wholly uncomfortable holding up that shelf.

"I was hoping she would help me," he said forlornly.

Lane moved toward the linen closet and put a hand underneath the broken shelf so her dad could inch his way out. He pulled the stacks of towels down, then took the shelf from her and set it on the floor. When he straightened, he faced her, broader and taller than Lane, but shorter and smaller than she remembered.

"I'm glad you're home." His smile was slight and hard to decipher underneath his bushy gray mustache, but she saw it in his eyes. "It's been good having you around again, even if you are always rushing around or staring at that phone or buried in your computer."

"Thanks, Dad."

A pause, and then, "Not everything is the way it seems, you know."

Lane wrapped her arms across her stomach, suddenly feeling on edge. "What do you mean?"

"I know you think we all chose Lindsay over you, but that's not the case."

"I don't really want to talk about this." She started to turn away, but his hand on her shoulder stopped her. She stared down the hall, refusing to meet his eyes.

"We lost you that day, and I still haven't forgiven myself. For a long time I refused to speak to either of them—"

"You walked Lindsay down the aisle. If that's not a show of support, I don't know what is." Lane didn't like this. She didn't like the way her emotions were still so raw after all these years. She didn't like the anger that bubbled just beneath her surface or the tears that clouded her eyes.

"We'd already lost you, Lane. I couldn't bear the thought of losing another daughter."

Lane's mouth had gone dry. "Then I was right. You made your choice." She faced him. "I'm fine, Dad. I've moved on. You don't have to worry about me at all anymore."

His eyes looked sad. "I will worry about you until you're back for real. You can't hold on to your anger like this. It's not good for anyone."

Lane didn't want to hear any more of what he had to say. She didn't want to relive any of this humiliation for one more second. "I have to go milk a cow," she said, and then she walked away.

Church. Lane hadn't been in months. She'd been raised in church, raised to believe in the importance of surrounding herself with like-minded people. But somewhere between the cliques in her youth group, the well-meaning but insensitive remarks of her parents' friends, and the day Lindsay and Jasper walked down the steps as a married couple, church had lost whatever appeal it once held.

She'd never tried to explain it to anyone, but the truth was, she'd found God in the strangest of places. In the shower. On the elliptical machine at the gym. Right in her own loft in the middle of the night.

But like she did with everyone, she kept him at arm's length too. Relationships were tricky and emotional, and she was careful to maintain a safe distance from heartbreak.

You get that, right, God? You understand?

Somehow she had to believe he did. After all, he'd given her this job and these responsibilities. It was up to her to do them well.

Lane dragged her feet as she walked into Harbor Pointe Community Church. The old wooden building had been painted white—and repainted many times over the years. The people of Harbor Pointe kept it in good shape, though it didn't have a particularly traditional feel inside. In the summer, the entire congregation often met down on the beach of Lake Michigan under an oversize white tent the church had purchased ages ago.

Lane had never admitted it, but the services on the beach had always been her favorites, even as a kid. There was something about abandoning their sandals on the landing at the dunes and plodding through morning-cool sand to meet with Jesus. She supposed in some ways those were the services where she'd felt closest to him.

Something inside her twisted at the memory. Part of her missed the way those services had made her feel.

Things were simpler then. She didn't know much about the world, but she knew God loved her. He'd made her and he loved her. How simple it sounded now.

She pushed it away. She was fine with her casual conversations with God.

"You probably don't even remember what the inside of this church looks like, do you?" Her mother's joke fell flat, sounding more like an accusation to Lane than anything. Lane ignored her, and her mom walked off in the direction of a small group of older women, who enveloped Dottie and started in with questions about Nate.

Her dad made a beeline for the same pew the Kelley family had occupied since she was a girl, probably assuming Lane would follow. But she didn't, instead standing alone at the back of the small sanctuary. Rows of wooden chairs had been set up to face the stage, which wasn't deep or wide but still served its purpose. Lane took it all in, wishing she could vanish and wondering if there was a way to slip out without her parents noticing.

She caught her mother's eye from across the room and had her answer. No way her mom was letting her slide out of this one. Another thing that would never change.

Her phone buzzed.

Are you on your way home? Chloe had texted. I blocked off today. I'll be at your place whenever you need me.

Lane quickly typed back a reply. I'm at church. I'll text you when I leave.

I wish you could just stay there. You deserve the break.

Too much to do. It's going to be a late night.

"You might want to put that away in here."

The deep baritone of Brooks's voice startled her, but it was the nearness of his body at her side that had her nerves on edge. What was going on with her lately? This was Brooks, for pete's sake. Hot but annoying Brooks.

"You shouldn't sneak up on people." She took a step away, but he was still close enough she could smell whatever woodsy soap he used. Too faint to be cologne, but still potent enough to make her want to continuously inhale. "People aren't allowed to use cell phones in church?"

"It's an older crowd. They frown on Sunday morning technology."

When she dared a glance in his direction, she saw the lazy tilt of his grin and she knew he was just messing with her.

She gave him a shove and looked away, hopefully before he saw her smile. Truth was, she found him as amusing as she did annoying. It was rare that she found anyone amusing.

"Any word on Nate?"

Lane shook her head slightly.

"No news is good news, I guess."

She followed his gaze to the front of the church.

"But it sure isn't the same up there without him."

"I still can't believe he plays the guitar, especially in front of people. Nate was the most rebellious of all of us. He hated coming to church." Lane remembered those rebellious years well. There were times Lane was the only one in the family he could really talk to.

Ryan shrugged. "He hates being told what to do, but he's a true believer at heart. Hey, did you think any more about my job offer?"

She had. A lot. She'd practically gotten a virtual download to her brain full of ideas—from colors and accents to furniture placement. And she'd rejected all of it. She did not have time to design twelve cottages, especially not in the month Ryan had left before his first guests arrived.

"I have to go," he said. "Service is starting. We can talk about it at dinner."

"You still come to family dinner?"

He grinned—lazy, lopsided, and electric—as he walked away. "Of course. I'm part of the family."

She watched as Ryan walked onto the small platform and slung his guitar over his shoulder. He stood behind the microphone and welcomed everyone. Then his eyes met hers. "And especially those who haven't been back in a very long time—welcome home."

Home. Her body tensed. Not for her. Not anymore.

Lane did her best to focus on the church service. The music unexpectedly drew her in. Ryan certainly had a gift. "Anointed," her parents would say. But the buzzing of her phone kept her only partially engaged during the pastor's message, and it warranted many a dirty look from her mom.

Lane looked around the small church and saw Betsy sitting in the row behind Ryan, Hailey, and Jack. Betsy glanced at her, and for the briefest moment, Lane remembered how important their friendship had been to her at one time. Betsy probably had no idea. Lane had never told her.

Since she left Harbor Pointe, she'd searched for a friendship like the one she took for granted, only to decide such a thing didn't come around twice. She'd never dwelled on it before, but sitting here in the church they'd attended as kids, a deep loneliness washed over her, one that was always prevalent but usually easy to push away.

Not today.

Today the reality of it stung.

After the truth came out about Lindsay and Jasper, Betsy had tried to be a good friend. She'd even driven to Chicago one Saturday and Lane practically turned her away. She didn't want to be reminded of home or her family or the fact that anyone knew of her humiliation. She didn't want to be close to anyone or give another person the power to hurt her the way she'd been hurt.

"I won't tell anyone, Lane," Betsy said. "I know how hard this must be for you."

Lane had been ugly to her—it was the only way to make Betsy go. Told her she could never understand because she'd never been in love. No one had ever cared for Betsy the way Jasper cared for Lane. She'd said hurtful things, but it had done the trick. Betsy stopped calling, and Lane hadn't talked to her since.

At the time, it had been the one thing Lane could think of to protect herself, but her methods had been faulty. She knew that now. But now it was too late.

She'd behaved so badly and it had crushed her friend. No wonder she refused to wait on Ryan and her at Hazel's the other night. Some wounds reopened as easily as if they were fresh, regardless of how many years had passed.

Lane understood that better than most people, didn't she?

CHAPTER

17

POST-CHURCH CONVERSATION had Lane inhaling deep four-count breaths and exhaling for as long as she could. She stared at the ground as her parents stopped to talk to *every single person* they saw, and she tried to be polite and answer all the questions that came her way.

"Yes, I live in Chicago."

"Yes, I actually like it there."

"No, it's not a dirty city. I don't mind the people. My career is going well. How did I lose all my weight? I moved out of Harbor Pointe." Pause for laughter. "Of course that was a joke. Just diet and exercise."

Nellie Lampkin practically felt her up trying to determine "where she'd put all that weight," despite Lane's repeated attempts to move out of reach of the old woman's grabby hands.

"I simply don't understand it." Nellie's head moved in short bursts, wobbling on a too-thick neck like a bobblehead doll, as she pinched and poked around Lane's torso. "There was so much fat on you before. Where'd it all go?"

Lane pressed her lips together and imagined herself back in the loft, wearing her comfiest yoga pants and her worn-out purple Northwestern sweatshirt, poring over the designs for Solar's new space.

But even as she did, the image of the cottage at Cedar Grove popped into her mind. She shook it away. She hardly had time to think about that right now.

"You're just so thin now." Nellie's tone was one of disdain, as if Lane had morphed into something wholly ugly and undesirable. And this after spending her life being equally ugly and undesirable in a differently shaped body.

"I'm healthy now." Lane tried to keep her tone calm. She didn't have to defend herself to Nellie Lampkin—why did she feel like she did? The woman had a knack for sticking her nose where it didn't belong. When Lane was a kid, Nellie was the one who pulled her brothers home by their ears to tell their parents the boys let the dog "dirt in her yard."

Lane could still remember the look on her mother's face when she explained—not so politely—that her boys had absolutely done no such thing and that she expected an apology, which, of course, never came. Nellie was a tough old bird, and Lane hated that she was in her crosshairs.

"What'd you do, stop eating gluten? That seems to be the hot button for weight loss these days. It's a bunch of hooey, if you ask me. A life without bread is no life I want to live." Nellie's eyes narrowed as she stared at Lane. "You're not bulimic, are you?"

Lane felt a gentle hand on the small of her back. "There you are. I was looking for you."

She froze as Ryan's body pressed into her side, his touch warm and safe like a harbor for a ship that had been out in a storm all night. Lane often felt like she was being tossed on the sea, her nerves shot, as if that was simply how life was. She'd gotten used to it.

But with one touch, it seemed he'd calmed the storm that raged inside her.

Of course that was ludicrous. No man had that kind of power over her. She was just thankful for the distraction.

"Mrs. Lampkin, I'm sorry to rush her off like this. We have lunch plans and we don't want to be late." Ryan smiled at her—a real smile, with his eyes—and gave Lane a soft push to the side. "You do look beautiful in that pink dress, Mrs. L. You should wear pink every day."

Lane tossed a glance at Nellie, whose cheeks had turned red as she soaked in Ryan's compliment. He gave her a wave and moved with Lane toward the front door and out onto the lawn of the church. Churchgoers gathered in small groups in the grass, and her own family hovered by their car, parked in the gravel lot. She turned away, embarrassed that Ryan had heard and seen Nellie's invasive hunt for fat. She'd cringe about that for years to come.

The same way she'd cringed all those years ago when women like Nellie would tell Lane's mom to take food away from her daughter, get her on an exercise program, and do something about those extra pounds.

"It's okay; you don't have to thank me." He stopped walking once they'd cleared the majority of the crowd outside the church.

She glanced at Ryan, who was the kind of disheveled good-looking that wasn't fair to the rest of the human race. Lane had a feeling the guy woke up like this—sandy-colored hair, stunning green eyes, bright-white teeth lined in perfect rows, and just the right amount of stubble on his chin to keep him from looking preppy.

"You're expecting a thank-you?"

"It's the least you could do after I just saved you in there." Ryan crossed his arms and looked at her. "We've all been cornered by Nellie Lampkin, though I'm not sure everyone has the same kind of relationship with her that you do. She seemed awfully comfortable with you." He waggled his eyebrows as he said it.

She sighed. "I would say she means well, but I don't think she does."

"No, she's kind of a terrible woman." Ryan's eyes flickered and Lane couldn't help but laugh.

"You're the one who told her she looked good in pink."

"A little payback for the nasty things she said to you."

Lane felt her smile skitter away. "I can't believe you heard all that."

"She's not exactly quiet." Ryan stood several inches taller than her, broad and strong, but she didn't dare let herself imagine there was safety in his arms. She'd made that mistake before. Besides, she was leaving that afternoon. All this nonsense running through her mind about Brooks had to stop.

"You shouldn't let people like that make you feel bad about yourself."

Lane waved him off. "I should go. My parents will wonder where I am."

But as soon as she said the words, she saw her parents' sedan pull out of the parking lot and away from the church.

"Unbelievable." Lane watched the car disappear down the hill. "They left me."

"Must've thought you were riding with me." He nodded toward his motorcycle.

"I'm not getting on that thing." Lane looked away.

"Scared?"

"Aren't you?"

He stilled. "I'm not going to let fear stand in the way of doing something I really love. And your brother wouldn't either."

That was true.

"Let's do it. It's warm out today. It's the perfect day for it." He unstrapped an extra helmet and handed it to her. "I'll drive safely, I promise. Or do you have a transportation rule?"

Lane snatched the helmet from him but didn't put it on. "And why should I trust you?"

"I've given you no reason not to." He smiled.

Yet. She'd be smart to keep that in mind.

"You can walk if you want to." Ryan swung a leg over the bike and started the engine. "Up to you."

It was not like Lane to get on a motorcycle with a man who'd basically become a stranger to her, especially not this soon after the accident. In college she'd developed an incredible sense of control—and she liked it.

Getting on the back of Ryan's bike meant giving over control to someone else. And that unnerved her, no matter—or maybe because of—how good he smelled.

"Last chance?" He revved the engine.

"Didn't you have a concussion or something?"

He shook his head. "No. Just a gash on my leg and a headache."

"You promise to go slow?"

"I promise to keep you safe."

"That's not the same thing."

He grinned. "No, it's not."

This was stupid. She should walk. She absolutely should not get on his bike. She shouldn't wrap her arms around him, press herself into his back, inhale the masculine smell that even now danced around her nostrils.

She shouldn't do any of those things. So why was she putting on the helmet? Why was she swinging her leg over the bike? Why was she awkwardly trying to figure out where to put her hands?

"They go here." Ryan took her arms and wrapped them around his torso. When he let his grip on her go, she loosened them, but as soon as he pulled away from the curb, she realized loose wasn't an option.

"Hold on," he said, turning his head toward her.

She did as she was told as he accelerated down the street, and her stomach somersaulted the way it did when her dad had driven them on "Butterfly Hill," the road he loved to take because its curves and bumps promised butterflies to even the slowest of motorists.

Ryan braked for a stop sign, fixed his feet on the road, and leaned back. "You okay?"

She nodded, self-conscious in the helmet yet thankful it hid the way she was feeling—defenseless, vulnerable, excited.

But this was Ryan Brooks. She was not allowed to feel this way about him.

Then again, she was leaving in a matter of hours. She might never see him again. That gave her instant protection from any silly attraction she was battling at the moment.

He returned his attention to the road, and they were off again. With each passing block, she grew more and more comfortable with the movement of the bike and with Ryan's nearness.

"Care if we take the long way?" he asked at another stop.

She shook her head. Secretly she was thankful for any diversion that kept her from her parents' Sunday dinner even for an extra few minutes. Also secretly, she kind of liked being on the back of his bike. He was right not to let fear keep him from getting out there again. He loved this, and she could see why. Nate loved it too. She knew as soon as he was able, he'd be here at Ryan's side. Not that she'd ever admit any of those things out loud.

They drove through town and onto country roads that were dotted with farms and cornfields and vast amounts of green. The lake came into view and the road wound parallel alongside it for several miles, each one drawing her closer to Ryan and more exhilarated by the speed of the bike. As they drove, her mind wandered until it reached the end of itself. For the first time in years, she didn't have that buzzing pressure to do more, to be more.

It had been replaced by the feeling of the wind, the smell of the lake, the heat of the spring sunshine, just starting to warm up in time for summer. The whirl of busy drifted away as if she'd left it on the curb before they even pulled away.

Finally, after forty-five glorious minutes of forgetting every responsibility she had, they started back toward town. Before they reached the city limits, he slowed and turned down a long paved driveway leading to a large white house overlooking the lake.

Surely he didn't live here. Where were they?

She sat up straighter until the rest of the home came into view. Her parents' car was parked in the grass next to several others, and her mom was unloading food from the backseat.

In the distance, Lane saw Noah and Emily's kids running around the yard, chasing two big yellow Labs. A shirtless Jett came tearing out from behind the garage and tackled one of the dogs. Lane wondered if the dog would retaliate, but it didn't. It pulled away and ran off with its companion, Jett trailing close behind, trying to catch its tail.

Otis ran out from the side of the house, determined to keep up with the other dogs. "How'd he get here?"

"Guessing your parents went home and got him when they picked up the food."

It was a thoughtful gesture, though she wasn't sure why she felt a sudden twinge of emotion because of it. Otis was just a dog. Yet knowing they'd thought about something she loved—it made her feel included. And she hadn't felt included in her family for years.

Ryan parked the bike, put the kickstand down, and turned off the engine.

She loosened her grip around him and took off her helmet. "Where are we?"

"Sunday dinner."

"I thought it was at my parents' house."

"We rotate."

A blue Honda Civic came into view and drove toward them.

"Did they invite the whole town?" Lane remembered Sunday dinner. It was always right after church, but it was the only real meal they had all day, which was why her mother called it "dinner" and not "lunch." Her parents filled their table with neighbors and relatives, but judging by the number of cars, the amount of participants had only grown. Lane had forgotten the way she'd sat through those meals, as quiet and unmoving as if she weren't there at all.

She'd listen as they all spoke, telling stories and being social, and she had wondered how they did it—shared themselves so readily with other people. Ryan had that same talent. She might even admire it a little. It had always been so hard for her, yet it was what she wanted more than anything—to fit in. To belong.

"Your parents are well-loved," Ryan said. "And they make everyone feel welcome."

Well, that was ironic.

Lane shoved the pitying thought aside. She'd done well for herself, and if she'd felt welcome here, she might never have spread her wings. After all, she'd practically been pushed out of Harbor Pointe, so leaving had never been as difficult a prospect as staying would've been.

Still, her mother's comment about work being the only thing she had nagged at her.

Hailey and Jack emerged from the blue Civic.

"Uncle Ryan!" Jack raced over to the bike, and Ryan held up a hand of warning.

"It's still hot, buddy; remember."

"I got it." He raised his hand and Ryan slapped him five. "Mom, can I go play?"

Hailey gave him a nod and he ran off toward the other kids.

"He got you on the back of that thing?" Hailey shook her head at her brother.

"She hated every minute." Lane could tell Ryan was smiling as he said the words. Something in her body language must've given her away.

"It was more out of necessity than anything." Lane lifted herself up and off the bike. "My parents left me at church." She placed her feet firmly on the ground but still felt like she was floating.

"Oh," Hailey laughed. "That was nice of them."

Ryan dismounted the bike and took the helmet from Lane. "I knew you'd love it. You just gotta loosen up a little."

She narrowed her eyes. He was cocky. Or maybe it was confident. Whatever it was, he was sure of himself in a way that Lane never had been. She'd learned to fake it, but deep down, she always knew it was phony.

"Who says I loved it?"

Ryan's eyebrows popped up. "You didn't have to *say* anything."

Lane's mind spun back to one particularly tight curve. He'd navigated it beautifully, but it had required that she tighten her grip around his torso. She wondered if he'd taken that route for the sole purpose of forcing her to hold on more firmly.

"Don't mistake the thrill of the ride with affection for the driver," Hailey said. She glanced at Lane. "He's so ridiculous." She walked off toward the house, carrying a tray of deviled eggs.

Lane watched her go, mostly to avoid meeting Ryan's eyes.

"Why are you afraid to admit you had fun?"

"I'm not." She straightened.

He raised an eyebrow as if to question her reply.

"I'm not afraid. It was fine. We have different versions of fun, that's all."

"Fun is fun, Lane Kelley. And that was fun." He set his helmet on the seat of the bike. "Even you have to admit it."

"This is a beautiful home." They walked through the yard around the side of the house. "Who lives here?"

But before Ryan could answer, she saw Jasper standing at the grill, a bottle of beer in one hand, a large spatula in the other.

Lindsay emerged through the back door, stepping onto the deck wearing a white sundress and no shoes. Her long blonde hair was pulled up into a messy bun, a white headband positioned near the front of her hairline. She set a tray of meat down beside the grill and said something to Jasper.

Jasper barely acknowledged her. Lindsay stared at him for a long moment, then finally walked away. As she did, her eyes fell on Lane, standing dumbly off to the side of the deck, horrified that somehow she'd been tricked into coming to dinner at Lindsay and Jasper's gorgeous, expensive, sprawling home.

"This is Lindsay's house." Lane practically whispered it.

"Your parents didn't tell you?" Ryan raked a hand through his hair. "Oh, man, Lane. I'm sorry."

She looked at him. How much did he know? Obviously he knew the man she'd thought she loved hadn't wanted her after all. Wasn't that enough? Ryan hadn't been in the country when Jasper and Lindsay got married. Lane remembered because she'd stupidly come to Harbor Pointe that day, and after she saw Jasper and Lindsay leave the church in their wedding attire, she actually wished she'd had his shoulder to cry on.

Somehow she had a feeling he never would've supported that marriage. The only other person whose support she had was Nate's. He'd found her in her car outside the church. Dressed in jeans and an old T-shirt, it was clear he hadn't been at the wedding.

He didn't say anything. Just sat with her in the car until she got tired of sitting, then made her go get a burger with him at Hazel's. He chattered on about who knows what and made her forget, if only for a few minutes, that her entire family had betrayed her.

It wasn't right that he was lying in a hospital bed while the rest of them were here, having Sunday dinner like nothing had changed.

"You okay?" Ryan had paused when Lane stopped walking, but now he stood in front of her, forcing her attention. "You look green."

Lane glanced toward the swimming pool beyond the deck. "Jasper and Lindsay live here."

She thought of her loft apartment in Chicago. She loved that place. She loved the tall windows and the view of Lake Michigan. She loved the way natural light streamed in even when she was trying to sleep past 6 a.m. She loved that it was open and perfect for entertaining, even though she never had anyone but Chloe over.

It was a sign of success that she could afford a place like that in the city. And it was safe. To her, it was the safest place in the world.

But this house was something else entirely. *It* was a sign of success no matter where you lived. The yard stretched on forever, and they obviously had every amenity a person could want—swimming pool, three-season room, outdoor showers for the days they spent at the pool or beach. She could only imagine what the inside was like. She bet Lindsay had hired a professional decorator to come in and make the place look even richer.

Lane would've gone for a more cottage feel. White woodwork, distressed furniture. She would've pulled some of the ostentatiousness out of the place and created a home.

Had Lindsay turned this house into a home?

Lane always knew Jasper would be successful. He was a financial adviser. He knew money. Obviously he'd given her sister a good life.

Did it matter if it was the life Lane was meant to have? That pool, that grill, that deck, those dogs—they all should have been hers.

"Lane?"

"I'm fine." She shook the thoughts away. "I don't feel so great. Do you think you could run me back to my parents' house?"

"Lane, you don't have to keep running away." His hands found her arms.

Lane glanced over to the deck, only a few yards away, where her mother, Lindsay, Emily, and three women Lane didn't recognize were standing.

"What are you doing over there?" Her mother motioned for her to join them. "Come eat, Lane. Lord knows you could use the calories."

Lane's breathing hitched.

"She is awfully thin, Dottie. Don't they have food in Chicago?"

Lane didn't move. She didn't want to be the center of attention. Especially not here.

"She just put away an Arcto-Burger from Dairy Dream," Ryan called out. "With fries and a chocolate shake."

Lane tried to hide a smile.

"That should shut them up, right?" Ryan stared at her with helpful eyes—too gorgeous for his own good.

"Most of them know I'm lactose intolerant, but it's the thought that counts." She smiled just as her phone buzzed.

He pulled it out of her hand before she could respond.

"I need that for work."

"It's Sunday."

"I have a big presentation—"

"That will still be there after we eat."

She folded her arms in front of her, not unlike a petulant child. "I bet you haven't thought about this stress box once since church. Why ruin it now?"

She frowned. "Stress box? It's a phone."

"It's a ball of stress. Every time it goes off, you drop whatever you were doing and disappear for a few minutes. No one should be available 24-7. It's not healthy. I'll just hold on to it till after lunch."

She eyed him, firmly planting herself in front of him. "Fine. If you get to hold on to my phone, then I get to hold on to yours."

His head tilted as he regarded her for a long moment. "Deal." He reached in his back pocket and pulled out a flip phone that had to be at least five or six years old.

"I can't believe this is your phone."

"I'm a simple guy, Lane Kelley. I don't need any bells and whistles to shine up what I've got to offer." He grinned at her and she resisted the urge to give him a playful shove. She couldn't risk any more physical contact with Ryan Brooks, not after that motorcycle ride.

She snatched the phone from his hand and examined it. She was surprised the thing still worked. "Is this even on?"

He shook his head.

"Why not?"

"It's Sunday."

She frowned. "So?"

"I'm off the grid on Sunday."

She stared at him, trying to decide if he was kidding, but his steady expression didn't change. "You're serious."

"Are you intrigued?" His expression had gone lazy again, and something about it made her a little weak in the knees.

Oh, please. What a cliché. Weak in the knees for a man? She knew better than that. She silently reprimanded herself for her middle school–esque behavior and stuck his phone in her purse. "We'll trade back after we eat."

He smiled at her, and somehow she knew she'd just been conned into not only giving up her lifeline but also eating lunch at Lindsay and Jasper's table.

And the only thing that made it okay was the man whose hand had once again found the small of her back.

CHAPTER

18

"YOU LIKE HER." Hailey's singsongy voice reminded Ryan of when they were kids.

Sometimes his sister could be so obnoxious.

"Would you knock it off?" Ryan pulled a Coke from a galvanized tub filled with ice and cans of soda.

"You're completely smitten with her; I can see it all over your face."

Ryan's attention wandered across the yard to where Lane stood, chatting with Emily and sipping a bottle of water. Every once in a while, her eyes found his, but she always pulled them away before acknowledging a connection.

He found this flirtatious dance they were pretending not to do completely intoxicating, but that was not his sister's business.

"Why don't we talk about something other than my love life?" Ryan took a seat next to Hailey, who'd claimed a lawn chair by the pool and was watching Jack like a hawk.

"Stay in the shallow end," she called out, then to Ryan: "I hate pools."

"Let him have fun. He's got those stupid floaties on."

"He could still drown."

"Jeremy's in there," Ryan said with a nod toward Lane's youngest brother.

Hailey's gaze fell on Jer and he could've sworn her cheeks turned pink.

"Maybe we should talk about *your* love life. . . ."

Hailey shot him a look intended to shut him up.

"Little sister, you have a crush." There was nothing he loved more than teasing his sister, but when her face turned serious, he stopped. "What is it?"

She gave a soft shrug, then glanced back at Jack. "I can't think about dating anyone right now. Jack is the only man I'm going to have in my life for a long time."

Ryan watched as his nephew pulled himself out of the water onto the top step, then launched himself straight into Jeremy's arms. Jer picked him up and tossed him but somehow managed to be there before Jack's head went underwater. Jack squealed with the delight of a small child who still had hope of seeing his dreams come true.

"Hailey, just because Jack's dad was a jerk doesn't mean you're going to spend the rest of your life alone."

Hailey's smile came with glassy eyes. "Of course not. I've got you."

He heard what she wasn't saying. Ryan didn't have much room to talk. It wasn't like he'd made great strides in putting himself out there—lately none of his "relationships" had gone beyond two or three dates. Even his interest in Lane Kelley seemed safe. After all, she was going back to Chicago that afternoon.

Besides, they were friends. They'd always been just friends.

"If you're not careful, Lane Kelley is going to see through the cracks in your armor."

Ryan leaned forward, elbows on his knees, eyes still focused on the young swimmers. "What's that supposed to mean?"

"Everyone here knows you as this happy-go-lucky, super-charming guy," Hailey said. "But I know the real you."

"You're saying I'm not charming?" He grinned at her.

"I'm saying you hide behind your sense of humor." Hailey reached over and put a hand on his. "I think it's great if you like her, big brother. She's smart, successful, beautiful, and if I remember right, you kind of always had a thing for her."

A dangerous combination. Especially for him. Hailey was right: he was attracted to Lane. He found himself thinking about her whenever she was—and wasn't—around. He told himself it was the thrill of the chase, but even he knew better. This girl had gotten under his skin.

If he wasn't careful, this infatuation could turn into the real thing. And then what? Did he really want to deal with that kind of rejection?

Get it through your head, Brooks. She's off-limits to you. Lane had a boyfriend and lived hours away. Ryan had a business to get off the ground, family members to watch over, and no plans to move to the city. He didn't have time to acknowledge, let alone act on, these feelings. And yet there was something about her . . .

He stood and glanced down at his sister. "You're wrong, kid," he said. "It was just a motorcycle ride."

Lane hated to admit it, but every time Ryan walked away from her, she found herself searching for him as if he were her lifeboat in a sea of sharks. Emily had rushed off to tend to one of her kids, leaving Lane feeling even more exposed. People she didn't know milled around a table that had been filled with food—the kind she used to enjoy but would not allow herself to eat now. It was an odd assortment of picnic foods and breakfast items, as though nobody could make up their mind which meal they were hungry for. Potato salad and deviled eggs were on one side while freshly made cinnamon rolls and sausage-and-egg casserole were on the other.

Not too many years ago, Lane would've helped herself to all of it, but now she knew better. She eyed a bowl of fruit and the chicken on the grill. She'd allow herself those things. Nothing more.

Ryan sat by the pool with his sister, watching while Jack swam. Everyone looked so content here. Happy and peaceful. But all Lane could think about was the phone in Ryan's pocket and the presentation she wasn't working on.

And Jasper. And Lindsay.

And the way it had felt to have permission to wrap her arms around Ryan Brooks while he navigated sharp turns on a motorcycle.

He was right—she didn't want to admit it had been fun. But why?

She glanced at Lindsay and Jasper every so often, doing her best to appear nonchalant, but mostly still humiliated by what they'd done to her. Did everyone look at her like the cast-off sister who couldn't keep her fiancé's eyes from wandering? Did they tally up her faults to explain Jasper's choice? Was there a chart out there somewhere detailing her flaws compared to Lindsay's perfections? A number system to compare the two sisters in all the categories that mattered when choosing the person you wanted to spend the rest of your life with?

Her eyes found Jasper again, whom she'd caught looking at her more than once. He still stood at the grill, nursing another beer and talking with a guy Lane didn't recognize.

Jasper wasn't just her first boyfriend—he was her first everything. Her first kiss. Her first slow dance. Her first "I love you."

They'd met at school at the very end of her freshman year. He was a year older, working as a resident assistant on one of the guys' floors of her dorm. Most of the students were already preparing to leave at the end of a long week of finals, packing, saying good-bye. Lane wasn't in a rush. She'd arranged to stay on campus and take a few classes over the summer, much to her mother's dismay. But Lane knew if she went home, she'd fall back into her old habits, and the reminders of what she'd been were still too fresh. They'd surely sidetrack her progress.

Earlier in the year, at the suggestion of her roommate, Shannon, she'd started exercising as a way to deal with the stress of school, of growing up, of figuring out what came next. The constant pressure to get better grades, accumulate more service hours, make a better impression, build her résumé, weighed on her like a pile of bricks in her backpack, always dragging her down, nagging for her attention.

"Come with me," Shannon had said. "It'll be fun. And you need to take a break. You've been sitting in that chair for hours." Lane had been working on her first major college paper at that point, and Shannon was right. She needed a break. But kickboxing? With her athlete of a roommate?

But Shannon was so encouraging and kind, Lane found herself agreeing to go.

She put on a pair of old yoga pants and a T-shirt and trudged over to the field house where the class was being held. She stood in the back, doing her best to stay hidden and avoid the mirror in front of her. The music started and the teacher, Amber, took her spot at the front of the room. Amber was one of those girls, the kind Maddie and Sabrina and Ashley would've welcomed into their circle, no questions asked. Spunky, bubbly, thin, Amber was a physical therapy major with a keen interest in fitness, and she was not messing around.

"I don't want any excuses today!" her chirpy voice shouted into a headset microphone. "If you want to get fit, you're going to have to work for it! Are you ready to work?"

Amber spoke in exclamation points for forty-five minutes straight, and more than once Lane thought for sure she was about to literally die. But every time she lost some of her luster, Amber shouted, "There's no excuse not to live your best life, and your best life starts by not giving up! Let's move!"

Lane glanced up toward the front of the class and met Amber's eyes. She expected Amber to judge her—overweight, struggling, hiding in the back—but Amber gave her a "You've got this, girl!" and it gave Lane the strength to power through until the end of the class.

Afterward, the limber instructor bounced—the woman hadn't even broken a sweat—over to Lane and handed her a bottle of water. "I haven't seen you here before."

She wanted to assure Amber she would not be back, but instead she just said, "I came with my roommate."

"So it was your first class?"

Lane nodded and took a drink of water, wondering if a person could drown by drinking water while they were trying—and failing—to catch their breath.

"Wow, usually people have to sit down at their first class."

Lane stopped midswig. "I didn't know sitting down was an option."

Amber laughed. "You did really well. I hope you come back."

She smiled, a genuine smile that shamed Lane because she'd pegged her for one of the fake, dull types.

This girl with rock-hard abs who could pass off tight shorts and a sports bra as a legitimate outfit had just paid her a compliment. And it was all the encouragement she needed.

By the time she met Jasper, Lane had turned into a gym rat. She was a different person, and the exercise had given her something besides her studies to focus on. She never missed a day. With Shannon's help, she started making better food choices, and before long, she had dropped four sizes.

She'd probably seen Jasper on campus or in the dorms at some point over the past year, but she knew the guys at her school weren't looking for girls like her, so she didn't pay attention. That day, though, after a lengthy week of finals, she headed into the nearly empty cafeteria and poured herself a cup of coffee. It was still early enough for scrambled eggs and a banana and maybe reading something that wasn't about the ancient Mayans. She had filled her tray and was making her way to a table in the back when the door opened and a small group of guys walked in, laughing loudly the way immature college guys did.

Something about group laughter always made Lane cringe.

She sat down as they approached the food line, where a large woman named Janice served them biscuits and gravy. Lane's eyes darted from her tray to the group of guys when she noticed one of them seemed a little older, the one the others followed. He wore black athletic shorts and a Bulls T-shirt and had a swath of chocolate-brown hair cut short at the edges.

Something about him was vaguely familiar. Maybe she'd passed him in the stairwell or seen him on campus. Or maybe he was one of the guys whose attention she avoided as she still, after all these shed pounds, kept her head down, her eyes on the floor, her nose in a book like the one she was reading now.

She didn't realize she was staring until his head turned and his eyes met hers.

Snapping back to the page in front of her, feeling caught and vulnerable, she pretended to read as the guys found a table kitty-corner from where she sat. They were loud and made it impossible to concentrate, but Lane knew her inability to focus had less to do with the noise and more to do with the deep-brown eyes she could sense were focused on her.

She ate quickly, wishing for a chance to escape, finding it difficult to hide when she was the only other person in the cafeteria besides the workers.

Lane had gotten good at staying firmly planted behind the wall she'd built around herself. She'd mastered the art of putting out a leave-me-alone vibe, which felt safer than putting herself out there, but this guy didn't seem fazed by it.

Looking back, she imagined that's the only reason she and Jasper had ever even spoken. Lane certainly wouldn't have made the first move. If he hadn't sauntered over with that casual nonchalance and quiet confidence, she would've left the cafeteria that day unscathed.

But that's not what happened.

He did saunter over, and he stood beside her table without speaking. When she glanced up from her book, she threw a brick on the top of her wall, but somehow it fell right back down to the ground.

"I've been trying to get you to notice me for months." He sat across from her. "You never look up from those books of yours. What is it today? Shakespeare?"

She held out her book. A mystery she'd been meaning to read for weeks. He looked surprised.

"You're Lane."

He knew her name? Just the realization of it set off something inside her—something unfamiliar and a little bit exciting.

"We had Western civ together."

"We did?"

He laughed. "Ouch."

"Sorry." She didn't have an explanation. She didn't look around during class. She didn't look around during anything.

"It's okay—I get it. You're too cool for guys like me."

She closed her book and forced herself to look at him. "This is a joke, right? Did your friends send you over here?" It had to be a joke—a prank, something she'd never get used to no matter how many times she found herself in the middle of one. What would it be this time? More snorting at her? Or maybe they'd bet this guy fifty bucks he wouldn't come over and talk to her, the fat girl.

His eyes held her hostage, a smile playing at the corners of his lips. She assumed he was ready to burst out laughing, but instead, he positioned his hands on the table barely an inch from hers. "The first time I noticed you, you were standing at your mailbox. You dropped your backpack on the ground and tore open an envelope and the look on your face when you read whatever was inside—I think about that look every single day."

Was he serious? Her stomach wobbled just thinking this might not be a prank.

"I've almost talked to you a hundred times, but today, last full day in the dorm, I figured it was now or never. So what do you say, Lane Kelley? Will you have dinner with me tonight?"

She glanced at his friends, none of whom seemed remotely interested in anything but the food on their plates. They hadn't put him up to this?

Things like this didn't happen to her.

"Are you sure you've got the right person?"

His brow furrowed only slightly, and his face lit with a smile. "Oh, I'm sure." The way he looked at her, like she was someone to adore, was intoxicating.

"I'll have dinner with you on one condition," she finally said, aware that her wall was at great risk.

"Name it."

"You have to tell me your name."

He'd kissed her hand then behind a mischievous smile, a hint of their future together, a future of stolen kisses and comfortable touches, the kind that come from spending countless hours together. Jasper had become the one person in the world she'd trusted, the one person she loved above everyone else.

She'd given him everything.

The thought shamed her now, standing on the deck of his giant house, the one he shared with her only sister. How could she have been so naive?

In that moment, she looked at Ryan just as he looked at her. He didn't turn away. He had that same confidence Jasper always had, as if he knew exactly what to do to make her knees weak.

That was enough of a reason to run straight home to Chicago and never turn back.

She and Jasper had been so good for so long, but now every memory of him left a sour taste in her mouth.

If she didn't get ahold of herself, she knew the exact same thing would happen to her memories of Ryan Brooks, and those were some of the only happy memories she had.

CHAPTER

19

TO SAY THAT DINNER at Jasper and Lindsay's was awkward could've possibly been the understatement of the century. Ryan sat at the large outdoor table between Hailey and Jack with Lane across from him. In his pocket, he could feel her phone buzzing with the kind of madness that demanded attention. How did she function with this constant noise? It was like having a small child tapping on your shoulder nonstop until you gave him exactly what he wanted.

Across from him, Lane pushed food around on her plate. Today the friendliness of the family and friends seemed like a put-on, like everyone was trying to ignore the air, thick with tension.

"How's Nate?" Hailey hated silence, so she was going to jabber her way through it despite the fact that he'd given her an update on Nate's condition that very morning.

His sister had never done well with conflict or tension. She chattered on to fill the space, constantly wanting to make sure everyone was okay. She'd always been that way, maybe because when they were kids, everyone was not okay.

"The doctors are hopeful," Dottie said from her end of the table. "And so are we. That's why we decided to go on with Sunday dinner. We're believing God is going to take care of Nate."

"Amen." Aunt Clarice's reply was somber, her face grave.

Ryan had no doubt they truly believed Nate was in God's hands no matter what happened, and they'd taught him to believe it too. But that didn't keep him from praying for a miracle.

"Lane, some of Nate's friends are at the hospital now, but don't forget it's your turn to sit with him this evening," Dottie said.

Lane's fork clanked on the plate. "Mom. I'm heading back to Chicago today, remember?"

Dottie swallowed the bite of food in her mouth and took a sip of water. "I thought perhaps you'd reconsider."

"I can't. My presentation is tomorrow. I told you this."

"You're really going back when you don't know if he'll be okay?" Jeremy's question was a valid one, but Ryan could practically see the inner turmoil Lane suffered as her phone continued to vibrate in his pocket.

Lane stared at her plate. "I was given a second chance at a big presentation. I have to be there tomorrow." Her words were quiet, barely audible, as the rest of the table weighed in on her choice to leave.

"Can't they Skype you in or something?" Noah asked. "I mean, you're on that stupid phone twenty-four hours a day anyway."

"Oh, give her a break. Work is important. If she didn't care about her job, we'd all be talking about how lazy she is." Emily had always been the reasonable one.

"It's just a shame how young people's priorities are so out of whack these days." Aunt Clarice had always been the most condescending of the bunch.

On and on it went, and Ryan watched the words pile on top of Lane one after the other, like too-heavy weights she didn't have the strength to carry.

Debates like this weren't uncommon at Sunday dinner. If it

wasn't religion, it was politics. If it wasn't politics, it was the way schools were run nowadays.

But Ryan knew how much Lane hated to be the center of attention, and having the debate focused on her was probably excruciating.

The noise had escalated, the remarks growing more and more heated, when finally a voice at Ryan's right spoke out louder and firmer than all the others.

"Let her go."

Heads turned toward Lindsay, who had stood and was now looking at Lane.

Mousy, spineless Lindsay sticking up for Lane, of all people? It was enough to shut the whole table up.

"She has a life in Chicago—a job that depends on her. Don't make her feel guilty for going back to it," Lindsay said, still facing Lane.

Slowly Lane looked up, her eyes meeting her sister's, and while Ryan expected to see gratitude there, he saw something else instead.

Lane pushed her chair away from the table and turned to Lindsay. "I don't need anyone to stick up for me." Her chin quivered. "Especially not you."

She threw her napkin down on her plate and walked back the same way they'd come, around the side of the house and toward the front yard. But she had no phone and no transportation.

Now what? Did he follow her?

One of Lindsay's friends, Morgan, stood and put an arm around Lindsay. "That was pretty awful of her."

Lindsay sniffed, then excused herself, walking toward the house with Morgan at her side.

"When will those girls ever move past their differences?" Dottie sighed. She didn't even try to make excuses for them. Not this time.

Ryan's eyes trailed down to the end of the table where Jasper sat smugly, eating his burger and sipping his beer as if nothing unusual had happened. Ryan had only gotten bits and pieces of what had happened over the years: Jasper and Lane were dating. He dumped her for Lindsay. That was the gist of it, but judging by the hurt in Lane's eyes, there was more to the story.

"I'm her ride," Ryan told Hailey.

"Go."

He quietly excused himself, and when he walked around to the front of the house, he found her standing near his bike, her back to him. He assumed from her hunched-over posture that she was crying.

So he did what he always did when the emotions were too thick and the load too heavy to bear.

"Wanna egg the house?"

She quickly wiped her cheeks dry, obviously embarrassed he'd found her this way. "What?"

"Not raw eggs, either. I'm thinking we take Hailey's deviled eggs and just chuck them at the front door. No one eats them anyway—they're really gross and they smell—so that's a bonus."

Lane laughed, though he could still see broken sadness in her eyes.

"Look, Lane, I know it's been a while, but if you need to talk—"

She shook her head, stopped him with an upheld hand. "It's fine. I need to get home. I'm just feeling overwhelmed and out of place." Her eyes turned glassy. "But what else is new?"

He stilled. He knew she was leaving—this wasn't a surprise—but how did he tell her he didn't want her to go? That he wanted to know all the things that made her sad, all the things that made her laugh? That he wanted to reach over and wipe those tears away?

What would it take to earn the right to touch her? He was doing a poor job of getting the idea of her out of his head.

They stood in the quiet for a few long seconds. "What do you need?"

She looked at him for a moment as if she had no idea how to answer that question. He got the impression she wasn't accustomed to asking for help.

"Actually, could you take me to the hospital? And then help me figure out a way to get Otis back to my parents' house?"

He studied her. It was as if every buoyant, floating feeling she'd had on their motorcycle ride had been tied down like a balloon to a post.

"I want to see Nate before I go."

"Of course." He handed her the helmet, his mind racing through a script of things he would not say out loud. "Hop on."

20

LANE ARRIVED BACK in Chicago early in the evening, knowing it would be an all-nighter, but hopefully the kind that left her feeling energized and not exhausted.

She'd said good-bye to Nate and made Ryan promise to text if anything with his condition changed. He told her he didn't text, but he'd be happy to call her.

"You don't text?" She heard the surprise in her own voice. She'd never met anyone who didn't text. Even Mrs. Pim had mastered the art and she was many years older than Ryan.

"I prefer actual communication," he'd told her. She could practically hear the wink in his tone. Was he trying to get under her skin?

"Texting *is* actual communication," she'd argued.

"Is it, though?" They'd been sitting in Nate's room having this conversation when a nurse walked in to check the machines her brother was hooked up to.

Lane stole a glimpse of Ryan, who watched the nurse's every move, until the second he caught her staring and she had to look away.

She could not figure him out, but one thing was certain—he was bad news.

It doesn't matter how charming he is or for how many years you've known him. He will break your heart.

When the nurse walked out, he wore that lazy smile on his face, the one she'd started to think about in the moments she was supposed to be working.

"Why do you have that goofy grin on your face?"

He looked at her then, the kind of gaze that told her he knew too much about what she wasn't saying aloud. "Some moments just wouldn't translate in a text."

Like the unspoken flirtation he seemed intent on having with her?

He had a point. She'd never felt vulnerable or exposed because of a text, but that's exactly how he made her feel in that moment.

Later, when she was leaving, she put her number in that ridiculous grandpa phone of his, put his number in her phone, and thanked him for his help.

"Think about my offer, okay? I'll keep looking for someone else, but I'd rather hire you."

"Ryan, you know I'd love to help you, but there's just so much going on at work."

He nodded, but she could see her words stung.

"I'll have my assistant send over some names for you, though."

Another nod. He opened her car door and Otis hopped inside. "Take care of yourself, okay?"

"Of course," she said, her heart pounding. What should she do? Should she hug him? Should she just jump in the car and drive away, knowing there was a good chance another ten years could pass before she saw him again?

He stood on the other side of her door, latched on to it, looking at her a little too intently. Maybe he didn't know how to say goodbye either; after all, he was the one who'd gone off to the Army without telling any of them he was leaving.

She got in the car and he shut the door, then knelt down, bringing his eyes level with hers. "Let me know about the job, okay?"

She nodded. "And keep me posted about Nate."

She'd driven away then, leaving Harbor Pointe and all its unwanted emotional turmoil in the wind.

Seeing Jasper had been a healthy, if painful, dose of reality. Life for her did not include love. It included simple rules, and if she followed them, she would be okay.

While Ryan held her phone hostage, Marshall had called four times and sent a whole string of "Why aren't you responding?" and "Where are you, Lane?" texts. She sent him a quick message that she was on her way back and she'd let him know when she got in.

He'd responded with Finally. I don't appreciate you blowing me off today.

She tossed the phone on the passenger seat of her car, wishing she had the guts to throw it out the window. Ryan's words raced through her mind.

"I don't know how you get anything done with that thing in your pocket," he'd said when he handed it back to her.

Lane had frowned. "It tells me exactly what I need to get done. It's my lifeline."

He narrowed his eyes and took his time before he responded. "Disagree."

"You wouldn't understand. Look at the phone you carry." He seemed unfazed by her judgmental comment. Scratch that. He seemed amused by it as though he knew he was pressing her buttons and a part of him liked it.

She told herself she didn't care about his opinion. What did he know? He didn't even work weekends. He probably spent Saturday and Sunday lying in a canoe somewhere, while she slaved away for clients like Mrs. Pim who scheduled huge dinner parties "in three weeks" and who needed "a completely new outdoor space before I let anyone over here."

Never mind that every space in Mrs. Pim's restaurants was nearly brand-new and perfectly put together. The woman simply loved to change her mind.

She didn't doubt Ryan had worked hard on renovating the

cottages at Cedar Grove, but he had a nonchalance about him, the kind that suggested his feathers were rarely ruffled, his pace was rarely hurried, and his work was most likely not hard for him.

She didn't know if she could ever respect someone who didn't value hard work. Perhaps it was his fatal flaw. She'd cling to it in an attempt to rid her memory of the way she felt on the back of his bike with her arms wrapped around his muscular torso.

Now, standing in the elevator that would take her to her apartment, Otis quietly panting beside her, she turned the phone over in her hand. There was nothing wrong with building a career and wanting to be successful at it. People in Harbor Pointe weren't career people. They had businesses supported by tourists. Jobs that were different from careers. They would never understand.

Besides, work wouldn't hurt her. Not the way people could. It was safe and she was in control, just the way she liked it.

She got off the elevator and Otis pulled her down the hallway toward her door, where she saw Chloe sitting on the floor, piles of papers strewn out in front of her. She'd missed so many texts and phone calls from Chloe while Ryan had her phone, she felt even more behind now.

Her assistant glanced up when she heard Lane's footfalls in the hallway. "Oh, thank goodness." She started gathering the papers and stacking them in a neat pile. "I was starting to think you were never going to get here."

Lane reached her apartment and opened the door, wishing she'd left Harbor Pointe that morning like she planned or, better yet, days ago. Before the uncomfortable dinner with Lindsay and Jasper. Before the memories of life in that town. Before the motorcycle ride that had sent her emotions into a tailspin.

She would've been much better off.

"We have a lot to do," she said as she dragged her bags inside, Chloe trailing close behind.

"First things first," Chloe said. "How's your brother?"

Lane threw her keys in a small glass bowl on the table near her door, kicked off her shoes, and set down her bags, all the while trying hard not to internalize Chloe's question. "He's the same."

Chloe paused. "No change at all?"

Lane looked away. Chloe's genuine concern seemed to have triggered something inside her. Her assistant was the only person who knew anything about her life. And while she still knew very little—and would hopefully never find out about Lane's humiliating past—she did care about Lane the way a friend would.

She supposed she valued that a lot more now than she had before her stay in Harbor Pointe.

"Are you okay?"

Lane could sense Chloe's eyes on her.

It wasn't good news and she knew it, though she hadn't allowed herself to think about the fact that the longer Nate stayed in this coma, the worse it was.

What if he died?

It was like the thought had only really occurred to her now, in that moment, removed from it all. She'd assumed he'd be fine. Told herself it was so. Perhaps she'd been bewitched by her mother's blind optimism. She'd even taken to talking to him when it was her turn to visit. She figured he'd answer all her questions when he woke up.

Her heart started to race, and her fingers trembled as she was overcome with the most profound fear she'd ever felt in her life.

"Lane?"

She dropped onto her plush sofa, her chest hollow as if there were a large, cold hole carved out of the center of it. *What if he dies?*

"You look like you're going to be sick." Chloe sat down next to her but kept her distance. She knew Lane didn't like to be touched.

"I'll be right back." Lane stumbled toward the bathroom. She couldn't fall apart in front of Chloe.

She closed the door and flipped on the light, catching a glimpse of herself in the mirror. The bags under her eyes were more noticeable than usual and she looked tired. Exhausted even.

Somehow the trip to Harbor Pointe had sucked the life right out of her.

Her phone buzzed, pulling her attention. Or maybe it was the constant connection that had sucked the life out of her. That would've been Ryan's theory.

She looked down at her phone, still taking slow, deep breaths. Marshall.

Home? I'm going to stop by and check on your progress.

Her head spun, her heart pounding as she struggled for the next breath. She closed the lid and sat on the toilet, phone still in her hands, fingers cold.

Her stomach turned. Marshall could not come over. He would just make her second-guess herself.

He should know by now she didn't need him to check on her progress.

She dropped her head down between her knees and did the only thing she could think to do—she prayed.

It was a short, burdened prayer, one that probably didn't even make sense and one she had no business praying given her distance from God these days.

But even a quiet "Help me, Lord," began to calm her panicked heart, and her breathing eventually evened out.

She texted Marshall: Just got in. Don't come over. Too much work to do.

So much work to do.

She splashed water on her face, steadied herself, and focused on what had to be done. She had a job to do, and if she wanted to land that account, she needed to pull herself together.

Just breathe.

She dabbed some concealer under her eyes, pulled her hair up into a loose bun, and emerged from the bathroom, wholly different from when she went in, even if that buzz of anxiety still lingered.

Chloe sat in the same spot on the couch, watching Lane, wide-eyed, as she sat down next to her and pulled the laptop out of her bag.

Lane glanced at her unmoving assistant. "Are we going to work?"

"Are you okay?"

Lane toggled her laptop to life. "Of course."

"You didn't look okay."

"How do I look now?" Lane opened the mood board she'd begun for JB Sweet.

"Creepily better." Chloe frowned. "Did you have a panic attack?"

Lane patted Chloe's closed laptop. "Work. We have lots to do."

"You didn't answer my question."

"Have you ever known me to have a panic attack, Chloe?" The last thing she needed was for her assistant to lose faith in her. She wasn't one of those people with anxiety, the kind who needed medication. Whatever had just happened, it was not a panic attack.

She was born for this—it was time to prove it. No racing heart was going to tell her otherwise.

Lane turned her attention to the images on the screen: a business space that was elegant without being stuffy and trendy without being cliché. She pulled up Marshall's notes on her designs.

"How many of these changes were requested by the client and how many were Miles's idea?" Lane scrolled through the e-mail Marshall had sent with his thoughts.

"It's been a weird week, Lane," Chloe said. "JB and Marshall took Miles to lunch on Friday."

She thought of her own lunch on Friday—standing at the counter of the cottage Ryan had been so excited to show her. It was almost like he'd been waiting to share this piece of himself with her. She wasn't used to feeling included like that. But while she'd been smitten by the possibilities for Cedar Grove, Miles had been swooping in to steal her promotion.

"But these changes aren't from Miles. He's doing something completely different. Apparently they're letting him present a separate idea to Solar."

"What?" Lane stood. "Why would they do that? We're supposed to be a team."

Chloe shrugged. "I don't know. I guess they see value in giving them a variety of options to choose from."

This was not the way they'd ever worked before. What had changed? "There's . . . talk."

Lane pressed her lips together and faced Chloe, hands on her hips. "What kind of talk?"

"That they've already decided about the promotion."

Heat rushed to Lane's cheeks.

"They haven't announced it, though, so the way I see it, if you knock this one out of the park, you still have a great chance."

Lane plopped down on the couch again and let out a heavy sigh. Her phone chirped at her.

"Maybe you should put that away," Chloe said.

"It's Julia Baumann," Lane said, reading a series of tweets that seemed pointed directly at Lane. "She acts like she landed Solar already."

"And she wants the world to know it," Chloe said.

"She's very confident." Lane glanced at her new, unfinished design. She'd been so in love with the original images when she'd finished them, but all of Julia's tweets combined with Marshall's "concerns" had led to a complete overhaul—one that wasn't even close to being done.

The new design didn't give her that same feeling of excitement, but she thought it was more in line with what the Solar execs wanted, so she was going with it.

She turned the laptop around and showed it to Chloe. "What do you think?"

Chloe's eyes landed on the screen, then darted back to Lane. "What happened to it?"

"I fixed it."

Chloe took the computer and studied the image. "It looks so . . . sterile."

Lane could feel the bubble of panic return to her center. "Really? I don't think so."

"I thought we were going for upscale trendy?" Chloe had spent hours helping on the campaign. She knew Lane's designs almost as well as Lane did. "What happened to the bicycle wall?"

"Things . . . changed. This is better."

"But it's not you. Actually this looks like something Miles would pitch."

Lane took the laptop back. "I designed it, so that makes it me."

Chloe looked away. "I'm not trying to be difficult, Lane. You know I just want what's best for you."

"Landing this account and proving I deserve that promotion are what's best for me. So let's concentrate on finishing up the new designs so we at least have a fighting chance."

"I just don't want to see you trade away your aesthetic to land this account. Your artistic eye is what people love most about you. Miles doesn't have that, and honestly neither does Julia Baumann."

"Marshall said the client might respond better to something more sleek. That was his impression after the preliminary meeting last week."

"Lane, how long has it been since you've heard Marshall give one good design idea?"

Lane frowned. "What are you saying?"

"I'm saying Marshall needs you to make him look better. It's *your* gut instinct that's gotten him where he is today."

"Then why would he question my designs now?"

Chloe shrugged. "I don't know, but I don't think you should change a thing. Give your original presentation and get some sleep tonight. You've earned it."

Lane stared at the rendering on her screen, remembering the way she felt when she finished the original designs, the ones she was going to pitch last week. She'd been so excited about those, and a part of her still believed if she'd been able to give the pitch, Solar would've loved them too.

Had she been obsessing over new designs simply to keep herself occupied while she was dealing with the turmoil of being back in Harbor Pointe? Or had she allowed Julia Baumann and Miles to get inside her head? How easily they'd revealed her insecurities.

She needed to stay busy—always busy—but what if Chloe was right? What if all her busyness was for nothing and the designs were fine as they were?

Chloe turned her own laptop back toward Lane. "This is you, Lane."

The image of Lane's original design—trendy, youthful, modern—shone back at her, a reminder of how it felt to truly be proud of her work.

Lane's phone buzzed. Another social media update from Innovate. *At this hour?*

Lane clicked over to view Julia's most recent post—a photo of her standing in front of a huge presentation board depicting a very masculine-looking room, decked out with deep jewel tones and accented with gold. It was ornate, rich-looking, and there was nothing particularly special about it at all. It looked like every other business out there.

Had Lane misread Solar altogether? Maybe the young executives wanted to be taken more seriously.

Chloe looked up from her own phone, where she'd obviously just seen the same image.

"There's a Solar logo in the corner of that presentation board." Lane squinted at the photo.

"The curtains have fringe on them," Chloe said dryly.

Lane read the caption. "'Innovate goes life-size for its clients, especially the sunny ones.'" She glanced at Chloe, who rolled her eyes, but Lane didn't know how to be flip about her competition. It only made her want to do better. She had an overwhelming desire to win, to be the best. But Innovate was their biggest competitor and Julia was no junior designer.

"How do I compete with this?" Lane asked, clicking her phone's screen off.

"Maybe you should turn off your notifications for a while," Chloe said. "You shouldn't focus on Julia Baumann or Innovate or any of this. You should do a real Lane Kelley design—that's what you're known for. Wouldn't you rather win the account without sacrificing your own artistry?"

The thought stung. Of course she would. But part of her job was giving the clients what they wanted.

"I'm going to keep going on these," Lane said, turning her attention back to the new designs on her laptop. "I need to make sure it's perfect."

Chloe got up and walked toward the kitchen. She grabbed a Coke from the refrigerator—something Lane kept in there only for her—then plopped back down on the oversize white sofa and cracked it open. "It was already perfect."

But Lane had moved on.

She didn't have time to linger on old ideas. Not when she had twelve hours before the Solar meeting and about fourteen hours of work to do. She began working with the design program on her computer, creating an animated digital walk-through, first of a sample reception area and then of the office suite and conference room. Each had its own unique traits, but they were perfectly branded in a way that Lane felt reflected a sleeker version of her original impressions of Solar.

Chloe looked up sources while Lane worked on the creative design. Lane moved quickly, opening tab after tab on her computer, checking with suppliers she wished kept middle-of-the-night hours and doing her best to guess prices on the items she couldn't confirm in the moment.

She made a pot of coffee and drank until it was gone, then felt wired and high-strung, but she couldn't take a break. She didn't have time.

Every once in a while, she'd think of Nate in his hospital bed or Lindsay and Jasper in their pseudo-mansion or Ryan Brooks and the way his hand on the small of her back had seemed to steady her, but she forced herself to stay focused.

Marshall texted until about one in the morning, then—thank goodness—he must've gone to sleep or given up because she wasn't quick enough in texting him back.

About 4 a.m., Chloe drifted off to sleep on the couch, the way she had so many times before, and Lane wondered if she should buy her assistant a week away somewhere. The massage was kind, but Chloe deserved more for how hard she worked. And like Lane, she never took any vacation time.

Without Chloe, Lane had no friends, and she didn't want to run her off too. If Chloe got tired of working these long hours or suddenly realized she wanted to have a life outside JB Sweet, Lane would be left alone.

Completely, utterly alone.

And yet, Lane had made the choice to be a career woman—and career women had their careers. She'd always found a way to take solace in that.

Why, after all this time, did it suddenly seem like it wasn't enough?

Just before nine that morning, Lane sat on the sofa outside the conference room at JB Sweet with Chloe, her laptop, and a to-go cup of coffee from Dillon's, her favorite little café near her loft.

"Did you go to sleep at all last night?" Chloe asked. Her assistant always looked put together, but then, she did run her own fashion blog. She just had a way about her. Today she wore a mod-style navy-blue dress with white polka dots and a red belt. If Lane didn't know better, she never would've guessed Chloe had gotten herself ready in about twenty minutes because she overslept after Lane had already woken her up twice.

"I might've drifted off for a few minutes," Lane said.

Chloe shook her head. "I don't know how you do that. It's like you're Superwoman or something."

Lane didn't know if Chloe's comment should make her feel as gratified as it did, but she couldn't help it. She worked hard. She was always busy. She wore that busy like a badge of honor, hoping someone would recognize it.

"You feel good about this?" Chloe asked.

Lane had completely overhauled her original design. Her new presentation was flawless. She was going to land this account. She nodded.

The elevator opened and Marshall appeared, that typical stoic expression on his face. Marshall was all business. It was a wonder he'd ever asked her out in the first place, and sometimes Lane wondered if he approached their relationship the same way he approached business deals. She was surprised a contract wasn't involved.

Lately she could feel him getting impatient with her. They'd been dating five months, and apparently in his world, that meant they should be sleeping together. Lane had put him off, though, for so many reasons. He wouldn't wait much longer, she was sure. But she'd be fine if their romantic attachment slowly faded away.

"You're back."

She stood, feeling like she should probably hug him, though he didn't make a move to suggest he felt the same. Instead, he motioned for her to sit back down, then took the chair next to her. "Are you ready?"

"She's ready," Chloe answered before Lane could.

"Good. Can I see the new designs?" Marshall leaned toward Lane, who held her computer and portfolio tightly on her lap, feeling suddenly possessive of her work.

"No."

His eyebrows popped up, surprise on his face. "Funny. Let's see them." He laughed as if she were kidding.

"You can see them during the presentation," Lane said.

At her side, she could feel Chloe's shock, but she kept her eyes on Marshall.

"Lane, this is my name on the line here too." Marshall lowered his voice. "I need to be confident you've got this right."

"I can make sure everyone in there knows these designs are my own. I can keep you out of it completely so it's just my name on the line," Lane said, thinking about what that meant. She'd worked so hard to build a reputation she could be proud of. Her name now represented certain things in the design community, and though that community might be somewhat small, it was where she lived and worked and spent her days.

Was she really willing to put her name on these new designs? Did she believe in them that much?

She glanced at Chloe, who stared at her in shock.

"Why the hostility, Lane?" Marshall leaned back in his seat.

"No hostility," Lane said. "I just know the team is now under Miles's direction and they'll be presenting a separate design, so I'd like to go on record with this one as my own. You can put your name on his."

Marshall shook his head and stood, peering down at her. "We'll talk about this later." He left her on the sofa with a racing pulse and sweaty palms.

Once he was out of earshot, Chloe let out what sounded like a laugh. "That was awesome." She jumped to her feet. "Did you see the look on his face?"

Lane's nerves turned into an involuntary laugh of her own. "What did I just do?"

"You stood up for yourself." Chloe grinned. "It was epic."

Lane glanced at the oversize, sleek silver clock on the wall. It was already nine. "I should've listened to you all along, Chlo."

Her assistant sat again. "What do you mean?"

"I want to go back to the original design."

Chloe's face brightened. "You do?"

"They're going to call us in any second, and I didn't bring all the visuals for the original design."

"You sure about that?" Chloe glanced at Lane's portfolio with a raised brow.

Lane unzipped the sides and opened the black leather case. Much of her presentation would be done digitally, but Lane still loved a tangible visual aid or two. On the top of the pile were the new designs—the mood board for a sleek, mature business space that resembled any other.

Chloe picked them up to reveal the original boards, the ones that had been on display last Monday, the ones Ashton apparently told Marshall they liked. Why had Marshall gotten her so far off track if the Solar team liked the original direction? Did he want her to fail?

If the Solar execs didn't prefer her designs after all, then she wouldn't land the account. And while that idea made her a little sick to her stomach, Chloe was right—she'd rather lose an account with a design she believed in than win it with a design she didn't even want to execute.

"Did you put these in here?" Lane asked, moving the original designs to the front of her portfolio.

Chloe smiled.

"Thank you." Lane made sure her smile was genuine to match her gratitude.

"Lane?" Marshall appeared from around the corner. "You can go on in. We'll be there in a minute."

Lane glanced at Chloe. "I hope this isn't the worst decision I've ever made."

$\mathcal{21}$

RYAN WOKE UP EARLY MONDAY MORNING. If things went according to plan, this would be the week Esther was completed and Cedar Grove was ready for finishing touches. He'd already hired a crew of painters, but he was still hoping Lane would tell him what color paint to use.

It kept him up last night, wondering how he was going to pull any of this off. Maybe it was too lofty a dream. He didn't want to guilt Lane into helping, but he sure could use her artistic eye right about now.

His phone rang. He didn't recognize the number on the screen of his flip phone, but when he answered, he heard Lydia Beckett's voice on the other end.

"Ryan, how are you?"

"I'm doing well. How are you? How's DJ?"

"Fine. We're all fine. Just had a couple of questions for you about Harbor Pointe. I was trying to come up with activities for DJ, and I had a few ideas I wanted to run by you."

Ryan had already thought of that. Drum's son was a rambunc-tious six-year-old who deserved to have the week of his life. He'd arranged water sports rentals with Noah, a fishing excursion with Tucker Delancey, and if his mom said it was okay, a hot-air balloon ride on their last night in Harbor Pointe.

He relayed his plans to Lydia, who naturally told him it was all "too much."

"At least let me pay you, Ryan. You're giving us this whole week in your cottage for free—don't think we believe for one second someone isn't footing the bill."

It was the least he could do for the family of the man who'd saved his life.

Lydia's voice shook as she said a quiet thank-you, and at the sound of her tears, a lump got stuck in his throat.

This was his dream for Cedar Grove—to rent it out, run a good business, and boost the town's economy, of course, but along with that, to offer vacations for the families of the men he'd served with, many of whose wives were now widows and single mothers.

It seemed fitting that his very first week, Cedar Grove would be filled with these families.

Maybe if he did it long enough and for enough veterans and their families, he'd stop feeling guilty that he hadn't come home in a body bag.

"Sounds like everything is just going to be perfect, Ryan," Lydia said. "You have no idea how much good you're doing. Drum would be so thankful to you."

He couldn't respond for fear of his voice breaking. It was Ryan who was thankful to Drum. The man's bravery had kept Ryan safe—one more reason he was determined to use his life well and not turn out like his dad. After several seconds of silence, Lydia said good-bye and Ryan ended the call, more anxious than ever to make sure everything was perfect for their stay in Harbor Pointe.

If he could do for these families what the Kelleys had done for him—what this town had done for him—it would all be worth it.

He helped Jerry unload boxes of tile for Esther's bathroom, his mind wandering back to the day he'd returned from Afghanistan after two tours that had lasted a total of five years. The bus dropped him off at the Newman station, and from there, he planned to find a ride to anywhere else.

There weren't many from Newman who went off to fight in the war. Ryan and one other kid, Tommy Kemper. He and Tommy had a lot in common, thinking back on it now. Neither had many prospects—no money for college, no great job waiting for them—and both wanted out of their parents' houses more than anything in the world.

Tommy's mom had done her best for him, but the string of losers she'd brought home to play house with over the years had turned Tommy into a withdrawn, brooding kid with a chip on his shoulder. Ryan was one of the few people the guy had ever even talked to. They'd enlisted the same day, after hearing an ROTC recruiter at an assembly at Newman High.

That's my ticket out of this dump, Ryan had thought.

Tommy must've thought the same thing because after the speech, they both found themselves waiting to sign whatever paperwork the recruiter had that promised them freedom from life as they knew it.

Tommy didn't make it back to Newman. He was killed in action.

When Ryan returned, he wore his guilt like an invisible cloak, wrestling with the whole idea that he'd been spared when a man as good as Drum, a man with a wife and a son, had died just months before.

Much to Ryan's surprise, the mayor of Newman, Gerald Jeffries, met him at the bus station.

"If you don't mind, we've put together a little welcome home for you," Mayor Jeffries said.

"Oh, that's not necessary, sir."

"We heard about what you did over there, Brooks," the mayor said. "Mighty proud of you. And we're thankful for your service."

"Just doing my job, sir."

The mayor picked up his duffel bag. "Follow me."

Ryan didn't argue. He didn't much feel like going to a welcome home party, but it was thoughtful, and he'd never been Newman's pride and joy before.

He'd been wounded only a few days after he found out the truth about Hailey's boyfriend—took it as a sign it was time to go home and protect the family he should've been protecting all along.

As he entered the Post House—an old post office that had been converted into a reception hall—Ryan used a cane and walked at a much slower pace than he used to. The doctors said he would heal, but in that moment, he wasn't so sure.

The mayor led him into the reception hall, and the crowd that had gathered erupted into applause and cheering. Ryan stood just inside the room, facing a large, handwritten banner that read, *Welcome Home, Ryan Brooks*, and shook his head at the scene in front of him.

Never in a million years did he expect to make his hometown proud.

"Mr. Dobbins's fifth-grade class made the banner and the cheerleaders made the cupcakes. Hundreds and hundreds of cupcakes." The mayor clapped a hand on his back. "Can't promise they're edible, but it's the thought that counts." Mayor Jeffries led him through the crowd and Ryan recognized a number of familiar faces—former teachers who'd probably expected him to turn out like his dad, former classmates who'd aged ever so slightly, and at last his eyes fell on Hailey.

She bounded out of the throng of people and into his arms. "You're finally home." Her smile stretched the entire width of her face—it was the best view he'd had in years. Hailey had always been so cheerful and easy to please, even in the midst of their circumstances. He was relieved at the thought that maybe she was the same old Hailey. He'd been afraid that the way her life had turned out could've stolen that from her.

"Would you say a few words, Ryan?" Mayor Jeffries asked.

"Wow. I'm not really prepared."

The mayor hopped onto the small stage at one end of the room. "Come on up here." Then, into the microphone: "Would you all like to hear from our hometown hero?"

"I'm not a hero," he said, though he was pretty sure no one heard him.

"Go on, Ryan." Hailey gave him a shove. "Don't be modest. We're so proud of you."

Seconds later, he found himself on the stage, staring into a sea of faces, his mind full of nothing.

He inhaled a deep breath and let it out slowly, careful not to exhale into the microphone. "This is all pretty unbelievable." He glanced at Hailey, who was still beaming, hands clasped in front of her face. "But really, I'm not a hero. I'm just a guy who had a job to do."

The mayor leaned forward. "Anyone who risks his life to serve our country is a hero in our book. Am I right?"

The crowd cheered.

Ryan looked across the modest crowd. Newman was hardly even a village, but they'd managed to assemble a respectable number of people. For him.

One face was unmistakably absent, though.

His father's.

"The truth is, I feel kind of strange standing up here when so many of my buddies will never have the chance to stand again. Those men and women are the real heroes. Those are the ones we should be . . ."

A loud noise from the back of the room drew Ryan's—and everyone else's—attention. The door was flung open and a drunk Martin Brooks stumbled in. Ryan's eyes darted to Hailey, whose face quickly crumpled.

"Where's . . . my . . . son?" If Kenny Fowler hadn't caught him and set him upright, Martin would've fallen down.

There he was. The reason Ryan had left Newman in the first

place. A reminder of everything Ryan hoped he wouldn't become, on display for everyone in town to see. A reminder that the town had made a mistake. Ryan Brooks was no hero—he was just a kid who grew up in a trailer park with a dad who was a mean drunk and a mom who took off when he was too young to remember her.

He'd left the stage then, probably to the pitying stares of every well-meaning person in town.

The next day, he drove to Harbor Pointe for a weekend away, and he'd been there ever since, working for a local construction company, going to school, and only venturing into Newman when he had to.

Today was one of those times.

And he was dreading it.

After his morning breakfast at Hazel's, Ryan set his crew to work. He knew they could handle the day's tasks, but he wanted to be there while they did.

Unfortunately, he had something more important to tend to.

He hopped on his bike and headed out on the highway toward Newman, the same route he and Nate had ridden the day of the accident. Flashes of what he'd seen that night spun through his mind like an old-time movie reel edited to show only a few details at a time. Everything had happened so quickly, and he didn't have all the pieces.

He'd been putting off thinking about it, choosing instead to fantasize about winning over the girl who got away. But with Lane back in Chicago, he had nothing to focus on but facing the truth.

Walker and another deputy had come by his work site on Friday to probe him one more time, apparently not buying his story that he didn't know anything.

Noah was especially concerned with figuring out who was responsible for the accident, and with every day that passed, every day Nate didn't wake up, the urgency to pin the blame on someone only increased.

A week had passed. Ryan couldn't avoid his fears for another day. He had to find out the truth about what he remembered.

First he stopped at Scooter's and checked the parking lot, almost relieved when he didn't see any sign of his father. Drinking this early in the morning would be a new low, even for good old Martin.

Ryan didn't even know if his dad was still working. Had he been able to hold down a job? Every month when Ryan left an envelope of cash in his mailbox, he said a prayer that more of it went to food than to booze.

He drove into Newman and then to the outskirts, on the other side of a set of railroad tracks that ran through the small town. That cliché had never escaped him. He and Hailey really did come from the wrong side of the tracks. It was only when he was with the Kelley family that he let himself forget that for a while.

He crossed the tracks and entered the trailer park where he and Hailey had grown up.

He didn't want to be here. Didn't want to confirm his worst fears. Didn't want to be faced with the ethical dilemma that was sure to follow. But he had to. He had to know the truth.

Last night, his mind replayed the accident so many times he finally got up and watched *SportsCenter* to try to fill his brain with something other than the sound of metal meeting with asphalt. But once he lay down, it all came back again.

He'd been so close to finally falling asleep when the image of the blue truck jumped into his mind. He was lying on the road, staring at the taillights, and then the image narrowed and his eyes fell to the spot just above the right of the license plate. A red-and-white bumper sticker. He couldn't read the words, but the colors were unmistakable.

Now, as he turned in to the trailer park, he asked God to guide him, whether what he feared was true or not.

He rode through the rows of trailers toward the back of the park, to the lot where he'd lived for too long. Their trailer jutted up next to a large stretch of woods, which he and Hailey had often run to on the nights their dad turned mean. How many times had they run off and hidden in the cover of darkness?

How many times had Martin stood in the doorway yelling for them to come home? When they were young, they'd done as he said, out of fear mostly. But as Ryan got older, he realized they could stay hidden for hours, and in the morning, their dad wouldn't remember yelling after them at all.

By middle school, he'd met the Kelley family, and Ryan and Hailey never slept outside again. He'd call and Frank would pick them up at the bus station in Newman. Sometimes they'd stay in Harbor Pointe for several days at a time, especially during the summer.

Martin never once came looking for them.

How could he have left Hailey in this place without him? She was barely twelve when he left for the Army. All those nights he'd stood watch over her while she slept, oftentimes outside . . . No wonder she'd gotten herself out of there as fast as she could.

But her escape had only led to more pain. And Ryan vowed not to let that happen to her again.

Off to one side, he spotted the blue Ford F-150. The truck faced him, but a dark shadow of suspicion hovered overhead as if he already knew what he would find when he checked the back of the vehicle.

A part of him had known all along.

He told himself to check the back of the truck and go. No need to hang around. Get his proof and turn the man in.

As he parked his bike and killed the engine, though, the front door opened. The sound of that flimsy metal door unlatching set off something inside him—all his memories of those terrible nights rolled into one. The image of his father standing in the doorway, backlit by the dim lights inside, shouting into the darkness for Ryan and Hailey to get inside.

But he wasn't that scared kid anymore. He wasn't afraid of this man. He'd learned the truth since leaving Newman—that his worth wasn't wrapped up in Martin Brooks's words.

Still, sometimes the fear of turning out just like his father was so great it crippled him.

Martin stood at the door, glaring into the sun. "This is private property."

Ryan could hear the slur of his words.

"You can't be back here." He stumbled off the steps and into the yard until finally a splash of recognition washed across his face. "Ryan?" The word came out thin, barely a whisper, as if he couldn't believe his eyes. "What are you doing here?"

Ryan looked away. He hated this. He didn't want to stand in front of this man. He wanted to forget they were related and move past every vicious memory that still tortured him in the quiet nights. He'd done such a good job of shoving it all to the back of his mind and not thinking about it.

"I just need to check something on your truck," Ryan said.

"What's wrong with my truck?" Martin wore baggy jeans and an old gray T-shirt with a stain on the front. Did he ever do laundry? Shower? Or was drinking the only thing that mattered to this man?

"Nothing's wrong with it."

"Then what are you doing snooping around it?"

Ryan locked eyes with his dad, who glared at him, hands lifelessly hanging at his sides. "Where were you last Sunday?"

Martin looked away for a split second, then back at Ryan. "How am I supposed to remember last Sunday?"

"It's not a hard question, Dad."

"I don't know. Here, I guess?"

Ryan walked around the truck and there it was, above the license plate, just off to the right: a torn white bumper sticker with red lettering.

He stared at it for several long seconds, reliving the memory of the accident and its aftermath. The way Nate's bike sounded as it skidded across the pavement. The way Ryan lost control of his own bike and narrowly missed colliding with his friend. The sound of the machines that now breathed for Nate in a steady pattern of fabricated inhale and exhale.

His own father had been responsible for all of this, and a part of Ryan must have known the whole time. If it weren't for this man—this incompetent, miserable excuse for a human being—that terrible night never would've happened and the Kelley family wouldn't be perched on seats throughout Harbor Pointe Hospital praying their son would wake up from his coma.

"Do you know what you've done?" Ryan glared at his father. "Do you have any idea what you've done?"

"I don't know what you're talking about, Son."

"Don't call me that." Ryan shot out from behind the truck and grabbed his father by the shirt. Martin stumbled backward until they were edged up against the side of the trailer. "Don't you ever call me 'Son.'"

"What do you want me to call you then? Hero?"

The way he said the word—it reeked of disdain as if Ryan were the one who had something to be embarrassed about and not the other way around.

"Don't call me anything," Ryan said through clenched teeth.

Martin laughed like a bully in a schoolyard. "Kid, you're no better than me. Look at ya, ready to rip my throat out." He leaned closer. "You've got a temper just like your old man."

"I'm nothing like you."

Martin laughed and Ryan could smell the alcohol on his breath. "Keep tellin' yourself that, Son."

Ryan gripped harder, slamming his dad into the trailer. "You put someone in the hospital. Someone I care about. And you almost killed me."

"What are you talking about?"

"Don't pretend you can't remember running us off the road."

"I don't know what you're talking about."

"Last Sunday at dusk."

No response.

"I saw your truck. I was lying on the highway next to my bloody friend and you drove off."

Martin's face fell, eyes searching off in the distance until they landed on Ryan's bike. "Two motorcycles . . ."

Was he only now remembering? How drunk had he been?

"Two motorcycles. It was so dark." He pulled away from Ryan's grip and staggered toward the bike. "So dark."

Ryan studied the older Brooks for a few seconds, but he averted his eyes as the man processed the memory of what he'd done. It was too painful. He didn't have it in him to relive it one more time.

Martin turned back and faced Ryan, eyes glassy, forehead creased. "That was you?"

Ryan looked away.

"Are you going to turn me in? Is that why you're here?" Martin asked after a long pause.

"I should've turned you in a long time ago." The words sounded sharp on his own tongue.

"I promise I'll get help." Martin walked toward him. He'd been a hulk of a man when Ryan was a kid, but now he seemed smaller, thinner, a shell of who he'd once been.

And Ryan realized in that moment he wasn't scared of him at all.

"Yeah, I've heard that before."

"I mean it. I've saved some of that money you left in the mailbox. I can check myself in somewhere. Go to meetings. I'll get better—I swear."

Ryan didn't look at him. "How did you know it was me who left the money?"

Martin's chin quivered. "No one else cares if I live or die, Son."

"I don't want you to starve to death," Ryan said. "That doesn't mean I care about you."

Martin wavered as if his knees were buckling underneath him. By instinct, Ryan reached out and caught him just as the older man collapsed. Ryan dragged him, reeking of alcohol and cigarette smoke, toward the front of the trailer, then pulled him inside.

"I made a mess of everything, Ryan," Martin said, dropping his head into his hands. "I'm sorry about your friend."

"I'll give you a week to come clean. And if you don't step up and say something, then I will."

Ryan couldn't bring himself to console this man—not after all he'd done. And yet, standing there, looking down on him, he could sense something deep inside him telling him not to leave.

He knew that still, small voice. He'd learned to pay attention to it; he lived his life by it. But even so, in that moment, he did the only thing he could do.

He turned and walked away.

CHAPTER

22

LANE STOOD IN the conference room at JB Sweet, trying not to remember the last time she'd been there.

Miles was standing at the front of the room next to a large-screen television, where whatever new images he and the team had come up with would be displayed.

He sauntered over to her as she set her things down on the glass-topped table.

"No hard feelings, Lane, right?" He wore a stupid grin on his face.

"Of course not, Miles. You've been pushing your own ideas since we started this campaign." The fact that Marshall had warmed up to them, making her question her own work, was what really irritated her.

"Gotta fight for my ideas." His eyes darted to Chloe. "Anyway, good luck today."

Lane gave a nod and he walked off.

Marshall, Ashton, and the rest of the Solar team filed in. They chatted about some tech project they were working on as they sat down, most carrying coffee cups like the one Lane had thrown away on her way through the door.

Miles had returned to his seat in front of the big screen, wearing his slick salesman smile.

Once everyone was situated, Marshall stood and explained that they had a unique situation on their hands—two different pitches from two of JB Sweet's brightest and best. He glanced at Miles, who was still wearing the same pasted-on smile, and motioned for him to begin.

"Thank you, Marshall." Miles had competed on the speech team in college. He was very polished. A little too canned for Lane's taste, but nobody else seemed to mind.

"And thanks to the Solar team for allowing us to reconvene today after our unfortunate mishap last week." Miles glanced at Lane. "It's given our team time to go back and reevaluate our designs and really strengthen what we have for you."

He clicked a button on his laptop and an image appeared on the screen behind him. The mood board Lane had created for their original presentation.

Chloe grabbed her hand and squeezed. Lane swallowed, her mouth suddenly dry.

"As you can see, my team has taken a very trendy, very upscale approach, one that says, 'We don't take ourselves too seriously, but we take your business very seriously.'" Miles glanced at Lane. She'd coined that line during one of their earliest team meetings.

He'd stolen her presentation.

She looked at Marshall, who sat stoic, nodding along with Miles's pitch.

Miles had stolen everything right out from under her—her images, her words, her plans. She could go with the updated version she'd put together last night, but looking at her original pitch on the screen in front of her, it was clear which one was the winner.

As Miles finished speaking, Lane turned to Chloe, a *Now what?*

expression on her face. Lane's thoughts whirled as she searched for some solution neither of them could find.

"We love your take, man," Ashton said. "Looks like the extra week did you guys some good."

The extra week? Miles had changed nothing. He'd probably spent the whole week staying out late and sleeping in. Lane thought Solar wanted changes—had they seen any of the original designs? Maybe Marshall shut down the meeting before they even had a chance to get a preview.

So why did he tell her to change everything? Did he want Miles to be able to claim these ideas as his own? Did he, for some reason, not want Lane to become creative director? Did he know what he'd put her through?

Stay in control.

She would. She always did.

"The floor is all yours, Lane." She recognized Marshall's voice, but when she looked up to meet his eyes, a sharp pain ripped through her temples as if her brain were suddenly too big for her skull. The pressure in her head was so great it made her sick to her stomach.

She stood, unsteady on her feet, aware that Miles was wearing a smug grin, watching her struggle to get her bearings. She reached the front of the room, the idle chatter of transition slowly coming to an end.

She glanced down at her tablet, where her identical-to-Miles's presentation waited for her.

For a moment, the words stopped being words as the letters jumped off the tablet like a shark in a newly mastered 3-D movie, only less vibrant and a little fuzzy around the edges. She told herself to focus, to zero in on the speech she'd practically memorized, but a darkness began to cloud her vision at the edges and the pain in her temples blossomed into a brain-breaking headache.

The door of the conference room swung open and a stout man with a bushy white mustache walked in.

"JB." Marshall stood. Lane's head spun, her eyes unable to focus. Not JB. Not today.

"We didn't expect you today, sir." It was still Marshall.

The pressure in Lane's head pulsed. Her stomach rolled.

"Thought I'd check out our rising stars before I head down to Mexico for a few days."

Lane stared at the table, where her tablet and notebook began to blend together, barely listening as Marshall and JB discussed Miles's stolen pitch.

"We're about to hear from Lane Kelley." Marshall stopped talking, and in the pause, Lane lifted her head, knowing all eyes were on her. She thought her head might explode, the pain only increasing.

Just breathe.

Lane forced a smile, but as she did, she noticed her mouth felt strange—numb. She touched her cheek but couldn't feel her fingers on her skin. What was going on? Why was her face tingling? She looked at her fingers, turning her hand over in front of her, clenching and unclenching a fist she couldn't feel.

Why was her hand tingling now?

"Lane?" There was worry in Chloe's voice. "Lane? Are you okay?"

Her hand involuntarily covered her eyes, her forehead, as she applied pressure to where it hurt, which seemed to be everywhere. Nausea rolled through her like a child tumbling down a steep hill in the middle of summer, only without any of the laughter or joy.

"Lane?" The voices sounded hollow. They asked if she was all right. Did she need water? The right side of her face tingled. What did that mean? It wasn't good. Tingling numbness. Was she having a stroke?

"My face is numb," she heard herself say with a voice that didn't sound like her own. She tried again. "My face is numb." Was she slurring?

The tingling spread to the fingers of her right hand.

My hand is numb. I can't feel my face or my hand.

But she couldn't say the words. Was she going to be sick? Why was she so dizzy? Her legs turned noodle-like, loose and gelatinous underneath her. They could not be trusted. She reached for the chair and Marshall was at her side in an instant to steady her. Marshall. She'd cared for him once. Hadn't she?

She couldn't remember, but she was thankful for his help getting her to a chair.

"I think you should call 911," someone said.

She shook her head, feeling like the victim of a wisdom tooth extraction someone forgot to tell her about. Had she been drugged? Sabotaged?

She touched her cheek. Still nothing. She felt nothing. Was it drooping? Was she going to turn into one of those people with a droopy face?

Her entire body seemed to be floating above itself in a perpetual, circular, dizzying motion that had her wishing she'd foregone that last cup of coffee.

What felt like seconds later, there was a man standing over her. He wore a black polyester jacket and a serious expression. He met her eyes and she told herself to concentrate. He was handsome-ish. His eyes were crazy green and reminded her of Brooks's.

Brooks. Why had he come to her mind?

"Lane, how are you feeling?" Mr. Green Eyes's entire face turned warm then, as though he knew it had the ability to calm her with a single smile. At least he was using his powers of charm and seduction for something good.

She thought of Jasper, whose powers of charm and seduction had broken her heart.

Someone must've told him her name was Lane. Marshall probably. Or Chloe. Her head turned ever so slightly and she was practically touching Chloe's strappy-heeled sandals. She recognized them because she'd admired them so much Chloe had bought her a pair.

"I think they'll make your feet look thin," Chloe had said when she handed them over. "They do to mine."

Wait. Why was she so close to Chloe's shoes? Was she on the

floor? Had she fallen on the floor? Did anyone cover her up? She was wearing a skirt, after all. What if she accidentally flashed JB or the hipster executive from . . . What was that business's name again?

"Lane?"

"Mmm-hmm?"

He stared into her eyes, unromantically. "I think you'd better come with us to the hospital. We need to check you out." His tone reassured. That was nice of him, to make her feel better about being on the floor in the conference room when she was supposed to be upright and delivering a career-making presentation. Very thoughtful. "How's the numbness? Can you feel your face?"

With her left hand, she pushed against her right cheek.

Nothing. She shook her head. No. No, she could not feel her face.

"Is she having a stroke?" It was Chloe's voice that asked Lane's question.

"We want to rule it out," Mr. Green Eyes said. "Could be any number of things."

"Is she going to be okay?" Chloe's tone sounded slightly frantic, matching the way Lane felt about the scene unfolding before her.

She was twenty-nine. People her age didn't have strokes.

There was commotion then, off to the side, and Lane closed her eyes—only for a second, because Green Eyes was back. He shook her shoulder. "We're going to put a brace around your neck, just to keep everything as still as possible."

He slid something underneath her neck, then fastened it on the side, making it impossible for her to move her head.

Was this really necessary? She was fine. She just had a momentary . . . a passing . . . "I think I'm going to—" Just like that, the entire contents of her stomach were now on his pants.

"Sorry." Her voice still didn't sound like it belonged in her body. The darkness seeped further into her peripheral vision, invading her eyesight like an unwelcome intruder. She tried not to panic, head throbbing, face numb.

And the world went black.

CHAPTER

23

RYAN RODE BACK to Harbor Pointe from Newman, still needing to blow off steam. Had his dad really had the nerve to make more empty promises? After everything he'd put them through?

That man didn't deserve his sympathy and he hadn't earned a second chance. If Nate didn't pull through this, Ryan's father could be tried for vehicular manslaughter. Or worse.

And he should be. He should be locked away—should've been locked away years ago. It was a wonder he'd stayed out of jail this long.

Ryan made the turn to Harbor Pointe. He should pull over and call Walker right away. Now that he knew what he'd feared was true.

But he'd created a nice life for himself here, stayed under the radar enough that nobody really knew where he'd come from or what he was destined to become. And how would Noah and the rest of Nate's family react when they learned the truth?

What if the Kelley family somehow blamed him for his father's actions? What if they thought he'd known all along? What if a part of him *had* known all along? Would it change how they felt about him? Would his safe world crumble at the admission?

It didn't matter and he knew it. He believed in justice, and his father had broken the law, caused a life-threatening accident, and driven away.

Of course he'd call the cops. As much as he hated it, he'd just have to deal with the fallout. He'd give his dad time to come forward on his own. And if he didn't, Ryan would have to step in.

Ryan parked his bike next to the model cottage at Cedar Grove and took out his phone. He wanted to focus on something else. And while he couldn't exactly confide in Lane about what he was going through, he wanted to hear her voice, to remember there was something good in the world, even if she didn't belong to him.

He'd just call to say hi, check on how her presentation went. Talking about her presentation would be a welcome distraction.

The phone rang and he considered hanging up. But he'd never been one to worry about looking too eager. He liked her. He didn't care if she knew.

Besides, once the truth came out about the accident, who knew if Lane would even take his calls anymore?

"Lane Kelley's phone."

"Lane?"

"No, this is her assistant, Chloe. Can I help you?"

"Can I speak to Lane?"

There was a pause on the other end.

"Hello?"

"I'm sorry. Who's this?"

"Ryan Brooks. I'm a friend of Lane's from home—"

"Oh no. Did something happen with Nate?"

Ryan paced into the backyard and stared out across the lake. "No, no change yet."

"Oh. Thank God. That would be terrible right now. I mean that would be terrible anytime, but especially right now." Chloe sounded preoccupied. "Wait. You're the hot friend. With the motorcycle."

"Oh, am I?" Ryan smiled. "Is Lane around?"

Another pause.

"Chloe?"

"She told me not to tell anyone." Her voice was low, quiet, as if she didn't want the people around her to hear what she was saying.

"Tell anyone what?" He straightened. "Is something wrong?"

Yet another pause.

"Chloe?"

"She collapsed just before her presentation this morning."

"What?" Ryan's stomach sank. "Is she okay?"

"We just got to the emergency room, but it's been a zoo. We've been waiting around for someone to tell us something. I think they're going to take her back to have an MRI."

"Did you call her parents?"

"No." Chloe's voice was firm. "And you can't either. She was very specific. She doesn't want anyone here. She's convinced this is nothing and it's more important they stay with her brother." She hesitated. "I would never say this to her, but I think she's really scared. Her whole right side was numb and tingly."

"Where are you?"

"You can't come here, Ryan. She'll kill me if she finds out I told you."

"I won't tell her parents."

He heard a sigh on the other end of the line.

"Fine. I'll text you the address of the hospital."

"Thanks."

"And, Ryan?" Chloe stopped him as he was about to disconnect.

"Yeah?"

"You're not so annoying after all."

Three hours later, Ryan parked his bike outside a hospital that was much larger than Harbor Pointe's. Chloe had texted him instructions on how to find them, and he followed signs for the ER. At least they hadn't admitted her. He supposed that was a good thing.

He raced through the hallway until he found the check-in desk. Seated behind it was a large woman with short hair and a sour expression.

"I'm here to see Lane Kelley."

The woman didn't look up from her computer keyboard. "Are you family?"

"I'm a friend."

She eyed him. "Have a seat. I'll let you know when you can go back."

Ryan doubted it, but he did as he was told. He assumed they were still at the ER, though it had already been three hours since Lane was supposedly going back for an MRI. He texted Chloe just to make sure.

He watched the flurry of activity behind the small windows in two large doors, nursing his guilt over not calling Lane's parents before he left. He'd promised Chloe, but if the situation was worse than she'd let on, he'd decide for himself whether that promise was worth breaking.

He didn't need to give them any more reasons to be upset with him.

The doors opened slowly from the inside, and a younger woman wearing a navy-blue-and-white polka-dot dress looking like something out of a fifties movie appeared in the doorway.

She walked over to him. "Are you Ryan Brooks?"

He stood. "Chloe?"

She gave him a once-over, then met his eyes. "We've been here forever, but I think they're sending her home. Finally."

"Can I see her? Is she okay?"

"I don't know. The doctor told her some things she didn't want to hear."

Ryan's heart dropped. "What kind of things?"

"Like, she's going to have to make a serious life change. Went on a long rant about stress and the physical toll it takes on a body.

I know we're all relieved she didn't have a stroke or something worse, but it sounds to me like this is just as serious, especially for someone like Lane."

Someone like Lane.

He'd known her his whole life, but a week ago, she'd practically been a stranger. A stranger attached to a phone that kept her connected to everyone—and not really to anyone—all at the same time.

"Does she ever rest?"

Chloe shook her head. "It's what she's proud of—how hard she works. It's like she's got something to prove, and no matter how much she does, it's never enough."

He thought about all the teasing she'd endured over the years. The nicknames, the mocking, the friends who'd turned on her, and Jasper's betrayal. It didn't seem far-fetched that Lane would think she had something to prove.

She had no idea she was loved just the way she was.

"It's in her DNA," Chloe continued. "And she's been this way as long as I've known her."

"Do you think this is enough of a wake-up call for her to make some changes?"

Chloe shook her head again, slowly. "I think she just sees this as an annoying disruption in her day."

Ryan sighed. She always had been thickheaded. It was part of what he loved about her.

"I'll take you back," Chloe said. "Follow me."

They walked through the big, slow-moving doors and into the ER, past a number of small rooms with people lying on beds, waiting for explanations, treatments, answers. Knowing Lane was one of those people set something off inside him. He wanted to protect her, but he knew she'd never let him.

Chloe led him around a corner and into a darkened room where Lane Kelley lay on a hospital bed, somehow managing to make a hospital gown look sexy.

"Brooks?" She sat up, confusion on her face.

This was the most impulsive thing he'd ever done. Why was he here? He hardly knew her anymore.

And yet, seeing her like that—alone and scared, whether she admitted it or not—he knew there was nowhere else he was supposed to be.

"What are you doing here?"

He took a few steps into the room. "Came to see what all the fuss was about. You've always been pretty dramatic."

Lane looked at Chloe, whose eyes widened. "I'm going to leave you two alone." She stepped out of the room.

Lane frowned.

"Don't be mad at her. I called to see how your presentation went and she answered your phone. I made her tell me what happened."

"You called to see how my presentation went?"

Something about the surprise in her voice made him wonder if she had a single friend. He nodded, not caring so much if she exposed his feelings. He hadn't exactly been shy in his pursuit of her.

Never mind that it terrified him. A relationship with Lane—it would be the kind of relationship he'd work for. He'd find a way to make sure it didn't end.

But a whole lot of things would have to change before that could happen, namely her seeming disinterest in him.

Still, every once in a while, a smile, a look, a gesture gave him that little bit of hope he needed to keep from giving up.

Lane looked away. "It was nothing, really. The doctor is filling out the paperwork to send me home. You drove all this way for nothing."

He sat down on the edge of the bed. "You're right. I should've just texted."

She tried—failed—to hide her smile.

Ryan watched as her smile faded and her head drooped. He took her hand. "You okay?"

Her face was pale and there were dark circles under her eyes. She looked exhausted.

But still beautiful. She had no idea how beautiful.

"They think it was a severe migraine brought on by stress." She closed her eyes, which looked like they could shed tears at any moment. He had a feeling she wasn't used to showing any kind of emotion. How hard this must be for her—to appear weak, even for a moment.

He understood. There'd been a time once when he thought he had to hold everything together too.

"So you've got to make some changes." It wasn't a question. Someone had to drill that into her head or she'd go right back to the life she'd been living since the day she graduated from college.

Before she could respond, the door opened and a tall guy wearing a suit walked in. He glanced at Ryan, then back at Lane. She pulled her hand from Ryan's.

"Marshall." Lane's expression didn't change. "Where've you been?"

"Talking with JB and Ashton's team."

She turned away.

Marshall looked at Ryan. "Could you give us a minute?"

"He can stay," Lane said without so much as a glance at Ryan.

"Who are you?" Marshall took a step toward Lane.

"Ryan Brooks." He stood, stretched a hand out toward Marshall. "Friend of Lane's."

"Friend from where?" Marshall stared at Ryan's hand but didn't shake it.

"From home, Marshall. Just a friend."

Lane's annoyed tone didn't faze Marshall. "Uh-huh. Is he the reason you stopped answering my texts when you were away last week?"

Oh, brother. This guy wasn't only pompous; he was insecure. He was going to do this right now?

"I'm going to wait in the hallway." Ryan started for the door, but Lane's hand on his arm stopped him before he could move farther.

"No. Please stay."

Something about her request sat him back down, made him wish he had the right to wrap his arms around her and promise he'd stay as long as she wanted him to. Even if she wanted him to stay forever.

CHAPTER

24

THERE WAS A CHANCE Marshall's head might explode.

Lane hated that she was in this hospital bed. She was fine. The MRI didn't show anything out of the ordinary. Where was the doctor with the paperwork? What would happen if she just got up and left? Because the consequences of that couldn't be worse than sitting in this room listening to whatever it was Marshall was about to say.

That was, if he ever got back to paying attention to her instead of puffing up his chest for Ryan's benefit.

Maybe she'd asked Brooks to stay just to get under Marshall's skin. Maybe she was mad that her so-called boyfriend had only now shown up at the hospital, after several hours, after everything at JB Sweet was squared away.

Or maybe she'd asked him to stay because as soon as he walked in the door, something inside her shifted, as if somehow his being there made her feel like everything would be okay.

It was ridiculous, of course. No one—especially not a man—could do that for her.

But at the sight of him, everything else drifted away. He'd driven all that way at a moment's notice . . . for her?

"Lane, I need to talk to you about a few things." Marshall directed a pointed look toward Brooks. "Private things."

The silence in the room was tense and awkward. Marshall wasn't going to let this go. She glanced at Brooks, surprised how badly she didn't want him to walk away.

"I'll just be in the hallway," he said, his hand on hers. She looked up at him and felt instantly foolish. She didn't like how very much she liked him. It scared her. She could not let herself get hurt again.

And yet there was a protective kindness in his eyes that made her feel safe, like even if she never worked another day in her life, it didn't matter. It wouldn't change his opinion of her one bit.

She nodded and Ryan left her alone with Marshall. He stood as stiff and straight as ever. "What's going on with that guy?"

"I told you. He's a friend from home."

"A friend of your family?"

"Yes, actually." She didn't want to talk about it. She didn't want Marshall to chip away at feelings she hadn't figured out for herself.

He ran a hand over his clean-shaven chin. "Lane, up until a week ago, I didn't even know you had brothers. I feel like you're keeping things from me."

She was. She was keeping herself from him. Why? And more importantly, why didn't she want to change that?

After a long, silent pause, save Marshall's fidgeting, he finally seemed to get the hint this wasn't a topic she wanted to discuss.

"I didn't come here to talk about this," he said.

Well, thank God for that.

"The good news is JB Sweet has landed Solar, which was surprising after everything that happened."

He came here to talk about work?

"That's great," she said. And yet she felt sick she'd lost her chance. Sick that Miles had stolen her ideas. Sick that her breakdown had happened in front of JB Sweet, the man who ultimately decided who deserved to be the next creative director. Lane must look like such a train wreck to the Solar executives.

She forced a smile, but as she looked at Marshall, it was as if she was seeing him for the first time. Their similarities had drawn them together, but now she couldn't think of a single thing they had in common. The emptiness in their relationship had been magnified in the wake of this episode, and while she'd always known she didn't risk heartbreak with Marshall—he just didn't have that kind of hold on her—she now realized she didn't fit with him, even casually, at all.

He hadn't even asked her if she was okay.

Her eyes drifted across the room to the small vertical window in the thick hospital door. She could see Ryan leaning against the wall. He must've dropped everything to get there—what about his cottages, his schedule?

Marshall had been in her life for years and he'd been standing beside her as she collapsed, but it had taken hours for him to get across town.

"You're happy, right?" Marshall took her hand. "About Solar? I mean, you're a great team player, so I figured you'd be happy."

Lane nodded, then closed her eyes. Her head was still thick and cloudy. She didn't want to think anymore. She just wanted to sleep.

"Listen, I know you're going to hate this, but JB sent me here to let you know he wants you to take a leave," Marshall said.

Her eyes popped open. "A leave? Why?"

"He thinks you need it." Marshall's face turned sympathetic, but everything about his expression seemed phony. "After today, can you really disagree?"

"But what about Solar? You know Miles's presentation was full of my ideas, Marshall. That's my account." Her voice betrayed her, cracking under the weight of the acknowledgment.

"I tried to tell JB that. He thought Miles really had a connection with the Solar team. Does it really matter who thought of the ideas? As long as the right person manages the personalities, it'll all work out. We all have our place on the team, Lane." His smile was familiar, the smile of a man with a story to sell.

Lane watched as he stuck his hands on his hips and paced the small space next to her bed. She stilled. "You recommended Miles for the promotion, didn't you?"

The look on Marshall's face was all the answer she needed. She knew, ultimately, the decision was Marshall's.

And he'd given it to Miles, even after Miles had presented Lane's work as his own. Marshall didn't care about her at all. Lane willed herself not to cry. Not now, not in front of him.

She'd been working nonstop. She'd sacrificed sleep and food and any semblance of a social life . . . and for what?

"Tell me one thing, Marshall." She squared off with him, as much as she could from her hospital bed. "Did you ever have any intention of recommending me for that promotion?"

Marshall stopped fidgeting and focused on her. "Lane, listen." He sat on the edge of her bed. "You're an important part of our team. I couldn't do any of this without you—and I wouldn't want to."

"Why do I feel like there's a 'but' coming?"

Marshall sighed. "Your artistic eye, your creativity—we don't have anyone else on the team half as good. You make us all better."

Lane stared at him, her head still heavy—though she wasn't sure if it was from her episode or from what Marshall was saying.

"This is hard for me." Marshall looked away.

She had no pity for his predicament. "Just say it."

"I have to think about the *whole* team. You know that, right?"

She didn't respond.

He let out a heavy sigh. "I told JB I think you're in the best spot for your skill set right now."

Lane's eyes clouded with tears she was determined not to cry. "Did you ever intend to recommend me for the promotion? Was I even considered?" She met his eyes. "Tell me the truth."

Marshall pressed his lips together and held her gaze. "I considered it, Lane."

"How long have you known I wasn't going to get it?"

He looked away.

"Marshall."

"A couple of months."

A traitorous tear slipped down her cheek. "We've been working on Solar for more than a couple of months. You said this was my shot. You promised."

He stood, took a couple of steps away from her, facing the wall. "You know you do your best work when there's something big on the line."

She could feel the last of the breath she'd just inhaled drain from her body. "Get out."

"Don't do this, Lane." He faced her.

"I can't believe I ever listened to a word you said."

"This is business—*we* are us. They're two separate things."

She lifted her chin, feeling as if she were finally seeing things clearly for the first time in years. "There's no 'us,' Marshall. There never should've been."

"Lane."

"It's over. All of it."

"What do you mean, 'all of it'?"

"I mean you'll have my resignation letter on your desk as soon as I get out of here."

As soon as she said the words, a terrible cocktail of fear laced with nervous excitement swirled around inside her. What was she saying? She'd worked for years to get where she was—and she was just going to throw it all away?

"You're being impulsive, Lane."

She glanced through the long vertical window in the door and into the hallway at the same time Ryan glanced through the opposite side. The look of concern on his face shifted something inside her. How was she supposed to feel about any of this? It was as if that one trip back to Harbor Pointe had single-handedly turned her life into something she didn't recognize.

The door opened and the doctor walked in. "I've got the paperwork here, Miss Kelley. But promise me you'll think about what we discussed. Promise you'll make some changes."

She glanced at Marshall, who stood, dumbfounded, in the corner of the tiny room. "I've already started making changes, Doctor. And I already feel one hundred pounds lighter."

CHAPTER

25

RYAN STOOD IN THE HALLWAY, resisting the urge to go back into Lane's room. With every glance through the door, he had the distinct impression this guy was upsetting her. How self-absorbed was Marshall not to realize she didn't need this right now?

Chloe appeared at his side, also focusing on the tiny glimpse they could see inside the room. "We're only supposed to have two people back here. I hope they don't kick us out."

"I can go wait in the lobby," Ryan said.

"No, it's fine. Marshall probably won't stay long anyway." Chloe sighed. "I'm surprised he even showed up at all."

"Is this the first time he's been here?"

"Yep." Chloe crossed her arms and glared into Lane's room even though Ryan was sure she couldn't see much of what was going on in there. "Maybe she'll finally dump him. I don't know what she ever saw in that guy in the first place." She looked at Ryan. "She doesn't think I know they're a couple, but I know everything there is to know about Lane."

The phone in Chloe's hand buzzed and she glanced down at it. "Sorry; this is Lane's phone."

Chloe tapped around on the phone, just like he'd seen Lane do so many times over the last week.

"Unbelievable."

"What?"

She turned the phone and showed him a photo of Marshall standing next to a buttoned-up younger guy in a business suit. "That—" she pointed to the younger man—"is the guy who's been after Lane's promotion for months."

Ryan took the phone and read the caption underneath the photo: *After several years of excellent work, JB Sweet is proud to introduce you to our newest creative director, Miles McQuerry. You earned it, Miles. Congrats.*

"Looks like Miles finally got what he wanted." Chloe snatched the phone back. "Marshall promised her that promotion."

The door to Lane's room opened and Marshall stormed out, shooting Ryan a glare.

Chloe took a step toward Ryan as if she could somehow protect him, but he wasn't scared of this guy. He straightened to let Marshall know he wasn't backing down, and Marshall turned his attention to Chloe.

"I expect you'll be back at the office later this afternoon."

Chloe frowned. "I want to make sure she's okay."

"She's going home. If you value your job, you'll get back to work." One more pointed look at Ryan and Marshall sauntered away.

Man, Ryan wanted to punch him.

"I can't believe him." Chloe looked like she was going to cry. "He's going to keep me there all night."

"Sounds like a great place to work."

She let out a sigh. "I'm going to check on Lane."

"Okay, but maybe don't tell her about that photo you just saw," Ryan said.

Another frown.

"It might upset her. And right now that's about the last thing she needs."

"You're one of the good ones, aren't you?" She smiled at him, then opened the door and disappeared inside Lane's room, leaving Ryan standing in the hallway, whispering prayers that somehow he would have the words to help Lane, no matter what she was going through.

His grandpa phone buzzed in his back pocket.

"Hello?"

"Ryan, where are you?"

Hailey.

"What's wrong?"

"I came over with Jack after school and you weren't here."

"I had to go out of town for a few hours—sorry I didn't stop by and tell you. What's going on? You sound upset."

The silence on the other end of the line had him worried.

"It's Dad."

His stomach lurched. "What do you mean?"

"He's here, on your front porch. Says he's not leaving until he talks to you." Hailey paused. "I thought you didn't talk to Dad anymore, Ryan. What's he doing here?"

"I'll explain when I get back. Just go back to your place, Hailey. He'll leave eventually."

"I haven't seen him in a long time." She said it quietly, as if to herself.

"And you shouldn't. Get Jack and go home."

"Okay." Her voice was shaky as though she was remembering things she didn't want to recall. They'd worked so hard to get him out of their lives—to forget the things he'd done. If the truth came out about the accident—if there was an investigation and an arrest and a trial—it would force them to relive those things all over again.

He didn't want that for either of them, yet he didn't feel inclined to keep his father's secret, not when his friend's life hung in the balance. He didn't owe his dad that. He didn't owe him anything.

The door to Lane's room opened just as a nurse appeared in the hallway with a wheelchair.

Lane had gotten dressed and now stood right behind Chloe, who seemed determined not to leave her side. She didn't need a wheelchair; Ryan would just scoop her up and carry her home.

At the sight of him on his phone, Lane's eyebrows shot up.

"Hailey, let me call you back." He ended the call.

Panic washed across her face. "You didn't tell her about me, did you?"

"No, that was about something else. Are you okay?"

She smiled despite exhausted eyes. "I'm fine. Honestly."

"She's not fine," Chloe said. "She needs someone to sit with her and I have to go back to work."

"I'll do it." Might've sounded a tad bit eager with that reply.

Lane's eyes found his. "You don't have to do that. I don't need someone to sit with me."

"Yes, he does," Chloe said. "I'll relieve him after work, but I'm not sending you home alone. What if you collapse again?"

"He has a job. He has a life. He needs to get back to those." Lane's dark hair fell long and loose around her shoulders. He wanted to brush it away from her face.

"*He* can make up his own mind," Ryan said, flashing her a smile. "*He's* got people covering for him at work and *he's* got the whole day off." Not entirely true, but he'd deal with that later. He motioned for her to sit in the wheelchair. "Your chariot, my dear."

Her face went blank. "I am not sitting in that thing."

"If you want to get out of here, you are." The nurse, whose name tag read Donna, gave her a don't-mess-with-me look.

Lane sighed.

"You sure you've got her?" Chloe asked.

Ryan smiled. "Nowhere else I'd rather be."

Lane turned to her assistant. "Go. I'll be fine."

When Chloe hugged her, Lane stiffened, then eventually hugged her back. "Thanks, Chloe."

"He's a keeper, Lane," Chloe whispered, not very quietly, before she released Lane. She looked at Ryan. "I'll be over after work."

He nodded at her and she clicked off down the hall. Lane turned to face him. He gave the wheelchair a gentle push, and she finally sat down, purse in her lap.

Ryan pushed her through the hallways with Donna following close behind. Once they were outside, Lane stood and spoke to the nurse. "I'm good to go now, right?"

Donna glared at Lane. "I don't want to see you back here, young lady." She shook a finger in Lane's face. "That means you need to take better care of yourself. You hear me?"

Lane hugged her purse like a child clutching a worn-out teddy bear. She bowed her head. "I hear you."

"Good." She glanced at Ryan. "You take care of your girl, you hear me?"

Ryan nodded. "You can count on it."

Donna scooted her way behind the wheelchair, spun it around, and plodded away.

"You obviously don't have to come to my place," Lane said.

"Are you afraid I'll find out what a slob you are?" He grinned at her.

"I'm actually very neat." They started walking toward the parking lot. "I just don't want to waste any more of your time."

"That's the thing," Ryan said. "It's my time. So I get to decide if it's a waste or not." He led her toward the spot where he'd parked his motorcycle earlier in the day.

"I can take care of myself. Everyone is overreacting." She stopped beside Ryan's bike.

"I'm not so sure they are." He handed her a helmet. "Besides, I promised Chloe."

Lane heaved a sigh—very dramatically—and put the helmet on. "You're such a Boy Scout."

"I take that as a compliment." He put his own helmet on, swung his leg over the bike, and helped her on. "You're okay to ride on this, right? You're not going to pass out?"

She smacked his shoulder, then wrapped her arms around him. He sat for a second, marking the moment in his mind. He could get used to the way it felt to have her this close. Easily.

After navigating the city streets, he parked in front of her complex, an old, nondescript brick building with rows and rows of windows.

Somewhere between the hospital and here, she'd laid her head on his back—maybe too tired to keep it upright?—and now she shifted, pulling away from him. He noticed her absence and immediately wished they could rewind time.

She stood next to his bike, holding the helmet. "Thanks for the ride."

"You're not getting rid of me that easily." He kicked the stand down and got off the bike. "Lead the way."

No matter how many times he told her, she seemed incapable of believing he wasn't going to just drop her on the curb and go. Obviously she wasn't used to letting anyone else take care of her.

She led him toward the door of her building and into the elevator. She pushed the button for the sixth floor and the door closed.

Lane stood against the back wall of the elevator. Her eyes had lost a little of their luster, her skin was pale, and those dark circles only seemed darker.

"When was the last time you slept?" he asked.

She lifted her eyes to his. "Day before yesterday, I think."

"And ate?"

She shrugged.

"Do you seriously not remember?"

"I've been really busy, Ryan."

Something about her seemed so fragile, he decided not to push it. He wouldn't judge her. He'd simply help her get better. The elevator doors opened to a hallway with only four doors in it. She walked over to the second one—a barn door on a track—inserted her key, and pulled it open.

The sound of her dog's toenails clicking on the hardwood floor broke the silence.

Lane picked up the dog and hugged him. "Otis! Are you surprised to see me so early?"

As Lane reunited with Otis, Ryan looked around her loft. Light streamed in from the two walls of windows, illuminating the space. Brick walls had been painted white, keeping everything light and airy. It reminded him of the images Betsy had shown him of Lane's work—homey, cozy, cottagey. She could've gone sleek and modern with this kind of space, but she hadn't. Maybe she did carry a part of Harbor Pointe with her, whether she knew it or not.

"Wow, this place is incredible," he said, taking it in.

She set Otis down and the dog came over to Ryan and sniffed his shoes. "Thanks."

"I'm guessing you designed it yourself." He stopped near the desk and noticed a wall of awards on display behind it. This many awards and it still wasn't enough.

"Yes, it was empty and bare when I moved in." She closed her eyes for several seconds. "I think I need to lie down."

He took her bag from her and set it on the table near the front door.

"I should check the mail."

"I'll take care of it." Ryan followed her to the rear of the loft, where a large bed with a crisp white comforter was situated behind a short privacy wall. He pulled the covers back and Lane sat down. She started to protest when he knelt in front of her to take off her shoes, but he gave her a look that shut her up.

She scooted her legs underneath the blankets, laid her head down on the pillow, and closed her eyes.

He quietly went over to the windows and drew the blinds, though there was still so much light coming in from the other room. When he turned to go, he heard the rhythmic rise and fall of her breathing.

It had only been seconds and already she'd fallen asleep.

He pulled the covers over her and watched her sleep—just for a moment. He thought about Nate, still in a coma, still fighting for his life, with a waiting room full of people who had to take shifts for a chance to see him. Lane's collapse had been the exact opposite. Her own boyfriend hadn't shown up at the hospital until hours after she'd gotten there.

He needed to get back to Harbor Pointe—to the cottages, to his sister—but he couldn't leave Lane. Not when there was no one here to take care of her. He called Jerry and ran through the plans for the next few days.

"You're coming back tomorrow, right?" his contractor asked.

"Hoping to, but can't be sure. I know the timing is terrible, but you guys can handle it, right?"

"'Course. We've done eleven others; we've got this. You take care of what you need to take care of."

The man didn't ask any more questions, and Ryan hoped when he returned to Cedar Grove, he'd find his absence hadn't slowed them down.

Around 9 p.m., Chloe let herself in to Lane's loft at a manic pace.

"I'm so sorry it's so late. I know you've got to get back home." She dropped her bag on the floor near the sofa, where he and Otis sat, watching *SportsCenter* and drifting off.

"You're half-asleep," she said. "I knew Marshall was going to make me stay late—probably just to spite me because Lane quit and everything."

"Wait. What?" Ryan muted the television.

"She didn't tell you?" Chloe stopped moving for the first time since she'd come in.

"She fell asleep seconds after we got here and hasn't moved since."

Chloe walked over to the bed and peeked in on Lane, then returned, shaking her head. "She probably hasn't actually slept in days."

"I'm getting the impression she really doesn't take very good care of herself."

Chloe plopped down in the chair across from where he sat. "That is an understatement. She's the most driven person I know, though. It's inspiring."

"It's crazy."

"Same thing." She smiled.

"Did she really quit her job?" He couldn't imagine Lane leaving something that meant so much to her.

"I'm kind of hoping she'll wake up tomorrow and realize it was a huge mistake."

"Was it, though?" Ryan didn't say so, but he hoped she woke up feeling completely free. No job should keep a person chained like hers did. Less work, more life—that was his motto.

"Of course it was. Lane is a rock star at what she does. She's the creative force behind almost everything Marshall puts out there. She's the reason he looks so good to JB."

"Huh."

"What?" Chloe leaned forward. "What are you thinking?"

"Maybe Marshall didn't promote her because he was scared to lose her. I mean, if she makes him look good—why would he let her get away? I'm betting he'll be begging her to come back by morning."

"I don't know. He was really angry."

"He'll get over it. That was just his ego."

Chloe stood and headed to the kitchen. "Did you find something to eat? Lane doesn't keep much in the house."

"I got some groceries."

"You did?" She opened the door of the newly stocked refrigerator and glanced inside. "Wow, you did." She turned to face him. "You probably don't want to drive home now, do you?"

"I'm going to stay till she wakes up."

Chloe eyed him. "What's the deal with you two?"

"There is no deal. We're old friends."

"So, what was she like—you know, before she was kicking butt and taking names? Was she always amazing? Everyone at work wants to be her, you know."

"I'm sure she's told you about her childhood."

Chloe's eyebrows popped up. "Um. No. I found out last week that she had a brother. She doesn't talk about herself. Ever."

At his side, Otis twitched in his sleep. Ryan let a hand rest softly on the animal, thinking about how much the small dog meant to Lane. Next to Chloe, the dog was probably her only true friend in this life she'd built for herself. With her carefully constructed wall of protection and her everything-in-its-place set of rules, Lane had created a world where she'd never be hurt again.

Like him, she'd put her past behind her, but unlike him, she'd run away from her past and just kept running. The people in her life knew only what she allowed them to know, which, from the sound of it, wasn't much.

Instead of seeing the gift she had in her childhood, in her family, she saw only the pain. The realization set something off within him. He wanted to give her back everything she thought she'd lost— everything that was waiting for her if she'd just open her eyes.

But he had no idea where to begin with someone so fragile.

"Ryan?"

Chloe's voice pulled him back to the present. "Sorry. To answer your question, yes, she was always amazing."

"I knew it." Chloe grinned.

"She just didn't know it for herself."

CHAPTER

26

SUNLIGHT STREAMED through the cracks in her blinds, pulling Lane out of a deep, deep sleep. She rolled over in bed, the foggy memories of what had happened slowly returning.

She touched her face, aware of her fingers on her skin, thankful that the numbness had subsided. There was no trace of that debilitating headache either, only the growl of a ravenous stomach.

She vaguely remembered staggering to the bathroom in the darkness last night, but other than that, it had been the most restful sleep she'd had in months, possibly years. As if the frantic pace of her life had finally caught up with her, rendering her completely useless until she caught up on her sleep.

As she stood, the memory of her conversation with Marshall poked at her. She'd been rash and impulsive—maybe even emotional, which wasn't like her. She rubbed her temples and stumbled toward the kitchen. She'd scrounge up something to eat and then she'd face the day.

Though what would she do without a job?

"Well, look who's up."

She gasped. She'd thought she was alone, but one look at her sofa told her otherwise. Ryan sat next to a pile of folded blankets and a pillow, Otis on his lap and the remote in his hand.

"You're still here?" *Why didn't I look in the mirror before I walked in here?*

"Yes, and I feel so welcome. You've been a great host." He picked Otis up and set him on the floor, and the traitor stuck right by his feet.

"You've put a spell on my dog." Lane couldn't remember the last time she'd walked into a room and Otis didn't come running.

"We've bonded the last couple days."

She frowned. "Couple days?"

"You've been asleep since Monday afternoon."

"What? What day is it today?" Where was her phone? How much had she missed?

"It's about ten in the morning on Wednesday." Ryan followed her into the kitchen. "And I hid your phone."

She spun around and faced him. "Why would you do that?"

"The doctor said you have to make some changes. Figured that was a good one to start with."

Her heart sped up. She needed her phone. She'd slept Tuesday away—she needed to know what had happened.

Yet, without a job, what could she possibly have missed?

Ryan opened the refrigerator, and to her surprise, there was food in it. Fruit and vegetables and almond milk and juice.

"What's all that?"

"Those are called groceries." He tossed a grin over his shoulder.

"Almond milk?"

"You said you were lactose intolerant."

Did he listen to everything she said?

"Sit down. I'm going to make you something to eat."

"You really don't have to do this, Brooks."

He pulled a carton of eggs from the fridge, along with a green pepper and an onion. "Someone has to take care of you, Lane. And if you're not going to do it, then I am."

She searched for an argument, but nothing came. Ryan moved around the kitchen like he knew it—finding and using utensils she didn't realize she had.

"I'm making you an omelet." He cracked an egg into a small glass bowl. "It's been days since you actually ate."

"Where did all this food come from?"

He cracked another egg. "They have these things called grocery stores. Even here in Chicago." One more egg. "You do eat eggs, right? I figured those were probably in your rule book."

She didn't respond to his comment or his smirk. As he poured the eggs into a small pan, she took the briefest moment to admire the way his blue T-shirt showed his defined muscles. He had the physique of a man who cared about his body, though his comfortable, disheveled style might suggest otherwise.

"You like having me in your kitchen." He leaned against the counter, facing her, that grin on his face. She'd been staring, her brief moment of admiration for his form turning into several long moments, which he'd clearly noticed.

"Don't flatter yourself," she said. "I'm just hungry."

"Well, sit down."

She did as she was told, watching as Otis hung close to Ryan, who tossed more than one treat at the lucky dog.

"I don't give him that many treats."

"That's why he was so easy to win over." Ryan tossed another dog treat to Otis.

"He's going to get fat."

Ryan picked up the pan and flipped the omelet without a spatula.

"Are you showing off?"

He set the pan back down on the burner. "Is it working?"

"We'll see how it tastes."

A few minutes later, he set a plate in front of her with an omelet, a side of fruit, and a glass of juice. He sat across from her, an expectant look on his face. She stared at the plate, then the man across from her, and an inexplicable wave of emotion rolled through her.

She didn't want a man to take care of her. She could take care of herself. She always had. She couldn't stop now.

And yet, being taken care of was . . . nice.

"Are you okay?"

Her eyes had clouded over, and she now sat there, wondering how to explain to him that she'd never eaten a meal at this table with another person. It hadn't bothered her before, but his presence—his goodness—set something off inside her. Quietly she slid her plate closer, blinked away tears, and said, "Everything is perfect."

She ate under his observant eye, certain he wasn't going to let her move until she'd finished every last bite.

"You must be starving," he said.

She was. So hungry. "This is really good, thank you. Nobody has ever cooked me breakfast before."

Otis nestled himself at Ryan's feet, and they sat a few moments in silence.

"Chloe came by a couple times."

She tried to listen, but mostly she was thinking she liked the way he looked in her apartment, like he'd been carved to fit perfectly in her space. She pushed the food around on her plate, reminding herself that this was dangerous territory she found herself in. She had to keep her wits about her or she'd get lost in his green eyes.

When had Ryan Brooks become so wonderful?

She glanced up at him, watching her. Maybe he'd always been wonderful and she just never noticed it before.

"She said you quit your job." He studied her, maybe waiting for some reaction, but she had none. She should probably feel panicked or worried, but she didn't, as if for the first time in her entire adult life she'd done something truly remarkable.

"I guess I did." She took another bite.

"How are you feeling about that now, after two days of sleep?"

She shrugged. "I feel fine."

By the look on his face, he wasn't buying it. And why should he? She'd lived for this job since she graduated college. She'd given everything to it, thinking that unlike Jasper or Lindsay, this career did not have the power to hurt her. She'd counted on it.

But it had hurt her, hadn't it? All the times she'd been passed over. Hearing Marshall admit he dangled that promotion in front of her because she did better work when there was something on the line . . . it stung. And now it was gone. She didn't even know who she was without her job.

"So what now?" He settled into his chair as if he wasn't going anywhere until they had this conversation. She wasn't accustomed to conversation with her meals.

"I guess I'll have to find a new job." Well, that was weird. She hadn't really thought about it, but she needed to do something for an income.

"Right away?"

She met his eyes. "What are you getting at?"

"I have an idea."

She set her fork down. "And you've had two straight days to think about it."

He smiled. His face showed excitement as though he'd been waiting to tell her a secret and, at last, here she was. She had to look away. She didn't like the way his smile stirred up her feelings, feelings she hadn't experienced in years.

"Why are you still here, anyway? What about Cedar Grove? You have a deadline." She finally dared another glance in his direction.

"I have a great team," he told her. "They're very competent."

She still felt bad. He should be there, working on this huge project—not sitting in her apartment babysitting her while she slept. "Okay, what's your idea?"

"Come back to Harbor Pointe with me."

"No."

"That's it? You're not even going to think about it?"

"My last trip to Harbor Pointe was probably what caused all this in the first place. I'm not at my best when I'm there." She didn't like the reminders, the memories. She didn't like watching everyone seamlessly float into each other's lives while she was anchored on the edges of it all like she had bricks in her shoes. She had never fit in there, and that hadn't changed. Last week proved it.

He leaned toward her, his hands dangerously close to hers. "I don't think that's true."

Did he know the whole truth about Lindsay and Jasper? Did he know she'd gone to Harbor Pointe on their wedding day and, hidden in her car a safe distance away, watched them leave the church? Did he know that Jasper had turned out to be nothing like the man she thought he was and that Lindsay had betrayed her in the worst possible way? Did he realize the pain of their betrayal still influenced nearly every decision she made?

She didn't want him to know. She didn't want anyone to know that the man she'd loved so loyally didn't choose her. If people found that out—if Ryan found that out—then he wouldn't choose her either.

The thought surprised and upset her all at once. She didn't want Ryan Brooks to choose her. What was she thinking?

Although . . . she met his eyes. "I'm sure someone told you what happened."

"I don't know the whole story." His gaze was still intent on her. "But I think I've put most of the pieces together."

There were those clouds in her eyes again, darn it. She did not want to cry over this. She had never cried over this—why was the pain of it just now resurfacing? Why was his kindness bringing out something in her she couldn't wrap her head around? Was it so unfamiliar for someone to treat her this way that she'd grown to view kindness as a rare, priceless gift? Unlike Marshall, Ryan needed nothing from her.

He was solely focused on what she needed, and she didn't know how to feel about that.

"I saw how you reacted when Jasper was at the hospital. And how hard it was to be at their house."

She needed to be logical, not emotional. "I don't want to talk about it." She'd been through it all in therapy, with someone who wasn't really a part of her life. That was enough.

"But maybe you should."

"What do you want me to say? Do you want me to tell you that I gave him everything and he broke my heart? That I couldn't have predicted what happened in a million years but feel like I should've seen it coming? That every person I meet isn't a potential friend—they're just someone else I refuse to get close to because I never want to feel that way again?"

"Lane, it was awful. I get it."

"Do you, though? She's my sister, Brooks. He didn't just break my heart; he took my sister." A knot caught in her throat as the words hung in the air. Words that surprised even her. All this time, she thought she'd been grieving the loss of her fiancé, but was it possible she'd really been grieving the loss of a sister she'd always hoped would become her best friend?

He was watching her; she could feel it. "I'm so sorry."

A tear streamed down her cheek and she quickly wiped it away. She would not cry over this.

"I can't imagine what you went through."

Thoughts turned to those days leading up to their wedding—the wedding that should've been hers. She'd thrown herself into work, but every night she came home—alone—and forced herself not to cry. So long she'd been holding this in, and now, in the wake of Ryan's kindness, her resolve had come undone.

She covered her face with her hands, unable to keep the unwanted tears locked away for one minute longer.

Nobody had comforted her during that time—not because they hadn't tried, but because she wouldn't let them. Even Nate, with his surefire methods of distracting her, eventually came up short. The pain was just too deep. She'd been hurt too many times and decided relationships weren't worth the pain.

Looking at Ryan, she wondered for the first time if her logic had been faulty. But the thought of reliving that pain terrified her.

He sat unmoving. "He's lucky I wasn't here when that happened."

She laughed through her tears, thankful for the release of emotions that had built up behind her wall. "I have three brothers, remember?"

"Didn't they defend you?"

She shrugged. "Maybe. I didn't stick around long enough to find out. By the time they got married, I think my family had decided not to choose sides—well, except for Nate. He boycotted the wedding with me." She smiled, though the memory still hurt her—the lack of support from the rest of her family. "But I took their not choosing as a choice, I guess."

"I think there was a lot more to it than you realized."

She wiped her cheeks dry. "What do you mean?"

"Something changed. I knew it the second I got home from overseas. Nobody would talk about it for a long time, and once I had an idea of what had happened, I kind of hated Jasper because he didn't seem to care."

"Sounds like Jasper."

"I think they're all still grieving that there's this broken piece of their family."

Lane didn't respond. She found it hard to believe that anyone was grieving over the loss of her.

"Look, all I'm saying is that you've got something really great— you just don't realize it. I don't want you to throw away everything good with the bad."

She eyed him. "Tell me what's good about Harbor Pointe, about me being in Harbor Pointe."

"Well, for starters, you would be with me."

She let out another quick laugh. "You're something else, you know that?"

He leaned back. "That's what I'm trying to tell you."

"Brooks, I can't build my career in Harbor Pointe."

"Well, maybe you should hold off on that search for a few weeks."

"I can't; I—"

"Just hear me out," he cut in. "You come with me and help me decorate my cottages. I'll pay you for your time. While you're there, you get more rest than you would if you were here, you can visit your brother, and I can make sure you're eating every day."

She pulled her legs underneath her on the chair. "It's a nice thought, but living in my parents' house could very well land me right back in the emergency room."

"Is it the cows?"

She laughed again. "It's everything. The constant stream of people. The noise. And yeah, maybe the cows." She finished her last bite and took a drink. "In a way, I always felt like a guest there, even as a kid."

He looked at her like he didn't understand.

And it was stupid. If her family hadn't had their open-door policy, she and Ryan never would've known each other in the first place. She was happy for what her parents were able to do for him and Hailey—she didn't begrudge them one moment of happiness given what their home life must've been like. "You wouldn't understand. You always fit in seamlessly, like you were born to be a part of my crazy family."

"I've thought that before too."

She stilled. She couldn't wish that things had been different for her—because if they had, they would've been different for him.

"Your family loves you, Lane."

The words hung there, right on the edge of the bubble around her, and she refused to let them penetrate her heart. She didn't believe it, and she wasn't going to pretend for a moment she belonged with people who had betrayed her the way they did.

"I know you're only half-listening to what I'm saying, but it's true. Just because you're different from them doesn't mean you don't belong."

She shook her head. "I've made peace with all of this. We don't need to talk about it." She stood and walked to the coffeemaker—mostly to get out from under his attentive eye—but he followed her over and reached for her mug.

When she turned toward him, she realized he was dangerously close, and they were both holding her mug.

"I can pour my own coffee," she said into his chest, not daring to meet his eyes.

"You might have to get used to letting other people help you." His nearness stirred something in her that she wasn't willing to feel, and he showed no signs of backing away. "Come with me, Lane. You can stay in one of the cottages at Cedar Grove. You can rest. Maybe remember who you are."

"I know who I am, thank you." She gave him a soft smile. "I'm a really amazing interior designer, and I—"

"That's not who you are, Lane. That's what you do."

She edged away but felt the counter against her back. She didn't understand. What she did *was* who she was. "It's a really bad idea."

He inched the mug away from her, and she glanced up. His eyes were full of her—had anyone ever looked at her the way he was looking at her now? Like she was something special, something to be treasured? She could see how much he wanted to take care of her, to protect her.

But letting him in was only going to end in heartache.

Why, then, did she hear herself say, "Fine. I'll come back with you"?

His eyes lit and his face spread into a victorious smile. "You will?"

"On one condition."

"Name it."

"You have to let me get my own coffee."

His gaze fell from her eyes to her lips, then back. Slowly he handed her the mug and took a step away, leaving her dizzy and wondering why her heart seemed intent on betraying her.

CHAPTER

27

"OH, I HAVE ONE MORE STIPULATION," Lane said as she wheeled her suitcase out from her bedroom, a second bag hanging over her shoulder.

"Another one?"

So far, she'd added, "You can't comment on my phone usage" and "I'm not milking any cows" to the list.

Ryan had no idea how he'd convinced Lane to come to Harbor Pointe with him, but he wasn't about to question it. "What is it?" He took a few steps toward her.

She stilled. "I don't want my parents to know about my . . . episode or whatever you want to call it."

"Lane—"

"This is nonnegotiable."

He could see she'd dug in her heels. Whatever lies she'd been telling herself for years had caught up to her while she packed her clothes for a trip to Harbor Pointe. She thought they didn't deserve to know what was happening in her life, that they didn't love her,

271

Just Look Up

that she didn't fit in with them. How could he show her none of that was true?

"Brooks."

"Fine. But I have a stipulation of my own."

She glared at him. "I don't think that's how this works."

"There are no rules, Lane." He walked toward her and took the suitcase. He liked being close to her. He could see it made her uncomfortable, but he didn't care. He was intent on proving to her that he wasn't going to hurt her like Jasper had. "You have to take one hour in the middle of every day to rest."

Her jaw went slack. "You can't be serious."

"Nonnegotiable."

Her eyes had narrowed, but that hint of a smile was back, playing at the corners of her mouth.

"Can I break the hour up into fifteen-minute increments throughout the day?" She pretended to be annoyed. At least he thought she was pretending.

He shook his head.

"This is totally ridiculous."

"Nonnegotiable."

After a long pause, she finally relented. "All right, let's go before I change my mind." She picked up her bag, which she'd set on the floor beside her, but he swiftly swiped it from her and slung it over his own shoulder.

"You have to let me do some things for myself," she said.

"I will. But carrying luggage isn't one of those things."

"I work out, Brooks. I'm very strong."

He held her gaze. Standing right in front of her, the way he'd done earlier in the kitchen, once more he wanted to kiss her. He wanted to drop the bags on the ground, pull her toward him, and show her how he really felt without using a single word.

With his free hand, he brushed a strand of hair away from her face. She tensed at his nearness and he was reminded once again that she was skittish and unavailable. This would take time, gaining her trust.

272

And he was just fine with that. He'd wait as long as he had to.

"We should go." He started for the door. "Do you have everything?"

She nodded and picked up Otis, a confused expression on her face.

Don't freak her out, Brooks. "Let's go." He purposely kept his tone light, even if the air between them was not.

They drove separately, but he kept her in his mirrors the entire time. He knew he had so much to deal with when he got back to Harbor Pointe—he only hoped Jerry had kept everyone on task—but Lane was more important than work, so a few extra days of scrambling was fine with him. They had almost a month to finish and a good team in place. They'd be fine.

At least he hoped they would.

Hailey had called again last night, asking about their father. How long could he put her off? With everything that had happened with Lane, he hadn't given his father a second thought, but the clock was ticking for his old man. If he didn't come forward, Ryan had to make a decision about what to do next. Was he really going to turn him in?

He shook the thoughts aside. Right now, the only thing he wanted to focus on was getting to Harbor Pointe and taking care of Lane. Everything else would just have to wait.

It was late afternoon when they pulled into town. Ryan parked in front of the model cottage and Lane pulled in behind him. She turned off the engine and let Otis out to run around the yard.

"How was the drive?" Ryan opened the trunk and tugged out her suitcase.

"It was fine." Lane leaned against the car.

"Well, you had a good view."

She turned her face away from him, once again failing to hide her smile.

"You can admit you think I'm funny." He slammed the trunk shut.

"Ah, but looks aren't everything." She shot him a glance, then started for the front door.

"Good one, Kelley."

She tossed a smile over her shoulder and kept walking. That smile—it could light up a night sky. Maybe his sister was right. He had it bad.

He'd called Hailey that morning and asked her to arrange for a cleaning service to come in and make sure the place was spotless.

"Do you have an investor coming over or something?" she'd asked. "Why can't you do this yourself?"

"I'm still out of town," he'd told her. "And it's not an investor. It's Lane."

Hailey went silent, but only for a moment. "Lane's coming to stay with you?"

"Not *with* me. Just in the cottage. I'm going to have to crash with you for a little while."

"You've got it bad, Ryan."

"Can you call the cleaning service or not?"

She assured him she'd take care of it, and he hung up on her before she could give him any more grief about whatever feelings she thought he had for Lane. He knew he'd have to field a ton of questions about it later, but now, as he unlocked the front door, he only hoped his sister had come through.

He pushed the door open and was instantly greeted with a fresh, clean-linen smell. *Thank goodness.* He wasn't a total slob, but he was a single guy living alone in this place. The last thing he needed was to whisk Lane away with the promise of rest only to be met with a bachelor pad that desperately needed a deep clean.

"Are you wanting the other cottages to match this one?" she asked. "I mean, your designer did some things really well."

"Whoa, slow down." He set her bags down and closed the door.

"What?" She sounded confused.

"We just walked in. Why don't we get you settled before we jump right into work?"

She looked genuinely perplexed.

"We do things differently up here, Lane." She might have trouble adjusting to their slower pace. "I'm going to take these bags upstairs. Are you hungry? I could make you dinner quick."

"I just ate."

He paused midstep. "That was breakfast—hours ago."

She moved away. "I'm still full."

He wasn't going to argue. He put her luggage in the room at the top of the stairs. Barb had painted it a bright yellow, and though he'd originally been opposed to the idea, it had grown on him. With the thick white woodwork, the color really popped, and there was just something happy about the space now. He hoped Lane liked it.

He turned and found her standing in the doorway. "Is this me?"

"It's not the master. I hope that's okay. You can move into the master if you want to—I just need to get some stuff out of there." It wasn't much. He purposely had very few belongings in this house.

She frowned, then started down the hall toward the other bedrooms. She pushed open the door to the dusty-blue master where he'd been staying, then faced him. "You're living here?"

"I couldn't afford a separate place while we were renovating, so I just moved in here. But I'm going to stay with Hailey while you're here. You'll have the place all to yourself."

She shook her head. "I'm not putting you out of your own house."

"It's fine, Lane. I'm hardly ever here anyway. I've got so much to do to get these cottages ready."

"And you just gave up three straight days to come sit in my apartment." She crossed her arms. "I'm thankful, Brooks, but you don't have to take care of me anymore. I'm fine."

She sure was stubborn. He moved toward her. "What if I like taking care of you? What if there's nothing else that matters as much to me as that?"

"Well, that's silly."

"Is it?"

"I don't want to be the reason you can't make your deadline. This project is too important to you," she said, arms still crossed, feet still planted.

"It is." He stood directly in front of her. "But so are you." He only just now realized how much. Did she feel that too? Whatever it was that was going on between the two of them? Was he imagining it?

"Ryan, why are you doing all this? You don't even know me anymore." She pressed her lips together—full lips he wanted to taste.

"I've always known you, Lane." He reminded himself that once he crossed this line with her, he couldn't go back. He'd decided to win her trust slowly, but it would demand all his willpower not to take her face in his hands, press her body close to his, and kiss her.

"Brooks?"

"Are you still dating that guy?"

"What?"

"You quit your job—does that mean you quit him too?"

She looked cute when she was perplexed. "If you must know, no, I'm not still dating him. Why?"

His eyes fell to those lips. "Just curious."

"Well, you didn't answer my question."

Before he could, the front door opened and someone came inside. Normal people would worry, but normal people didn't have Hailey as a sister.

"Ryan?" she called out. "You here?"

"Be right down." He looked at Lane. "Either room is yours. I'll see you downstairs."

He knew Hailey had probably just saved him from making a huge mistake—so why did he come down the stairs thinking she had the worst timing in the world?

CHAPTER

28

BROOKS LEFT THE ROOM just in time. Lane wasn't sure what was going on between the two of them, but she knew it was dangerous.

She put a few things away in the dresser and hung up some of her clothes in the closet, then went in search of Ryan and Hailey. She'd gotten settled—and she was restless. They needed to make a plan for designing these cottages.

She heard them in the kitchen as she came downstairs, but as she approached, they both stopped talking.

"Everything okay?" she asked, feeling like she'd interrupted something.

"Hey, Lane." Hailey left Ryan standing on the other side of the kitchen and pulled Lane into a sisterly hug. "I'm glad you decided to come back. That way you'll be here when Nate wakes up."

She certainly hoped so.

"I didn't mean to interrupt you guys," Lane said.

Hailey waved her off. "I was just leaving. Sounds like you both have a lot of work to do. You're saving Ryan's tail—you know that, right?"

Lane frowned.

"With the cottages. The whole town is talking about how important this community is going to be."

"Hailey." Ryan sounded like he was warning her about something.

"What?" She shifted. "It's true. Tourism is down. You know how it is around here. All the local businesses are hoping that with new places for people to stay, we'll have more people coming to town this summer."

Lane glanced at Ryan. He was leaning against the counter with his arms folded, and if she had to guess, she'd say he wasn't too happy with his sister.

"So you're saving him and in turn, saving the town." Hailey grinned. "No pressure. See you tonight."

Hailey left and suddenly the cottage felt like a huge, empty mausoleum, just her and Brooks and the awkward tension that hung between them.

"You didn't tell me how much pressure you're under to pull this thing off."

"Let's find something to eat."

Lane didn't push it. She watched while he whipped together a huge taco salad and then proceeded to scoop half of it onto her plate and set it in front of her spot at the table on the porch.

"I can't eat all that," she said, laughing.

"It's salad. It's healthy."

She shook her head. "You have no idea what you're talking about."

"Just eat what you want."

"You also have no idea what it's like to be a girl."

"Thank goodness for that." He laughed.

She liked this casual rapport they had between them. Sometimes nothing about it seemed dangerous. But then she'd catch that look in his eyes.

"When can we talk about this project?" Lane asked after swallowing her first bite. "This is really good."

"I know." He grinned at her. Smiling came so easily to him. She envied that. "We can talk about it tomorrow."

"Shouldn't we get started today? I mean, you've got guests scheduled for less than a month from now, and you heard your sister."

"I already talked to my contractor—they've got their marching orders. Work is being done, just not by you."

Did he know how hard that was for her?

"It'll be fine." He smiled.

She set her fork down. "It will?"

"Sure. I have complete faith in us."

Us. She wasn't used to that. She'd worked on a team at JB Sweet for years and rarely felt a sense of camaraderie, only competition. "You aren't worried at all?"

He shrugged. "It won't change anything for me to worry about it. We'll do what we can do, and it will be enough."

The conversation lulled and they ate in silence, the sun starting to look heavy in the sky.

"Maybe that's not completely honest," he said, staring off toward the lake.

"What's not?"

"Saying I'm not worried. The first week the cottages are open, I have some really important people coming to stay here. That's the thing I fall asleep thinking about."

She took a sip of her water and watched him for a long moment. If she wasn't careful, he might fool her into believing there were genuinely kind and good men out there when she'd spent the last seven years believing the exact opposite.

"Like, investors?"

"More important."

She considered this. In the past week, she hadn't often seen a serious side of Brooks, but she was pretty sure that was about to change.

"I should be dead right now."

She frowned. "What?"

He stared past her as if reliving a painful experience. The somber expression looked like it belonged on someone else. Never on Brooks.

"We were out on patrol, same as every other day, when we came under enemy fire."

Ryan's smile had gone and taken his playful flirtatiousness with it. She had a feeling she was witnessing something rare, something very few people ever saw.

"It all happened so fast. I was about to take cover behind a small shed when I felt someone yank me backward. One of my friends—Drum, a guy I'd gone through basic training with—he must've seen something I didn't. He shoved me in the opposite direction just before the explosion. That shove saved my life. But Drum . . ."

His voice trailed off and Lane realized she'd been holding her breath. She'd been so self-absorbed she'd never even asked what it had been like for him over there. The things he'd seen, the way he'd lived—what kind of toll had that taken on him?

She'd assumed that he was always happy-go-lucky. But what if his casual charm masked a deeper pain?

"Brooks," she whispered.

"He has a wife and a kid." He shook his head. "I can't figure out why he was killed and I'm still here."

He turned away from her for several seconds and she could see that his eyes were closed, and she wished she knew how to comfort him. Everything that came to mind seemed so trite in comparison.

"His family is coming here next month." Finally he turned back toward her, wearing what must be a forced smile. "So I guess I do want everything to be perfect for them and the rest of the veterans who are coming."

"Are there veterans and families of vets in every cottage?"

He nodded. "I wanted them here as my guests. I thought we could give them a peaceful, relaxing week in Harbor Pointe. Maybe this place could do for them what it's done for me."

How ironic the town she'd sought to escape was a place of refuge for him.

And he probably wasn't making a penny off of them. He simply wanted to give these people—his people—a gift.

She'd never done something that selfless in her entire life. The thought shamed her. Her pain had consumed every aspect of her life, so much so that it prevented her from valuing anyone else.

"Then that is exactly what they'll get," Lane said.

He leaned back in his chair. "Don't get all crazy. You need to take it easy, remember?"

She shrugged. "I'll be fine."

"I shouldn't have told you about this," he said. "You're going to be nuts until everything is finished. Pressure is the last thing you need."

"Actually, I think for the first time in my professional career, I feel like I can use my skills for something worthwhile. It's not just about making some rich guy happy or some business look good. It's about doing something really wonderful for people who deserve it."

The knot was back at the center of her throat. She didn't even know she'd felt that way until she said the words.

"Okay, then we'll get started tomorrow. First thing." He stood and picked up the empty plates. She followed him inside with the water glasses.

After they loaded the dishes into the dishwasher, Brooks turned and looked at her the same way he'd looked at her that morning in her apartment and then later in the hallway upstairs. If it were any other man, she might think he'd developed feelings for her, but this was Ryan Brooks. Her old friend. Her brothers' friend.

He was like this with everyone—wasn't he?

"I'm going to go," he said. "I want to run by the hospital and sit with Nate for a while. You'll be okay here alone tonight?"

She laughed involuntarily. "I live in the city. I think I can handle Harbor Pointe."

"Right. I forgot."

"Ryan, thanks for everything." She pushed her hair out of her face. "It meant a lot to me that you came to the hospital."

"Hey, I'd never miss the chance to see you in a hospital gown." He raised his brows.

"You're terrible." She gave him a shove, but as she did, he grabbed her arm and pulled her toward him, stopping just inches from her face. They were close—too close—but she didn't want to pull away. He loosened his grip on her arm but kept a hold on her. His hand slipped into hers. He moved even closer and her heart raced. What was happening? This was Brooks.

She stared at their hands, intertwined. *Oh. This was Brooks.* Brooks, who had beautiful green eyes and a nearly undetectable scar underneath the right one. Brooks, who'd paid such close attention to her—not just this past week, but even when she was young. Brooks, who knew all her secrets—all the things she was embarrassed about or ashamed of—and didn't seem to mind one bit.

And he'd been here all along.

He lifted her chin so he could meet her eyes; then his hand moved to her neck, the feel of it on her skin turning her stomach upside down.

"I don't want to mess this up," he said, both hands on her face now, his eyes searching hers. "But I've wanted to kiss you since I was sixteen."

Lane inched back slightly and studied his face. Was he serious? "Since you were sixteen?"

"That day on the beach—that stupid game of truth or dare."

Lane's stomach turned. She remembered. Another day of humiliation for her.

"Don't do that," he said, lifting her chin again, forcing her gaze. "Don't let that old memory have control over you. I'm telling you *I* was the idiot. I am the one who should be ashamed."

She shook her head. "No, you didn't do anything wrong."

"I didn't do anything right either." His thumb traced the edges of her lips, then rested on her cheek. "I wanted to kiss you that day.

I was so nervous, and I didn't want everyone watching. And I wasn't sure I wanted our first kiss to be on a dare."

This couldn't be true. She'd been overweight and awkward. She conversed better with adults than kids her own age. She preferred books to people. What was there for him to like about her? She couldn't think of a single thing.

"This is a bad idea," she whispered. But even as she said the words, he covered her lips with his own, his kiss unhurried and soft, as if he wanted to take his time, to experience the fullness of a kiss he'd waited so many years to have.

She closed her eyes and within seconds she was lost in him—lost in the way his lips moved over hers, the way he backed her up to the counter, the way he wrapped his arms around her like he couldn't get close enough.

She wound her arms around him, the muscles in his back taut underneath her hands, her mind wandering all the way to nothing as if she didn't have a single care in the world.

But she did have a care. Many cares. And this feeling—this caught-up-in-something-new feeling—was risky. It was what had led her to heartbreak with Jasper.

Ryan wasn't Jasper, though. Ryan was Brooks. Someone she'd known all her life. He'd never hurt her the way others had. And yet . . . she'd thought that about Jasper once too.

She pulled away, eyes on his chest.

He must've sensed her apprehension because he straightened, concerned gaze on her. "You're freaked out."

She leaned back. "No, no, of course not."

"I'm sorry. I shouldn't have—" He ran a hand over his mouth and chin, searching her eyes. "I'm sorry, Lane."

He walked past her, picked up his duffel bag, and headed out the door, leaving her with nothing but silence and an unwelcome desire to run after him.

CHAPTER

29

THE NEXT MORNING, Lane woke up with the memory of Ryan's kiss fresh in her mind. She'd replayed the moment over and over before finally drifting off to sleep, and never with the kind of disdain her head told her she should have.

Now, as thoughts of the day ahead pulled her out of bed, she realized she'd liked kissing him. And if she was honest, she wanted to do it again.

The thought alarmed her. What if Brooks discovered—like Jasper had—that she wasn't worth loving?

She shoved the question aside and got ready for the day. Visiting Nate was her top priority. Unlike the first time she'd been home, she didn't feel obligated or put out in being here. She actually *wanted* to be in Harbor Pointe. The thought surprised her.

Nate's stream of visitors had slowed down by the time Lane had left town, but thanks to Dottie, there was still rarely a moment when he was alone. Lane remembered the first day she'd walked into the hospital, over a week ago. So much had happened in that time, she could hardly wrap her head around it.

She exited the elevator on the third floor and strode toward Nate's room. She pushed the door open and found her parents standing by Nate's bed with Walker Jones.

"Lane?" She couldn't be sure, but her mom almost looked relieved to see her.

"You're back." Her dad drew her into a hug—the kind of hug only he could give. For a long moment, she didn't respond, her arms limp at her sides. Her dad only held her tighter, until finally Lane hugged him back. Then he pulled away and studied her. "Good. Where you belong."

Lane chose not to dwell on the comment. In her displaced state, she was likely to give it more weight than it deserved.

"Is everything okay?" She glanced at Walker, who wore an annoying smirk.

"Better now that you're here." Walker winked at her.

"Mom?" Lane asked, ignoring him.

"We were just discussing the progress on Nate's case," her mom said. "We really want to know who's responsible for this." Her voice shook as she finished the sentence.

"Any new information?" Lane knew Noah was intent on finding whoever had run Nate and Ryan off the road, but last she heard, nobody knew anything.

"Trying to lean a little harder on Brooks. He seems to know more than he's letting on."

Lane remembered how at the farmers' market Walker had implied Ryan knew something. The comment had gotten under her skin, but she couldn't believe it was true. If he knew something, he'd say so.

"Ryan?" Dottie practically gasped his name. "There's no way he knows something and isn't telling us. He wouldn't do that. I'm sure he wants to figure out who is responsible as much as we do."

Walker looked unconvinced. "I'm just telling you what my gut is saying to me."

"Well, your gut is wrong," Lane said. "You obviously don't know

Ryan very well if you think he'd keep something this important from our family."

"That's cute," Walker said. "But he acts like someone with something to hide."

"What are you saying?" Dottie asked. "That Ryan is somehow responsible for the accident?"

Walker shrugged. "It's a possibility. Either that or he knows more about what happened."

A nurse entered the room, drawing their attention. Lane was thankful for the distraction. She didn't like Walker in the first place, and his suggestion that Ryan was a liar made her furious.

After the nurse finished checking on Nate, Lane's mother stood and looked at her father. "I could use a cup of coffee."

Frank nodded. "Lane, you'll stay with Nate?"

"Of course."

Lane's parents followed the nurse out of the room, leaving her with Walker Jones.

"You should probably go now, Walker," Lane said.

"You want to go to dinner sometime?" He hitched his thumbs in his belt loops and eyed her like she was a perfectly cooked prime rib.

"With you?"

"'Course with me. I'll show you a good time. You seem tense. I can help you with that."

"No."

His brow furrowed. "Why not?"

"So many reasons."

He took a step toward her. "I see how it is. You're not fat anymore, so you think you're better than the rest of us." He'd emphasized the word *fat* like it was heavier than the other words.

Lane's face flushed and she was fifteen again, wearing a skirt that had gotten tighter since the last time she wore it and wishing Mr. Dobbs hadn't called on her to solve a math problem on the whiteboard at the front of the class.

She'd stood there, back to the rest of the group, aware of their stares, their comments, their jokes—but she could've tried to ignore them if it weren't for Walker Jones, who always seemed to have it in for her.

She solved the problem, and as she returned to her seat, Walker covered his face with his hands and snorted—something that happened a lot those days when Lane walked by. There was a ripple of laughter as Lane finally took her seat, trying desperately not to cry.

She lifted her chin and pretended not to notice or care, wondering how high school kids could act so juvenile, but fresh tears stung her eyes.

Her mind strained as she played through the rest of that day. After school, Brooks came by Summers and her dad told her to make him whatever he wanted. They'd gone down to the dock to eat their sandwiches with their feet dangling in Lake Michigan, and Ryan made her forget all about Walker and her rotten day at school.

Recalling it now, she realized he'd most likely had a pretty bad day himself, but as soon as he saw her sullen face, it was like his only goal was to cheer her up. How had she forgotten that kindness?

"Are you thinking about it or . . . ?"

Walker's question pulled her back to reality. She wasn't that girl anymore. And while she'd felt so alone in those years, her memory reminded her she wasn't. She never had been.

"You can go, Walker," Lane said, ignoring his question.

He strolled over to her and got much too close, looked her up and down, then—finally—walked out of the room, taking with him the memories she'd worked so hard to forget.

CHAPTER

~~~

30

RYAN SAT IN HIS BOOTH at Hazel's, waiting for Hailey, who was now
ten minutes late. Betsy strolled over and refilled his coffee mug.

"What's wrong with you?" she asked. "You look like you haven't
slept in a week."

That was fairly accurate. He hadn't slept well at Lane's apartment
because he was worrying about Lane, and after his massive mistake
last night, he'd welcomed dawn from the comforts of Hailey's sofa,
where he'd sat for most of the night, wide-awake and kicking himself for kissing her in the first place.

It had been some kiss, though. Mostly he was searching his mind
for a way to do it again.

But he'd scared her off. So much for slowly earning her trust.

"I'm fine," he lied.

Betsy's face said she didn't believe him, but he didn't need to get
into it with her. Or anyone. He was too humiliated.

Hailey rushed in—Jack-less—and sat down across from him.
She wore her Hazel's uniform because her shift started in forty-five
minutes.

"Sorry," she said. "I dropped Jack off, but I forgot his lunch at home and had to run back and get it for him. Why do they save all the field trips for the very last month of school?"

"Great question," Betsy said. "Another great question is 'What's wrong with your brother?'"

Hailey frowned, then turned her attention to Ryan. "You do look awful."

"Thanks. You girls sure know how to make a guy feel good about himself first thing in the morning."

"Sorry," Hailey and Betsy said in unison.

"What's wrong?" Hailey echoed Betsy's concern.

"Nothing's wrong. Let's order and eat so I can get to work."

Hailey and Betsy exchanged a look; then Hailey moved over and Betsy slid in next to her, both of them staring at Ryan.

"Oh, man." He took his baseball cap off and raked his hands through his hair.

"We know a lovesick man when we see one," Hailey said. "And you, big brother, are like the poster child."

"It's Lane, isn't it?" Betsy folded her hands on top of the table like they were about to have an important talk.

"You don't have to answer. We already know it's Lane," Hailey said.

"It's been Lane for a long time," Betsy confirmed. Another knowing look between the two of them.

"I haven't seen Lane in years, you guys." Ryan took a drink of his coffee, mostly because he didn't know what to do with himself under their watchful gaze.

"Okay, so it was Lane a long time ago and now it's Lane all over again," Betsy said. "You don't have to be embarrassed about it."

"Really?" His eyes darted from Betsy to Hailey and back. "The two of you are going to give me advice on this topic? How are your love lives again?"

Hailey waved him off. "We're not talking about us here."

"No, of course not," Ryan said. "Bets, I'm on a schedule. Can I get my—?"

But before he could finish the sentence, one of the other waitresses set a plate in front of him.

"You underestimate me." Betsy smirked.

Hailey narrowed her gaze. "Okay, you were up all night—something is obviously bothering you."

His food didn't even look appetizing anymore.

"We know you went to see her in Chicago," Betsy said.

"And you brought her back here with you."

"And you gave up your house for her."

"I didn't give up my house for her," Ryan said. "She's helping with the design of the cottages. That's all."

"That is so obviously not all," Hailey said. "Why don't you ask her out?"

He drew in a breath and avoided his sister's irritating stare.

"You did ask her out," Hailey said triumphantly as if she'd just solved a Rubik's Cube for the first time.

"Not exactly," Ryan said, the memory of the moment his lips touched Lane's haunting and exciting him at the same time.

Hailey and Betsy shared a quick glance.

"It was stupid. I don't want to talk about it."

"You kissed her," Hailey said.

Betsy gasped.

"Or . . . was it more than a kiss?"

"No, it wasn't," Ryan said. "Not that it's any of your business."

Hailey smiled. "You kissed her."

"Was it romantic?" Betsy asked. "How'd it happen?"

"Did you take her down to the dock and kiss her under the light of the moon?" Hailey's voice had gotten weird and breathy.

"Or maybe you were out on the porch, ready to leave, and she grabbed your hand and stopped you before you could go, and when you turned around, you looked in her eyes and you couldn't help yourself . . ." Betsy's tone matched Hailey's as she practically acted out the scene she described.

"You two have officially lost your minds," Ryan said, shaking his head. "Both of you need to get out more." And he needed to find some guy friends.

"That's actually true," Hailey said, "but since we don't, we have to live vicariously through you."

"Great." Ryan took a bite of his eggs, swallowing before he could taste them.

"So what's the problem? You should've kissed her years ago," Betsy said. "I mean, I admit, when she left for college, I figured that was the last we'd ever see of her, but the day you two walked back in here, it was pretty obvious there was still something between you."

"You think?" Ryan washed his eggs down with a swig of orange juice.

"I think everyone knows it except the two of you," Hailey agreed.

Ryan let out a sigh. "I don't think she's interested."

Betsy shifted in her seat. "Look, Ryan, I used to know Lane really well, and even when we were kids, she was always strong-willed, but she's also really shy."

"But not with me," Ryan said. "She's never been shy with me."

"All I'm saying is Lane is independent. If you want her, you're going to have to pursue her." Betsy met his gaze. "Because she thinks she's better off by herself."

"Maybe she is," Ryan said.

Hailey huffed. "You don't believe that, so don't even pretend."

"You're right. I don't. I think she needs someone in her life to balance her out a little—remind her that there's more to living than work."

"Then go do that." Hailey clapped a hand over his.

"How?"

"Don't give up on her," Hailey said.

"Just show her you're one of the good guys," Betsy added. "Because after Jasper, she's probably decided there's none of those left."

Ryan finished the last of his breakfast and fished a ten-dollar bill from his wallet. He set it on the table. "I have to get to work."

"Is that for our counseling services?" Hailey asked as he threw the money on the table.

Ryan stood. "Thanks or whatever."

"We're here whenever you need us," Betsy said.

"Whether you want us or not." Hailey grinned.

31

ONCE WALKER HAD GONE, Lane let out the breath she didn't know she'd been holding and dropped her bag on the floor next to Nate's bed. She sank into the chair and drew a deep breath. Maybe this was a mistake. She'd been back one day and already she'd ruined her friendship with Brooks and had a run-in with Walker Jones.

But, she remembered, she had nothing in Chicago to go back to.

She pulled out her phone, which had been eerily silent, and opened her social media accounts. Also eerily silent. It had been days since she'd posted anything—would her followers forget all about her?

"Oh, I didn't realize anyone was in here."

She didn't have to turn around to recognize the voice that came from behind her. *Lindsay.*

Slowly Lane turned toward her sister, who hung back in the doorway. With one look she could see Lindsay had been crying.

"What's wrong?" She asked the question more out of habit than genuine concern. She didn't care what was wrong. Not with Lindsay.

That made her an ugly person, and she knew it. Lane was probably the last person in the world she wanted to talk to.

"I'm actually glad you're here." Lindsay took a few steps into the room and closed the door behind her. It would be a matter of minutes before someone else showed up, Lane was sure, but she didn't like the thought of being alone with Lindsay even for seconds. It would bring out the very worst in her, and she didn't need to be reminded of her very worst right now.

Or maybe it just hurt too badly.

Lindsay hugged her black leather handbag to her chest and avoided Lane's eyes. Finally Lane returned her attention to Nate. If Lindsay wanted to talk to her, fine, but she wasn't going to try to pull it out of her.

Lindsay cleared her throat.

Lane didn't move.

"I thought you'd gone back to Chicago."

"I did."

"You came back again?" Her voice shook as she said the words. What was going on?

Lane didn't respond, figuring the answer was obvious, but she noticed Lindsay didn't move from her spot near the door. Seconds later, she heard her sister sniffle.

"Are you just going to stand there?" Lane asked, doing nothing to hide her irritation.

Lindsay hovered behind her like she didn't know where she was supposed to go unless someone told her.

"Did they say anything about Nate? Is he any better?" Lindsay dared a few steps closer, then moved around to the other side of the bed. She still clung tightly to her purse and avoided Lane's eyes.

Surprisingly, Lane saw no need to avoid Lindsay's. She lifted her chin and watched her sister, the memory of the day Jasper told her what he'd done rushing at her as if the floodgates had opened. She braced herself for impact, remembering the look on his face when she showed up at his door. She knew instantly something was wrong. She just had no idea what it was.

Jasper had been away for the weekend—camping, he'd said.

Never mind that Jasper wasn't a camping kind of guy. That should've been her first clue.

"You look like you're about to be sick," she'd said when he answered the door. He didn't move out of the way to let her in. He didn't pull her into an I-missed-you-so-much hug, which was, she thought, what a fiancé should do. Instead he just stood there silent, and she knew whatever it was, it was going to hurt.

"Jasper?"

He avoided her eyes, opting to stare at his feet. "We need to talk, Lane."

Her throat went dry. "Can I at least come in?"

He finally looked at her. "There's something I need to tell you."

"Okay." She paused then. "You're scaring me, Jasper."

He glanced away. "I met someone, Lane."

His abrupt words shook her foundation. "What are you talking about?"

"I think I've fallen in love with someone else."

She was getting the worst news of her life, standing in the hallway outside his apartment. Doreen from next door was probably eavesdropping through her keyhole. "Can I come in? We can talk about it."

"It's not a good idea, Lane."

"What are you talking about?" She tried not to sound hysterical. "When did all this happen? This weekend you met someone new? Someone you're in love with?"

He let out a heavy sigh. "Don't do that, Lane. Don't make me feel bad about this."

She felt her jaw go slack. Was he serious? "You don't feel badly about this?"

"What? Of course. Of course I do." A noise from inside the apartment startled him and he closed the door a little.

Lane eyed him, her stomach wrenching, her heart pounding like the bass drum in a marching band. "Unbelievable. Is she here now?"

"I didn't think you'd be by until later," he said as if that were an acceptable answer to her question.

A calmness came over her, the kind of calm that was a bit frightening given that it was so out of place. "Get out of the way, Jasper."

He resisted, but he had to know she wasn't going to leave until she knew what—or who—he was hiding.

She finally pushed past him and found Lindsay sitting in his kitchen wearing one of his white button-down shirts and nothing else. She was perched at the table with her legs pulled up under her, hair in a messy bun, and Lane realized Jasper had never gone out of town that weekend at all. He'd only told her that so he could spend a few days with Lindsay without having to worry that Lane would find out about it.

Lindsay stood, a dumbfounded, confused expression on her face. "Lane, it's not what it looks like."

Lane's mind rushed to piece it together. She'd brought Jasper home with her twice the previous summer. She'd introduced him to her family. They got along. Hit it off. Had there been sparks between him and Lindsay that she hadn't noticed? Had this started then? When he was there with *her*?

"It looks like you two spent the weekend together."

Lindsay looked helplessly toward Jasper, who smoothed his hair and sighed. "Lane, let's be rational here. We're all adults."

"She—" Lane pointed at Lindsay—"is not an adult."

"Technically she is," Jasper said.

Lane met his gaze. After several seconds of glaring at him, she smacked him across the face. Hard.

"Lane!" Lindsay rushed over and stood next to Jasper, giving her a clear picture of how this whole scenario was going to end. The two of them on one side, Lane on the other.

"You both make me sick," Lane said, doing her best—which really wasn't very good—not to cry. "I never want to see either of you again."

Apparently Jasper loved Lindsay's bubbly personality. They had fun together. They just had a spark he'd never felt with Lane. He said it all as Lane struggled to wrap her brain around the words, the scene in front of her. Like he needed to get it off his chest to make himself feel better.

She'd been too paralyzed to say or do anything else—all the things she should've said came to her afterward, but by then it was too late. She didn't have an audience for her pain anymore.

A few months later, Jasper and Lindsay announced their engagement. A few months after that, they got married. And now, years later, she was sitting in the same room with one of the people who'd caused her the greatest pain she'd ever known.

Yet Lindsay was her sister. It had never mattered before, so why now?

"Lane, are you ever going to talk to me again?" Lindsay asked, interrupting Lane's much-preferred silence.

Lane glared at her. "I really see no reason to, no."

Lindsay nodded, eyes on the ceiling, the way she did when she was trying not to cry. "It's just that I could really use someone to talk to right now."

Lane glanced at Nate, the rhythmic breathing of the ventilator the only sound that broke the silence hanging between them.

"I think I made a terrible mistake." Lindsay slid into the chair on the opposite side of the bed. Lane kept her eyes on Nate. She wouldn't engage. She couldn't.

"I never should've betrayed you the way I did, Lane, and I'm so sorry."

A lump lodged itself squarely in the center of Lane's throat like someone had inflated a balloon there, making it hard to swallow.

Out of the corner of her eye, she saw Lindsay wipe her cheeks dry, and she resisted the urge to feel sorry for her.

A long-forgotten image rushed back at her. The two of them huddled together in a single sleeping bag, camping in the backyard. It was well past midnight and their brothers had made a sport of scaring their sisters.

"I'll protect you," Lane had said when Lindsay crawled into her sleeping bag. "It's just the boys being silly. We're not going to give in. We're going to prove to them we're strong enough to stay out here."

"All night?"

"Yep. If we stick together, we can do anything."

Now Lindsay pulled a tissue from her purse. She'd become someone Lane didn't recognize—a shell of an actual person—as if Jasper had stolen her identity away and molded her into who he wanted her to be.

Was that it? Lane was too strong for him?

"I don't think he ever got over you, Lane."

Lane folded her hands in her lap. "Don't be ridiculous."

"I've spent my whole life trying to live up to his memory of you. In the beginning, he sometimes slipped up and called me Lane. Or one time, I made him dinner—Italian, because all I knew how to cook was pasta. You would've thought I was feeding him something foreign, like squid or octopus, and I knew he was thinking, *Lane and I don't eat pasta.* Because you don't anymore, which is why you're so thin and gorgeous now. That's hard for me too, because you know, I was always the thin one, and then I had Jett and now my body looks like this." She flopped her hands in the air, having grown a bit more hysterical with each word.

Lane glanced at her, not telling Lindsay she still looked like a model. She said nothing.

"I feel like your ghost has followed me around ever since that day in Jasper's apartment. It's been Jasper and me and your ghost, this constant reminder of the person he should've married, this strong, brilliant, beautiful person who didn't deserve to have her heart broken." Lindsay's eyes were bloodshot. She closed them and another tear escaped. "I can't measure up to you, Lane—not for Jasper and not for anyone else."

Words she'd been waiting years to hear did nothing to soothe the aching of Lane's spirit. Shouldn't Lindsay's admission warm her heart in some way? Why didn't it?

"I don't think Jasper and I are right together." Lindsay balled up her tissue and pulled at the edges the way she'd done even when they were kids. "I know it's too late to say that, but . . ." Her voice trailed off and she dabbed the corners of her eyes, crossed her arms, and leaned back in her chair. "I've tried to make this work, but Jasper . . ." She looked at Lane.

Jasper what?

"It's just not. Working, I mean."

Lane's heart raced. For years, she'd dreamed of one of them realizing what a ridiculous mistake they made by getting together behind Lane's back. She'd dreamed of the day Jasper finally admitted how horribly he'd treated her and offered an apology, which she absolutely would not accept. She'd imagined the day Lindsay did exactly what she was doing right now—admitting to Lane that their marriage was a mistake.

So why did it feel so unfulfilling to hear her say the words?

"What's not working?"

"Me. Him. Us." Lindsay sighed. "He's so distant and he hardly ever pays attention to me anymore. He doesn't do what he says he'll do and he never helps out with Jett. My friend Morgan talks about her husband all the time—how he does the laundry and makes the kids' lunches. He's a present husband and father. Jasper isn't." Lindsay shifted in her seat. "You wouldn't understand, Lane. You've never been married."

That stung. She wanted to lash out with *Well, whose fault is that?* But she bit back the words, her gaze landing on their brother, whose life hung in the balance. Suddenly their rift—no matter how hurtful—felt silly and unimportant.

"Do you remember when I was in eighth grade and I decided to go out for basketball?"

Lindsay shrugged. "Kind of."

"I told Mom and Dad I wanted to play sports because it looked fun, but really I thought maybe I'd lose some weight and everyone would stop calling me Pudge." Lane's mind wandered back to the way the uniform had fit her—too tight, too revealing. It was embarrassing. "I wanted to quit after the first week. I hated it so much, and I was so bad at it."

"That, I remember. You'd come home in tears every night."

"It was awful. I just knew I'd made a mistake, and I wanted out of it."

"I know what you're getting at, Lane, but this isn't the same thing."

"Mom and Dad refused to let me quit," Lane said, ignoring her sister. "I stuck it out the entire season. I even scored two baskets, which was pretty impressive given the fact that I hardly ever actually played in a game."

"Yeah, you're a real Kobe Bryant," Lindsay said dryly.

"My point is, nobody gives you a guarantee that it's going to be easy. Giving up would be easy. Leaving would be easy. Sticking it out—that's a lot harder."

"You sound like a motivational speaker."

Lane could practically hear her sister's eye roll in her tone. "You wanted this life so badly you hurt our whole family to get it. Walking away now would just be cruel and selfish, Lindsay. To me and to Mom and Dad, not to mention to your son." Lane stood. "You don't get to quit just because it's not easy or Jasper isn't paying attention to you twenty-four hours a day. Why don't you focus on other people for a change? Figure that out and I'm betting the rest of it will fall into place."

Lindsay knit her fingers together. "It's not that simple."

Lane studied her for a long moment, wondering if she'd ever been happy at all. Had her marriage to Jasper been some weird effort to try to one-up Lane? Was she so tired of being in Lane's shadow that she purposely sabotaged her?

Lindsay got up. "For what it's worth, Lane, I am sorry."

Lane leveled her gaze. "If you're really sorry, then prove it."

"How am I supposed to do that? Divorce Jasper? Wouldn't that prove it? Would you forgive me then?"

"No, Lindsay." Lane slung her bag over her shoulder. "You don't get to give up on the life I was supposed to have. If you really want to prove to me you're sorry, then you'll do everything you can to make your marriage work."

She glanced at Nate one more time before she turned and walked out.

CHAPTER

32

IT WAS TEN MINUTES PAST NOON, and Ryan had started to wonder if Lane was going to show. He sat on the front steps of the model cottage, but there was no sign of her. What if she was so freaked out by their kiss that she was set on avoiding him? Or worse, what if she'd left town? He'd call her if he had his phone. He wasn't sure where he'd set it down.

Finally, after about fifteen minutes of waiting, she pulled up in front of the house, and she and Otis got out of the car. She carried a brown paper bag, and she looked like something out of his dreams.

Hailey and Betsy—as annoying as they were—were right. Having Lane back in his life felt like a second chance. He wasn't about to let her get away that easily.

"You're late," he said, keeping his tone light. He didn't want to let on he'd actually been worried about her.

"Sorry. The girl my dad has working the register is not so bright. I had to come around to her side of the counter and ring myself up."

"You didn't do that."

She looked puzzled. "Of course I did. She was taking forever. I rang up the next three customers too, then showed her a couple shortcuts on the register."

"I bet she loved that."

"I was nice." Lane smiled. He'd never get tired of seeing that. "I brought lunch." She held up the bag.

"I see that. Should we eat out on the back porch? I think there's bottled water in the fridge." He opened the door and led her through the house and into the kitchen, where they both lingered just a hair too long. It was impossible not to think about that kiss, standing in the same spot where it had happened.

Lane's cheeks were undeniably pink, and he knew it was up to him not to make this awkward.

He grabbed a couple bottles from the refrigerator and motioned toward the screen door that led to the porch. Barb had picked out a set of wicker gliders and a love seat, and there was a small table and chairs for eating on the porch. Lane sat cautiously in one of the chairs as if she wasn't sure she wanted to be there anymore.

"Look," he said. "I know you feel weird about what happened last night."

"Oh, we're talking about this?" She looked away.

"Do you not want to?"

She hesitated. "I thought you felt weird." Her voice was quiet. He guessed she wasn't used to actually discussing her feelings.

"I do. Sort of. I mean, I don't regret it, but I feel bad if I made you uncomfortable."

She didn't respond.

"I'm sorry if I was out of line."

"No, you weren't. It's fine."

He lifted his chin and faced her. "So I can do it again if I want to?"

She smiled, then looked down.

"I'm not Jasper, Lane."

She stiffened at the mention of his name, but he wouldn't let that deter him.

"I know what I want, and even though you may not be able to accept it yet, I'm not going anywhere. I'll wait till whenever you're ready."

She pressed her lips together, then raised her head. "What if I'm never ready?"

He shrugged. "I guess I'll be waiting a long time."

Her phone buzzed from somewhere inside her purse. She didn't jump to get it the way she usually did. Instead, she pulled the sandwiches from the bag and set them on the table. "I hope you're hungry."

"I've got some ideas to show you." Lane felt exposed as she said the words, as if she'd never done this before. Her desire to please him was alarming. She was usually much more sure of herself when it came to work. But this was so important to Ryan, and she wanted to get it right.

She took out her laptop. After she left the hospital, she'd gone down to Davis Park and sat in the gazebo, sketching out her ideas, then searching for images on her phone, which she saved to later turn into a makeshift mood board. It wasn't fancy, but they were working on a deadline.

"Let's see what you've got."

"I used the model cottage as inspiration," Lane said, turning her laptop toward him. "But I tweaked the ideas a bit. Your designer chose some really nice foundational pieces. The hand-scraped, dark wood floors and crown moldings are perfect. The kitchen cabinets are beautiful, but I'm glad most of the details—the counters and appliances—aren't in yet."

She showed him the farmhouse sink she'd found, then the tile for the backsplash in the kitchen, then the rustic, galvanized light fixtures—which he said looked like barn lights—and towel bars and mirrors for the bathrooms. She scrolled through ideas for planked wood paneling on the walls and ways to make each cottage uniform but unique, then took out a book of paint chips.

"You did all this today?" Ryan swallowed the last bite of his sandwich. "This is amazing, Lane."

She thought she might fold underneath the weight of that simple compliment. "I've been designing these cottages in my head since you first showed them to me."

He smiled. "So you had a head start."

She nodded.

"Well, it's still really amazing. I'm so glad Barb quit."

She laughed. "We have a ton of work to do to make this happen."

He was mid-drink but shook his head. "No, *we* don't."

She frowned. "Ryan, if I'm going to actually design this, I have to be a part of the work."

"You're the supervisor, Lane. Let's call you the 'creative director.'" He crumpled up the paper his sandwich had come in and stuffed it in the bag. "That means you get to tell everyone else what to do. The crew is coming first thing on Saturday, so that gives us a day to get a plan."

"Your crew works on Saturday?"

"Every day but Sunday at this point."

"It's not much time, but I can call in some favors. I looked at inventory from suppliers I've been using for years," Lane said. "I think we can do it. I want everything to be perfect for your opening week."

"You do?" He looked surprised.

"Of course I do. Those people deserve to be spoiled. Let's spoil them." The excitement that welled within her was unexpected, but she'd never used her skills for such a worthy cause before. She was thrilled with her designs and wanted them to be good, but mostly she wanted to see the looks on the faces of the families they'd be hosting that first week.

Maybe she'd been working for the wrong incentive all along.

"I like the way you think," Ryan said. "Should we get started?"

He reached a hand toward her, and when she took it, he pulled her up, but he didn't take a step back and he didn't let go.

"I'm ready when you are," she said quietly, trying not to relive the kiss but desperately wanting it to happen again.

"This is going to be a lot more difficult than I thought." His gaze was fixed on her, his body close. His thumb traced the edge of her hand with such softness she almost didn't feel it.

She lifted her chin slightly, entering extremely risky territory. She searched her mind for all the reasons she'd given herself that this attraction to Ryan Brooks was a terrible idea, but in that moment, she couldn't think of a single one.

He drew in a deep breath as if he were inhaling the very essence of her; then abruptly he took a step back and let go of her hand. She felt his absence instantly. She knew he was giving her space because that's what he thought she wanted.

That's what *she'd* thought she wanted.

But looking at him now, she couldn't think of a single thing she wanted less.

"Would it be such a bad idea?" She stared at her feet, unwilling—or maybe unable—to look him in the eye.

"Would what be such a bad idea?"

What was she thinking? This was a mistake. A huge, scary mistake. But in that moment, it didn't seem to matter.

"What, Lane?"

"You and me. Would *we* be such a bad idea?" Her heart raced as she finally dared to look at him.

He smiled but didn't move. "I think it's the best idea you've ever had."

"But I live in Chicago."

"Yeah, you do." He took a step toward her.

"And you live here. And we're friends, and I don't want to mess that up. And now, technically you're my boss, and I've done that before and it didn't work out so well. And I've been really good about making sure I didn't feel this way ever again. And I swear, Ryan Brooks, if you hurt me—"

"Are you finished?" He smiled, then placed a hand on the small of her back and pulled her closer, their bodies touching as he closed the gap between them.

"Probably not." She grabbed a fistful of his shirt, inhaling his distinctly masculine scent. "There are so many reasons why this is a bad idea."

"Lane?" His gaze, intent on her, nearly stole her breath away.

"Yeah?"

"Shut up." He smiled, then leaned down and kissed her, hands still wrapped around her possessively as if he wasn't willing to allow space between them. His kiss began carefully but quickly turned into something deeper, more intense.

She got lost in it, and for several minutes she was able to push away every fear she had and pretend like there was no way this could ever end badly. Her hands slid around his back as she drew him closer, savoring every gentle touch, every movement of his lips on hers.

She loved kissing him. Why hadn't she realized it sooner?

Finally he pulled away, and if she had to guess, it wasn't easy for him to do so. They were breathless and wilted, yet hungry for more of each other. She'd never felt this way before—not even about Jasper. Had she ever really loved him at all?

With Ryan, it was different. He made her want to wrap herself up in his strength and goodness and never let go. She didn't mind him taking care of her. She found herself yearning for his protectiveness.

"I have to calm myself down," he said, his forehead pressed to hers.

She replied with gentle kisses on each of his cheeks.

"I'm glad you didn't make me wait long to do that again." He stepped back.

She smiled, regarding him for a long moment. "I'm terrified of whatever this is, Brooks. I've been thinking about it nonstop."

"Well, stop thinking about it. You don't have to figure everything out. You don't have to make sense of it all. Just let me love you."

She stuck her hands in her pockets and turned away. "That's a big word."

He grabbed her arm and spun her back around. "It's the way I feel. I knew it the day I saw you at the hospital. Some part of me has always known it, but I guess I gave up thinking it would ever happen."

"What are you saying?"

"I'm the kind of guy who knows what I want." He shrugged. "It's you, Lane. It's always been you." He took her face in his hands and kissed her again, this time softly, gently, and in a way that made her want to accept every type of kiss he had to offer.

When she leaned away to search his face for any sign that she should run the other way, she found none. Nothing waiting for her there but affection.

And she felt a piece of the wall she'd built around herself come crumbling to the ground.

CHAPTER

33

THE FOLLOWING DAY, after a restful night of sleep, Lane woke up early to meet Ryan at Hazel's, which was where he apparently started every morning.

The plan was to buy paint, then spend the rest of the day shopping for the details that would make the cottages truly special. She'd told Ryan—twice—that he didn't have to come with her, but he'd insisted.

"I can't think of a better way to spend a Friday."

"Than shopping the vintage market?"

"If you're there, it'll be perfect."

She'd given him a playful shove, which led—as most of their physical contact had that day—to another kiss. She had a feeling she'd never get tired of kissing him.

Dressing for work that morning had been an exercise in mourning, something she hadn't given herself a chance to do. While she loved helping Ryan with the cottages, she didn't know who she was without JB Sweet & Associates, without the race to win or the competition of having her ideas chosen. She didn't know how to put on a sundress and strappy sandals instead of a black pencil skirt and a high-necked, ruffled gray top. When she looked in the mirror, the blue eyes staring back at her were unfamiliar and a part of her felt lost.

Still, she could tell her body hadn't fully recovered from her episode. Where there was usually energy, there was now lethargy. She required great care—and as much as she resented her body for not keeping up with her, it hadn't given her a choice. Right now, she had to go slow.

She'd get better and she'd be unstoppable.

She walked over to Hazel's, mostly an attempt to calm her racing mind, but as soon as she arrived, she wished she'd asked Ryan to pick her up after he ate.

Betsy Tanner stood right inside the doorway talking to an old man Lane didn't recognize.

Lane had been thinking about Betsy a lot lately, wishing things were different between the two of them, wishing she hadn't allowed their friendship to disintegrate.

How would she ever apologize for the way she'd treated Betsy?

"Good morning, Lane," Betsy said after excusing herself from her conversation. "Here to meet Ryan?"

Lane did a once-over of the diner but didn't see Brooks. "I am. How'd you know that?"

Betsy took two menus off the hostess stand and smiled at Lane. "Lucky guess. Follow me."

She did as she was told, following Betsy back to the same booth where she and Ryan had sat the first night she was in town. It felt like a lifetime ago.

"He should be here any minute. Can I get you some coffee?"

"Decaf would be good."

Betsy's eyebrows shot up. "Decaf? I didn't think women who wore power suits drank decaf."

"Doctor's orders," Lane said without thinking.

Betsy's face filled with concern. "Are you okay?"

The question triggered something unwanted within her.

Regret.

The kind of regret that came with a realization that she'd thrown away something she should've fought like crazy to protect. Her friendship with Betsy had been a gift—and her instinct, surprising as it was, was to fold herself back into it, to pretend they could pick up where they left off, even though she could still see hurt in Betsy's eyes.

"Lane?" Betsy sat down across from her, fully attentive like she always had been.

"It's nothing," she said. "I'm okay."

Betsy's face fell. She sat still for a long moment, then finally scooted out of the booth. "I'll go get that coffee for you."

Lane watched her walk away, heartsick that she hadn't been able to confide in Betsy the way she had for so many years. Betsy had never once betrayed her trust—that had to count for something.

A few moments later, a young girl showed up at the table with an orange-topped coffee carafe and filled Lane's mug. She slid a small container of cream—which Lane couldn't drink—and a tub of various sweeteners toward her.

Lane thanked her, but her eyes wandered over to the front counter, where Betsy was now waiting on a young couple with a small child.

She watched as her former friend made change and smiled and asked questions about her customers. She marveled at how Betsy connected with people so easily, the way everyone but Lane seemed able to do. She could see it on their faces—Betsy had won this family over, just by paying attention.

Lane, on the other hand, found it difficult to look people in the eye. She struggled to talk about herself. She'd created a world in which she was wholly self-sufficient.

And the crises of the last two weeks had shown her how empty that world was.

She hadn't been the kind of friend to Betsy that Betsy had been to her. Betsy deserved better, but still, Lane wondered if she might be willing to give her a second chance.

The bell over the door jangled, and Ryan walked in and made a beeline straight for her. He sat down across from her. "What's the matter?"

Was it that obvious? "I'm fine."

He covered her hands with his own. "That's probably not going to work with me. I know you too well."

"Can you just give me a second?"

He pulled his hands away. "Of course."

"I'll be right back." She made her way over to the front of the diner, where Betsy now stood behind the counter, wiping it down. Lane stood on the other side, between two old men who nursed cups of coffee and sat on stools that pulled up to the counter.

"Betsy."

Betsy stopped moving and looked at Lane.

Lane didn't know what else to say. How did she properly convey her regret? What words would make it okay? Images of all the times Betsy had been her only shoulder to cry on flashed through her memory, like a movie in her mind.

Betsy stared at her now, waiting for Lane to say words she didn't have.

After a long moment, the old man on Lane's right snapped his newspaper open. "Are you two gonna stand there and look at each other all day or what?"

"Is it a staring contest?" the man on the left asked. "My grand-kids always want to have staring contests."

"Well, that's annoying."

"You know what else is annoying? Having to wait five minutes for a refill on my coffee."

Lane saw the twitch of Betsy's mouth, the slightest hint of a smile, and she pressed her own lips together in a failed attempt to keep from laughing. One giggle from Betsy, and Lane felt her stoic expression disappear.

They both laughed, and Betsy reached across the counter and grabbed Lane's hand. "I'm so glad you're back."

And Lane knew she didn't just mean "back in Harbor Pointe."

"Betsy, I—"

"You don't have to say it, Lane. I already know," Betsy said, cutting her off. "But we have a lot of catching up to do." She nodded toward Ryan, and Lane found him staring at the two of them from his spot in the booth.

"Are you two about done?" The old man on the left pushed his empty mug toward Betsy.

"Of course, Mr. Shields." Betsy grinned at Lane and refilled the man's coffee. After she finished, she looked at Lane again.

"I'm sorry, Bets," Lane whispered.

Betsy shook her head. "Forgiven. Forgotten. Now let's go back to being friends, okay?"

Just like that? She forgave her like it was nothing—like Lane had never even hurt her feelings in the first place. She forgave her like it was something she'd been wanting to do for years.

"Yes. Let's." Lane swallowed hard. No one had ever shown her that kind of grace before.

She walked back to the table where Ryan sat, confusion on his face.

"You okay?" he asked.

She glanced at Betsy, who smiled as if they'd always been friends, the kind who could communicate without words, the kind who knew what the other one needed whether anyone said so or not. "I'm good, Brooks." She looked at him. "Really, really good."

CHAPTER

34

LANE'S WORK ETHIC was unlike anything Ryan had ever seen.

Mostly, she found it impossible to sit back and watch anyone else do anything unless she was right in there, doing it with them. He regularly had to force her to take breaks, kick her out when the team took over, and remind her that *rest* wasn't a dirty word.

His reminders were always met by feigned annoyance, but by the middle of the following week, he thought he'd gotten through to her. Maybe.

It had been less than a week, and already Ryan could see a hint of what the cottages were going to be. And it was all thanks to Lane.

They spent their days together, eating lunches she packed and dinners he grilled. They shopped for supplies and checked in on the crew. They took breaks and sat in the hospital room with Nate, talking to him, keeping him updated on the progress at Cedar Grove, just in case he could make sense of what they said. They'd even attended church together last Sunday, followed by family dinner at Noah and Emily's.

People in town were talking, and neither of them seemed to care. He was falling in love with her, and the only thing that worried him was that she, in her fearfulness, would run away.

They'd steal kisses in half-finished pantry closets or "accidentally" brush up against each other as they navigated small and crowded spaces on the job site. She'd allowed herself to become more accessible to him, and he wasn't taking a single moment of it for granted.

But in all of his newfound happiness, there was one thing still nagging at him, especially when they visited Nate in the hospital. He had to take care of this thing with his dad. He'd hoped the man would step up and come clean on his own, but the deadline had passed, and he knew that wasn't going to happen.

He dreaded it, but he had to go to the police and tell them what he knew. It was the right decision. He set it in his head that he'd go first thing in the morning.

And then he said a silent prayer that Lane—and the rest of her family—wouldn't hold it against him.

It was late Thursday afternoon, three days after the deadline he'd given his father, and Ryan had just walked through Lois, the cottage his crew was focusing on today. The paint had made a huge difference, and now they were installing the farmhouse sink Lane had ordered.

He had to hand it to her: she knew how to make an old cottage feel brand-new without losing any of its charm.

Outside, he walked toward the model cottage. He was early for dinner with Lane, but he didn't care—any excuse to see her for even a few extra minutes was good with him.

As he neared the front porch, Hailey rode up over the yet-to-be-paved hill and waved at him. As soon as he saw her face, he could tell something was wrong.

She got off the bike and put the kickstand down, meeting him near the front of the cottage.

"What's wrong?"

She was winded from the uphill ride, and she was still wearing her Hazel's uniform. "Walker Jones just came to see me at work."

Ryan's gut twisted. "Why?"

"Ryan, he thinks you know something about Nate's accident that you're not telling. He's even wondering if you made up the whole story about the truck because you don't have any details about it." Hailey's brow knit into a tight line.

"Well, that's just stupid," Ryan said.

"What if he starts thinking you actually caused it?" Her face fell. "Ryan, what if Nate doesn't survive and they try to blame you for his death?"

Ryan rubbed his hand over his stubbled chin. There was obviously no evidence Ryan was responsible for the accident—so why did he suddenly feel nauseous?

"Ryan?" Hailey's voice kicked up a notch, the way it sometimes did when she was scared. "It wasn't your fault, was it?"

"How can you even ask me that?" He shook his head.

"I don't know—you're acting weird. Walker said if Nate wakes up and tells a different story than you're telling, then they're going to charge you with reckless driving or something."

Why couldn't Walker just leave it alone?

"Noah is the one pushing for answers," Hailey said.

"Did Walker tell Noah his theory?"

"I don't know."

"Hailey, I didn't cause the accident." He pushed his hand through his hair. "Dad did."

Her face went blank, the color rushing from her cheeks. "What did you say?"

He explained what he remembered—how he wasn't sure at first, but that he'd gone to confront Martin and now he was certain. It was their father who had put Nate Kelley in the hospital. Their father was the reason their friend was fighting for his life.

"Why didn't you say anything?"

"He begged me not to turn him in, and I told him he had one week to do it himself. Then Lane collapsed and we started working and everything went sideways. It just kept getting pushed to the back burner, and I know that's no excuse, but I was planning to tell Walker everything. I gave Dad plenty of time to step up and confess. If I turn him in, he'll go to jail, Hailey."

"Where he belongs." Her eyes brimmed with tears.

"I know, but it's not that simple. He's still our dad."

"He ruined our lives, Ryan. How many times did he come home drunk and use you for a punching bag? He's the reason Mom left. He's the reason I've never had a normal relationship in my life."

All true. All horribly, unspeakably true.

"And what do you mean 'Lane collapsed'? Is she okay?"

"She's fine. It was a stress thing, and I wasn't supposed to tell anyone, so keep it to yourself."

"What do you think she's going to say when she finds out you've been hiding this from her?"

Ryan looked away. He didn't want to think about that—not when their relationship was so new, so fragile. He should've told her right away. Why hadn't he just told her?

Before he could formulate a response, the front door opened and Lane—beautiful Lane—walked onto the porch, pulling their attention from the tense conversation.

"Ryan," Lane said, eyes full of tears.

"What is it?"

Her face lit with a bright smile. "Nate just woke up."

Word must've spread quickly through town because the waiting room on the third floor of Harbor Pointe Hospital was packed. Friends, family, familiar and unfamiliar faces—the whole place was buzzing with activity and everyone wanted to know if Nate was going to be okay.

Lane had shot off the elevator as soon as the doors opened, with Ryan and Hailey close behind.

"I'll go to the waiting room," Hailey said, turning left toward the noisy crowd, which no doubt included half the high school faculty and the entire basketball team. Ryan followed Lane toward Nate's room.

Fortunately the two-visitors-only rule hadn't been enforced for a while.

They rounded the corner and turned in to the room where Nate had lain unresponsive for more than two weeks. Lane's parents flanked the bed, both looking flushed and grateful, tears of relief in their eyes. Noah and Jeremy stood at the foot of the bed, with Lindsay off to the side, and Nate sat propped at an angle.

Lane's eyes welled with fresh tears and she covered her face. Her brother gave a tired smile but didn't speak.

"His throat is very sore." Dottie's voice wobbled. "From the tube."

Lane rushed to his bedside and hugged him. "Are you okay? Is everything okay?"

"He's not brain-damaged if that's what you're thinking," Jeremy said.

"That's not funny, Jer," Dottie scolded.

"Thank God," Lane said. "I'm so glad you're okay."

Nate attempted to clear his throat. "You're here." His voice was hoarse and the words came out as a whisper.

"I couldn't leave you—not till I knew you were okay. Pretty hard to see Superman lying in a hospital bed." She wiped her cheeks dry.

Nate's gaze made its way over to Ryan, and he softly shook his head. "You okay?"

All eyes turned to Ryan. "Don't worry about me, man. I've recovered. We're just glad you're back."

Lane looked at her mom. "When did he wake up?"

"I tried calling you earlier," Dottie said. "It might've been the first time I actually wanted you on your phone. It all happened so fast." She squeezed Nate's hand. "He's going to be all right."

Ryan let out a heavy sigh. "I'm so relieved."

"Look, Brooks, maybe you should go." Noah took a threatening step toward Ryan.

"Noah!" Dottie put a hand on her oldest son's bulky arm. "Ryan is a part of this family. He is more than welcome to stay."

"Is he, Ma? Part of the family?"

Ryan swallowed, his throat dry.

"What is wrong with you, Noah?" Lane straightened. "You're being really rude."

"Do you have something you want to tell your *family*, Brooks?" Noah crossed his arms and glared at Ryan. They were all watching him, waiting for an explanation they didn't even know they needed.

"What are you getting at, Noah?" Jeremy asked.

"Walker thinks our friend here is hiding something. Thinks maybe Ryan is responsible for the accident. Nate can't remember, so we've got nothing but Ryan's word."

"That's ridiculous," Lane said.

Noah's glare was still locked on Ryan like a sniper who had him in his sights. "You got anything to say for yourself, Brooks?"

Ryan looked around the circle, all eyes on him. Everyone waiting for an answer to a question he didn't remember. While he hadn't caused the accident, was he responsible somehow? Was the distraction of Newman, with all its ghosts, enough to have made Ryan a poor driver? He'd given his dad money over the years—what if that money had gone to buy the liquor that night?

He couldn't say for sure that he *wasn't* responsible. At the very least, he'd known more than he let on, and he could see now that his silence had caused the Kelleys pain. He'd almost told them several times, but something had always gotten in his way.

Noah crossed the hospital room and got right in Ryan's face. "You better go."

Lane tried to pull her brother away, but he didn't move.

He glanced at Nate. "I'm sorry, man."

Lane's mouth opened and Dottie let out a slight gasp. Before he had to see any more of the disappointment on their faces, he turned and walked out into the hallway, every ounce of oxygen rushing from his body. He forced himself to breathe—a deep, controlling breath—but it did nothing to calm his nerves or chase the nausea away.

His father's actions had stolen everything away from him. Again.

Somehow he'd figured out how to manage that when he was younger, but the stakes were so much higher this time.

And as he walked down the hallway, the weight of what he stood to lose followed him like a heavy burden he wasn't able to carry.

CHAPTER

35

LANE STAYED AT THE HOSPITAL long enough to hear Noah's case against Ryan—a case it sounded like he'd been building for several days now, no doubt with Walker's help.

She didn't want to believe any of it, but what if it was true? What if Ryan *had* caused the accident?

"You don't remember anything, Nate?" Lane asked. "I can't imagine that Ryan would keep this a secret. He's not the type not to own up to his mistakes."

"If his mistakes landed him in jail, he might be," Noah said.

"Why are you being like this, No?" Lane asked. "This is Brooks. We've known him since we were kids."

"All the more reason he should've come clean."

"All right, enough," Dottie said. "We aren't in the habit of pointing fingers."

"He practically admitted it, Ma," Noah said, hands on his hips like he had something to prove.

"You didn't give him much of a chance to defend himself,"

Dottie said. "If he was responsible, I'm sure there's an explanation. It's not like he set out to run Nate into a telephone pole."

A nurse entered the room, a scowl on her face. "I'm sorry. He really needs to get some rest."

"Are you kidding?" Noah huffed. "He's been asleep for almost three weeks straight."

"Dude." Jeremy shot Noah an irritated look intended to shut him up, but when Noah was angry, he was immune to that sort of thing.

"You can come back in the morning," the nurse said and strode back down the hall.

They all said good-bye to Nate, leaving Lane at the end of the line. She walked over to his bed, sat down, and hugged him again, his arm limp on her back, no strength to speak of.

"Try to get some rest," she said. "And if you can remember what happened, I think that would be really good right about now."

He nodded, then squeezed her hand. "Glad you're here."

She smiled. "Me too." So glad. It shamed her to think that she'd almost missed this because of work. She stayed still for a long moment.

"What is it?"

"I was just thinking about the night you and Brooks dragged me out back to tip cows with you."

Nate's laugh quickly turned into a cough.

"And the weekend we were camping at the lake and you put a frog in Mom's sleeping bag."

"You've had a while to walk down memory lane." He strained when he spoke as if it really hurt his throat.

She nodded. "All the times you invited me places with your popular friends or came home early because you knew I'd spent another Friday night by myself. You always watched out for me. You were one of the only people who didn't seem to care that I was a social outcast."

It was good to watch him inhale and exhale without the help of a machine.

"I'm sorry I threw that all away."

"You didn't," he whispered. "You just took a break."

She smiled, her eyes cloudy. "Well, I'm back now, okay?"

He nodded.

Commotion in the hallway drew their attention, and Lane turned to find Betsy standing in the doorway. Her face was as white as the whipped cream on the tops of her famous pies.

"Someone said you were awake." Betsy stood unmoving as if her feet were frozen in place.

"Bets." He said her name so quietly Lane wondered if Betsy heard him.

"You're awake." Betsy clapped a hand over her mouth and burst into tears. "Oh, thank God."

"Betsy?" Lane walked toward her and took her by the arm, and as she led her into the room, Betsy's knees buckled and she almost collapsed.

Had Betsy and Nate become close since Lane left?

"I've been praying every day that you would wake up, that you would be okay. I've been so worried." Her voice was shaky, bordering on hysterical, as she released emotions that seemed to have been locked up for days. "I've been so worried about you."

Nate lifted his hand slightly, and she stared at it as if she didn't dare touch him.

"It's okay, Betsy," Lane said. "He can't really talk because he was intubated for so long. His throat is really sore."

Nate gave her a tired smile and Betsy took his hand in both of hers and pressed it to her mouth. Lane felt her eyebrows shoot up.

"I'm sorry I haven't been over to visit at all," Betsy said, still worked up. "I was afraid to come. I was afraid seeing you like this would be too much to handle, but I realize now I should've been here. I should've been here the whole time. I've been such an idiot, Nate—a really stupid idiot—but . . ." She seemed to be working up her courage for something important. Lane had never seen Betsy like this. "The truth is, Nate Kelley . . ." She swallowed. "Well, the truth is, I love you."

Lane's eyes widened. What? Betsy loved Nate?

"I've always loved you. Sorry, Lane." Betsy tossed her a look, then refocused on Nate, this newfound boldness clearly something she wanted to hold on to. "And I don't even care if you don't feel the same way about me. I'm just glad you're okay. I'm just so glad you're okay."

When Nate swallowed, it looked like it hurt, and it took several long seconds that must've been painstaking for Betsy. Finally he looked up at her, the trace of a smile on his lips. "I do," he whispered.

Betsy stilled, eyes on their hands but slowly moving toward Nate's. "You do what?"

"Feel the same."

She gasped. "You do?"

He squeezed Betsy's hand, and though his eyes looked heavy and tired, he appeared genuinely happy. He nodded. "For a long time."

Betsy shook her head. "Why didn't you say something? Why didn't you tell me?" She leaned toward him.

He only shrugged. "I guess I was scared."

Lane squeezed Betsy's arm. "I'm going to leave you two." She smiled. "But you should know that this—" she waved her hand between the two of them—"makes me very happy."

Lane's happiness for Betsy and Nate almost made her forget her confusion and sadness over what had happened only moments before with Brooks.

Almost.

She couldn't make sense of Noah's accusations, and she needed to believe they weren't true. But Ryan hadn't denied it—even she had to admit he'd looked guilty. She hadn't wanted to believe Brooks would hide something—not from her—but she might have been blinded once again.

She knew the familiar sting of betrayal all too well. Had she been a fool to believe Ryan was different?

Her head was spinning, and though she half expected him to be waiting at the cottage when she got there, she was a bit relieved to find it empty. She needed time to think, to process.

They'd gotten so close so quickly, spending this past week together, working on the cottages, eating meals together. They'd gone to Jack's birthday party together, run on the trail, shopped for the cottages. And he'd never mentioned anything about his role in Nate's accident.

Had Noah's near-obsessive need to find whoever was responsible scared him silent? Was he the reason her brother had nearly died?

Her heart lurched at the thought. She'd trusted him cautiously, believing that he wouldn't hurt her.

Had she made a terrible mistake?

Lane went inside and grabbed a bottle of water from the refrigerator. It was past dinnertime, and she wondered where Brooks was. Perhaps his absence was the only answer she needed.

The knock on the door startled her. She drew in a deep breath. *Brooks.*

She pulled the door open, expecting to see him standing there with explanation in hand, but instead she saw an older man wearing baggy jeans and a dusty tan-colored coat, toothpick dangling from the side of his mouth.

"Can I help you?" Lane kept the door in front of her as if that were any protection. Why hadn't she checked to see who was there before opening it?

The man eyed her. "Where's Ryan?" he growled, the stench of alcohol and cigarette smoke accosting her nostrils.

"He's not here," Lane said. "Can I give him a message? I'll see him tomor—"

"Ryan!" he yelled into the house. "I know you're in there!"

"Sir, I'm sorry; he's not here." Lane's pulse quickened.

"Let me see my son!" He pushed on the door, and though his

speech was slurred, he was still stronger than Lane, who stumbled back and fell into the stairs.

This was Ryan's father?

Lane could picture Ryan as a young boy, cowering as she was now, struggling to get away from this man's angry clutches, and her heart filled with sadness and fear. She'd been teased, sure, but this was something else entirely.

She'd never let herself imagine his life, always assumed it was bad and left it at that. But this? How was it possible this hadn't ruined him?

Lane scrambled to her feet as the man stormed through the cottage. He stumbled into a vase on a table and knocked it to the floor, where it shattered.

"Ryan! Get out here, Son!"

Lane raced after him, heart pounding, pulse like a metronome in her ears. "Mr. Brooks, he's not here."

Ryan's dad was standing in the kitchen, growing more and more agitated, his balance questionable. "Where is he?" He turned to Lane, his eyes dark.

"I'm not sure. I haven't seen him for an hour or so."

He sized her up as he took a few steps toward her. "You his girlfriend?"

"I'm his friend."

"Yeah, right," he snarled. "Take a good look, sweetheart. See what you're in for if you stay with my son."

Lane steeled her jaw, lifting her chin to meet his eyes. "Your son is nothing like you."

He squinted at her, then let out a loud, drunken laugh, stumbling forward, knocking into her. She caught the weight of him and tried to push him back to a standing position, but his body had gone limp and he slipped farther forward as if he'd fallen asleep.

Seconds later, his whole frame twitched and he jerked backward, but as he did, his elbow caught Lane's eye, knocking her into the double stove and onto the ground.

He tumbled forward again, but before he could land on top of her, he was yanked back as if by an invisible cord and thrown to the floor.

Lane peered up from her spot on the floor and saw Brooks standing over the man.

"What are you doing here?" His voice was frantic, as though his worst fears had been realized.

Ryan's dad pushed himself up, but Ryan shoved him down again. "Stay there." He looked at Lane. "Are you okay?"

She nodded. "I'm fine." Her eyes welled with tears as she saw the shame wash over him.

"Your face is bleeding." Ryan's eyes flashed black as he grabbed his dad and pulled him upright, holding him by two fistfuls of his coat. "What did you do to her?"

Lane stood and put a hand on Ryan's arm. "It's nothing. I'm fine. It was an accident."

"Look at you, still the great protector," Ryan's dad spat. "You always did think you were a hero."

Ryan's grip on his dad tightened, as did Lane's on Ryan.

"I should've turned you in when I first figured out the truth," Ryan said through clenched teeth. "Why did I even hesitate? Why did I give you time to do the right thing?"

"Because you're weak."

"No. Weak would be running two people off the road and leaving them there to die."

Lane let out a slight gasp. It wasn't Ryan—it was his father. His drunk, good-for-nothing father. And Ryan hadn't had the heart to turn him in.

"Lane, call Walker Jones," Ryan said without looking at her.

"Don't do this, Son."

"I told you not to call me that," Ryan said. "Lane, pick up the phone."

"Ryan, are you sure—?"

"Lane, please."

She did as she was told and they sat there in silence for five solid, awful minutes until a squad car pulled up in front of the cottage.

Walker strolled in, thumbs hitched through his belt loops. "Domestic dispute here?"

Ryan turned his dad to face Walker. "This man is responsible for Nate Kelley's accident."

The shame in Ryan's eyes had only deepened. Lane could practically see the boy he'd been, forever making excuses for an unfit father.

"That right?" Walker took Ryan's dad by the arm and glared at Ryan. "I knew you were hiding something."

"Just get him out of here," Ryan said as Walker dragged a drunk Martin Brooks out the front door.

Once they were gone, Ryan turned to Lane, eyes glassy and panic on his face. "Are you all right?"

She looked at him and nodded.

He reached over and touched her cheek. "Did he hurt you?" His voice caught in his throat as he said the words.

She shook her head. "I'm okay. It was an accident, really."

Ryan folded Lane into his body, holding on to her tightly, seeming afraid to let her go. "I'm so sorry, Lane."

The memory of that boy she'd known all those years ago—the one who loved without condition, who always seemed to see her despite her attempts to hide—scrolled through her thoughts. Now, having a real picture of the way he'd been raised—it only made her love him more. Because in spite of it, he'd turned into the best man she'd ever known.

Even now, in the midst of his own pain, he was only concerned for her.

Had she ever loved anyone so selflessly?

"I'm fine, Brooks. I promise."

He pulled back and studied her face. "I'm so sorry I didn't tell you the truth about the accident."

"No, I'm sorry I didn't trust you enough to give you the benefit of the doubt," Lane said, still locked onto his eyes.

He shook his head. "It's my fault. I promised him time to come forward himself. I was going to tell Walker soon; I just—"

Lane put a hand on his lips. "I don't care, Ryan. I don't need you to explain. You had your reasons." And she didn't care what those reasons were. She only wanted him to know that he was safe—that in this place, with her, he was safe.

And something told her the same was true for her.

CHAPTER

36

LANE STOOD ON THE FRONT STEPS of Lindsay and Jasper's home, gift in hand, wishing she and Ryan had driven here together. It had been a week since his dad had been hauled away by the police, and in that time Lane had watched a peace wash over him, the kind that comes with finally letting something go.

It had convicted her somehow, knowing that she'd been holding on to years-old anger and pain, allowing it to seep into every aspect of her life.

She rang the doorbell, and a few seconds later Jett pulled the door open and stared at her. He took one look at the neatly wrapped box she held and shouted, "Presents!" Then he snatched it out of her hands and took off in the other direction.

Lindsay had texted Lane an invitation to Jett's half-birthday party, and while Lane thought celebrating a half birthday seemed a bit over the top, she decided to show up.

It was a step.

Maybe there was peace waiting for her, too, if she could finally let a few things go.

Lane stepped inside the house, and it was, as she expected, ostentatious. Perhaps that was simply Lindsay and Jasper's taste, but she couldn't help redecorating it in her mind.

"Back here," Lindsay called out.

Lane followed her sister's voice to the kitchen—a true gourmet kitchen with practically more space than Lane had in her entire Chicago apartment.

When Lindsay saw her standing there, she stopped slicing strawberries. Her shoulders dropped as if she'd just let out a breath she'd been holding for years. "You came."

Lane smiled—not even a forced one—and accepted her sister's hug. "Jett already has my present."

When Lindsay pulled away, Lane saw the tears in her eyes. "I can't believe you came."

Lane hadn't been kind or forgiving with Lindsay at the hospital. She'd found it difficult to part with the pain that had defined her for so long.

But having been forgiven with such ease after barely whispering an apology to Betsy, Lane understood the freedom that could come with that gift. And somehow she wanted to extend it to her sister. If she didn't, she'd wind up bitter and angry for the rest of her life.

And that wasn't a life she was interested in living. Not anymore.

"Where is everyone else?" Lane looked around the nearly empty house.

Lindsay fidgeted with the watch on her wrist. "You're a little early."

"I am?" Lane pulled her phone out to check the text again. Sure enough, she'd misread it, putting her at Lindsay's half an hour before the party started.

She glanced at her sister. "Okay, then. What can I do? Put me to work."

Lindsay nodded and walked back to her spot behind the counter. "Cut up this watermelon?" She rolled it toward Lane. "Everyone will be here soon. I'm thankful you came early."

Lane sliced into the watermelon. "You are?"

Lindsay nodded.

They worked in silence for a while.

"You were right, Lane," Lindsay said without looking at her. "I'm going to work on things with Jasper. We're planning to get away for a weekend and talk things through."

"I'm glad." Lane's pulse quickened at the thought. There was still a part of her that didn't like thinking about Lindsay and Jasper together, but when her eyes caught a glimpse of Ryan outside, heading to the deck with a poorly wrapped present for her nephew, it seemed to matter less.

Jett raced over and grabbed the gift from Ryan—Lane bet he didn't thank him either—then darted away.

"So you and Brooks?" Lindsay said quietly.

Lane waited until Ryan looked up and saw her through the glass door. He smiled and waved at her. "Yeah," Lane said. "Me and Brooks." She went back to cutting the watermelon, still unsure how to make conversation with Lindsay. They'd never had the chance to really get to know each other as adults, so in some ways, Lindsay felt like a stranger.

"Your house is beautiful," Lane said with another slice.

Lindsay had moved on to cantaloupe. "It feels like a museum."

Lane didn't argue.

"Hey, could you help me with it? I haven't done anything to it since we moved in."

Help Lindsay create a home for her and *Jasper*?

"I've seen your work, and everyone is talking about Cedar Grove. I'd pay you, of course."

Lane's gaze caught the living room, where a beautiful stone fireplace was wasted on a poor layout that did nothing to direct the eye to the room's true focal point. Within seconds, she had ten ideas on how to make that space beautiful and cozy, the way a family home should be.

"I'll think about it."

"Please, Lane? It would be fun."

"I said I'll think about it." Lane gave her an exasperated look, and Lindsay's eyes lit as she gave Lane a bright smile.

"Think about what?" Dottie had let herself in through the front door. When she found the two of them standing there alone, her brow knit.

"I asked Lane to help me with my house," Lindsay said cheerfully.

Dottie's eyebrows shot up. "And you're thinking about it?"

Lane scraped chunks of watermelon from the cutting board into the bowl. "I'm thinking about it."

Dottie covered her mouth with her hand, and her eyes filled with tears. "You're thinking about helping Lindsay?"

Lane felt her shoulders relax as she saw the joy on her mother's face.

"It's what I've been praying for, Lane," her mom said. "That you would come home to us, that you could find a way to forgive. Not just Lindsay, but all of us."

Lindsay looked away, her guilt still obvious.

"I'm working on it," Lane said.

Dottie pulled her into a hug. "I'm so sorry you were hurt, sweet girl. That's what I tried to tell you all those years ago."

"When I was too stubborn to listen." Unexpected tears sprang to Lane's eyes.

"Yes, when you were too stubborn to listen." Dottie stepped back and looked at her. "We never stopped loving you, Lane. You always, always have a home here."

The words lodged themselves in Lane's heart, and surprisingly she believed them. It was what she'd wanted for so many years—had it really been hers all along?

Dottie hugged her again, this time tugging Lindsay close too. "I'm so thankful my family is back together."

After several long seconds, Lindsay pulled away, wiped her eyes dry, and picked up a plate of cookies. "I'm going to take this out to the deck."

"I'll help you." Dottie grabbed a bowl of pasta salad and followed her, tossing one last smile at Lane before closing the sliding-glass door behind her.

Lane continued to cut the watermelon and put the chunks in a big glass bowl. From where she stood, she could see people arriving for Jett's party—people she now recognized and most of whom she even enjoyed. Sure, they were quirky and a little bit nosy, but they were her people.

What if she didn't go back to Chicago at all?

Well, that was a crazy thought. She belonged in the city, working. What would she do with herself if she lived here? She found her value in her work. It was the only thing she was good at.

Her phone buzzed several times. She didn't recognize the number, so she sent the call to voice mail.

She picked up the bowl of fruit, propped it against her hip, and had started outside when her phone beeped with a new message.

She dialed her voice mail and stepped through the sliding door, managing to pull it shut behind her, before the voice on the other end stopped her in her tracks.

"Lane, this is Julia Baumann from Innovate. I understand you're no longer working with JB Sweet."

Had she called to gloat?

"What a huge mistake they made letting you go. Listen, a creative director position has just opened here, and I think you'd be perfect for it. I'd love to set up a time to get you in here and tell you all about it, but I can assure you that's just a formality. We want to offer you the job, and we think you'd be a great fit for our team. I'll be waiting for your call."

Lane must've looked as shocked as she felt because when Brooks came over, he was wearing concern on his face.

She clicked the screen off and regained her composure. Now was not the time to think or talk about a job offer that would take her back to Chicago.

Never mind that they both knew this would probably happen.

She supposed a part of her just didn't think it would happen so soon.

"Is everything okay?"

Lane waved him off. "Yes, of course."

He leaned over and kissed her, a gentle hello—but she still got excited by his nearness. He took the bowl from her. "I'll go put this down on the table."

She moved closer to the edge of the deck, overlooking the huge yard. Kids were tearing toward the swimming pool. Adults were standing in small social circles, greeting each other like the old friends they were. And for some reason, Lane wasn't overwhelmed by the scene in front of her at all.

Instead, she almost felt like she belonged with these people— a feeling she wasn't sure she'd ever experienced before.

"You're here."

Jasper's voice was unmistakable. Lane didn't even have to turn around to know it was him. He stood beside her, bottle of beer in hand, and she stiffened at his nearness.

"I'm surprised you came."

"I am too, actually." She avoided his eyes, focusing instead on the birthday party scene unfolding below.

"You still holding a grudge?"

She caught a quick glimpse of Ryan, who was helping Lindsay set up chairs on the deck—something that seemed more like a job for Lindsay's husband. "No, I'm actually not holding on to any part of what we had. I'm starting to realize it was a good thing that you and I didn't end up together."

"Really?"

She finally met his gaze. "Yeah. I don't think we were ever right for each other, Jasper."

He scoffed.

"It would've been a mistake, me and you. I know now that I'm with the right person."

"Who? Brooks?"

Lane didn't want to seem like a goofy teenager, but she couldn't help but smile at the mention of his name.

"You and Brooks."

She nodded. "And you and Lindsay. Don't mess that up."

"I can't believe *you're* giving *me* relationship advice." He leaned his elbows on the railing.

"She's my sister, Jasper. Treat her right."

He took a swig from his bottle and walked away.

Lane's eyes wandered across the yard to Ryan, who greeted Jack and Hailey on the deck. He picked Jack up and turned him upside down, all the while carrying on a conversation with his sister.

From her bird's-eye view, she could see the stark contrast between the two men she'd loved, or thought she loved, and for the first time ever, she was genuinely thankful Jasper had broken her heart.

It had taken years away from it all to see that her pain—her gut-wrenching heartbreak—had actually been a gift and that gift had led her back to Ryan Brooks, which was perhaps where she had always belonged.

CHAPTER

37

RYAN SAT ON THE DOCK, Cedar Grove behind him, aware that his work was nearly finished. With Lane's help, the crew had transformed the twelve cottages into more than he could've ever imagined. He should be joyous, but with tonight's grand opening celebration just hours away, the part of him that knew Lane's time in Harbor Pointe was temporary began to inch ahead of the part that could pretend what they had was permanent.

Over the last couple of weeks, he'd fallen even more in love with her—if that was possible—and now, imagining a life without her seemed on par with torture.

He heard her footfalls behind him and tried not to think about how seldom they would share this lunch-on-the-dock tradition if she did decide to go back to Chicago. Why had he fooled himself into believing this place could ever be enough for her?

Still, when she kicked off her flip-flops and sat down beside him, dangling her feet in the water, there was a part of him that hoped . . .

"I think we're all ready for tonight. I've prepped the tour guides, and the photographer already shot the cottages, so your new website is going to be absolutely gorgeous." She stared out across the water. He stared at her. "I really loved being a part of this, Ryan."

Did she sense it too? The end of what they had?

"Is everything okay?"

He nodded.

"You're quiet. That's not like you." She studied his face for a long moment. "What's wrong?"

"You're not staying here, are you?"

Her face fell. "Brooks . . ."

"No, it's okay." He took her hand. "I knew we couldn't keep you to ourselves for long."

She scooted closer and let her head rest on his shoulder.

"What are you going to do?"

She sat up. "I was offered a position with Innovate, the firm I've been competing with since I started at JB Sweet." Her smile was sad. "They want to make me a creative director."

His stomach rolled. He was thrilled for her—genuinely happy—but those feelings had a hard time surfacing for the devastation he felt for himself. He couldn't move to Chicago—his life and family were here. But Lane couldn't give up this opportunity. It was what she'd been working for all along.

"That's so great, Lane. You deserve it."

"Really?" She still wore her happiness cautiously.

"Of course. You've earned it. And they're lucky to have you." Hardest words he ever had to say.

She stared toward the lighthouse. "So you think I should take it?"

It would be selfish to say otherwise. "I think you'll be amazing."

"I didn't know how you'd feel about it," she said. "But I was thinking we could still spend weekends together? I can come up here or you can come to the city."

"Definitely." But in his heart he knew they'd start off with those good intentions, and then, as happened with so many long-distance relationships, romantic or otherwise, they would eventually grow apart. And all these feelings they had for each other would slowly drift out to sea, taking with them the memories of what they'd shared.

"You don't look convinced," she said. "I actually think we can make this work. I mean, you might have to be willing to text me once in a while."

"You know I hate texting." He smiled, then drew her close and kissed her unapologetically, knowing that while what he really wanted was to keep her with him forever, he had no right to hold her back from what she really wanted.

Still, it occurred to him that sometimes doing the right thing sure felt wrong.

Lane did one last walk-through of all the cottages, anxious for the general public to see what they'd been working so hard on. As she closed the door on Mabel, one of the homes in the center of Cedar Grove, she drew in a deep breath of late-spring air.

Tourist season was just around the corner, and her time here in Harbor Pointe was coming to an end. Though she'd told Julia she needed a few days to think about her offer, the truth was, the second it had come in, Lane knew what she would do. She had never been in the position to negotiate before, but Innovate really wanted her—and she had used that to negotiate a better deal for herself, one that included weekends off.

Even Brooks had agreed it was a perfect fit, exactly what she'd wanted all this time.

So why wasn't she more excited about it?

The plan for tonight's open house was to have everyone meet in the adjoining Cedar Grove backyards, which Lane had set up with tables and chairs underneath a large white tent. White lights had been strung in the trees, creating a canopy over the fire pit, which was encircled with several Adirondack chairs. They'd gather together and Ryan would thank everyone for coming; then the visitors would tour the cottages, the goal being to hopefully entice the locals in Harbor Pointe to tell their friends and relatives about a beautiful new community that was perfect for a week away. If enough families booked the cottages every week, everyone would win.

Lane wanted to see Ryan succeed almost more than she wanted it for herself. Knowing she'd played a small part in his happiness had filled her up enough to last a lifetime. At least that's what she told herself.

She, Lindsay, Dottie, and Emily had gone shopping earlier in the week for the perfect party dresses, and though there were moments when Lane still thought she'd been born into the wrong family, she'd begun to feel like a part of the crazy Kelley clan, a part of Harbor Pointe.

Leaving would be harder than she thought.

After she'd returned to the model cabin and dressed in her form-fitting black-and-white dress, she hurried down the stairs and found Brooks waiting for her in the kitchen. "I'm going to meet the caterer outside and just make sure they set everything up in the right spot."

He shook his head. "You don't get to come in here looking like that and expect to have a normal conversation."

She smiled. "You're looking pretty good yourself." While he wasn't exactly clean-shaven, he had cleaned up, and there was no sign of the baseball cap tonight. Instead he wore a pair of gray dress pants and a white button-down shirt with an unknotted tie dangling around his neck.

"You forget how to tie that thing?"

"I was hoping you would do it for me." He grinned as she came closer. She avoided his eyes while she secured the tie around his neck. Once she'd finished, she stepped back and gave him a once-over. "There. Now you look respectable."

"Well, that's a shame." He tugged her toward him, welcoming her into his arms. She thought about the look in his eyes when she'd told him about the offer from Innovate. She'd assumed he would put up more of a fight, though she supposed it was good he didn't. Her resolve wasn't strong, and she was thankful he wanted the best for her.

Each time he kissed her now, she prayed it wasn't the last time. Maybe it was naive to think they could overcome long distance, but she couldn't stand the thought of letting him go.

His kiss was soft, perfectly placed. His lips had begun to recognize hers and they moved in a rhythm, the kind that accompanied familiarity but would never grow monotonous or mundane.

She pulled away. "You're going to make us late."

He kissed her again. "I don't care."

She laughed, then headed for the back door and out onto the patio, knowing that in just another couple of days, this view would be nothing more than a fond memory.

The thought was unwelcome, as was the lump that had formed in her throat.

She quickly shoved them aside and focused on the caterer, who was nearing the tent. The preparations for the party would be her saving grace tonight, keeping her mind occupied.

Everything was perfect by the time people began arriving just before 7 p.m. As she stood off to the side and watched Ryan greet the guests, her heart swelled, so gratified was she with the response and with his success. Together they'd created something incredible. No amount of miles between them could take that away.

Her family arrived, each of them clearly excited for Ryan. Noah had apologized for his outburst at the hospital, and in true Brooks fashion, he'd waved it off as if it were nothing.

Even Nate showed up, still in a wheelchair, and Lane couldn't tell if his happiness was for Ryan, because he was with Betsy, or because he was finally out of that hospital bed. Regardless, seeing him there served as a well-placed reminder that life was short and people were what mattered most.

How had she ever convinced herself otherwise?

One by one, familiar faces filtered into the tented area, the buzz of excitement thick in the air. So many sought out Lane to thank her for sharing her gifts with Harbor Pointe, which, of course, embarrassed her but made her feel validated at the same time.

Once the tent had filled, Brooks stood and waited until he had everyone's attention.

"I'd like to thank you all for coming tonight," he said. "We've worked so hard to bring this place back to life, and we hope you love it as much as we do. We've got tour guides in eleven of the twelve cottages, waiting to take you through and show you just how beautiful these spaces would be for your friends and family who come to visit. Our goal is to show them what we all know to be true—that Harbor Pointe is truly a special place."

The crowd applauded.

"One more thing, since we're all family here." He looked at Lane. "I want to thank the beautiful, elegant, and classy Lane Kelley for lending her artistic eye this past month and turning Cedar Grove into this stunning community you see before you."

More applause.

"Once you tour the cottages, feel free to come back here and join us for dinner and dessert."

The crowd dispersed, and Lane kept an eye on Brooks as he talked to a guy in a black suit who Lane thought might be one of his investors.

"Tell me it's not true."

Lane turned and found Chloe standing behind her. "What are *you* doing here?" She pulled her friend into a tight hug, realizing in that moment just how much she'd missed her.

"Your beautiful boyfriend texted and asked me to come. I was hoping he was going to ask me out, but he said he was sure *you'd* want me here, so there went that dream." Chloe wore an adorable black floral dress that hugged her torso and flared at her hips. It looked like something straight out of another decade. It looked like Chloe.

Lane laughed. "How are you?"

"I'm okay. You look wonderful. This small-town, slower-paced-living thing really agrees with you." They started walking toward the cottages. "Which is why I'm wondering about a rumor I heard at work the other day."

Lane groaned. "Are you going to give me grief about it?"

"Someone has to. What's the boyfriend say about all this?"

"I don't like the word *boyfriend*. And he's fine with it. He thinks I should go." She caught a glimpse of Brooks, genuine smile on his face, shaking hands with the man in black.

"Sure he does." Chloe folded her arms and followed Lane out onto the sidewalk. People zigzagged from cottage to cottage, filling the little community with such excitement, Lane could hardly keep from grinning.

"I've been reading your blog," Lane said.

"You have?" Chloe linked her arm through Lane's.

"Of course. It seems like it's going really well, Chloe. You're going to quit JB Sweet one of these days and become a real entrepreneur."

Chloe let out a sigh. "That's the dream."

"Have you been inside any of the cottages yet?"

Chloe shook her head. "Had to find you first—see if I could knock some sense into you."

Lane gave a soft shrug. "This was always going to be temporary, Chlo. You know that. Brooks and I both knew that."

"But things change, Lane. Look at you. You're positively glowing."

Lane wished it were true, wished she could be content here, but she never had been before. She'd accepted that she belonged in the city, where she could work for something important. She needed her work. She could hardly further her career or feel a lasting sense of accomplishment in Harbor Pointe.

"Lane! Oh, Lane!" A small, stout woman Lane recognized as her mother's old friend Laura Danvers plodded toward them. "Lane Kelley. You simply must come work your magic at my cottage."

"Oh, thank you, Mrs. Danvers, but I'm heading back to the city soon."

The woman's shoulders slumped. "I've been wanting to redo our cottage for years, and I just never felt the inspiration hit. After walking through these cottages and seeing your work, let me tell you, the inspiration hit."

Lane thanked her but quickly moved on, doing her best to avoid Chloe's knowing stare.

"You've found something really special here, Lane," Chloe said, slowing her pace.

Chloe's words hung in the air between them, begging Lane's attention, but she shoved them aside. She couldn't think about what she'd be leaving behind this time—not if she wanted to stay on course.

"I have to go back, Chloe." Lane faced her. "You know I do."

"But why? There's nothing left to prove." Chloe waved her hands toward the beautiful cottage community that had come to feel more like home to Lane than anywhere else she'd ever lived. "Look what you've done."

Lane fought tears. It would be hard to say good-bye to this place. To Brooks. Even to her crazy family.

"Lane." Chloe's earnest eyes studied her. "It's okay to want a simple life." She stood unmoving, her words resounding somewhere at the back of Lane's mind.

"I know that," Lane said, wholly aware it was a lie. *Simple* had never been on her agenda.

"You're not going to change your mind about this, are you?"

Lane shook her head, unable to ignore the part of her that was saddened by this.

Chloe put her hands on Lane's shoulders. "Well, if you decide to start your own design business and relocate to Harbor Pointe, I'd happily quit my job to be your assistant."

"Just like that?" Lane couldn't imagine Chloe leaving Chicago for sleepy Harbor Pointe.

"Just like that."

"You wouldn't miss the city?"

Chloe shrugged and let out a harrumph that would've suited an old lady. "I'm over it."

If only it were that easy.

If only Lane were that brave.

CHAPTER

38

SATURDAY MORNING, the day after the grand-opening party, Ryan was up before the sun. He wanted to make sure everything was perfect for his guests—especially Lydia and Drum Jr.—who were arriving later that day. If he was honest, he was nervous.

Cedar Grove practically glowed in the early morning sunlight. It was as if the cool breeze and promise of warmth had been a gift, hand-wrapped just for him. He had been praying that the details of this day would fall into place, even the ones he hadn't thought of, so why was he surprised to see that they were?

After a final walk-through of each of the cottages, he saw Lane sitting out on the dock. It was a sight he'd never tire of, having her close enough to touch. And though a part of him thought it would've been easier to watch her go back to her old life if he'd never given in to his feelings for her in the first place, another part of him wouldn't trade their time together for anything in the world.

He'd prayed about their relationship—confused about why their timing was so off—but he hadn't been happy with the answers he seemed to be getting.

Lane had a strong, independent mind of her own—it was one of the many things he loved about her. And as much as he wished things were different, as much as he wanted her to stay, he'd never ask her to give up her dreams for him. What if she resented him for it? He couldn't live with himself knowing he was the reason she wasn't doing what she loved.

Still, he'd miss this view. He'd miss her nearness, her unexpected laugh, her beautiful blue eyes that always seemed to know exactly what he was thinking before he even said a word.

Man, it was going to be hard to let her go.

He made his way to the dock, the same place they'd sat together so many times before. She didn't turn around, though something told him she knew he was there.

He sat down next to her and took her hand, following her gaze to the skyline, the first rays of the sun now bathing the lake in golden light.

"I'm going to miss this place," she said quietly.

The unshed tears in her eyes made him want to beg her to stay, to promise his life's mission would be to make her happy. Instead, he wrapped an arm around her shoulder and pulled her close, placing a gentle kiss on her forehead. "You're going to be so amazing, Lane."

It killed him to say it. He didn't want to believe it. He wanted her to live right here in Harbor Pointe so he could see her anytime he felt like it. He wanted to spend every single day with her, stealing kisses in the alley behind Hazel's on the way to the farmers' market and dreaming about the kind of life they would create for themselves.

His heart ached knowing she was leaving later that day.

"But what about us?" She looked at him.

He gathered every positive thought he could find and put on a reassuring face. "You said it yourself. We'll see each other on the weekends. You'll come back here, and I'll visit you. We'll make it work."

A tear streamed down her cheek, and he wiped it dry with his thumb.

"I think we both know that won't work forever," she said.

He didn't want to have this conversation. Wouldn't it be easier to face the truth somewhere down the road?

"Ryan, I don't want you waiting around here for me."

"I've waited for you this long," he said.

"But how does this end? You're not going to move to Chicago. I'm not going to move here."

"I don't want to talk about this, Lane. I can't think about losing you."

She reached up and put a hand on his cheek. "You'll never lose me." She was talking about loss in the abstract you'll-always-be-in-my-heart kind of way. That wasn't good enough for him.

He liked it better when she was being positive about their relationship. What had happened to that version of this scenario?

She rose up on her knees and drew him toward her, kissing him with such softness it had to be good-bye.

He responded to her kiss, pulling her body close. He didn't know when—or if—he'd get to kiss her again, after all. She made him feel like he could do anything, and now that he'd seen just a glimpse of what they could be, he didn't know how he'd manage otherwise.

How did he exist in a world without her?

After several minutes, he broke away and saw the tears that had streamed down her face. She didn't need him to fall apart right now. She needed him to be strong. He wiped her cheeks dry and held her face in his hands, marveling again at her beauty.

"You're getting the promotion you finally deserve, Lane. You're going to blow them all away."

Her smile looked forced.

"I'm excited for you—and so proud. I can't wait to hear what happens next."

"And this place—it's going to explode, I just know it is." She kissed him again. "I'm just sorry I won't be here to see it."

He didn't tell her that his investor from Summers Bay was thrilled with the way Cedar Grove turned out. Just as Ryan had hoped, he'd specifically requested that Ryan and his designer work together to create another cottage community there, to boost tourism the way the investor was sure they'd done in Harbor Pointe. Ryan didn't want to confuse Lane or seem like he was trying to convince her to do anything but what she'd always wanted to do.

"You have an open invitation," he said. "Anytime."

They finally stood. She picked up her flip-flops and wrapped her arms around him for one more kiss.

"I'm really going to miss you," she said when she pulled away.

He could tell by the lump in his throat that responding would be unwise, so instead he held her, drew in the scent of her, marked the moment in his mind so he'd never forget how she felt in his arms.

And then he let her go.

Lane hadn't expected leaving Harbor Pointe to be so difficult. She'd been there almost a month, and in that time, something inside her had shifted. When she was with Ryan, half the time she didn't even have her phone with her. She knew very little about what was going on at JB Sweet, and oddly she didn't care.

And not caring felt really good.

But that all ended today. Today was her first day at Innovate, and she needed to impress Julia Baumann and the rest of the team.

She'd been hired after a brief phone interview, but she still didn't have a feel for the place or the people, so naturally that morning she was nervous. So nervous she spilled her coffee twice, once on a newly dry-cleaned white blouse that had to be traded out for a dark-purple one, less likely to show stains.

As she walked to work that morning, her thoughts turned to

Brooks, who'd stolen her heart without a word of warning. She was surprised by the depth of her feelings for him, knowing that if he'd asked her not to go that morning on the dock, she would've called Julia and declined the offer immediately.

But he hadn't said that. He seemed excited for her, as though he wanted her to go back to the city and live the life she'd always dreamed of living. After all, it was what she wanted too.

Wasn't it?

Innovate was on the eighteenth floor of a tall building that faced Lake Michigan. The view would be beautiful, naturally, but as she peered across the street, she marveled at the contrast between the lake here and the way it looked in Harbor Pointe. Surrounded by people and commerce and buildings and cars, Chicago was its own kind of beautiful, and she'd thrived here once. She could learn to do it again.

Never mind that part of her ached for the lighthouse, the dock, the green of the trees and fields that surrounded Harbor Pointe. She shoved the thought aside. It was ludicrous—crazy, really, to even think like that.

She was walking into the first day of her dream job, and she needed to stay focused.

She took the elevator up to the eighteenth floor and told the receptionist, a sharply dressed young woman with short, jet-black hair and bright-red lips, that she was there to see Julia Baumann.

"Is she expecting you?" the woman asked dryly.

"She is."

"Name?"

"Lane Kelley."

"Sit." The woman nodded toward the sleek, modern waiting area with its black-and-silver chairs and perfectly placed magazines. She admired the open floor plan, the sharp lines, the attention to detail.

But it struck her how different it was from the aesthetic she'd cultivated in Harbor Pointe. There was no shiplap, no hand-scraped wood floor, and not a single piece of distressed furniture.

"Lane?"

Julia Baumann appeared in the waiting area. Lane stood and shook her hand. "It's good to see you, Julia."

Lane's phone dinged three times in quick succession.

"Sorry; I can silence that."

"No, don't," Julia said, motioning for Lane to follow her down a long, narrow hallway. "I put you in a few text groups. I hope you don't mind having that thing chirping at you all day." She smiled at Lane over her shoulder, then led her into a posh, white office with two big, solid windows across the room from a glass door.

"I'm used to it." As soon as Lane said the words, she realized she wasn't so used to it anymore. Somehow her phone seemed to have lost its pull. She no longer felt the need to be connected at all times.

The freedom of that didn't escape her.

"I've been a big fan of your work for a long time," Julia said, her no-nonsense tone causing Lane to straighten. "When I heard you'd left JB Sweet, it was a no-brainer to snatch you up. I think you're going to be a great addition to our team."

Lane's phone dinged again. And again.

"You should probably look at those before they get too out of control," Julia said. "We like prompt replies in our communication."

Translation: Meet your new master.

The thought jarred Lane as she pulled the phone from her bag and scrolled through messages about projects she wasn't familiar with yet, then saw one unread message from Ryan.

Missing you this morning. Good luck at the new gig. Knock 'em dead. Attached to the text was a photo taken from their dock, the lighthouse in the distance. A knot swelled in the center of her throat.

"All caught up?" Julia sat behind her desk and slid a few papers toward Lane. "Take a few minutes to fill out this paperwork and then I'll show you your office."

Lane glanced up and nodded, afraid if she spoke, she'd burst into tears. She did her best to complete the new-employee paperwork while Julia clicked off text after text on her own phone.

Moments later, she slid her completed paperwork across the desk and Julia shut her phone's screen off. "Very good. Follow me."

The whole scene did nothing to settle Lane's weary nerves.

This was crazy. She had to pull herself together. And fast. She was walking down a sleek glass hallway toward *her* new office. She was finally getting the job she'd always wanted. She should be leaping for joy.

But her heart ached to be sitting on the dock in Harbor Pointe, enjoying that familiar view alongside a man she actually thought she loved.

"We'll take a look at your responsibilities as our newest creative director," Julia said. "As soon as you're all settled, I'll introduce you to the team. You've got a few important people to meet before we make the rounds."

Lane forced herself to stay focused. She'd never been the day-dreaming type. She'd be wise not to start now.

"This is it," Julia said, leading her to the opposite side of the building from where they'd been.

"This is my office?" Lane was used to a cubicle in the middle of a room full of cubicles. This office wasn't much different from Julia's, and while Lane had a street view, if she strained a bit, she could see a sliver of the lake.

"We've all found ways to make these glass boxes our own, so feel free to do whatever you like," Julia said. "As you know, you're taking over the position I vacated."

Lane hadn't realized that.

"I'm here if you need anything, but now that I've been pro-moted, I'll be very busy. I trust you're self-sufficient and won't need much training."

Lane hoped not.

"There is a stack of files on the desk. Look through those this morning, and around eleven we'll have a meet and greet with your team. We're throwing you right into the thick of it—I hope that's okay."

It didn't sound like a question, so Lane didn't give an answer. Instead, she listened, smiled, nodded, and prayed she was actually ready to do this job. She'd forgotten how quickly things moved, having abandoned her urgency for a much slower pace in Harbor Pointe. She and Brooks had been up against a tight deadline at Cedar Grove, but he still found time to spend Sundays without a phone, to take walks, to admire the way the sun hit the lighthouse *just so* at four o'clock in the afternoon.

Perhaps a bit of her sharp edge had been dulled in those quiet moments.

She'd readjust, of course, but it was a bit shocking, like jumping into a cold lake instead of wading in slowly.

"I'll leave you to get settled," Julia said. "I'm looking at another all-nighter, so I want to get a head start on my pile."

Julia was gone before Lane could respond. She sank into the desk chair in her new office, surrounded by the buzz of creative activity, the electricity of work being done, and she couldn't help reflecting on the sound track she'd been listening to only days before: lapping waves, gentle breezes, Brooks's voice.

Why did she suddenly feel like she didn't belong here?

She reminded herself that a month ago, she'd felt exactly the same way about Harbor Pointe: out of place and anxious to return to her version of normal. She just needed to throw herself back into it—to get the sleepy lake town out of her mind and do what she'd been born to do: work.

Her phone buzzed for her attention and she quickly responded to the text messages, letting the team know she'd just arrived. She'd catch up and they would meet to discuss current projects later that morning. She toggled her computer mouse and her screen jumped to life. She pulled her planner from her bag and set it on the desk. Most of her appointments were on her phone, but her planner held any notes, ideas, sketches, or photos she came across.

As she opened it, she saw the paint chips she and Ryan had settled on for Cedar Grove. A dusty gray that wasn't too blue and wasn't too brown. How many samples had they brought back, searching for the perfect shade of gray for those cottages?

Brooks had diligently painted small squares all over Esther's living room wall and sat even more diligently, listening while Lane went through the pros and cons of each one. He'd seemed content to listen to her talk, even though she knew he probably just wanted her to hurry up and pick one.

The memory made her smile.

"Whoa." A voice pulled her from her daydream. She looked up and saw a man in a gray suit and blue tie standing in the doorway. "We don't see a lot of genuine smiles around here. It's kind of nice."

Her smile faded and she stood to greet him, affecting the same professional tone Julia had used when greeting her. "Lane Kelley." It made her feel like she was playing a role and maybe she'd been miscast.

"New creative director, I know. I've seen your work. I'm Jared Spencer." He stepped in and shook her hand. "Chief architect. We'll work together on new builds."

Lane didn't have much experience with new builds.

"I understand you spent the last month on a little cottage project?" His tone condescended. "You're probably going to have to step up your game here. I noticed it's been a few weeks since you posted anything on social media."

"Is that a problem?"

"At Innovate, we like our employees to be part of our image. If a client loves you, they're more inclined to call us for a consultation. But your side projects will have to stop. That's frowned upon."

Lane sat back down. What if Brooks needed her help again? Was Jared saying she wouldn't be allowed? She was about to ask him when he took a step toward the door.

"Just wanted to introduce myself," he said. "Maybe we can get a drink after work sometime." He smiled and walked away.

Lane's not-exactly-quiet office suddenly felt empty, except for the buzzing of a busy phone that demanded her attention.

CHAPTER

39

RYAN STOOD IN THE CENTER of the run-down cottage. He'd closed on the single-family property only hours earlier, thankful to have another project to keep his mind occupied. His Summers Bay investor was working out the financial details of a new cottage community, but while he waited, he needed to work.

The past three weeks without Lane had been torture, the only bright spot being Lydia and Drum Jr.'s vacation at Cedar Grove. Before she left, Lydia had thanked him and told him it had been months since she'd seen her son that happy.

"You gave him back his smile, Brooks," she'd said.

"It's the least I could do."

And while he was thankful and happy with how things had gone, he wished Lane had been there to share it with him. He'd done what he felt like God wanted him to do—let her go—but nothing about it had been easy.

He wanted to call her when the office manager told him Cedar Grove was sold out for the summer. He wanted to tell her they'd already begun booking for next year. He wanted to celebrate the fact that a large family from the South had rented out every cottage for Christmas because they wanted to spend the holiday together in a place where there was snow.

He wanted to, but he didn't. They'd agreed to go their separate ways. He had to honor that.

This cottage had been beautiful once. It had belonged to a couple who only used it in the summer, but the past two summers, with their declining health, the place was empty most weeks. Their kids finally convinced them to sell. They were all just too busy to make use of a house that practically begged for peace and relaxation.

Ryan found it sad that none of them had time to relax anymore.

It sat near the top of a sand dune, so the back deck overlooked the lake. The problem was, the deck wasn't quite safe anymore, the roof needed to be replaced, and the landscaping was overgrown. Not to mention the old-fashioned decor inside—like something straight out of the eighties. Most of the furniture was still in the house: a dark-brown and dated table in the entryway, an old tan sofa and a dark-brown chair positioned around a glass-topped coffee table in the living room. A squeaky old rocking chair on the front porch.

He had a knack for this kind of work, and he loved finding the beauty in things everyone else had discarded. In so many ways, it was a metaphor for his life. He'd been discarded by his mother, neglected by his father—and yet, somehow, God had brought the Kelley family into his life, and they'd seen something in him. Where would he be if he hadn't had their kindness?

Maybe it was too much of a stretch, but these cottages reminded him of who he could've been. Maybe that's why he was so passionate about transforming them.

Or maybe he just needed to hit something with a hammer.

He walked through the cottage again, making notes and getting ideas. He'd take out a couple of interior walls and create an open floor plan. He'd bring in the natural light and let it wash across the entire space. He'd repair the deck so the view could be properly enjoyed. He'd try not to call Lane and ask her what colors to paint or what fixtures to buy. And when he was finished, he'd either move himself in or he'd rent it out and move to Chicago.

The thought seemed ridiculous. He'd hate living in the city. His sister and nephew would be hours away, not right up the street. But if it meant he could be close to Lane—actually make a go of their relationship—wouldn't it be worth it?

He was coming down the stairs, still contemplating how to open up the tight hallway between the bedrooms, when he realized someone was standing in the entryway.

The man had his back to him, but his broad shoulders and wide gait gave him away.

"What are you doing here?" Ryan didn't care to be polite. His father, out on bond, didn't deserve his sympathy. And yet, looking at him now, standing with his hat in his hands and that forlorn expression on his face, Ryan couldn't help but feel pity. He'd likely end up in jail, where he belonged.

Why should that upset Ryan? He hardly knew him anyway.

"I stopped by the office at Cedar Grove," his dad said, surprisingly sober.

"You shouldn't go there. It's a place for families."

His dad looked away.

Ryan walked down the rest of the stairs and faced his father beside the front door. "So why are you here?"

"Your employee at the office told me where to find you. Said you'd bought another property to fix up and rent out." He looked lost, like he wasn't sure what else to say. And why would he? They'd never had a real conversation in his life.

"I'm proud of you, Son."

Ryan bit back a sarcastic response, choosing silence instead.

"What you've done with that place—it's impressive. You've really made something of yourself."

"I hope you're not going to try and take credit for that."

His father's face fell. "No, I know better. I know you did this all on your own—it was no doing of mine."

Ryan sighed. "I didn't do it all on my own. I had help. Lots of help. Lots of good people God put in my life over the years."

The words resonated within him. The Kelleys had seen past all of Ryan's faults and mistakes. Heck, he'd been trying to steal from Frank the day they met. They'd given him a second chance. They'd shown him the love of a father.

He prayed God wouldn't ask him to do the same . . . not yet.

"Well, I came to tell you I was wrong about you. You're nothing like me, Son. You're your own man, and I'm proud of you for that too."

"Thanks," he mumbled.

"And I'm sorry I hurt your girl." Martin turned away, obvious shame on his face. "It was an accident."

What could he say? That everything was okay? It wasn't. Would it ever be?

"I know you've got no reason to be proud of me," his dad said, eyes glassy with tears of regret. "But I wanted to let you know I'm working on giving you one." He reached into his pocket, pulled out something small, and set it on the rickety entryway table that had come with the house. He met Ryan's eyes, gave him a nod, then turned and started for the door.

Ryan glanced down and saw a one-month sobriety chip from Alcoholics Anonymous. He picked it up and turned it over in his hand.

"Wait." Why was Ryan stopping him? He wanted him to go. He wanted him out of his life—for good.

But when his father turned around, Ryan saw all the words he couldn't say written right there on the older man's face. He saw the years of regret, the unsaid apologies, the grave knowledge that he'd wasted so much of his life.

How do I fix this, Lord? This is beyond me.

His dad watched him, waiting for a reason to stay there, but Ryan's mind had gone blank.

"Show me the house?" Martin asked, looking like a boy in search of a friend.

Ryan drew in a deep breath, then gave him a nod. "Let's start in the kitchen."

"Miss Kelley, I need your approval on these designs." Jemma, a bright young intern Julia had assigned to Lane, stood in front of her glass-topped desk with a tablet. She turned the iPad toward Lane and pointed to a number of images, all put together by Lane's team for a pitch they were giving later that week.

Lane's phone buzzed and she held up a finger to Jemma, indicating she needed a minute. Jemma nodded, set the tablet on Lane's desk, and darted out of the office. Lane spent the next several minutes responding to a flurry of incoming texts over a crisis with a hotel project they'd been working on—the vanities they'd originally picked out were no longer available and the new ones they liked were more expensive.

Lane tried to remember she didn't have to fix every crisis, that she could empower her team to handle it, but the stress of dealing with it was still considerable.

She set her cell phone down and checked her e-mail. How was it possible that in the last ten minutes, twenty-two new e-mails had come in? Of those, fifteen were marked *urgent.*

She opened her social media accounts, pausing on a series of photos Betsy had posted. It was from the Kelleys' most recent Sunday dinner—this one down at the beach. Noah had opened his shop and they'd spent the day on the lake. She scrolled through the pictures. One of Betsy and Nate made her smile. Her brother looked so happy and healthy, she could hardly stand not to be there. He was walking with the help of a cane and, Lane had a feeling, bugging the doctors to tell him the exact day he could get back on that stupid motorcycle.

She kept scrolling, stopping at a photo of her parents. Her mom was facing the camera and her dad was facing her mom. Both were smiling as if they'd just shared a secret. She'd spent so many years feeling out of place in her family, she'd failed to see it for what it was—a gift.

She wished she could change that now.

The next photo nearly took her breath away. Brooks and his nephew, from behind, sitting on a remarkably familiar dock. They looked like two guys in deep conversation, though Lane knew conversation for eight-year-olds only went so deep.

Lane had done a good job convincing herself she'd gotten Brooks—and Harbor Pointe—out of her system. But knowing if she'd been there, she would've been out on that deck with him, celebrating her brother's recovery, spending time on the lake with people who were nothing like her but seemed not to care—it stirred something she wasn't sure she liked.

Loneliness.

"Lane, what are you doing still sitting there? We have to go." Julia rushed past Lane's office, pulling her back to reality. She had work to do, a pitch meeting in the conference room. It was her first since she'd started at Innovate, her first since the day she'd collapsed at JB Sweet.

Her adrenaline kicked into high gear and she gathered her things. Her heart raced as she headed down the hall to meet their client. Jemma hurried behind her with the tablet Lane had neglected to even glance at.

"They need your approval to move forward," Jemma was saying as she followed Lane.

"I don't want to rush through this. Can I get them to you after the meeting?"

Jemma shook her head. "They're on a tight deadline."

Lane stopped in the middle of the hallway and took the tablet. She scrolled through the designs, marking what she loved and what needed to be changed in record time. That ball of nervous energy had returned to her belly, a constant companion again now that she was back at work.

She needed a break. Maybe a trip to Harbor Pointe to check on everyone. Say hi. See if Ryan had forgotten her.

"Jemma, can you check my schedule?" she asked, handing back the tablet. "I'd like to get out of town for a few days. What can we clear to make that happen?"

The intern took the tablet and opened Lane's calendar as Lane began heading for the conference room again. Still scanning the calendar, Jemma caught up with her. "I guess we could block off some time in September?"

Lane took the tablet and looked at her calendar—a community calendar that allowed other people to add things to her schedule. In theory, the idea was perfect for a community office like theirs, but in reality, all it meant was that Lane had no control over how she spent her own life.

"Can we move anything around? When I started this job, I made it clear I needed weekends off." So far, that hadn't happened.

"Is working weekends a problem for you, Lane?"

Lane found Julia standing behind her, just outside the conference room. Lane's pulse buzzed like she'd been caught. She should remind Julia of their original agreement, but she didn't.

"Not at all," Lane said. "Just trying to sort some things out."

Julia raised an eyebrow. "Good, because we need you focused. We'll be here all weekend, but we should be able to get you out by nine on Saturday. Are you ready for this meeting?"

Lane nodded. "Of course."

"Let's go."

When Lane left the office that night, it was already dark outside. She rode down the elevator with Jared the architect, who insisted she come out for a drink with him.

She refused, of course, given the fact that she didn't enjoy drinking or going out—and because she had the feeling he wasn't asking her as a friend, and her heart was hardly available.

She pushed open the door to her apartment and found Otis waiting for her, looking neglected and irritated she'd been gone all day.

"I'm sorry, boy," she said, feeling like she'd let him down. The dog walker was no substitute for her and she knew it.

The apartment was quiet, too quiet—a reminder of her unwanted loneliness.

Her phone vibrated. Pulse quickening, she responded to a question from Julia, who clearly hadn't read the e-mail Lane had sent her earlier in the day in hopes of not being disturbed that night.

Ryan had always made it seem so easy to disconnect, but if she did that now, she'd be more behind.

She stood at the counter in her quiet kitchen, wondering what he was doing in that moment. It had been weeks since she'd heard from him, and she assumed that meant he didn't want to hear from her.

She held her phone in her hand, staring at his name in her contact list. She could just call to say hi. They were still friends, even though they'd decided not to be anything more.

But she was only prolonging the inevitable, only dragging out the awful truth that it wouldn't work between them, and she needed to stop fantasizing that it could. She didn't have a free weekend until September. How could she hope to maintain even a friendship under those conditions?

She set the phone aside and picked up a stack of mail she'd

dropped on the counter, eyes landing on the lone envelope that didn't look like a bill.

The postmark read *Harbor Pointe, MI.*

Something tugged at Lane's heart—that same unexpected and unwelcome homesickness from before. She tore open the envelope and found inside nothing but an old photograph of her, her siblings, and Ryan and Hailey. She remembered the day it had been taken, but she hadn't seen it in years. For the most part, Lane tried not to look at photos of herself as a teenager.

But seeing it now, she was struck by something other than her heaviness or wide frame. Her imperfections seemed to wane in the light of the smiles on their faces. The whole family had gone camping one weekend at the insistence of her parents, and Ryan and Hailey had come along. Every day they'd swim in the lake, and every night they'd catch fireflies and eat whatever dinner they'd cooked over an open flame.

At the time Lane hadn't realized it, but she'd been genuinely happy that week—as if the pain caused by the outside world had simply melted away. One night at dusk, after swimming all day, her parents made them scrunch together and pose for this photo. Lane looked at their young faces, still dripping wet, skin tan from long days in the sun. They were all looking at the camera, smiling large, toothy smiles—except Brooks.

She drew the photo closer. Brooks, with his bright-green eyes and raspberry-colored lips, was looking at her. And the expression on his face told Lane what a part of her had known for a while.

Everything she'd been searching for—a family, a place to belong, the promise of true, unconditional love—it had been there all along. But she'd never looked up long enough to see it.

She'd rushed out of Harbor Pointe, determined to leave, anxious to start over with so much to prove, and she had. She'd proven she was strong and independent and successful. But what had that gotten her?

She glanced around her loft, spotting a bored Otis curled up on the couch.

He was the only family she had here.

She walked over to the desk in the corner. On the wall, in between the windows, she'd put her many awards on display. Framed pieces of paper she'd been so proud of. A trophy that had seemed so important. Sometimes she looked at them when she felt down, and they made her feel significant. Special. Worthy.

Those accomplishments had become the thing she lived for. And she had mistakenly thought *they* were what made her who she was. She'd been so wrong.

This was the life she'd carved out for herself? This empty, fast-paced, high-anxiety life that left her feeling hopelessly alone?

She'd convinced herself that work could never hurt her. That people were disposable. That titles and accolades and self-sufficiency were what really mattered. That she didn't need anyone.

Lord, I need them. I need you.

The prayer was reluctant, of course, but so true. She needed more than herself, no matter how much she didn't want to admit it.

She flipped the photo over.

Found this in a box of my stuff when I was cleaning and thought you might like it. I hope you can see yourself the way I've always seen you—even when I was a kid. Smart. Beautiful. Independent. I loved you even then. Don't forget to turn your phone off and rest. Miss you every day.

Brooks

She tried to swallow the lump in her throat.

He'd loved her? Did that mean he could still love her, although she'd left yet again?

The thought scared her—terrified her, really. She didn't know how to be loved, but as she looked back at the photo, she realized she wanted to try. She belonged there, in that group, with those people. She belonged on the dock, surrounded by lighthouses and green fields. She always had.

She just hadn't known it until now.

God had shown her, through Brooks's unconditional love, that it wasn't what she *did* that made her important, special, or worthy. It was simply who she was.

What if who she was really had been enough all along?

CHAPTER

ANOTHER MONTH HAD GONE BY, and Ryan was making considerable progress on the new cottage. He stood in the living room, admiring the way it looked now that the walls had been knocked out, new drywall had been installed, and beams had been added to the ceiling.

The back deck had been repaired, the bathroom gutted, the upstairs opened to a loft overlooking the main floor. He'd been here before—the foundation was all in place, but it was time to start thinking about the finishing touches. Today they were preparing to redo the stone fireplace, which was, as Lane had taught him, the focal point of the room.

Jerry had just pulled into the driveway, and as Ryan walked outside to greet him, a familiar blue pickup truck parked in the street in front of his house.

Jerry gave him a wave and hauled his tools inside while Ryan greeted his dad, who came bearing two to-go cups from Hazel's.

"Brought you some coffee," his dad said, handing him one of the cups.

His way of making amends, maybe? He'd stopped by almost

every day since Ryan had given him the tour. Never mind that Ryan always had some caffeine before he even showed up on the job site. It was the thought that counted—and his dad's thoughts had never been about Ryan before.

"Thanks. Did you go to your meeting yesterday?"

"Yeah. The donuts were stale."

"I gotta get to work."

"I know it, Son. I'll get out of your hair." Before he walked off, Ryan set down his cup and took the second coffee from his dad's hands, as he'd done every other day the man had come out to his job site. He took off the lid, smelled its contents, and gave it back.

Still out on bond, his dad seemed determined to keep his promise to make Ryan proud, and for some reason, Ryan felt compelled to help him if he could. He'd even put in a good word for him with a buddy who ran a feed plant between Harbor Pointe and Newman. His dad now worked there part-time, and so far, he hadn't missed a shift.

Ryan walked the perimeter of the cottage, thankful it had a good-size backyard with a private staircase that led to the beach. The landscaper would be there later that week, and while some of the wooden stairs needed replacing, it was still mostly functional.

He made the familiar trek down to the beach, same way he did every morning, fresh coffee in hand, taking off his shoes at the last step. He'd been thinking a lot about Lane, about the fact that two months had gone by and he still missed her every day.

He had done what God asked—let her go—but he still hadn't figured out a way to stop thinking about her.

He'd e-mailed her a few photos of the cottage and its progress, wishing she were there to drag him around to her specialty shops and flea markets, the way she had when they were working on Cedar Grove. He'd added two built-ins because he knew she liked them, and last week he'd had Jerry create a faux-shiplap look in the kitchen just because Lane loved the way it looked.

Her responses were always immediate and encouraging. She gave the occasional design idea and kept everything very professional. He hated it. He didn't want her to be professional with him.

He missed her. He'd fallen in love with her, and that hadn't changed. He'd started to believe no amount of time could change it.

As he stood there, staring out over the water, he asked God one more time to take his feelings for Lane away. If he had to let her go, he didn't want to think about her all the time anymore. The dull ache had become too familiar, and he needed it to be gone.

That, or he needed her back.

But the last two months had made it clear—*something* had to change.

The new project was already under way, and while Lane did much of her work from behind a desk, this one was different. It required a more hands-on approach, and Lane could hardly wait. She'd mocked up the designs based solely on photographs of the space, but she had a pretty good idea of what her client was looking for.

"I think this is your best design yet," Chloe said from the passenger seat of Lane's car.

"Really?"

Chloe grinned at her. "Seriously, it's brilliant. It's more 'you' than anything else you've ever designed."

Lane didn't take compliments well, but she appreciated Chloe's encouragement. Everything about the design was risky, and she wasn't the type to take many risks.

"You look like you're going to throw up."

Lane glanced at Chloe, then back at the road. She followed the instructions on her GPS and rounded the corner to the new work site. "That's pretty accurate."

Chloe reached over and squeezed her shoulder. "You're going to be just fine."

"You think?"

"Would I have quit my job to be your assistant again if I didn't have complete faith in you?" She grinned.

Lane parked and drew a deep breath. She got out of the car and grabbed her laptop case. All her designs were carefully thought out, and she could hardly wait for her presentation. Chloe was right— this project was very much "her," which, she supposed, was part of the risk. It terrified her to put herself out there this way, but she knew she had to at least try.

Never mind that her palms were clammy and her mouth was dry.

"Here goes nothing."

"I'm so excited," Chloe said.

They walked up to the front door and rang the bell. When there was no answer, Lane pushed the door open, figuring this work site wasn't unlike all the others she'd been on—people coming and going all day long, no one waiting to be let in or out.

She called out a quick hello but was met by only the sound of power tools at work in the next room.

"This place is going to be amazing," Chloe said, looking around.

"It really is." The smell of sawdust wafted to her nostrils.

She walked toward the kitchen, Chloe on her heels, both admiring the incredible potential in the space.

"Lane?"

His voice could have stopped her heart. How long had it been since she'd heard him say her name?

She turned and found Brooks standing just inside the screen door—the kind that banged in the wind—that led out to the deck.

"What are you doing here?"

In that moment, she felt self-conscious. Had this whole past month been a huge mistake?

"I have something to show you." She set her bag down on the old table in the kitchen and pulled out her laptop. "Do you have a few minutes?"

He still looked shocked she was even there. She couldn't tell if that was a good thing or not.

"Of course."

"Please, sit." She motioned toward the chair and caught a glimpse of Chloe, whose expression told her to calm down. Was it obvious she was panicking inside?

She hadn't seen him in two months. She wanted to rush into his arms and tell him she'd stay there for the rest of her life if he'd let her, but she wasn't here on a social call. This was business.

She opened her laptop and sat down next to Ryan. His bewildered stare unnerved her.

"What are you doing here?"

"I'm about to show you." She smiled at him, hoping he wouldn't think less of her for what she was about to say.

She opened the program with all her designs and found the one she'd been poring over for the past three weeks. She clicked on it and her adorable new logo popped onto the screen.

"What's Memory Lane?"

She smiled. "That's my new business."

Chloe was stifling a squeal, Lane could tell.

Brooks frowned. "What do you mean? I thought you worked at a place called Innovate."

"I did. And now I don't."

"Lane, what about your promotion?"

She turned the screen toward him. "What you see in front of you is a compilation of ideas I've put together for the very cottage we're sitting in now. With a little help from your sister, I was able to snag individual photos of each room, and I've designed them all to create a cohesive, welcoming, and very relaxing environment, not unlike what we did at Cedar Grove."

She flipped through a series of photos, showing Ryan what the space could look like if she were to take over designing the project.

"Chloe, do you have the contract?"

Chloe pulled a set of stapled papers from her bag and slid a copy toward Ryan.

"What's this?"

"If you choose to allow Memory Lane to create a custom design for your space, we'll need you to sign right here." She flipped to the last page and pointed to the dotted line.

He skimmed it quickly, then looked at her. "Why is your business address in Harbor Pointe?"

Chloe stood. "I'm going to check out the living room."

His question left Lane feeling naked and exposed. She hadn't allowed herself to be this vulnerable with anyone since Jasper. How would she navigate the things she knew she needed to say?

"Can we go for a walk? Show me the view?"

"Sure." He led her outside, onto the deck. "There's private beach access this way."

She followed him down a long flight of stairs and kicked off her shoes at the bottom. Her first step onto the warm sand reassured her that she'd made the right choice. She was home.

"What's going on?"

"I quit my job." Lane stared out across the lake, drawing in a deep breath and finally—for the first time in two months—feeling a much-needed peace wash over her. She closed her eyes for a moment, letting the warm air fill her up.

"I figured that much. But why?"

She turned to him. "Turns out my dream job wasn't so dreamy after all." She started walking down the empty beach, the morning sunshine promising a beautiful day ahead. "I'd been working my whole life for that job—trying to prove something, trying to become something maybe I was never supposed to be."

She told him about the panic, the nerves, the urgency, the constant dinging of her phone, the late nights, the long weekends, the never-ending need to do, be, and obtain more.

"I really thought that without those things, I wasn't good enough."

His sigh was barely audible, but she heard it.

"I guess I thought God—and maybe everyone else—would only love me for the things I did. My accomplishments. My trophies."

"That's not who God is, Lane."

"I know that now. I know he loves us just because of who we are. Even when we mess up. And I've really messed up." Her eyes filled with tears as she thought of the relationships, the people, she'd neglected over the years. All in the name of selfish ambition. Driven by a pain that had been buried for too long.

"Anyway, my job suddenly didn't feel like the most important thing anymore. And I guess I want to remove myself from it all," she said. "The things I've really been searching for—they were here all along. I was just too busy to realize it the last time I was here."

Ryan stopped walking and faced her. "What kind of things?"

"It's hard to explain. I've been looking for a place where I fit in my whole life, and it turns out, I don't have to be like everyone else to be included. My family isn't so bad after all."

He smiled. "Is that all?"

"No." She met his eyes. "That's only part of it."

He stepped closer. "What else?"

She took his hand. "I swore when Jasper hurt me that I'd never, ever let myself feel that way again."

"I know." His voice was quiet.

"But knowing you were out there and we weren't together was every bit as painful as if I'd lost you."

"You'll never lose me, Lane." He drew her to him, their bodies pressed close as if they were created to fit together perfectly. He brushed the hair away from her face, eyes searching hers. "So what are you saying?"

"I'm saying I don't know where this is headed, but I want to find out."

He smiled. "You're saying you're gonna let me love you?"

She stood, unmoving. "There's that word again."

"It's the only one that fits. I think I've loved you since the first day I saw you, the day your dad brought me home and let me eat dinner with your family. That day changed my life, Lane. You've changed my life. And I don't care if you've got a big fancy job in the city or you're working at Harold's General Store in downtown

Harbor Pointe. What you do doesn't mean a thing to me—only that I get to be with you when you do it."

She'd forgotten how much she missed his kisses, but now, as his lips found hers, everything came back to her, and it was like no time had passed between them at all.

Soft and gentle kisses quickly turned hurried and hungry as Ryan drank her in. In his arms, she felt safe, and even though her true heart had been exposed, she knew he'd never abuse that or take her for granted.

Minutes later, she pulled back, holding on to his gaze with a smile. "Does this mean I've got the job?"

He laughed, taking her face in his hands and kissing her one more time. "You definitely have the job."

She'd missed him, the way his arms felt wrapped around her, the way his skin smelled, the way he stared at her with those green eyes that made her feel like she was the only person in the world.

Something told her the days of their separation were over.

As they turned and headed back toward the cottage, her phone buzzed in her back pocket. She took it out and powered it down.

He gave her a sideways glance. "You're not going to answer that?"

Her eyes scanned the scenery around her—the peaceful lake and the sand beneath her feet, the cherry-red lighthouse in the distance, the lush green trees perfectly complementing the deliciously blue sky—and of course, the handsome man at her side. "No, I'm not going to answer it."

He slid his hand into hers and gave it a squeeze. "I was hoping you'd say that."

As Lane looked up toward the top of the staircase built into the side of the sand dune, she had the distinct feeling that she was heading toward something important—a life full of love she could've had all along. And she vowed to never again miss what was right in front of her.

Fall in love
IN AMERICA'S MOST ROMANTIC CITY

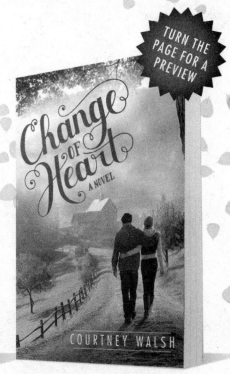

TURN THE PAGE FOR A PREVIEW

Could the loss of her dream lead to her happily ever after?

Sometimes a step back is the only way forward.

Available now at bookstores and online.

CHAPTER

Evelyn Brandt stood in her kitchen, the sound of uptight laughter filtering in from the dining room.

Hosting the Loves Park Chamber Ladies hadn't been her idea. Christopher told her a good politician's wife had to put herself out there. So she did.

And now she regretted it. It wasn't the first time that agreeing to something she didn't want to do had ended in regret.

She dialed Christopher's work line.

"Christopher Brandt."

". . . is in serious trouble," Evelyn said.

"Evelyn?" He sounded concerned, telling her he hadn't gotten her joke.

"This luncheon is pure torture," she whispered. "You owe me."

His laugh was forced. "I do owe you. Thanks for playing nice."

Of course she played nice. That was the only way she knew how to play. Learn the rules and follow them. Words to live by.

"Evelyn, do you have any more peach tea?" Georgina Saunders

appeared in the doorway, took one look at her, and frowned. "I didn't realize you were on a call."

Bad manners?

Evelyn said a quick good-bye to her husband and hung up. "I'm sorry about that. I'll bring more tea."

The caterer appeared to be occupied in the corner of the kitchen. So Evelyn took the empty crystal pitcher from Georgina, president of their philanthropic group, and moved to the opposite side of the room, thankful when the other woman returned to the dining room. If Evelyn had her way, she would've hidden out in the kitchen for the rest of the luncheon.

But the pecan-crusted chicken with chardonnay cream sauce hadn't even been served yet.

As Evelyn refilled and picked up the pitcher, it slipped from her hands. She caught it before it hit the ground, but not before the peach tea sloshed onto her black-and-white silk and cotton dress, the one Christopher had special ordered for this occasion. The one that made Evelyn feel like a child playing dress-up in her mom's closet.

Even after all these years of learning to fit the mold, she still felt uncomfortable in these scenarios.

"Evelyn, do you have that tea?" Georgina returned. "Oh, my. How clumsy of you. You should soak that before it stains."

Evelyn nodded. "I think I'll go change."

"Good idea." Georgina took the pitcher and left the kitchen.

Evelyn hurried upstairs, pulled off the dress, and stood in her closet. What she really wanted was a pair of worn-out jeans and her oversize light-gray sweater.

But that would never do, and she didn't want to embarrass Christopher. She knew how important these ladies were to his political career, both present and future.

She returned to the dining room, wearing a simple pair of black dress pants, heels, and a loose patterned blouse. A conversation was already in progress.

Georgina sat at the end of the table like a queen on a throne, chin tilted ever so slightly downward as always, eyebrows raised in judgment. "I hadn't heard that about Willa Seitz's husband," she was saying.

Evelyn frowned as she took her seat at the opposite end of the table.

"Did you know he was having an affair with Willa's sister, Evelyn?"

Evelyn felt her eyes widen. "I hadn't heard that, no." She should call Willa. Make sure she was okay. They didn't know each other well, but their paths had crossed enough for Evelyn to consider her an acquaintance at least, if not a friend.

And if the expressions on the faces of the women in her dining room were any indication, Willa Seitz wouldn't have many of those now.

"Seems it's been going on for quite some time." Georgina surveyed the rest of them. "We should all say a prayer of thanks for faithful husbands, ladies."

Yes. Evelyn was grateful for that, though she wished her husband was home more often. Being a state senator kept him busy. And away.

But then, weren't his position and his power part of what she loved about him? Her mind conjured an image of Christopher. Handsome and charming with eyes that sparkled and a smile that melted hearts. She'd never met anyone with quite so much charisma, and while she certainly didn't enjoy the days they were apart each month, the wife of a public servant had to make sacrifices too.

The main course was served, and the ladies around her table began eating the catered lunch. Evelyn mostly stayed quiet at these sorts of functions, meant for networking and planning the occasional philanthropic event. Christopher thought it was important she was involved.

"These women decide the who's who of Colorado," he'd told her. "Be charming and wonderful. We need their support."

She did as she was told, and while she never uttered a word of protest, she dreaded these luncheons more than dental work.

"Evelyn, will Christopher be home this weekend?" Lydia Danvers straightened. The woman might have been four years older than Evelyn, but she dressed fifteen years younger. All that time spent in the gym had certainly worked in her favor.

Evelyn shrank under her watchful eye. "He hopes to be," she said, then took a sip of her tea. "His schedule is always up in the air."

Lydia gave a curt nod, then a quick once-over. "Did you change your clothes?"

Evelyn smoothed her blouse. "I did. I just spilled some tea on myself."

The ladies laughed. "Oh, Evelyn, it's a good thing you had this meal catered," Georgina said.

More laughter.

Heat rushed to Evelyn's cheeks. She would tell Christopher she needed a break from the entertaining. She didn't have the gift of hospitality, and it was time she said so.

After this luncheon.

The doorbell rang, drawing all six pairs of eyes toward Evelyn.

"Are you expecting someone else?" Georgina asked.

Evelyn set her cloth napkin on the table as she pushed herself up. She'd never been more thankful for a doorbell in her life.

But when she moved toward the front door and spotted a man and a woman, both dressed in suits and looking quite official, her gratitude slowly dissipated.

She stood motionless on her side of the door, staring at them through the window until they flipped open badges, expectancy on their faces.

"Who is it, Evelyn?" Georgina called from the other room.

She cracked the door as her heart became a stopwatch set on double time.

"Evelyn Brandt?"

She nodded through the half-open door. "Yes?"

"Agent Marcus Todd, FBI. This is Agent Debbie Marnetti."

"What can I do for you?" Her stomach fluttered, and that familiar panicked feeling set in. And just like that she was eleven years old again, waiting for her father to come home, knowing her grades would not meet his approval. Her anxiety had turned to panic even then, and she'd been battling it ever since. Would she ever find comfort in her own skin?

Not now. She needed to keep it together.

"We need to speak to you about your husband. May we come in?"

"Christopher? Has something happened?" Evelyn didn't move from her spot in the doorway, her mind racing back to the quick conversation she'd had with her husband earlier today. He had seemed distracted—well, even more so than usual—but everything else was fine. He would've told her if it wasn't.

"Ma'am?"

Evelyn realized she'd been staring, mind reeling, and she quickly apologized. "I have guests."

The woman—Marnetti—rolled her eyes. The man gave her a warm smile. "It might be a good idea to ask them to leave."

Evelyn felt like she'd just been asked to return to the doctor's office for an in-person explanation of her test results.

"We really do need to speak to you immediately," Agent Todd told her.

"Of course. Come in."

She led them to the living room of their lakefront house. The house Christopher bought without telling her. He said it was a gift for her, but Evelyn knew better. The lake ran through Loves Park, and the homes surrounding it were some of the most desirable in town.

"It's a house worthy of a future governor," he'd told her on their first walk-through, confirming her suspicions.

"It's so big," she said. "What are we going to do with all this extra space?" The ornate fixtures certainly didn't seem like the kinds one would have in a houseful of children.

"We'll be entertaining," Christopher had told her. "Fund-raising. Campaigning. I've hired a decorator to come in and redo everything."

"Can we really afford that, Christopher?"

He pulled her into his arms. "You deserve a beautiful home, Evelyn. I want you to have the best."

She looked past him to the elaborate staircase at the center of the entryway. "I don't need all of this. I'd be happy with a small house in the country. As long as you're there. You know that."

His phone had chirped in his pocket and he'd excused himself to the other room, leaving her alone in the middle of a house she was sure would always feel more like a hotel than a home.

Now, in spite of the people surrounding her, Evelyn felt more alone than ever. She gestured for the agents to sit on the posh sofa Christopher's decorator had picked out.

"Can I get either of you something to drink?" she asked, trying to remember her manners in spite of her trembling hands.

"We're fine, Mrs. Brandt." Agent Marnetti's tone almost sounded like a reprimand.

Evelyn begged her heart to stop pounding.

"Evelyn, are you coming back?" Georgina appeared once more in the doorway. Her perfectly tweezed brows drew downward.

Evelyn's throat went dry.

"Who are you?" Georgina's superiority permeated the air.

"Georgina, I think it's best if we cut the luncheon short."

"We haven't even begun the meeting," Georgina said. "The others are still eating."

"Georgina, please." Evelyn practically pushed her out of the room, wishing she would just take a hint already. Her mind spun with possible scenarios. Why on earth was the FBI in her living room? And was there any way to get these ladies out without having to answer a million questions?

"Evelyn, I don't like the idea of leaving you alone here," Georgina said as they returned to the dining room. "Ladies, there are two strangers who've just barged into Evelyn's house. I think we need to get to the bottom of this."

Evelyn sighed. "They're from the FBI."

A collective gasp filled the room.

"What do they want with you?" Susan Hayes asked, rising from the table.

"I don't know," Evelyn said. "I haven't found out yet. Please go and let me call you all later."

"We should stay," Georgina argued.

"No." Evelyn's tone was firm for once. "Please go."

These women were really only here to help Christopher's political career, and whatever the FBI wanted, she had a feeling it wasn't going to be very helpful.

Evelyn suspected that before she discovered why the FBI was sitting on her sofa, Georgina and the others would have a litany of false explanations floating around town. She ushered them out, dismissed the caterer, and returned to the room where she'd left the agents.

"Do you know why we're here?" Agent Todd asked.

Evelyn shook her head. "You said it was about Christopher."

"Where is your husband now?" Agent Marnetti asked. She stood near the windows.

"Denver. They're in session. He's a Colorado state senator. He was elected three years ago. He worked hard to get where he is." She was rambling.

Something passed between the two agents in a silent exchange.

"What is it?" Evelyn folded her hands in her lap, feeling a rush of anxiety rise to the surface.

"This is quite the house you have here, Mrs. Brandt." Agent Marnetti walked toward the fireplace. "Is this marble?" She ran a hand along the mantel—a mantel most women would love. Evelyn had never cared for it. She'd tried her best to add personal touches—Christopher had allowed her to give three photos of the two of them to his decorator, a regal woman whose accent sounded like a cross between Britain and the Upper East Side. The photos stared at her from the mantel now.

"How do you suppose your husband paid for such a lavish home, Mrs. Brandt?" Agent Marnetti asked as she picked up a framed wedding photo.

"Would you mind telling me why you're here?" Evelyn stared at the agents. She had a right to know, didn't she?

The two officials exchanged another telling glance. Agent Marnetti looked away.

Agent Todd turned toward Evelyn. "We believe Senator Brandt has been embezzling money from the state."

Evelyn's stomach twisted. "That's not possible."

"We have evidence," Agent Marnetti said. "Lots of evidence. And we think it started long before he became a state senator."

Christopher adored Loves Park. Serving in city government had been a point of pride for him. Surely there'd been a mistake—he would never do anything to jeopardize his future.

Their future.

"I'd like to call my husband."

"There will be time for that, but right now we're going to have to ask you to step outside."

"Why?"

"We need to look around. Determine your involvement in your husband's crimes."

"*My* involvement? I don't even know what you're talking about." Evelyn's fingers were cold, like they always felt when she was nervous.

"Then you have nothing to worry about," Agent Todd said, his tone kind.

It was clear who was who in the whole good cop/bad cop scenario.

"Have you noticed any other elaborate purchases?" Agent Marnetti asked. "I mean, other than the house."

Evelyn frowned. "I don't know. Christopher's family has money. It's not so hard to believe he'd be able to afford the things he's bought."

"He lost all of his family's money a few years ago, Mrs. Brandt," Agent Todd said. "The senator made a few bad investments and lost it all."

"That's not possible," Evelyn said. "He would've told me."

"It seems there's a lot he didn't tell you," Agent Marnetti replied. "Or maybe he's just trained you really well on how to look innocent."

"That's ridiculous," Evelyn said. "Christopher handled all of our money. I never even paid attention." Her voice trailed off at the realization. She hadn't wanted to know about the money. Christopher assured her they were fine, and that was good enough for her.

She trusted him.

"Probably not the smartest choice." Agent Marnetti crossed her arms. "I find it hard to believe you didn't suspect anything. What about the cabin your husband purchased last month up in the mountains?"

"Our vacation home?" Evelyn had thought it was a bit excessive when Christopher bought that place, but she wouldn't tell them that.

"Quite a price tag on a home you rarely stay in."

"He was going to rent it out. Try to make some extra income. Christopher is a brilliant businessman."

"Spare us the rhetoric, Mrs. Brandt." Agent Marnetti pulled a walkie-talkie out of her pocket. "Come on in," she said.

Agent Todd stood. "Why don't we go outside? You don't need to watch this."

The front door opened, and a group of men in suits entered, rushing past Evelyn.

"You can't do this," she said, her voice barely audible.

Agent Marnetti stopped in front of her. "We have a warrant." She snapped open a folded piece of paper and handed it to Evelyn.

Her phone beeped. A new text message from Susan Hayes. Georgina would like a full report once the FBI leaves your house. We'll finish our meeting at her house. Join if you can.

"It'll be easier for you if you come with me," Agent Todd said.

"You're just going to go through all of our things?"

"We'll only take what's pertinent to the case."

A man walked by with her laptop.

"That's mine. Christopher has nothing to do with that computer."

"He might have hidden things on it, Mrs. Brandt. We have to cover all the bases." Agent Todd ushered her toward the front door. "You can wait in my car."

Evelyn's head started to spin, her heart raced, and she couldn't get a good, deep breath. *Not now.* She turned her phone over in her hand. "I need to call my husband."

Agent Marnetti snatched the phone from her. "Not a good idea."

"He won't answer, Mrs. Brandt," Agent Todd said.

"How do you know that?"

"According to our director, he was arrested about fifteen minutes ago."

Evelyn couldn't process what she was hearing. "I just spoke with Christopher. He didn't say anything. Why didn't anyone call me?"

"We couldn't risk you destroying evidence. Now, please, let's go outside." Agent Todd opened the door.

As Evelyn stepped onto the porch, she heard her name being called from the yard. She glanced up and saw four television cameras all fixed on her.

"Mrs. Brandt, did you know about the senator's embezzlement?"

"Mrs. Brandt, are you an accomplice to the fraud?"

"Did you know your husband was a crook?"

Wondering if she'd ever wake up from this terrible nightmare, Evelyn took a backward step into the house and slammed the door. "Get those people out of my yard."

"We're working on it."

Evelyn walked through the house, trying not to pay attention to the way these federal agents were carelessly searching through everything she owned. She went out to the rear patio with Agent Todd following close behind.

"Can you just leave me alone?"

"I'm sorry, Mrs. Brandt. My orders are to keep you in my sight at all times."

"You honestly think I had anything to do with any of this?"

He shrugged. "Stranger things have happened, ma'am."

"Not to me." Evelyn sat on a deck chair and let her head drop into her hands. "I can't believe this is happening."

A rustling in the bushes pulled her attention. She stood just in time to glimpse a man with a camera pointed at her.

She spun around, head whirling, black dots at the edges of her vision. She struggled to breathe. This time she couldn't keep the panic away. It was too strong. Every coping mechanism she'd learned in therapy eluded her, and she dropped into the chair, willing away the worry.

Her heart felt like it was being squeezed. Her airway, blocked. Her mind spun out of control, unable to latch on to one sane thought.

For a split second she was in her parents' house again, hiding under the bed, hoping her father didn't find her. He wouldn't abuse her—not physically—but he would tell her what a disappointment she was. He would point out that she wasn't living up to her potential, that what she needed was hard work and discipline. He would make her feel like the failure she was.

I'll never be good enough.

"Mrs. Brandt?" Agent Todd leaned in. "Are you okay?" He turned to the man with the camera and shooed him away. "Get out of here. I can arrest you. This is private property."

The cameraman rushed off.

"He's gone, Mrs. Brandt." Agent Todd stood a few feet away. "Do you need a doctor?"

Slowly Evelyn's panic subsided. It had been months since she'd had a panic attack, but they never got any easier. "I'm fine. I just want to be alone."

He lingered for a moment as if to assess her condition. "I'll wait over here," he said finally. "By the door."

But knowing she remained under his watchful eye was enough to prevent her from relaxing. That, coupled with the fact that her entire world had just come crumbling down around her, made Evelyn feel like she might never truly be at peace again.

A Note from the Author

YOU WOULD THINK the more you do something, the easier it gets, but that was not my experience in writing this book. *Just Look Up*, more than any other novel I've written, pulled from my own life experiences, and I suppose sometimes writing what you know is more difficult than making up what you don't.

I was on a trip to New York City for my husband's fortieth birthday when I first heard the words "just look up" in my mind. We were walking from our hotel to a restaurant down the street, and I was enamored just being back in my favorite city in the world. Granted, I've never been overseas, so I know New York has rivals, but for me, it's always been a place where my creativity can rise to the top.

So there I was, a small-town girl on the streets of New York for the first time in many years, taking it all in. The buildings, the traffic, the people, the overall "vibe" that is NYC—it was electric, and I was smitten. And I started to realize that everyone I passed had their eyes glued to their phones. They walked by, oblivious to the world around them, sucked into an online life instead of the real life happening right in front of them.

"Just look up!" I wanted to shout. "Look around at everything you're missing! Don't you know how amazing this city is?"

When you live in a place surrounded by the same sights and

people day after day, it's easy for life to become monotonous, even somewhere as glorious (to me) as New York. I started thinking about my own life and the ways I fail to look up. How I'm too busy or focused on my to-do list to pay attention to the important things in my life. I was confronted with my own inability to create margin in my life—how I say yes to too many things and put overwhelming pressure on myself to achieve.

And that's how this story was born. Lane's journey, though different from mine, is filled with much of what I've been through the last few years. The anxiety and stress, the need to *strive*, the inability to relax. That's all too familiar. And maybe you related to these things too.

We are a busy bunch of people. We love to pack our days and hours and minutes with *things to do*. We are always connected, always reachable, never unplugged.

And I don't know about you, but that hasn't served me well.

My prayer is that perhaps this story—my story as much as Lane's—might challenge you to search for that missing margin in your own life. To let go of the need to always be connected and to trade it in for a peaceful, restful, life-giving existence instead. To embrace the idea of the Sabbath and rest. Really rest, like all your work is already done.

And to remember the very best things are found when we just look up.

With love and gratitude to you for taking the time to read my book,

Courtney

PS—I *love* to hear from my readers! I invite you to sign up for my newsletter at my website, www.courtneywalshwrites.com, or to drop me a line via e-mail: courtney@courtneywalshwrites.com.

Acknowledgments

TO ADAM. For teaching me to slow down. For refusing to be hurried when it's not necessary or to live your life according to someone else's standards. For standing by my side "in sickness and in health" this past year and for helping me through all of it. Your belief in and encouragement for my writing is one of my life's greatest gifts. Plus, I think you're cute.

My kids: Sophia, Ethan, and Sam. You guys are pretty amazing. We often step back and say, "Wow. We have some really great kids." I'm inspired by each one of you for different reasons and am so thankful I get to be your mom. Thanks for cheering me on—and always remember, my love for you runs deep.

My parents: Bob and Cindy Fassler. Thank you for never discouraging my big dreams. And, Mom, thanks for being my first reader. Thank you for praying for us, and for training me up in the way I should go. I thank God for you every day.

Carrie Erikson. My sister. My friend. My wise counsel. Thank you for being the friend of my heart.

Stephanie Broene. I will always, always be grateful to you. You've made this story so much stronger (as you always do) and helped me figure out the best way to tell it. I am grateful I get to work with such an insightful, encouraging, and kind editor.

Danika King. For all the ways you make my stories better. I am eternally grateful.

Dr. Andrew Kong, my functional medicine doctor who helped diagnose my adrenal fatigue and anxiety and who also walked me through the long road to recovery. Because of you and your practice (and your very strict elimination diet, which nearly killed me), I am whole again. Thank you.

To Natasha Kern, my agent. Thank you for challenging me to be better and write stronger. I am so thankful to have you on this journey with me.

To Deb Raney. Always my mentor and always my friend. For all you've done to help me understand story—I am grateful.

To Katie Ganshert, Becky Wade, and Melissa Tagg, my precious writer friends whom I adore and love. Thank you all for brainstorming with me, for challenging me, for talking story and publishing and life with me. Because of each of you I feel so blessed to be on this journey.

To Jennifer Ghionzoli, for giving my books covers that make me absolutely swoon.

To the marketing team at Tyndale—Cheryl, Shaina, and Alyssa. Seriously. You guys are the best. Thank you for what you do every day to shine a light on our stories. Your authors are blessed to have you.

And especially to you, my readers. It humbles and amazes me every time I hear from one of you. I am so blessed to have the chance to share the stories God has given me, and I will never take for granted this opportunity. Thank you for choosing to spend time with my characters.

About the Author

COURTNEY WALSH is the author of *Paper Hearts*, *Change of Heart*, and the Sweethaven series. Her debut novel, *A Sweethaven Summer*, was a *New York Times* and *USA Today* e-book bestseller and a Carol Award finalist in the debut author category. In addition, she has written two craft books and several full-length musicals. Courtney lives with her husband and three children in Illinois, where she is also an artist, theater director, and playwright.

Visit her online at www.courtneywalshwrites.com.

Discussion Questions

1. Lane struggled with her weight growing up. How has that
   affected her adult life? Is there a challenge or situation from
   your past that still has some kind of hold on you? What steps
   can you take to work toward leaving that behind for good?

2. Lane is filled with an overwhelming desire to prove
   something. She spends her days striving to achieve more—
   especially at work, but also in other parts of her life. Are there
   areas of your life that can consume you in a similar way if you
   let them? What gets sacrificed as a result?

3. Lindsay's betrayal hurts Lane deeply. Do you think Lane is
   justified in feeling betrayed by her family? In what ways do
   holding on to these grudges change her life? What would
   you have done in Lane's situation? Could you have forgiven
   Lindsay?

4. Both Ryan and Lane have difficulty forgiving people close to
   them. Do you find forgiveness difficult to give when it comes
   to certain people? How do you keep from becoming bitter?

5. Lane often feels misunderstood, out of place, and left out—
   even as an adult, even by her own family. Why do you think
   that is? Can you relate? How are you different from the

people around you, and what can you do to celebrate those differences rather than allowing them to make you feel like an outsider?

6. Ryan credits the Kelleys with showing him unconditional love and a positive example of a real family. In what ways did different members of the family model that for him? How can you do the same for people God has put in your life?

7. When Lane finally gets everything she wants at work, it doesn't bring the satisfaction she thought it would. Why do you think that is? Describe a time in your life when you hoped and prayed for something, but when it finally happened, it wasn't all you imagined it would be. What did you learn from that experience?

8. At first, Lane's relationship with God is a lot like her other relationships—quick and hurried and not very deep. How does that change over the course of the story, and how does the change impact her life? How can you guard against this kind of surface faith in your own life?

9. When Ryan's fears about his father causing the motorcycle accident turn out to be true, he is faced with an impossible decision. Does he do the right thing? Have you ever had to choose between love and obligation? How did you make that choice?

10. The morning of Lane's big presentation, her stress and anxiety come to a head and she collapses. Many women struggle with fear and worry, but the Bible says that perfect love casts out fear. What does that mean to you? What are some habits you could develop to infuse your life with Scripture every time you start to give in to fear or worry?